INTERNATIONAL GUY

GUY

Volume 3

ALSO BY AUDREY CARLAN

LONDON • BERLIN • WASHINGTON, DC

INTERNATIONAL GUY

GUY

Volume 3

#1 *NEW YORK TIMES* BESTSELLING AUTHOR

AUDREY CARLAN

Montlake Romance

Published by Montlake Romance, Seattle

www.apub.com

Amazon, the Amazon logo, and Montlake Romance are trademarks of Amazon.com, Inc., or its affiliates.

ISBN-13: 9781503904651

ISBN-10: 1503904652

Cover design by Letitia Hasser

Cover photography by Wander Aguiar Photography

Printed in the United States of America

LONDON:
INTERNATIONAL GUY
BOOK 7

To Amy Tannenbaum,
my agent, my friend.

When things were very dark . . .
you were my light.
When hope was lost . . .
you promised me another way.

I believe you are a gift to this world.
I am but one honored recipient.

SKYLER

Tonight, my life path is laid out in front of me, split like a fork in the road. One direction leads to a happily ever after with the man I've come to love and trust, the other, a life without him. I brush my teeth and glance at the words I wrote on the mirror.

Trust your heart.

I hope those words don't lead him to leave me behind as a hollow shell of the woman I was when I met him. Over the past few months, I've lived large. Not in monetary ways, or as a celebrity, but with heaping bouts of happiness the likes of which I never anticipated having again after the loss of my parents. Up until Parker, my life felt like it was cut in half. Divided into the happier person I was before, and the woman with an uncertain present. With Parker by my side, that uncertainty changed. For the first time ever, I felt unbreakable. Living in a perfect dream. A man to call my own. One I felt deeply for. A new set of true friends, ones who didn't want something from me because of my fame. A great security team I trusted with my safety, and my muse was back, my craft better than ever.

Cloud nine.

Perhaps there's a quota of goodness each person is allotted in their life, and I have reached mine. The divine, God, the universe, Mother Nature, whoever made the rules, gave each person a happiness meter, and I hit the tippy-top when I fell in love with Parker James Ellis.

I've always believed there is a natural balance to the way the world works. Good, evil. Happy, sad. Love, hate. Because without one, the other could never be realized to its fullest potential. For me, Parker is everything good and right. Does that make me destined to be sad and wrong?

I close my eyes and take a full breath. Suddenly warmth invades the energy around me, a shift in the air sizzling along the fine hairs of my back and neck as hot male flesh presses against my skin. A familiar weight wraps around my waist, plastering me more firmly against his form. I keep my eyes closed, afraid that I'm imagining such beauty. I've craved this feeling, the caress of his hands over my bare skin in a loving, gentle manner, for what seems like endless days and countless hours.

The hairs on his chin abrade my neck as he leans his face into the crevice, a space on my body I've since dedicated to him. A sigh leaves me as if of its own accord, my subconscious knowing that in his arms is the most peaceful place in the world.

"I see you've left me a message of your own." His voice rumbles through my neck and down my chest.

I nod, incapable of speaking with him so near, the power of his energy mingling with mine all-encompassing.

"Trust your heart. It seems to be a recurring theme over this past week. Are you telling me to trust my own heart, or to trust yours since I already own it?" Both of his arms slide around my waist as he hugs me from behind.

I wrap my own arms over his, letting his warmth seep deep into me.

"Both," I say barely above a whisper, because he owns every inch of my battered heart.

He hums against my neck, and I feel the sound all the way down to my toes.

I open my eyes and find his blue gaze locked on mine in the mirror. "Are you ready for bed?" he says.

"With you?" My breath catches, and I'm not sure if it's because he's about to make love to me or do as he promised—hash out what got broken between us. At this moment, I'm not sure which I'd prefer more. "Always."

Parker places a gentle kiss on his spot, the crook of my neck, where it now feels moist and warmed from his lips and breath. He runs his hands down from my shoulders to my hands. "Come," he urges.

"I'd follow you anywhere." I admit the honest need burning in my soul. I turn so he can look me dead in the eyes. "Wherever you are is where I want to be. That is me, being honest, living my truth."

He tunnels one hand into my hair at my nape and lifts my chin up with his thumb. Time slows, and I can hear his breath moving in and out of his mouth as he leans closer. I imagine I can hear his eyelashes against his cheeks with each blink, until he closes his eyes completely and touches his lips to mine.

The initial press of his mouth is tentative, a greeting, his body offering a simple hello. I shift up onto my toes and place my hands on his bare shoulders. His skin is hot to the touch and warms me instantly. He curves an arm around my lower waist and holds me against him as he takes his greeting kiss to an all-out getting-to-know-you submersion of lips, tongue, and teeth. Each time my mouth opens his tongue plunges deeper, relearning what I like, taking everything I have on offer and then some.

My lungs burn with the need for air as the kiss intensifies, our tongues flattening against one another's in the most intimate of gluttonous treats. Parker eases back, allowing air to break the bond of our lips. He traces my bottom lip with his tongue before sucking it into his mouth and nibbling on the bit of flesh delectably. A zing of pleasure ripples through me, shooting like a zip line to the heat building between my thighs.

"Honey . . . ," I groan, not knowing what I need more, his mouth on mine, his cock inside of me, or his words sealing the cracks of our relationship back together. All seem to have top priority as my mind loses its hold on reality.

"Christ, I've missed hearing your sultry *honey*s when I've got my mouth on you. I fucking live to make you sigh. It feeds the broken pieces inside me."

I clench my arms around his neck and shoulders and kiss him hard before pulling back. "What do I have to do to make it right?"

He presses his forehead to mine, and we both close our eyes. "You're doing it. Being with me. Exposing the depth of what we have."

I run my fingers through his hair, my nails scratching down his scalp. He groans as if it's the best feeling in the world.

"Take me to bed." I can't think of anywhere I'd rather be than becoming one with him.

He grins that sexy smile that would make any woman's panties drop. He's so unbelievably handsome. "Pretty sure that's where this little impromptu make-out session is headed." He cocks an eyebrow and smirks.

I roll my eyes and push at his chest until he's walking backward. When his knees hit the bed, he falls down and tugs me right along with him until I land in a heap on his bare chest and boxer-clad legs. His hand runs up my back, and before he can put his mouth on me, I sit up and straddle him.

"First of all, before we do this, and believe me, I'm ready to go all night and heal some of those broken pieces in you *and me* . . . we have to be honest with each other about what happened, or we'll never move forward."

He sighs and puts a forearm over his eyes. I grab ahold of it and move it up and out of the way. "I did not cheat on you with Johan." His body tenses under me as he tries to shift away. I lock my legs at his rib cage and hips. "No. You're not getting away from this. Yes, I screwed up. Big-time. I thought I could go see him, talk him out of doing what he was threatening, and technically I did do that."

4

Parker grinds his teeth and speaks through a clenched jaw. "Sky . . ."
I shake my head. "No, you have to hear this. I went there. He told me he was destitute. In for a lot of money with some really bad guys. Owed millions. His family disowned him, and either he found a way to pay back his debts or his life was on the line."

"Fucking bastard made that your problem, and it wasn't!" He growls like a caged animal, his body twitching with anger.

"Be that as it may, long ago, I thought Johan was all I had. He got me through the worst time in my entire life. And maybe somewhere in my head it got all twisted up, and I felt as though I owed him something."

"You didn't owe him shit!" Parker barks, and I cup his cheek, stroking my thumb along the taut lines.

"After some thought and a couple of sessions with my therapist this week, I'm working through that. Regardless, helping him out of a horrible situation in a way that didn't take attorneys or slanderous images of me being plastered all over the papers seemed like the right thing to do."

Parker grips my hip in one hand, wraps an arm up my back with the other, and hauls us both up to the headboard so that he's sitting up against the back and I'm straddling his lap.

His voice dips lower. "You put yourself in danger and our relationship at risk." Parker's eyes sear straight through to my soul, and my heart pounds out a beat so hard in my chest I wonder if I'm about to have a panic attack.

Tears sting my eyes, and I nod, tracing his clavicle with my fingertips, needing to touch him in some way as I get through what I have to say. "I'm not proud of what I did. All I can say is, at the time, it seemed the right thing to do. I'm not used to having someone in my corner. A man to help me through the struggles, and"—I swallow as cotton coats my throat—"I wanted to fix it. Make it all go away. I didn't think . . ." I can't hold the tears back any longer. They rush down my face like turning on a faucet. "I didn't know how bad it would look. But I swear, I just paid his debts, set him up to get some help in a rehab facility so he could clean himself out from the drugs, and—"

"Why did you stay the night there, Sky? Why?" Parker clamps his lips into a firm flat line.

I lick my own, wishing I was kissing his instead. "Honestly, it was stupid. By the time we settled things, it was early morning, and I was practically seeing stars from exhaustion. I hadn't told my security team where I went, so they didn't know I was there . . ."

An animal-like growl leaves Parker's lips, and his brow furrows. I trace his brow until it shifts into a smooth line once more.

"Honey, I was tired. Weary. Emotionally and physically exhausted. He offered up his room, which had a separate door and lock, *one I used*, and I fell asleep. Alone. He took the couch."

Parker's body seems to loosen and relax under mine, and he brings his hands up to my face and neck, where he trails each fingertip along my skin. Caressing me. His touch is a healing balm, like calamine lotion over a rash. Every new inch he covers eases the pain that's flickering white-hot against my pores.

His voice is like sandpaper has rubbed his throat raw as he replies to my admission. "He told me you'd rekindled your relationship and point-blank stated he'd been with you intimately."

Putting a knife inside of a light socket couldn't have shocked me more. My heart sinks and my stomach churns.

This. This is why he believed wholeheartedly that I'd betrayed him.

I cup both of Parker's cheeks and look him straight in the eyes. "I would never do that to you, to us. You have brought me back to life. I was empty before you. My life hollow. I moved through the paces one day at a time, but honey, with you, I live. Every moment. I live and love. There's nothing that could lure me away from that or make me risk losing it. Nothing."

He closes his eyes, and I lean forward, putting my lips to his, sealing my truth with a cleansing, healing kiss.

1

Skyler's kiss fills me with life and happiness and settles the unbelievable ache that took root in my stomach when I heard Johan's voice in my ear. She pulls back and just stares at me, while her finger traces over my brow and temples, then down my cheek to caress my lips.

My woman never cheated on me.

I believe her with every fiber of my being. Her brown eyes glow with sincerity and a hint of sadness as her chin trembles.

"What happens next?" She sounds unsure in the wake of all she's revealed.

I run my hands from her thighs, up her waist and to her rib cage. "Now we make up." I jackknife up and take her mouth in a searing kiss. She gives everything to me, wrapping her arms around my back, pulling me closer, plastering our chests against one another.

When I pull back, she sighs and nuzzles my cheek. She digs her nails into the bare skin of my back. "I was so scared I'd lost you. Lost it all in one tremendous mistake."

I suck in a huge breath and dip my chin to where her shoulder and neck meet. "I'm not going to lie and say I didn't think it was over. If you'd cheated . . . that would be the end."

The word *cheated* rings like an alarm bell in my brain, and I tense up as memories of kissing Alexis prod my memory bank.

"Fuck!" I hiss and pull back, putting distance between us.

"What?"

I lick my lips and ease my hands from her shoulders, stroke down her arms and back up. "When I thought we were separated . . . ," I start, and her entire body goes completely rigid.

Skyler crosses her arms over her chest. "You slept with Ms. Big Boobs . . . didn't you?"

I shake my head, and her response is a shaking breath.

Her voice wobbles as she responds. "Something happened between you two. She mentioned an offer . . ." Her lips tighten and her jaw firms.

"Peaches, I didn't sleep with her. I wouldn't. Couldn't. You were always on my mind, but there was a moment of weakness. I was sleepy, dreaming of you, and she was there, and . . ."

Her voice cracks as she lets out a little whimper. "Just tell me."

"I kissed her. That was it, and I stopped it before anything more could go down and made it perfectly clear I was unavailable."

Skyler straightens her spine and firms her jaw. "Do you want her?"

My heart pounds rapidly in my chest, and my throat becomes dry; it's hard to swallow. "Fuck no."

Skyler tips her head, a lock of golden hair falling into her eyes. I push it back as she speaks. "She's gorgeous. Big boobs, fantastic body."

I close my eyes, and flashes of Alexis race across my mind, her voluptuous curves a definite highlight to her overall attractiveness. "Yeah, and she uses that body and her looks to play men. Not to mention she's currently using her body to play hide the salami with Bo."

Skyler's eyes bug out. "No way!"

I grin wide knowing that Bo's man-whore ways are about to give me a big, fat get-out-of-jail-free card with my woman. "Yes way."

"Ew, he banged Ms. Big Boobs?"

A chuckle slips out of my mouth. "Evidently. From what I understand, he's with her now."

Skyler eases her head down to my chest, placing her ear to my heart. "Okay."

I frown and cup the back of her head before playing with the strands of her silky hair. Little puffs of air come out of her mouth, teasing my nipple with each exhalation. The little bud tightens and throbs, wanting attention. "That's it. I tell you I kissed a woman that wasn't you, and all you've got for me is *okay?*"

She shrugs. "Honestly, I don't think that woman is the problem between us."

The word *problem* sets off a new warning I feel pinging at the base of my spine.

"You think we have a problem?"

She sighs. "Yeah, I do."

"Besides Johan and Alexis?"

Skyler shifts her body so she's back to straddling my thighs and staring into my eyes. "Why didn't you trust me?"

The question comes out of left field, though as it bangs around my head a little, it starts to make sense why she'd ask it.

"I trust you—"

She cuts me off before I can finish. "No. You believed Johan without ever even talking to me . . ."

I grit my teeth and then think back to what it felt like calling her that day. The helplessness and worry for her safety, that something had happened to her. And then to find out she was safe and sound, in the arms of her ex while I waited for her in her bed. The evil claws of jealousy scratch at the surface of my skin, and I breathe through the pain of the memory, trying to calm down, say what needs to be said without setting either of us off.

For a moment I think about my words carefully. "Baby, the circumstances were pretty harsh. You spent the night with your ex in his hotel room. He told me straight up that he'd been with you and was rekindling your relationship. Trust never played into it."

Her gaze narrows. "Except when the entire world thought you were cheating on me in Milan with that stripper, or with Sophie, and I had to wait an entire day to find out the details . . . not once did my faith in you waiver. Why was it so easy for you to take the word of my ex? Someone you know is a liar and a cheat himself?"

An arrow of guilt rips through chest and pierces my heart. My stomach drops, and that sinking, empty, twisty feeling sets up shop again.

"You're right." I cup her cheeks and look her in the eyes. "You're right, Sky. I should have had more faith. In you. In us. In what we've built these past several months. It's just . . ."

Her hand comes to my cheek, and I nuzzle into it, needing her warmth and her soothing touch. "Talk to me."

"My past is fucked. You know that. Even when we first started, I held you back. Kept you at arm's length. I figured we could just have fun together, when the whole time, deep inside, I craved so much more. Except, I was afraid. Hell, Sky, I'm still afraid."

"Afraid of what?"

"That you'll do what she did." The honesty comes out of my mouth like a dragon breathing fire and singeing everything in its path.

"Who?" She frowns and runs her fingers through my hair, her nails scratching along my scalp just the way I like.

"Kayla."

She blinks prettily for a moment. "The woman you were with in college."

I nod. "She messed me up, baby. Bad. I never knew how much until the past few weeks. Both Royce and Bo have been giving me advice, reminding me not to compare what you and I have to what I shared with her, but . . . it's fallen on deaf ears. I'm trying to change my mindset and not compare, but the fear is still there."

"Honey . . ." The one word is breathless, but it's filled with love and sadness. For me. Not for her. "I'm not Kayla. I'm never going to be Kayla. I'm not going to hurt you."

I lick my lips and close my eyes. "The only other time I was anywhere close to being this happy in my life was with her. You and I, what we have, is a million times heavier. Better. Stronger. It means more. And I . . . I worry about losing it."

Sky cups both of my cheeks, presses her forehead to mine and kisses me softly. Once. Twice. Three times.

"You're not going to lose me. The only way that could happen is if *you* leave *me*. I want a life with you, Parker. Nothing is going to change my love for you."

I wrap my arms around her until I feel her warmth against my chest, right where I need it. "I want so badly to believe that."

She kisses my neck and shifts back so she can look into my eyes. "Then believe it. Trust your heart. It will never lead you astray." She smiles sweetly, using the words she wrote on the mirror to me as a personal mantra.

Trust your heart.

"I think I'm going to have to get those words tattooed on my wrist, so I can remember them always."

She grins. "That can be arranged."

I push my hand into her hair, letting the strands spill over my forearm. "Are we going to be okay?"

"Do you love me?" she asks softly.

"More than I could have ever imagined." My chest tightens, and the overwhelming emotion of this moment in time makes every single one of my nerve endings come alive. I can feel each inch of her skin that is touching me. Hear her lovely breath as she inhales and exhales fluidly. Smell her arousal mixed with her peaches-and-cream scent.

"Then we'll be okay." Her thumb slides along my cheek and then down to the scruff on my chin.

I wiggle my nose against hers. "Simple as that."

"Love doesn't have to be hard. It can be simple and easy. And sometimes, it's both." She smiles, and I swear it lights up the dark room with an ethereal glow.

"All I know, Peaches, is whatever love has planned for the future, I just want it all with you."

This has my woman sitting up higher, pulling off her camisole until her bare breasts bounce free. Oh, how I've missed those rosy peaks. My mouth waters and I grip her hips tight.

"Good answer!" she growls, and attacks my mouth.

***

Rachel Van Dyken's black combat boots sound heavy against the hospital tile floor. Her long blonde hair is pulled back in a complex ponytail that contains a series of what I can only call warrior braids. Her T-shirt sleeves are rolled up, and you can't miss the cut muscles of her biceps and shoulders. She walks with purpose, a gun at her hip and a pair of handcuffs dangling from the belt loop at the small of her back. Each of her strides is taken with intention as she scans the hospital hallways. Several feet behind us, her husband pulls up the rear, making sure we're not interrupted or accosted. Skyler was able to come in under the radar yesterday, but the second people started tweeting and commenting that they'd seen her in the hospital, it required the protection of her personal Van Dyken security team. Both of them have yet to speak to me. I'm not sure if they're pissed at me or the situation, or trying not to get personally involved. At some point, I'll have to have a one-on-one with them both to smooth over the rough waters.

As we approach Wendy's room I'm startled to hear Wendy's voice ring out through the quiet space.

"I want my damn collar!" her raspy voice screeches.

Rachel stops in front of Skyler and shakes her head, basically encouraging us not to enter. We can see Wendy sitting up in bed, hands over her face and Michael by her side.

I push around Rachel and enter the room, Skyler moving hot on my heels.

"You're awake!" I rush over to Wendy's side and put my hand to her head.

She lifts a watery gaze to mine. "You're okay?" she croaks.

Tears fill my eyes, and I don't even care that I might look like a pussy as a couple fall down my cheeks. The joy of Wendy being alive and awake is an emotionally overwhelming sight. "Totally fine. No worries. I'm just glad you're awake. You scared the hell out of us all these past few days. When did you wake up?"

She swallows. "Last night. I told Mick not to call you guys. Wanted it to be a surprise."

I glance at Michael. He looks like a train wreck. Worse. He looks like a man who's been hit by a train and left for dead. His normally light eyes are red rimmed with dark smudges underneath coupled with some puffy bags. The generally neat hairstyle he keeps is a wonky mess that looks as though he's tugged and run his fingers through it a million times.

"How do you feel?" Skyler asks, running her hand down Wendy's shin.

She smiles when she sees Sky. "They're making sure I'm not in any real pain. Drugs are good for that." She winks and I chuckle.

Only Wendy could cop jokes and make the worried people around her feel better.

I run my hand over her short red hair again. "Why were you yelling a moment ago?"

Her face turns hard, and she presses back into the pillow. "They cut off my collar."

Michael lifts up her hand and kisses it. "I put your ring back on," he says, but even to my ears it sounds like a consolation prize. Which to me is a surprise, because he bought her a huge diamond. Most women would be worried about their rock.

She glances at her engagement ring, but it only garners a slight twitch of her lips. "Not the same, and *you* know it."

He sighs heavily. "Yes, I do. They cut it, Cherry. They had to in order to take you into surgery and repair the damage the bullet caused to your chest and lung." He sits up taller and leans closer. "Don't worry though, I'm going to get you a new one. Made to fit, with *diamonds* this time. Would you like that?"

She shrugs and then winces. Maybe those meds don't cover all the pain, but she doesn't complain. "I feel . . ." Tears fill her eyes and fall down her cheeks as she focuses on Michael. "I feel naked. *Exposed.* Alone."

He bites down on his lips, and the expression that flits across his face is thunderous. Then he pats his heart, and I swear that I can almost see the gears moving in his mind as he does so. As if a light switch has been flicked, the darkness and anger are replaced with sudden happiness. He reaches up against his collar and into his dress shirt, where the long beaded chain he wears resides. Her padlock is there along with his key. He removes the chain from around his neck, undoes the hook, and removes the key. He puts that in his dress shirt pocket and stares at her, focused on her gaze. "Right by my heart at all times. Because it's you, Wendy, that makes this useless thing beat. You know that. You *know* . . ." His voice cracks.

She nods her head frantically, tears falling from her eyes.

Watching them feels like Sky and I are intruding on a private moment, but the air in the room is warm, an electric energy whirring in the space between us and filling me with a sense of peace and love. It's safe, and so special, I can't move away. I'm glued to this spot, my arm around Skyler holding her close as Michael tries to settle the love of his life.

He latches the necklace, then places it over Wendy's head and spins it around once, then twice. The beads fall down against her chest, and she inhales and sighs, her hand clutching the padlock like her own personal talisman.

"Feel better?" He grins confidently, knowing damn well that she does.

She smiles and blinks sleepily. "Yes, I do. You always know how to take care of me."

He kisses her forehead and then holds her hand to his face. "The most important job in my entire life. I'll put you and your happiness first. Always."

"I know," she murmurs, before her eyes close. "So tired . . ." Her voice falls off, and a puff of air leaves her lungs as she falls asleep, hand still clutching her padlock.

Skyler grips my elbow and nods her head toward the door. "We should go, let them rest."

I clear my throat as the emotional tide bangs against my chest. Michael makes sure Wendy is covered with the blanket and follows us outside of her door.

"How is she really doing? What's her prognosis?"

Michael rubs at the back of his neck then rolls his shoulders. "She woke in the middle of the night. They tended to her—doc says everything looks good, there's no sign of infection—but they're giving her antibiotics intravenously as well as the pain meds. Wounds look clean and are healing normally, but it will take some time until she has full range of motion in her shoulder and arm. She has to take it easy for the next six weeks at least. Which, I'm telling you right now, may be forever."

Forever.

That single word hits me like a gunshot to the chest, almost bowling me over. "Wait a minute, are you saying what I think you're saying?"

He crosses his arms defensively. "If you're thinking that my future wife will be tending to our home and planning our wedding and nothing else? Then yes. She doesn't need to work. She chooses to—"

I cut him off before he can continue, because at this point, the possibility that Wendy may not come back to IG is devastating. "You think she's going to be okay with that?"

"I'll make it clear to her that it is in her best interest for our family. The one we're building and the one we plan to have in the future. Your business may be important to you, but she . . ." He points a finger to where Wendy is sleeping in the bed. "She's everything to me. If she's not breathing, they may as well set up a coffin for two, because there is no place I won't follow her, the grave included."

Jesus.

There's head over heels, and then there's this. I can't even explain the level of devotion and blind commitment Michael has for Wendy. Frankly, I've never seen it. Not even with my parents, and they've been in love for close to forty years. This is downright cosmic.

"I feel you, Michael, but ultimately it's Wendy's choice. And even if you try to sequester her away with all your millions, she's made it very clear that we are a part of her life, a part of the family you mentioned. And I'm not letting her go. She's like a sister to me now, and I've never had one of those. So yeah, be prepared to fight . . ."

Michael plants a hand on my shoulder. "I'm not taking her away from your friendship, but I'm not exactly keen on her going back to work. I didn't want her to work in the first place. This just proves how dangerous it is out there."

I sigh heavily. "It's not normally like this."

He huffs and runs a hand over his scratchy jaw. "Says the man whose girlfriend has to have not one but two security guards with her at all times?" He glances at Rachel and Nate, who are on either side of our huddle about five feet away, pretending not to be involved, when we all know that if there were a threat of any kind to their charge, they'd react faster than you can light a match.

Sky rubs along my bicep, soothing me while reminding me that she's there for support or whatever else I may need. I loop an arm around her waist. "We'll be back later when she's had some rest. Cool to tell the guys that she's awake? I'll let them know that she's resting for the next few hours."

He nods. "Just tell Montgomery if I hear so much as one smart remark or innuendo of any kind, I'm liable to take him down where he stands. His days of hitting on my woman are done. You hear?"

I bite my lip, trying to hold back the smile threatening to break free. "Got it. Will warn him."

"Appreciated. And, Skyler, always nice to see you. No offense about the security guards. I know you need them." He frowns.

She pats his shoulder. "None taken. I shouldn't need them, but I do. And you're right. Life can be dangerous, but so is not living every day to the fullest. I've done that too, and in a way, it was like dying a slow death no one could see. Now, I may be taking risks, but I'm living free and enjoying every moment." She eases out of my hold and wraps her arms around him.

At first, it's as if Michael doesn't know what to do with his hands or how to hug a person other than Wendy. Which makes me feel sad for the guy. To have all of your joy wrapped into only one person . . . it's no way to live. Just makes me want to bring the fella into the IG fold even more.

Eventually his shoulders droop, and he drops his chin to her shoulder and wraps his arms fully around her, accepting her comfort. His body trembles as if he's letting go of the built-up tension. "I thought I lost her," he whispers, and Sky cups his nape and nods.

"You didn't lose her. She's here. Safe and sound. Healing. And she needs you more than ever."

He nods, sniffs into her neck as the emotions spill out of him. I can practically feel the waves of distress pumping off him.

She hugs him for a full minute before she eases back. "You gonna be okay? Is there anything we can do for you?"

He shakes his head, then moves the few feet over to the glass windows that look into Wendy's room. He places his hand on the glass. "All I need is in there."

She smiles and pats his back. "Well, go to her. We'll be back later with the guys and some food."

"Okay." He turns around and holds Skyler's hand. He squeezes it and whispers, "Thank you," to her, and then nods to me.

Skyler moves back to me, and I wrap my good arm around her waist. "You were good with him," I whisper as we walk back down the hallway, Rachel in front, Nate in the back.

She shrugs. "I know what it feels like to lose everything you love. There's nothing scarier."

I kiss her temple and think back to how it felt to be without her. Even though I didn't technically lose her, for a while it felt like I had. I'd never wish that kind of pain and torment on anyone.

"No, Peaches, there isn't."

2

The guys are in a rush to get to Wendy later that evening. Skyler and I are a few paces behind them. I've got my bum hand loosely hanging on her hip, my other hand carrying a to-go bag with a sub sandwich, chips, and a Coke for Michael.

We get to her room, and without even knocking, Bo barrels right in, Royce following behind him, the two of us after.

Bo's holding a big squishy teddy bear, and Royce a bushel of wildflowers.

When Bo sees Wendy sitting up in bed alive, he opens his arms wide and hugs the sky, the bear hanging from one hand. "Thank you, Lord above! Hey, Tink, how the hell are you, beautiful?"

Wendy grins. "Is that bear for me, or is that the one you cuddle at night to keep you warm when you've kicked your chicklet to the curb?"

He waves the bear and comes to the side of her bed. He lifts her chin and leans forward, his lips dead set toward hers. Before he can reach her lips, Michael leans over her, puts his entire hand over Bo's face, and pushes it back.

"Don't test me," he growls menacingly.

Bo snickers. "What? I was just gonna kiss her on the forehead. Jeez. So territorial." He shakes his head mockingly.

"It would be wise for you to remember that. I barely tolerate you as it is, Montgomery, and only because she has a high threshold for bullshitters and a soft spot for idiots. I, on the other hand, do not."

Bo holds out the bear to Michael. "Here, I think you need this more than she does. Maybe it will warm your black heart."

Sky and I can't help but chuckle in the corner as we watch the sparring unfold.

Wendy snatches the bear and tucks it to her side. "I like him. Thank you, dick-for-brains. It's good to see you alive and kicking."

Bo runs a hand through his hair. "Nothing can hold me down." He winks.

"I'm sure I could find a straitjacket that would do the job," Michael mumbles, and Wendy grabs his hand and squeezes.

"Easy, tiger. I'm the only one you're allowed to tie up." She grins, and I swear to all things holy that the guy's gaze heats with a burning lust right before my eyes.

"Too true, my love." He leans over and kisses her lips sweetly.

"Aw," Skyler whispers, and I nuzzle her temple until she turns her head and looks at me so I can kiss her sweetly too. She smiles wide after the kiss, and right here, in this moment, it puts one of the broken shards of my heart back in place. There are a lot of them floating around that the two of us need to work on putting back together, but I think we're both up for the job.

"All right, brother, back yo' ass up so I can get some sugar from my best girl." Royce nudges Bo out of the way.

Wendy reaches a hand to Royce, and he grabs it between his two huge paws. "How you really doin', girl?"

She smiles up at him. "They have me on some awesome meds, so right now, I'm feeling mighty fine."

"All right, all right, that's what I like to hear. You took a slug to the chest and yet you're sitting here smiling those pearly whites at your bros.

You amaze me, girl. There sure is no woman on this earth quite like you." He pats her hand, then leans down and kisses the top.

"You better believe it!" Wendy sighs and eases back against her pillow. I can tell she's trying to be happy and outgoing, her normal self, but it's wearing on her. The woman was shot and had a lung collapse three days ago. She needs the rest.

"So, when are you gonna get sprung from this chicken coop and come back to work? You know we can't carry on without knowing when the heart of our operation is back in business, right?" Royce asks.

"Not soon enough," she says at the same time Michael responds with "Never."

"Huh?" She lets go of Royce's hand and focuses her attention on Michael. "I'm going back to work, as soon as the doc clears me to."

Michael shakes his head back and forth. "We'll talk about it when you're back home, safe and sound."

Wendy shimmies and winces, turning a bit more to the side. "No, we'll talk about it now. I am going back to work, Mick. You know I love my job . . ."

"And that job has put you in danger. You don't need to work. I have plenty of money . . ."

"You have plenty of money. *You* do, Mick, not me. I want to contribute to our life."

He cups her cheek. "Cherry, you do, baby. Every day you take care of me, our home, make this shit world we live in bright, but I can't lose you, and your job—"

"Is the best thing that ever happened to me outside of meeting and committing to you. These guys are my family now. I can't leave them. Not when it's just getting good. I'm now part of a real team . . ."

"Baby, you've always been part of my team."

She pats his hand on her cheek. "You can't lock me up in a gilded cage and hope I'll stay there. I wouldn't be happy, and you know it."

"Then you can come work for me. I'll clear out the office right next to mine. You can be my personal assistant. It would be perfect. We could work together, and live together . . ."

She shakes her head. "No, honey. You love your assistant."

"No, I *love* you, and only you. She will be given a new position. You'll see. I'll make it worth your while," he says with a hope and a prayer, but somehow, I know it isn't enough. Wendy is a spitfire who never backs down from a challenge. If she wants to stay with IG, she will.

Bo grumbles and broods in the corner, scowling at Michael. Royce just rubs at his bald head and sighs. Me, with Skyler's hand in mine and Wendy alive and well, I'm feeling rather optimistic. I'll let it all play out and see where the dice land. Could be a seven or snake eyes, but only time will tell. My money, however, is on Wendy.

"Mick, I need something of my own. To contribute to our lives alongside you, not under your thumb and careful watch. I'm not leaving IG or the guys. You're just going to have to get over this fear you have. Don't worry, it will be okay. We'll figure out a way."

His face contorts into a tortured expression, eyebrows pinched, lips pursed, but it all melts away under her heartfelt gaze. "Okay, Cherry, whatever you want. You know I can't say no to you, but don't be surprised when you end up with a bodyguard."

Her eyes light up. "Can I pick him? I would looooove my own personal hot beefcake opening all my doors, driving me everywhere like I'm someone important. Oh! Sky!" She turns to my girl. "Maybe we can share Rachel and Nate! That would be sooooo cool." Her tone is one of awe and excitement.

Michael cracks a smile and a chuckle. The first time I've seen that man laugh since he rushed into the emergency room three days ago, which, right about now, feels like a lifetime ago. "Your bodyguard will be ex-military, the size of a house, and ugly as sin. I will do the picking, thank you very much." He leans forward and kisses her. "You try my patience, sweet one."

She grins and bites her lip. "You love it."

"I love you." He kisses her again as a man in a white doctor's coat enters the room.

"Ms. Bannerman. Your color looks great, and based on the smile on your face, I see that you're feeling a little better."

Wendy smiles at the short man with snow-white hair and spectacles. "I am, Doctor, thank you. I'm sorry I missed you this morning. Last night's doctor told me I have you to thank for saving my life. Thank you."

Michael eases out of his chair next to Wendy and holds out his hand until the doctor takes it and shakes it politely.

His voice is rough when he says, "Michael Pritchard. Fiancé. I will be making a hefty donation to the hospital in your honor. If you want the funds to go to a specific area, just name it. I am forever grateful for your talent and expertise. You saved my fiancée."

The doctor smiles, but it swiftly turns to an expression of sadness. "I'm only sorry we couldn't save the child." He pats Michael's hand and lets go.

The entire room goes dead silent. Not even the air passing through any one of our lungs could be heard. Probably because every last one of us is holding our breath.

"What?" Wendy gasps, her hand flying to her stomach.

"Child?" Michael whispers.

Oh no. God, please no.

My stomach sinks, and Skyler squeezes my hand so hard I almost cry out but hold it back. Barely. This isn't about me, though it feels as though a knife has just been stabbed into my stomach and ripped up, filleting me like a fisherman gutting his catch.

Wendy was pregnant when she got shot.

Wendy miscarried her unborn baby.

Wendy lost her child . . . because of me.

My stupidity. My fault.

I should have figured out that Eloise was the one all along. If I hadn't been so gone over my own pathetic personal woes, I could have worked harder, smarter. Maybe . . . maybe it wouldn't have happened. Maybe Wendy and Michael would be celebrating the knowledge that they were about to become parents instead of learning about the loss of what would never be.

Jesus. No.

The doctor looks at Michael, then at Wendy, and back down at the chart. "Did Dr. Lopard not talk to you about this?" His voice is hard and yet sad at the same time.

Michael simply shakes his head.

"Um, perhaps we should discuss this privately—" he starts, but Wendy cuts him off.

"Tell me now. These people are my family . . ." Her words crack as the tears start to fill her eyes.

"I'm deeply sorry, Ms. Bannerman, Mr. Pritchard. Our records show you were approximately ten weeks pregnant at the time you were wheeled in." He clears his throat as if it's hard for him to speak. "Due to the trauma your body sustained from the fall, the gunshot, and collapsed lung, you miscarried. There wasn't anything we could do."

Michael lifts his hands into his hair and spins around before stomping over to Wendy, dropping to her side. Tears run down her cheeks, and her chin is trembling.

He grips her around the hips and presses his forehead to her stomach. "Get out." The muffled phrase comes from where he's hovering over his woman protectively. His body starts to tremble and quake, the storm inside of him mounting. "Everyone . . . get the fuck out!" he roars, his head still pressing against her stomach, arms surrounding her lower half. She dips her head as the tears fall, and her hands tunnel into his hair.

The doctor goes out first, and the rest of us follow.

I don't realize until I'm standing outside of her room in shock that Skyler is plastered to my front, her hands cupping my cheeks, thumbs wiping away the tears I didn't know were falling.

"I failed her," I state to no one and everyone within earshot at the same time.

"You didn't. That woman hurt her. You had no part in it." Skyler's voice shakes with sadness.

"Brother . . ." Royce's voice is hoarse and deeper than normal when he claps a hand to my shoulder. "If you're at fault, we're all at fault. We worked the case together."

"Yeah, Park, we can't take on this blame. It's not ours to take, though it hurts all the same." Bo clears his throat and rubs at his eyes.

I close my eyes, but the bright lights of the hospital bouncing off the white walls is burning straight through my retinas.

"Come on, we all need to get out of here. Give them some time alone. To rest and come to terms with this," Skyler suggests, and hooks her arm in the crook of mine.

"I don't think any of us is going to be able to come to terms with this. Especially them." I nod to the room where I can still see Michael hovering over Wendy's form, his back shaking with what I'm assuming are tortured sobs.

"We all need to go, get out of here. Get some sleep," Skyler says, emotion coating her tone with a heaviness we're all feeling.

Bo huffs. "Screw sleep. I need a fuckin' drink." He crosses his arms, the leather practically groaning against the pressure of his muscles underneath.

"Amen, brother," Royce adds, running both of his hands down the sides of his face, pressing them together, and resting his chin on the tips of his fingers.

"Drink sounds right up my alley," I admit on a weary sigh, the rawness of what we just witnessed squeezing my heart in a painful vise. "Sky?"

25

"Where you go, I'll follow." She rubs my bicep and kisses me there through my clothes. She nods at Nate and Rachel. "We're going to hit a bar."

Nate groans. "That sounds like fun," he mutters dryly.

Rachel, on the other hand, cracks her neck and rolls her shoulders. "Sweet. I've been looking for a reason to knock some heads. Let off some steam. Odds are good someone will try something stupid. When booze is involved, there's always an idiot ready to rumble."

"Oh, now this I gotta see. Hot warrior princess, kicking ass and taking down men twice her size?" Bo grins sexily. "I know just the place." He smirks and moves ahead of the pack.

"Take it down a notch, killer. That's my wife you're talking about," Nate growls, his jaw tight and his fists clenched, ready to do some serious damage. If I were Bo, I'd be *very* careful. I'm confident Nate could take down a herd of elephants with one hand tied behind his back. As if on cue, the muscles running the length of Nate's arms bulge and ripple, and his nostrils flare as a nasty scowl forms across his normally handsome face.

Bo glances over his shoulder as he struts down the hall and the rest of us follow. "I know. The matching tattooed rings were a dead giveaway. Besides, she's far scarier." He gestures to Rachel.

Rachel cocks an eyebrow and grins. "Yes, yes, I am. You don't even know the half of it. Now lead the way, sparky."

***

We arrive at Chez Serge, and I start laughing hysterically. Not only is the bar so packed it's body to body, there's a giant padded area in the back with a huge mechanical bull in the center. Nate, however, is undeterred by the number of people and has us all going to the bar with him in the lead. Rachel hangs close to Sky, her eyes flicking from person to person, probably assessing any potential threats.

In hindsight, this is probably a bad idea, coming here with a massive celebrity like Skyler. Though so far, she's gone unnoticed, but I can tell she's keeping tucked to my side with her hair falling in front of her face.

Nate says a few words to the bartender. His face jets up, his gaze zeros in on Skyler, and his eyes widen in his sockets. He nods a few times and disappears behind a door in the back. He returns with a big man who oozes authority. He nods to a roped-off section near the bull. Nate shakes his hand, and we follow him to the section that's cornered off from a lot of the crowd. I make sure Sky is in the darker corner. I sit to her left, and Rachel takes the chair on her other side, facing the patrons. Nate stands off to the side and crosses his arms, a menacing don't-fuck-with-me look plastered on his hard face. He is not happy about the decision to go here, but it's Skyler's life. She should be able to go where she wants, within reason, as long as she's safe.

"Baby, do you feel comfortable here?"

My girl smiles wide and nods excitedly. "I haven't been to a packed bar in . . . hell, I don't remember when. This is awesome!" she breathes into my ear, and hugs me hard.

Royce and Bo take up the chairs across from us.

"Drinks anyone? On me?" Bo offers, standing up.

The man who was behind the bar puts a hand on Bo's shoulder. "Not to worry, friend. Drinks are on the house." He nods to Nate, then assesses Skyler. "I'm the manager, Simon. Your bodyguard said you'd be willing to let us take a picture of you outside by the sign upon your exit if we kept things quiet about your presence. I'm very grateful to have you grace my establishment. What can I get you?"

"Of course I will. And thank you for being discreet."

He nods politely, and yet there are stars in his eyes as he rubs his hands together in a nervous gesture.

"How about Seven and Seven?" Skyler asks, and Simon dips his chin, then focuses on Royce.

"Whiskey neat. My thanks," Roy rumbles, trying to be heard over the loud rock music.

"Beer for me. Whatever's local," I say.

"Same for me," Bo adds.

"And you, little lady." He leans over to hear Rachel better.

"Water for me and the big guy." She gestures to Nate, who hasn't taken his eyes off the crowd.

Simon moves to go back to the bar when Bo stops him. He gestures to the bullring. "When does the action start?" He grins.

"Anytime you guys want. I was going to hang back from starting the bull rides, but if you guys are fine with it, I can get it going."

Rachel stands and plants her hands on the table. "As long as this section stays roped off from the crowd, we should be fine."

Bo grins wickedly, sizing Rachel up. "I bet you can't last five full seconds on the thing."

She smirks. "If I weren't working, I'd take you up on that bet."

Sky pats Rachel's side. "Oh, please do it!" She claps like a little kid about to receive an entire bag of candy.

Rachel shakes her head. "I'm here to work, not to play."

Sky makes a stink face. "And I want my bodyguard to show up my man's best friend. You know you want to. Look at him . . . you've got to wipe that smug look off his face!" she taunts.

"No." Nate's voice sounds like a threat from across the table.

Rachel squints and puts her hands on her hips. "You don't own me . . . ," she starts, and even I know this is going to be interesting. The words *you don't own me* are fighting words in any conversation.

Nate narrows his gaze. "I believe the matching tattoo on your ring finger and the vows we said a decade ago beg to differ, fireball."

She smiles, but it's one of those wicked smiles a woman gives right before she's going to cut off a man's dick and feed it to him.

Bo rubs his hands together and whistles. "Bring it on. Van Dyken battle! My money's on Rachel."

Nate's jaw tightens as if he's chewing on rocks.

Rachel stares directly in her husband's eyes when she says, "Ride-off, Bo. You against me."

"What are the stakes?" He leans back confidently.

"Whoever loses has to wear a skirt for an entire day. Winner decides when." Rachel twists her lips into a confident smile.

"Oh shee-it. I'd like to see that." Royce laughs behind his hand.

Nate growls loud enough to be heard over the thumping music.

"I'm not sure who I'd rather see in a skirt more!" Sky laughs. "Either would be equally awesome!" Her entire face is lit up and glowing with happiness. I've missed it so much I want to kiss her hard and deep, so I do.

She gasps into my mouth, and I take advantage, dipping my tongue in and tasting hers. Our tongues dance, and all too quickly she pulls away with a few pecks on my lips, then turns back around to the drama unfolding at our table. I hook my arm over Skyler's shoulder and keep her close.

"You're on, sparky. Let's do this. Nate, you've got the charge solo."

"Obviously," he grates through clenched teeth, irritation positively dripping off his body.

She winks at him and saunters over to where the staff are setting up the bull. Bo removes his leather jacket and tosses it over his chair before going after her with equal determination.

Royce and I pull out our billfolds and each toss a fifty on the table.

"Hey, I want in on this action." Sky pouts and dips into her purse, pulls out a fifty, and lays it on the pile. "Who are you guys going for?"

Both of us answer at the same time, "Bo."

Her mouth drops open in what I can easily assume is shock. "No way! I'm going for Rachel! Sister solidarity!" She fist pumps the air and screeches, "Go, Rach!"

The lights around us dim, and the ring lights up. Bo, surprisingly, goes first. He hooks a long denim-clad leg over the bull's wide body, grips the handle, raises his arm in the air, and nods at the staff member working the controls.

The bull starts to buck wildly, and the crowd counts out the seconds. By the third second the bull is rocking madly and Bo's slipping around but keeping his hold. His body arcs with the bull as the crowd gets to eight seconds before the thing does a superfast jerk to the right and flings him right off. His body goes sailing through the air and lands in a heap across the red padding. He jumps up, raising his hands in the air. The crowd cheers for him. With a smug look, he points at Rachel, his hand in the shape of a gun.

Rachel eases over the padding and pops onto the bull as though she's been riding the things her entire life.

Uh-oh.

She curves her legs against the beast's body and locks them in place while she rubs her hand along her pants leg, then wraps it around the strap. She closes her eyes, takes a calming breath, and then raises her hand. The bull shoots to life, moving left, right, up, down, gyrating. It starts to circle as the crowd reaches four seconds.

It bucks up and back on five.

Swings to the right on six.

Back to the left on seven.

On eight, Rachel's body flows like water, her arm swaying in a circle as the plastic animal jolts around and up and down. Her long braided hair follows her movements like a lasso. She's magical on the thing. Moving with the machine, not against it. I've never seen anything like it.

The crowd reaches nine . . . she's still going strong.

The bull finally comes to a stop at ten seconds.

Rachel flicks her braids over her shoulders as she glances at a stunned Bogart and winks. As though she does it every day, she raises her leg over the side and slides off.

"Give me all your money, boys!" Sky claps, grabs the money, and waves it at Rachel.

Bo walks back behind the blonde goddess. His face isn't sour with the fact that he lost, it's in awe of the incredible woman who just whupped his ass.

Rachel dons her gear, then eases back into her chair calmly and sips on her water.

Bo steps up to Nate and looks him right in the face. "You are one lucky man."

Nate smirks. "Just think what else she can ride like that."

"Fuck!" Bo runs a hand over the back of his neck.

"Exactly." Nate grins. "Nice ride, fireball." He grins at his wife.

"I'm thinking that's not the only ride I'll have tonight," she quips.

"No. No, it is not," Nate announces with promise.

Looks like someone's getting lucky. I turn to Skyler and nuzzle her temple. Her hand comes down to my knee and runs up my leg, high up on my thigh, where she leaves it. Looks like I'll be getting lucky tonight too.

Skyler squeezes my thigh, and even though we got some horrible information and are brokenhearted for Wendy and Michael, we can find moments to enjoy the good in life. I think sometimes that's what it's all about. Living for the moment.

3

We're back in Boston, and an entire week has passed since Wendy and I were shot. A full three days of fear that Wendy wouldn't wake up, only to have her wake and find out that she miscarried a child none of us knew she was carrying. She didn't even know. I thank the good Lord for that one tiny favor. It doesn't mean they don't miss what they lost, it just gives them more hope for the future. Something to look forward to.

It's funny how when we are faced with loss, we can take one of two paths. One path is to never find healing and understanding, or the courage and strength to move forward, accept the loss for what it is . . . loss. This can put a person in a never-ending circle of hell. Constantly reliving that loss every moment of every day, never giving it up or letting it go, which, to me, doesn't serve the love one had for the thing they lost in the first place.

Then there's the second path. Acceptance. Accepting the pain and hurt from that loss and letting it guide you forward, making you stronger, pushing you to live for the moment and let the past stay in the past.

Keeping the past in the past is easier said than done. It's a challenge I believe every person has to live with each and every day. Everyone has something they lost, a tragedy they have survived. The key is picking up the pieces of your heart, of your might, and moving forward.

One step at a time.

One day at a time.

Living in the moment.

I worry every day that I'm going to get an email from the government or a military officer at my door or my parents' door, stating that my brother Paul has died in battle. A shiver ripples down my spine, and my chest tightens. My brother is a hero of mine and of every American soul. He selflessly risks his life to protect our freedom and fight tyranny across the globe. Still, the not knowing is brutal.

In this situation, my fondest hope is that Wendy and Michael lean on each other to get through their loss and come out the other side closer, more connected. A part of me is sure they will. Her being shot, losing a baby they didn't know they had, will cement them to their future together. Life is short, and it was proven to all of us this past week. We have to live it like we will not get another day.

Which is also why I haven't told Skyler to go home.

I walk over to the side of my bed, where she's still sleeping, and set down the cup of coffee I made for her. God, she's ethereal. Her natural skin tone glowing, her golden hair shining in the rays of sunshine streaming in through the blinds of my bedroom windows. The white comforter is pulled to her chin, and slowly I peel the fabric back, finding her bare chest and perfectly pink-tipped breasts. A purple hickey the size of a quarter mars the side of one breast where I got a little needy and territorial with her naked body. There isn't an inch on her skin I haven't licked, kissed, sucked, or bitten in the last forty-eight hours. I know every freckle, each tiny scar and birthmark, the entire patchwork that makes up my woman's body.

Easing over her, I straddle her hips, pull the blanket over the back of me, and cuddle over the top of her but don't put down too much of my weight. My fingers are taped together, and my palm is nothing more than a glued-together red line that's scabbed over. I'll put the brace back on, since I'm going back to work today, but I needed that thing off while I spent the last two days loving my woman.

Skyler sighs and wraps her arms around me. I nuzzle between her breasts, then flick each tip with my tongue, sucking hard on each nipple until they are glistening wet and erect. The pink color has now darkened to a plum-rose tone befitting her excitement. With my good hand, I skim my fingers down her belly and to the space between her thighs. When I encounter wet, hot flesh, I can't help but groan and bite down on one of her nipples, piercing her core with two fingers nice and deep.

"Oh God . . . I thought . . . mmm . . . I thought I was dreaming for a minute."

I leisurely finger-fuck her until her body is squirming under mine, her hips lifting to aid my fingers in a deeper plunge.

She sighs and tips her head back. I know instantly when I find the spot inside her that makes her crazy, because her body goes perfectly still, every muscle strung tight.

"You want to come right now, or you want me to fuck you?" I lick up the side of her neck and suck the flesh until she trembles.

"I want to come now, and then I want you to fuck me." She moans and digs her nails into my back.

I shake my head and chuckle into her hair. "Greedy girl."

"For you . . . always." She sighs as I redouble my efforts and play with her G-spot until she's bouncing her body into my movements.

Her body is glorious in the moments before she comes, and I can never get enough. She always keeps her eyes closed tight, her mouth open in a soundless cry, neck fully extended. Except that's not what I love the most. I test it again, attempting to lift up and away from her, so that I'm only touching her center, but she won't have it. No. My woman prefers to be touching me at all times, especially when she's about to come.

"Come here . . ." Her breath catches as I move my hand more forcefully, my fingers fluttering against her sweet spot in a cadence she can't help but surrender to. "Parker . . . honey, come here." Her hands reach around my back and tug me over her, chest to chest, heart to heart. I can feel the wild beating against my chest, my own heart synchronizing with hers, becoming one beat as she slips over the edge. Her arms and legs lock around me as her hips slam against mine, making "the beast" weep at the tip.

I groan into her shoulder, remove my hand, and plunge inside her heated depths. She welcomes me on a cry, the walls of her sex still squeezing in pleasure. I take her fast and hard, keeping her coming until I feel the tension down my spine, the tingle at the base of my dick, my balls drawing up tight, and then she locks me in place, from the inside with her sex and the outside with her arms and legs. Wrapping everything she is around all that I am until I'm not sure if we're two separate bodies anymore. I come in a wave so intense I lose all train of thought and motion, rutting into my woman as though I'll never have another chance. It's always like this. A loss of time, space, everything around us. I see and feel nothing but her.

Only Skyler.

Sex with a woman has never been this good, this all-encompassing in my entire life. Maybe because, before, it was never lovemaking but the act of simply getting off. Two bodies rubbed together physically, and a biological response occurred. End of story. With Skyler, it's an adventure. Every time is different. When our bodies come together it's not only a meeting of our physical forms, it's our minds and hearts melding, our souls recognizing one another.

Some people believe that your soul knows when it's met its mate. I can't imagine any other experience could ever rival or be better than what I have with Skyler. She's it for me.

My only question now is, Am I enough for her?

In the long run, will what we have be enough to sustain her? Keep her loyal to me? And then of course there's her job. She's the most sought-after woman in the entire world, on and off the silver screen. How could I ever compete?

My thoughts scatter as the feeling of Skyler humming and running her fingernails down my scalp enters my mind. I smile against her neck where I've planted myself, then lift my head. "Good morning, Peaches. How are you this morning?"

She smiles. "Mmm, I'm very good." She stretches her legs, and my softening cock slips out of her, which causes a pout to cross her lips.

I chuckle and push back. "Don't worry, there's more where that came from." I kiss my way down her chest and belly before sitting up. "I've made you some coffee." I gesture to the end table while my phone buzzes on the other side.

"You're too good to me," she murmurs, lifting up to a seated position, wrapping an arm around my neck, and kissing me softly on the lips.

If only that were true, I think to myself, still battling the very real fact that when everything went to shit with us, I didn't trust her to be true to me, to us. Whereas the same situation was brought against her a couple of months before, and she didn't hesitate to believe me and ask to hear my side before she went off half-cocked, unlike me. I know Kayla did a number on me, but looking back, and looking at what Sky and I have, the situations were nothing alike. Skyler is not Kayla. And what I had with that bitch is nowhere near as beautiful and strong as what I have with Sky.

Sighing, I try to let it all go, because we're starting over, Sky and me. We're choosing to trust and believe in our love for one another and figure out the rest as we go. That's all we can do for now.

Twisting around, I let her go and roll until I can reach the phone and lift it to my ear.

"Yo!" I say happily, nothing but sunshine and rainbows happening over here.

"Brother," comes Royce's warm greeting. "I know this is going to put a damper on your time with Skyler, but the next client is coming in today."

"Yeah, I know, and you told me you were meeting with her."

He sighs. "She's demanding you, or no deal. It's another six figures, brother, and after all the hell we've been through in San Francisco and Montreal, I *really* want to put my attention on the business and the goal of securing my pretty silver baby."

The Porsche 911.

Royce has coveted that car for years, but even with the kind of money he makes, he's never taken the plunge. Part of me wonders if he's trying to hit some ridiculous goal he's set for himself that he's not copping to. Another more mature part of me realizes it's his own damn business and to just leave it be.

"Dammit. All right, but I have Sky with me, and the paps know we're here. We told Nate we wouldn't leave the building for at least three full days. She has them working on something in between. I can't leave her here unprotected. Did Andre send over a temp to fill Wendy's position until she comes back?"

"Yeah, yesterday. Seems sweet. Quiet. Too quiet. I want Wendy back."

A pang of guilt about Wendy's current situation twists my heart, but I push that to the side along with my trust issues. "Yeah, me too, brother. Me too. In Wendy's files there's a contact for an alternate security firm that the Van Dykens vetted. Have one of them and a driver be here in an hour, and we'll head in."

"On it. Thanks, man." Royce's tone is filled with gratitude.

"Hey, we're in this business together. You, me, Bo, and our girl, Wendy, yeah?"

"Yeah, brother. Peace," he grumbles, and hangs up before I can respond.

"What's up?" Sky walks out of the bathroom wearing nothing but her lacy white panties and my business shirt.

I lick my lips and bite down on the bottom one. All thoughts of work are gone in a flash at the sight of her fuckhot body. "My dick if you don't put some pants on."

She chuckles and bends over to pick up her coffee. Her heart-shaped ass appears as the hem of the shirt rides up.

"Christ, woman, you'll be the death of me. You've got to stop being so damn sexy or I'll never make it to work."

She pouts. "You have to go to work? I thought we had another day."

I stand up and pad over to her naked, the beast half rising to the challenge of another round with the hottest woman alive.

"I'm sorry, but the client refused to meet with just Royce." I run my hands up and down her arms in a soothing gesture. "He didn't say why, but he wouldn't have called if he didn't have to. He's sending over the alternate security team. You cool with coming to work with me?"

Skyler nods and presses her forehead to my chest. "I just want as much time with you as possible." Her hands run up my rib cage and down to my hips and back up. "I missed you so much, and I know we're okay, but . . ."

"You're not ready to be apart," I answer for her.

She shakes her head. "No, I'm not."

I grab her cup of coffee and place it back on the end table before cupping her cheeks. "I'm not ready either. So, it's 'take your girlfriend to work' day. Sound like fun?"

She grins and nods. "Except first . . ." Her hands skim down from my chest, over the bricks of my abdominal muscles, and down to the thatch of dark curls, where she finds the beast has fully woken once again. With the slyest glance and the cockiest smirk, she eases down my body, and she sits on the edge of my low bed. Her head is at the perfect height for my very eager friend.

She licks the tip, and a pearl of my arousal comes to the surface. Skyler wraps her lips around the bulbous head of my cock and takes me down her throat.

My hands fly into her hair as if they are on autopilot. I close my eyes. "Perfect. Fucking. Woman."

She sucks hard on my aching flesh and pulls her lips off with a plop. Her little hand wraps around the base and jacks me up and back while her mouth drives me insane. Ribbons of heat ripple from the center of my pleasure and out until my knees shake where I stand.

"Don't ever forget it." She hums and takes me into the haven of her mouth once more.

I swallow hard and tilt my face to the ceiling as her tongue swirls around the tip and flicks the sensitive bit under the crown. "Never," I gasp, and thrust my hips deeper into her mouth as she groans, opening her throat to my slick invasion.

"Not in a million years could I forget the woman I love making me see stars."

I grip her head, and she goes faster, a goddess at giving head if there ever was one. I grip her hair and cup her cheek, holding her where I want her as I thrust shallowly. She sucks me deep and hard, alternating her hand and mouth perfectly.

My vision darkens, and all I can see are stars flickering behind my eyelids as the tingles start, and I'm ready to blow. I tap her cheek to warn her what's coming her way, but she doesn't stop. My woman goes crazy for my cock when I'm about to come. I'm fully aware it's because she likes the control she has over me in this vulnerable moment. What she doesn't know is I like handing her the reins as often as she wants them. Before her, no way, never. I ran the show in the bedroom. With Sky . . . it's all about the give and take.

I come spectacularly down her throat, and she works me through it until I'm spent and there's nothing left.

Sky eases to a standing position and I take her mouth in a fierce, appreciative kiss. "You blow my mind, baby," I whisper against her lips, tasting myself on her sweet tongue. The salt to her sweet.

She hums. "And here I thought I was blowing your cock."

I wrap my arms around her and just hug her while I laugh. It feels so good to have her back in my arms. I never want her to leave, nor do

I ever want to be without her again. The new goal: push anything and everything away that doesn't help me move forward with this woman. I want a future with her, and I'll stop at nothing to have it. Regardless of whether I'm worthy or not, if she continues to give me her all, I'm going to take it.

***

We make it through the doors of the IG office holding hands and laughing like lovesick fools. When I see not one but two strange women in our office, I wrap my arm around Skyler's waist and hold her close.

The blonde one sitting behind Wendy's desk stands up immediately. Her eyes go to mine and then widen when they land on Skyler. "Mr. Ellis. Um, Ms. Paige, I presume."

"And you are?"

"Annie, Annie Pinkerton." She holds out a shaking hand. Her eyes keep flickering to Skyler, and her voice shakes as she responds. "I'm the temp from Canton Global. Andre sent me to fill the personal assistant position for a couple of months."

"Ah, yes. Welcome to IG." I turn around. "And you are?"

A petite brunette with intelligent dark eyes and straight cappuccino-colored hair stands up from the waiting area and approaches with her hand out. She's standing no more than five feet two, wearing a simple but perfectly fitted sheath dress and an intricate gold necklace, which serves as a nicely placed statement piece on her neck. On her feet are expensive but stylish ballerina flats that match her Coach purse. The woman exudes confidence and straightforwardness tied into a small but pretty package.

"I'm Amy Tannenbaum, literary agent to Geneva James. I have a meeting with you." Her tone is direct and professional. No hint of exuberance or fanfare over seeing a celebrity A-lister standing before her. I like her instantly.

"Thank you for waiting, Ms. Tannenbaum. Let me get my girlfriend settled, and I'll be right with you," I offer, moving toward the hallway where my office is.

"Actually, I'd like to speak with you both, if you wouldn't mind. My business proposal and request involve you both in a manner of speaking."

I frown, and Skyler tips her head up to me. "I'm cool with it if you are," she says.

"It's very unorthodox—" I start.

Amy rushes to add, "It's my understanding from my cousin Gabriel Jeroux's significant other, Sophie Rolland, that everything you do is unorthodox, is it not?" She smiles flatly and waits calmly as I digest what she's said.

Sophie. That girl. From a princess to a literary agent. What's next, a rich magician? I wouldn't put it past her. Which reminds me once again I need to get in touch with her. It's been too long, and I still haven't found out whether or not she's got a ring on her finger from her French scientist.

"All right, well, come on back. Annie, please tell Royce I'm here and if he needs me, we'll be in with Ms. Tannenbaum."

"Absolutely, Mr. Ellis." She beams and sits quietly, turning back to her, or rather, Wendy's desk. I clench my teeth and squeeze Sky's hand.

She runs her hand down my arm as Amy follows from behind.

"She's okay and will be back at work in no time. You'll see," she whispers, and I inhale fully, letting her words sink in. Wendy will be back. It's only a matter of time. We will get through this rough patch without her.

I open my office door and offer the seating area so that Skyler and I can sit side by side and Amy in the solo chair. Once we're settled in, I clap my hands and wince as I bang the two broken fingers together.

Skyler grabs my forearm, and I place my hand over hers and focus on Amy. "How can International Guy be of service to you, Ms. Tannenbaum?"

Amy opens up her briefcase and sets on the table between us a half-inch-thick ream of paper that's clipped together. "That is the first half of the last book in the coveted A-Lister Trilogy."

Skyler's mouth falls open as she sucks in a fast breath. "No way . . . ," she gasps.

Amy nods. "I see you're familiar."

"With Geneva James . . ." She swallows, and her words slip out in a dreamy quality I'm used to hearing in the bedroom, not in my office when talking about an author. "Only one of the best romance authors ever. I've read everything she's written."

Amy smiles and nods, pride filling her body language. "I'm glad you're a fan. It makes what I'm about to ask for easier."

I frown and pick up the novel, allowing the pages to float by as I scan them. There's nothing here I recognize. Though I've heard of this author before. Many of her books are turned into romantic big-budget films. "What is it that I'm looking at again?" I hold up the fat stack.

"As I said, it's *half* of the third and final book in the A-Lister Trilogy. The other two novels have been on the *New York Times* bestseller list for over a hundred weeks. This book, this was supposed to be published a year ago. The fans are furious, and the longer it takes to release, the more we risk losing followers. We've already sold the trilogy rights to Paramount Pictures, and they want to get started on creating the first film but are leery about doing so until the last book is completed."

"Okay. I'm following you, though I'm not sure why you're here."

She purses her lips. "Geneva is suffering from a case of writer's block. Career-ending writer's block. She keeps saying she doesn't know how the story ends. Her characters are no longer speaking to her."

Sky nudges my shoulder. "You've dealt with that before." She smirks.

I tilt my head. "It's not quite the same thing. I was dealing with your own personal muse and internal issues, not an author's story line. I'm not sure I can help with this."

Amy pulls out her checkbook. "My company is willing to pay you two hundred and fifty thousand dollars to try to fix our author. Get her out of her funk. Help her see what we all see . . ."

"Which is what?" I lean forward, focusing on Amy's words and the honest sincerity in her tone.

"That she's incredibly talented. Her gift is in the words and the stories she tells. Unfortunately, the publishing house that worked on the last project treated her horribly. Abused her trust and left her feeling less than. Now the pressure to finish this final book in something that's becoming an empire, a household name, has thrown her completely off. She's paralyzed with the fear of failing her readership at large and herself."

Skyler's hands go to her chest. "What? No. That's awful. She's an amazing storyteller. Honey, you have to read the first two books in the trilogy. They're amazing."

"I find it interesting that you think so, Ms. Paige, since you were the inspiration for Simone Shilling, the young blonde A-list actress in the book. The woman who millions of readers around the globe love to love, when the poor thing can't find love of her own. Until . . ."

Skyler's entire face lights up with excitement, and she finishes Amy's sentence. "She meets Dean Briggs, a businessman not in the industry, nor does he have any interest in dating someone who is."

Amy smiles wide, and her face goes from pretty to beautiful in an instant, her straight dark hair falling into a silky sheet down the sides of her face. It's a perfect contrast to her olive skin tone and tasteful makeup. If I had to describe this woman using two words, I'd say she was the epitome of confident elegance.

"I see you've read the story."

"Yes, yes, a million times yes! I've got my agent on the lookout for any new movies of hers that I might fit in the lead role."

"And therein lies what I'd like to request." Amy doesn't exactly smirk, but I can tell she wants to. She's got Sky in the palm of her hands.

Finally. I think it, but don't say it. "I'm all ears."

"If it would interest Ms. Paige, I'd like it if you and she could go to London to meet up and spend time with my client. She needs to finish this book, but there's something holding her back. I want you to figure it out and clear away her writer's block. There is a lot riding on this. And Ms. Paige, if you accompany him, I will ensure that Paramount understands that you were the inspiration for this character and are best suited for playing the part. The contract alone would be a multimillion-dollar take home for you."

"I'm in! Sign me up!" Skyler says enthusiastically.

"Peaches, I'm not sure you understand what this means. You have to skip work, which I know Tracey will be unhappy about. And I thought you had press junkets for the Angel movie coming up?"

She purses her lips and waves her hand. "I'll figure it out. Even without the possibility of doing a book-to-movie script, I'll get to meet and hang out with one of my all-time-favorite authors. Do you have any idea how cool that is? You have to let me come!" She pouts and pushes out her bottom lip to the point where all I want to do is kiss and bite that lip in retaliation.

I glance at Amy and sigh. "Two hundred and fifty thousand and two weeks. Nothing more. If I can't get her out of her funk, there's no harm to me, my company, or Ms. Paige's option to work the movie once she eventually finishes the book. Agreed?"

Amy sits up straight and holds out a small hand. "You drive a hard bargain. I respect that."

I take her hand and shake it. Skyler does the same.

"When do you need us in London?"

She stands up and runs her hands down her sheath, removing any wrinkles. "I've taken the liberty of having both of your flights booked first class on British Airways leaving at ten a.m. tomorrow morning."

"A bit risky there, don't you think, Ms. Tannenbaum?" I grin, loving the ball-busting side of this woman.

"Life is full of risks. When you have something worthy, the risk suddenly seems small. I look forward to regular reports on how my author is doing, Mr. Ellis."

"Then I shall give them to you. Provide your contact information to my assistant, and we'll be in touch," I offer.

"It was good meeting the two of you." She shakes both of our hands. "And Ms. Paige, you're a very talented actress. I love your work and hope to see you on the big screen bringing the A-Lister Trilogy to life."

Classy. Now that's how you present your appreciation for someone's work. She didn't make a huge deal about being a fan, just coolly shared her enjoyment of my girl's talent.

"Thank you, Amy. We'll do our best to get your author's creative juices flowing again," Sky says rather breathlessly.

Amy closes her eyes for a moment, smiles, and then opens them. "Yes, well, that would be lovely. Take care and safe travels."

The second the door closes, Skyler hops and does a jig, dancing around my office. "Do you know how badly I've wanted to meet Geneva James!"

I chuckle. "No. I figured Sylvia Day would be your unicorn author."

She shakes her head. "No, because I've already met her, and she's super cool. Geneva James doesn't do signings or fan events at all. Word is she's turned into a bit of an introvert. Now I get to meet her and be considered first for the movie trilogy! This is one of the best days of my freakin' life!" She jumps up in the air. "We need to celebrate. We need to go out and have champagne. Oh no." She frowns for a moment. "We need to pack!" She shakes her head and paces the floor. "Nah, forget it.

I'll have my personal shopper send clothes to London for me and just take the essentials. This is sooooo great!"

I stand up and come around to her and scoop her into my arms. "I love seeing you happy. It reminds me of when we first met, and I took you all over New York. Do you remember that?"

She smiles. "Yes, I'll never forget it. And now I can show you London! I'm very familiar with the city." She wraps her arms around my neck and focuses on my eyes with a contented look. "We get to work together, honey. How cool is this?"

I grin and kiss her pink lips. "It's very cool. Just remember, we still actually have work to do. We need to help this author, so on the plane tomorrow, I want you to give me the lowdown about what you know. Tonight, I'll start reading the series and hopefully have it completed by the time we get to London."

Her eyes widen. "We'll read it at the same time! I'll do a reread, and we can talk about it. This. Is. Epic!" Sky's entire body vibrates with excitement under my hold.

I'm glad she thinks so, but a warning tingle picks up at the back of my neck. How the heck am I going to get a worldwide-bestselling author with millions of fans and an A-list celebrity around the city of London without dealing with some serious fan issues?

On the list tonight, phone call with the Van Dykens to put a plan in place for Skyler and Geneva's safety.

I can feel the shit storm coming, I'm just not sure what's going to bring it on.

4

Skyler's phone rings at the same time there is a soft knock on my office door. Skyler puts the phone to her ear as she walks over and opens the door for Annie.

The new girl.

I wince and look back at my computer, not wanting to see a blonde receptionist instead of my fiery redhead who's become far more than an assistant or a receptionist. In the several months Wendy's been here, she's become not only part of the team, but part of our small extended IG family.

"Hey, Flower, I'm glad you called. You'll never believe where I'm headed tomorrow and who I'm going to see when I get there!" Sky walks over to the couch and flops into the seat, a veritable ball of excitement.

Annie glances at her and walks over to me with a stack of envelopes and folded papers. "Um, sorry to bother you, Mr. Ellis. I've opened your mail and gone through the ones that are bills and sent those to be paid, and the rest here are requests for proposal for you to review. And this one on top, I didn't open because it has 'confidential' marked on the front." She hands me the stack.

I shuffle through the RFPs and hand that stack back to her. "You're going to have to give these to Royce. I'm headed to London tomorrow for the Tannenbaum job."

"Okay. Uh, do you need me to book you a flight?"

I shake my head and look at the nine-by-twelve yellow envelope. It has only my name on the front, no postmark, which means someone dropped it off to the building. "Did this come directly to the office or with the stack of mail?" I hold up the envelope.

"With the mail from the business carrier."

"No, I will not need a flight booked. Skyler and I already have flights that were booked by the client. However, my girlfriend needs her security team, Nathan and Rachel Van Dyken, to be on that same flight. First class. If you cannot confirm it, we'll need the four of our tickets rebooked and billed to the client."

"Yes, Mr. Ellis. Should I contact the Van Dykens for their personal information?" she asks, but Sky's voice rising across the room has us both focusing on her.

"Tracey, remember you're not only my agent, you are also my best friend. I need this time with Parker. You know. You *know* what it was like . . ." She lifts her gaze to where I'm sitting, and the pain that rips across her gaze flashes for an instant. It's enough for me to figure out what she's referring to. She's talking about when we were on the outs recently.

"I don't care what you want, I'm going to London for the next two weeks. This could mean a three-movie contract deal working with Geneva James. You want to talk press . . . there's your freakin' press. Make it work. I'll do one or two of the junkets while I'm in London, but I won't go to the other countries until after the two weeks are up."

Annie's eyes widen at the tone in Sky's voice, and she twists her fingers where she stands in front of my desk. "Ms. Paige seems awfully mad. Is there anything I can get for her that would help? Tea or coffee?"

I nod. "Yeah, why don't you use the company card and visit the lobby coffee station, bring her a caramel latte and a large coffee with cream for me and a variety of muffins and bagels for the team. Check with Royce and Bo to see if they want anything."

After she smiles softly and nods, I watch her walk away. Annie is sweet, timid, and dresses well. She's wearing a midnight suit I've seen before—the lapel and pocket details are intricate, and I distinctly recall fingering one of the dangling gold zipper pulls over Skyler's collarbone. By the time Annie reaches the door to leave my office, it hits me. It's the same suit I remember Sky wearing in one of the interviews we did together. Sky pulled it off better, but Annie's got a nice form. Toned legs, tight ass. She's not Skyler Paige, but I'm sure the woman turns quite a few heads.

"Thank you, Annie, and there should be a file on the Van Dyken Security team in Wendy's documents along with their personal information."

She flicks her long hair over her shoulder and shoots me a beaming smile. "You're welcome, Mr. Ellis. I'll get right on it."

I finger the envelope and then slide my letter opener through the glued flap. I pull the sheet out and turn it over. There are only six words typed in a big black font.

I AM HER. SHE IS ME.

Odd. I have no idea what this means. I flip over the paper, and there's nothing on the back. I look for any descriptive marks on the envelope that will explain who sent the strange note. Nothing. No return address, not even personal handwriting on the front, just my name and the company name and address typed on an address label, as well as a red-stamped "CONFIDENTIAL."

Skyler groans, leans forward, and runs her hand through her long tresses. "Tracey, I'm sorry if this puts you in a bind, but I'm doing this project with Parker. I'll be doing junkets on and off over the next three months in preparation for the film release. In between them, I'm going to be spending a lot of time in Massachusetts, so you're going to need to get used to not being able to drop in on me in Manhattan. I'm where I want to be and happier than I've ever been."

Suddenly she smiles, and the rigidity of her body relaxes against the couch. "I love you too. Don't worry about me. I'm in good hands." She grins and then ends the call, saying, "Bye."

I drop the weird note into the bin I use for miscellaneous crap I don't have time to deal with right now, and go to my girl. "You definitely are in good hands. Come here." I sit down, and she crawls over my legs and straddles my lap, pressing her face into my neck.

She feels so good in my arms, it's hard to believe she's still mine. After the shit with Johan, I really believed I'd never have this again. Never feel this content, warm, at peace. I run my hands up and down her back and massage her neck. "Everything okay?"

Sky nods. "It is now. Tracey's not happy, but she's never happy. I think she needs to get laid. The woman is growing cobwebs between her thighs."

I tip my head back and laugh heartily. "Getting laid, the answer to the world's problems."

Sky maneuvers her hand between our bodies and cups my growing length. "If the entire world were fucking all the time, they wouldn't have the time to fight wars. Imagine a world with no wars."

I grin while cupping her cheek and smoothing the pad of my thumb over her plump lip. "Make love, not war, eh?"

She leans forward and presses her lips to mine while cupping me fully. "Yep."

"You wanna get out of here?"

Her hand strokes the length of my dick through my tight slacks. "Yep."

"How about dinner tonight, with my folks?"

Skyler stops her movements and leans back; a happy light takes over her lusty gaze. "They want to see me again?"

I frown. "Peaches, I never told them we were on the outs. Nothing has changed with my family."

She bounces in my lap, cups my cheeks, and lays a hard kiss on my lips. We're going at it pretty heavy when the door to my office opens twenty minutes later.

Annie is holding two paper cups of coffee and sporting a fish-out-of-water expression. "I'm . . . so sorry. I, um, yeah . . . I couldn't knock because of the cups . . . ," she rushes to say.

I pull my hand off Skyler's ass, and she swings her leg and body around, planting herself cross-legged on the seat next to me. She wipes at her lips where I smudged her lip gloss.

"Sorry. We're making up for lost time." She blushes beautifully.

Annie plants the cups of coffee on the table in front of us. "One caramel latte, and one large coffee with cream. Again, Mr. Ellis, I'll be sure to knock next time." Her cheeks pinken with what I assume is embarrassment, when in reality, we should be the ones embarrassed, so starved for one another that we can't keep our hands to ourselves even in the workplace.

"No worries. There will be a lot of interesting things you see and hear while working for IG. We're a strange bunch."

Annie jerks her head. "Yeah, that's what Wendy's been telling me. I have a lot to learn."

"Wendy?" I frown and count down the days in my head. She's only a week out of surgery and three days out of the hospital.

Annie licks her lips nervously. "She's training me from home. Sending me how-tos and notes on certain things to make it easier to be helpful right away. I'm picking it up really fast, so you don't have to worry."

I glance at Sky, and she purses her lips and shakes her head. "There's not a lot you can do about Wendy, Parker. That woman marches to the beat of her own drum."

I huff and pick up my phone. "Yeah, until Michael nails her ass *and* mine. The last thing I want to do is piss off her man when he's already rooting for her to quit altogether." The cell in my hand rings a few times before she picks up.

"Hiya, boss man."

God, it's good to hear her voice, but I don't mention that, going right into chastising her. "Wendy," I state on a growl. "You are not supposed to be working. At all."

She sighs. "It's my job, and someone has to help the new girl along until I can come back. Which I'm hoping is more like three weeks, a month tops."

I tip my head back and press my fingers into my temples. "Does Michael know you're working?"

She lowers her voice. "Um . . . yeah. Sure."

"So, if I text him that you're training the new assistant, he'll be fine with that information?"

"You. Wouldn't. Dare!" she states with a whispered menace that makes me want to laugh. I hold it back, but just barely.

"I would. I'm serious. Stop working and get better. We need you. No one could ever take your place." I turn around and realize that Annie is still standing there, a dejected expression crossing her face. I close my eyes and turn around. "Fuck."

"My temp was standing right there, wasn't she?" Wendy says.

"Yeah." I clench my teeth.

Wendy starts to laugh in my ear and then cries out. "Do not make me laugh. It hurts when I laugh."

"Then don't laugh at me. Damn, you know you're a pain in my ass."

Wendy fires back, "That's what she said!" followed by another bout of hysterical laughter. And once again she groans. "Look, dude, I need to go. Have fun in London. I'll be keeping tabs," she says, then hangs up.

Fuckin' Wendy. Always has the upper hand. Damn minx.

I turn back around and find Sky giggling behind her hand and Annie gone. Thank God.

"Wendy so has your number, pretty boy." She grins, and I grab my coffee as I ease down next to my girl and wrap my other arm around her shoulders. Sky cuddles against my side with her own coffee close to her lips.

"You ready to go to London?"

"Totally."

"Well, let's go get ready. I don't have a personal shopper, so I need to go home and pack so we can visit the folks at Lucky's for dinner. I also need to have a conversation with Nate and Rachel. What do you have them working on in Boston anyway?"

She bites her lip and smirks. "Can't tell. It's a surprise. You'll find out soon enough. I'll call them on the way to your house and get them to meet us. Tell them we're off to London tomorrow. They always bring enough clothes with them for seven to ten days, so I'm sure they'll be fine to jet to London in the morning."

"Sounds like a plan." I stand up and hold out my good arm with the busted hand. She takes hold, and together we leave the IG office.

I just got back, and I'm already gone again. I'm starting to wonder if I really even need an office with how much I'm traveling nowadays. Tomorrow London. The client after that could have me in Asia. With my arm around my girl and my love life back on track, I guess it doesn't matter where I'll be, as long as I've got this woman's heart.

Skyler's heart, that's my home.

***

We arrived in London at ten o'clock the next evening local time, crashed at the hotel at midnight, and now, exactly twenty-four hours after having gotten on an airplane, we're headed in a black Audi to the home of author Geneva James.

Skyler, practically jumping in her seat, can hardly keep still. I put my hand on her bouncing, denim-clad knee. "Peaches, relax. You're spazzing out."

She puts her hand over mine. "I'm just so nervous. What if she doesn't like me? You know, the real me, not the me she sees on the movie screen."

This is a common fear my girl has, one of the reasons we met and I had her do the *Bared to You* campaign in the first place.

I hold up her hand and bring it to my lips to kiss her fingertips. She settles the second my lips touch her skin. I hope she always responds that way to me.

"Sky, everything you are, and everything that she will see, is beautiful, because you're beautiful, baby. Inside and out. You have nothing to worry about. Besides, Amy said she's a fan of yours."

She sighs heavily and leans her head back against the leather seat. "Yeah, but people always imagine how you'll be, and if you don't fit into that perfect box, they could find you lacking." A frown flits across her glossy pink lips. She's dressed in dark-wash jeans, canary-yellow stilettos, and a green-and-yellow flowered silk blouse, complete with a white blazer. The sleeves are pushed up to her elbows, and an array of gold bracelets tinkle with each of her movements. Half of her blonde waves are pulled up and away from her face, giving me unhindered view of her pretty brown eyes and high cheekbones.

I turn in my seat and cup her cheek, making her look directly at me. "There is nothing lacking about you. Beauty . . . check. Stylish dresser . . ." I run my gaze down her trendy but chic outfit. "Check. Compassionate heart . . . check. Sweet smile . . ."—she grins, making it easy to admire her lips—"check. Gorgeous face . . . check. Bangin' body . . . ch—"

She covers my mouth with her lips and kisses me so hard I feel it all the way down to my toes. She holds my chin and runs her thumb across my lip the way I usually do to her. "I got your point."

I grin wickedly. "Good. Now relax and realize she's probably more scared to meet you than you are of her."

She shakes her head. "I doubt that."

"It's not like you're meeting the pope, or . . ." I wave my hand in the air until I come up with another celeb. "Oprah."

Skyler giggles. "True. Though I like how you relate a talk show host and actress to the leader of an entire religion."

I shrug. "Kinda the same thing." I wink, and she laughs.

"God, I love you." She half gasps and grabs my hand.

I hold it tight. "Good, because you're not getting rid of me."

She eases her head onto my shoulder, her body finally relaxing against the seat in a more reclined position. "Like I'd want to anyway. Pshhht." The last part comes out in a burst of air, but the words themselves ping around my mind as though they are a solemn promise, not just a throwaway response to something I've said.

Fifteen minutes later, Nate stops at a beautiful black iron gate in a posh, quiet neighborhood in the west side of London called Notting Hill. The borough became even more popular after the movie *Notting Hill* starring Hugh Grant and Julia Roberts became a hit. I can see why. The buildings in this neighborhood are well maintained, the streets clean and filled with trees and quaint businesses. This particular house is a semidetached five story that reminds me of a colonial. If I had to guess, I'd say the house was probably around six thousand square feet, which seems really large for one person. According to Skyler, the Geneva James stalker, there is no record of Geneva James having a family or a significant other, but I imagine over the next two weeks we'll find out why.

Nate communicates with someone on the black speaker box, and the gate magically opens. We're brought down a small path and up to a circular drive that goes directly to the second level of the home. Rachel and Nate get out of the car first and open our doors. As we get out of the car, we can see a pathway to the right that leads to what looks like a private garden. Birds chirp and sing as the wind sways the leaves on the surrounding trees. The air is crisp, and the sun is shining its warm rays.

"It's surprising that it's so sunny. London isn't known for its bright days." Sky holds her hand over her eyes to block the light as she stares at the large London home.

"Beautiful, isn't it?" I ask.

"Yeah, I've thought about getting a home in London. My accountant would die a happy man if I bought ten houses." She grins.

I loop an arm around her shoulders as Nate and Rachel follow us up to the door, their gazes checking the environment.

"Why haven't you?" I ask.

She shrugs. "Never had anyone to take vacations with away from New York City before."

I lean over and kiss her temple. "And now?" I whisper into her hairline.

She hugs me to her side and lifts her chin. "Now I have you, and Tracey, and your brothers, and Wendy. Maybe I can buy a vacation place, and everyone can use it? Seems silly to buy something so huge and have it just sit there all the time."

I nod. "Makes sense. Whatever you want to do, Peaches."

Sky spins in a circle, wraps her arms around my neck, and looks right into my eyes. "And what if I want to get married and have a horde of your babies?"

I swallow slowly and try not to let the instant panic of so much responsibility hitting me all at once push me into blacking out where I stand. "I'd say, one thing at a time."

She grins. "Not out of the realm of possibility in the future, though?"

In the future.

Whew.

Not only is it good that she sees me in her future but sees us married and having children. The first part is amazing, the second nerve-racking.

"No. Not out of the realm, though I'd have to spend a year or two wrapping my head around the idea of children."

Sky bounces up onto her toes and kisses me. "Yay! We're on the same page."

"For once, Sky, I think we are."

She laughs as I push her in the direction of the stairs. When we get to the bright royal-blue double doors, I press the doorbell. Rachel and Nate flank our sides as though a predator could pop out of thin air. Always ready, those two, which makes me happy as a lark that they are glued to Skyler's side, especially when I'm not around.

While we wait for the door to be answered, I'm expecting a house attendant or an assistant and am surprised when the door opens and it's the author herself.

The brunette's blue eyes are kind when she sees me, but her mouth falls open as her gaze zeros in on my girl. "Skyler . . . oh my God. You're Skyler Paige. At my door. At my house." Her British accent makes each word sound lovely when she's mostly just blathering on. Geneva blinks a few times and then looks at me and back to Skyler. "My agent told me a man from International Guy would be coming to help me through my writer's block and he'd be bringing a surprise. We made a bet. A bet. Oh my God! You're Skyler Paige? You're at my house. Why are you at my house?"

Skyler chuckles. "You're fangirling over me! I've been fangirling over you since we met with Amy the other day in Boston. I've read all your books."

"You've read my books. Skyler . . . Skyler Paige has read my books. Oh my . . . I think I need to sit down." She sways where she stands, and I step forward to brace her shoulder as best I can without seeming like a handsy stranger. She just looks at my hand, then at me, and back to Skyler like none of this could possibly be real, or she's about to pass out.

"Hi, I'm Parker Ellis with International Guy. I've been hired by your agent, Amy Tannenbaum, to assist you with your problem. Skyler's here to help as well."

She shakes her head and places her hand against her chest as if her heart is pounding a mile a minute and she needs to stop it.

"May we come in?" I ask.

She sucks in a huge breath. "Oh, bloody hell, of course. Yes. Please, do come in." She opens the door wide, and we follow her into a large living area outfitted with furniture and decorations in a soft color palette. Pastel blue, cream, green, and gold offer a serene and tranquil space.

"Can I offer you a drink?" The tall brunette walks over to a tray filled with glass decanters and pours herself one. "Sherry?" She gulps back the entire thing and winces before pouring herself another.

I chuckle and move to the couch. "May I?" I ask with a gesture to the furniture.

"Please do. Have a seat. Um, I have tea or wine."

"I'd love a glass of wine. Let's get this party started." Skyler rubs her hands together and sits on the couch next to me.

"Party? Are we going to a party?" The brunette's brows furrow together.

"No, silly, we're the party. According to your agent, we're here to loosen you up and bring back your words. When my agent hired Parker, the first thing we did was get drunk together. I think it was an excellent start to our time together, don't you agree, honey?" she gushes, laying it all out on the table like she always does.

Geneva sips her drink and points to Sky, then to me. "You're a couple, right? I mean, I've seen some of the tabloids. You mean to tell me that you were his client?" She directs the question to Sky.

"Yep, and fell in love in the process."

"Wow. That sounds like a good story." Geneva opens a bottle of wine, pours two glasses of red, and hands one to Sky and then me. "Would you mind sharing your story?"

Skyler looks at me, and I wave my hand. "Go ahead. You're dying to share it, I can tell."

Sky smacks me on the leg playfully. "Shut up," she scolds, and then turns back to Geneva. "You're never going to believe this. When we met, my agent had hired him. He came to my penthouse in New York City. I had no idea he was coming right then. My agent had just left, and . . ." She takes a big drink of her wine, so I do the same. The cherry and plum notes slide easily down my throat and warm my belly in the process.

"And then I hear a knock on the door not even five minutes later. Well, I had just gotten out of bed and assumed it was my agent possibly having forgotten to tell me something."

Geneva curls up on her couch, getting comfortable. "Then what happened?"

"I opened the door, and there stood the hottest guy I'd ever seen in my entire life." She hooks a thumb to me, and I can't help but sit up a littler straighter and smirk.

Geneva looks me up and down in an assessing manner as though she's cataloging my features, not taking them in personally. "I can see that. He'd make a perfect Dean, well, if his hair were darker."

Skyler focuses on my hair for a moment, pausing her story. "Totally," she says breathily. "Anyway, I open the door, and this hot guy is standing there. Only I'm wearing a tank, no bra, and a *thong*."

Geneva's lips twist until she's giggling behind her hand. "I would have had a heart attack!"

"I nearly did," Sky says.

I sip at my wine coolly while the women get to know one another.

"Right! It was so embarrassing! Then again, I can't say my *ass*ets didn't help me bag the hottie!" Sky's voice lowers to a sultry timbre that has my dick paying attention. Damn thing pops up every five seconds around the woman lately.

The two of them fall into a fit of giggles and somehow become fast friends in the way that only women are capable of. Me, I just sit back and enjoy the show. Seeing them become close over their shared love of books and romantic movies gives me a great idea for how to start bringing Geneva out of her funk.

5

Day 1 of bringing Geneva James
out of her writer's block.

I scribble the note onto a pad of paper.

Sky looks over my shoulder and snickers.

I nudge her shoulder as we move through Geneva's home the next day. "What?"

"You're logging this like you would in a journal? Do you always do that?" Her eyebrows rise up toward her hairline. "Did you do that on me?" She grabs the front lapels of my sport coat and contorts her voice into that of a military sergeant. "Show me my journal entries!" She laughs herself silly, then continues up the stairs into Geneva's sunroom-office. She has two offices. One that she uses when it's sunny out and she can take advantage of the light, another she calls "the cave" because it's surrounded by books and heavy draperies over the windows.

Authors are weird. I get that, accepted long ago when I watched my ma deal with aspiring authors in the library she worked in as I grew up. Hell, she still works there.

When we reach the sunroom, Geneva is sitting at her desk, a blank white page on the screen in front of her. She sighs and drops her head down into her hand, elbow firmly planted on the desktop. "I just can't do it. I don't know how to move forward." The curve of her spine, her shoulders hanging, give a damning picture of how torturous the situation feels for this woman.

Sky walks over to her and puts her hands on both of Geneva's shoulders. "When my best friend reached out to Parker, she was desperate. I was completely gone. No desire to act, to perform. The love of my life, which had always been acting, telling a worthy story, was no longer inside of me. I'd lost it."

Geneva lifts her face, tears clouding the view of her blue eyes. "What if I make the wrong choice? There is so much riding on this book. And I . . . I can't get it wrong."

Sky kneels on the floor, placing her hands on Geneva's knee. "Why do you think you're going to make the wrong choice? This is your story to tell. Whatever you decide is going to be the right path. It is as you mean it to be for Simone and Dean."

Geneva shakes her head, and the tears fall. "The way I left it, the cliffhanger at the end of book two, I . . . started to write what I thought would be their path in book three, but it doesn't feel right. It feels like I'm writing for what will bring me the most dollars, but not for the story that's in my soul."

Skyler inhales loudly and lets it out. "You can only write the story you feel in your heart, the one that speaks to your soul. That's the one that the readers want to read and the story the characters demand. I know when I'm playing a role, if I try to act against the character's nature, it doesn't fit. It's like putting a round peg into a square hole."

Geneva wipes her eyes and leans an elbow onto her desk, then lays her head in her hand. "You've read the first two books. What do you think happens?"

Both Sky and I spent the evening before we left the States and the entire plane ride reading the first two books.

Sky sits back on her heels and ponders the question.

I answer immediately, "We don't know. You left so many possibilities open, we're silently waiting for whatever path you have them walk. Let me ask you this . . ."

"Okay?"

"Do you see Dean and Simone together? Do they get their happily ever after?"

She looks at me in the face, but it's as if she's seeing through me. "Yes, I do believe they end up together. They deserve one another after the hell I've put them through."

Skyler grins and puts her hands in the air. "Yay!" she cheers softly. "You see, we don't care how you get them there, only that at the end, they find one another. Isn't that what life and love is all about? The path to finding your happily ever after with the one you're meant to be with?"

Geneva nods. "I always thought so, yes."

"What we need to work with you on is finding that light again. Finding the joy that your writing gives you. When was the last time you did a fan event? A book signing?" I query softy.

Geneva purses her lips. "Wow, uh, I don't know. At least two or three years. I've been focused solely on the books and spin-offs."

"Sky tells me that a lot of authors have prereaders or beta readers. Do you work with any of them?"

She shakes her head. "I have my editor, Catherine Martin. She reads through and works with me on everything I write."

Sky gets up off the floor and leans into the desk. "You pay her to help you work through these things, yeah?"

Geneva nods.

"And what has she said about your current predicament?"

She snorts. "My editor says to stop believing the garbage my last publisher made me feel." Her cheeks pinken as if she's embarrassed.

"Which is what?" I tip my head and lean against the couch in the center of the room, ensuring my stance isn't dominating.

"That I'm not good enough. That the only reason I'm where I am today is because of them and their marketing skills. So basically, they foreshadowed this series, without them, folding."

Sky clamps her jaws shut, and fists form from both hands. "That's total bullshit. They didn't write the books. They didn't weave a story so beautiful people wanted more. You can't possibly believe their crap."

Geneva shrugs. "When you're told over and over you are nothing without their money, their marketing of your stories, you believe it. Then you second-guess why you're even doing what you're doing."

"Their marketing and money don't change the fact that the series you're writing now is a worldwide bestseller. Your agent has Paramount on the line for a three-movie deal. That's huge! Your other books did well too. Not because of your publisher. Of course, they helped spread the word, and a good publisher, like a good agent, believes in their author and the story they produce, but the end result is that not one person would have bought book two if they didn't love the first one. Can you see the logic in that at least?"

Geneva lets out a long slow exhale and shrugs. "I guess. I don't know."

Sky stands up and puts her hands on her hips. "Well, I do know. I think you need to see a little bit of it for yourself."

"Exactly! I couldn't agree with Skyler more," I say. "Which is why I contacted Amy last night."

Skyler's questioning gaze flings to me.

"You were in the bath," I say.

"Ah. Travel takes it out of my body," she remarks randomly.

I smile at my girl and glory in the fact that she's here with me, working this case. And she's right; having her here is fun. Different. A definite change from the norm but entertaining nonetheless. I absolutely appreciate going back to the hotel and losing myself in her body, sharing dinner with her, watching a late-night movie before falling asleep. It's a novelty I haven't had with a woman before Skyler and one I'm coming to adore more and more when I'm with her.

"Anyway, I contacted Amy. From four to six tonight you're going to be doing a pop-up signing at a bookstore in downtown London. She's already had your graphics designer create some artwork, and we've blasted it across your social media platforms."

Geneva's eyes widen. "Seriously? Um, wow. Okay. I . . ." She stands up and smiles. "I think this will be interesting. I haven't spoken to readers in a long time. Do you think any will show?"

Skyler makes a loud scoffing noise as I bite my tongue, watching the dramatics of my woman's response play out. She grins. "Puh-leeeze . . . of course they'll show. And I'm going to be first in line! I need every book they have at that store signed."

Geneva waves her hand in the air and goes over to a door that looks like it might lead to a closet. Inside are rows and rows of shelves with copies of her books on them. She grins as Sky runs her fingers across the spines and practically drools at the titles.

Readers and their books. Strange but sweet.

"You can have one of everything if you'd like."

Sky nods numbly. "Oh yeah, this is awesome!"

While Geneva starts removing titles and stacking them on a table, I scan the covers of the two print books for the A-Lister Trilogy. I glance at the couple on the fronts. You can't see their entire faces; the designer cut off the top half from the eyes up.

"Why cut off their faces?" I spin the cover around to Geneva, so she can see what I'm talking about.

She grabs the book in my hand and looks at it. "If the readers can see the faces, it may not match what they envision. I prefer to have the readers use their own imaginations of what the characters look like, unless I have my exact perfect vision of the characters by way of a cover model. It's rare, though. Since Skyler was my celebrity cast for Simone, and I had no way of getting her on the cover, I had the designer get a couple whose forms and hair colors suited the characters. That's also why their faces are in profile and half-visible."

"Huh, interesting." Another idea comes to fruition about zapping the author's writer mojo, but I'll have to talk to Skyler about it and Bo if she agrees.

My phone buzzes in my coat pocket, and I pull it out and note Amy Tannenbaum's number.

"Ms. Tannenbaum. How are you?" I move out of the supply closet and back into the sunroom. Outside is a private, lush green garden that would be an excellent place to sit and have a meal or chat about life over a beer, or a glass of wine in Skyler's case.

I don't have a backyard. My apartment is just that, an apartment. There are walls and a slider with a balcony that exposes my girlfriend to paparazzi if she chooses to open the door and check on the atmosphere outside of my home. I frown and think about Royce and his three-bedroom house in suburbia. Maybe there's something to planning for the future. Having a beautiful home and environment to share with the one you love while you plan to fill it in the future with your own children.

Amy's reply knocks me out of my current reverie. "Wonderful. How is my client?"

I curve around the closet door and watch while Geneva stacks more books on a growing pile. We're going to need to have those books shipped to Sky's New York apartment. There is no way that huge stack is being dragged back in our luggage. We'd need a suitcase just for the books.

"Enjoying herself, talking books with my girlfriend."

Amy lets out what sounds like a relieved sigh. "And she's going to attend the signing today?"

"Yep. She sounded excited about it, though worried no one will show up."

Amy groans. "My author doesn't think very highly of herself. The announcement went out three hours ago. As of five minutes before my call to you, there was a line around the block at the bookstore. Fans are already waiting, and she doesn't sign for another three hours. The store had to call in security. I thought it best to notify you, but mostly Skyler. I can only imagine how bad it will get if she shows up."

"If?"

"I'm suggesting she stay back. The crowd is already crazy. Skyler Paige shows, and it could turn into something scary."

A pinprick of dread ripples along my spine, and I grind my teeth. "I'll talk to her and her security team. She is not going to be happy about this."

"Who's not going to be happy about what?" Skyler asks me, a stack of books in her hands, the smile on her face slipping the longer I stare and don't answer her question. She narrows her gaze. "Park . . ."

I close my eyes and rub at the back of my neck. "Okay, I'll let you know the end result," I respond to Amy.

"Good luck," Amy says before ringing off.

"Well, we have good news and bad news," I start.

Skyler frowns as Geneva comes up behind her with another stack of books and sets them on her desk. "What's the good news?" Sky says.

I attempt to put on a happy-go-lucky smile but fear I'll fail as Skyler sets down her stack of books, crosses her arms, and sucks her bottom lip into her mouth.

"There's already a line around the bookstore of fans ready to get their books signed."

Geneva stops in her tracks and gasps, her hand flying to her chest. "Really?"

Sky looks over to her. "Like there was ever any doubt."

"Wow. I mean, I haven't been to a fan event in forever. I guess I just thought they might have forgotten about me."

I walk over to Geneva and place my hand on her shoulder. "Guess your readers want to meet the woman who's written the stories they've fallen in love with."

She smiles wide. "I guess they do. Now I need to figure out what to wear!" Geneva looks down at her jeans and fingers the hem of her white V-necked T-shirt. "Not exactly hip author threads, are they?"

"I'm sure Skyler can help you pick something," I offer, knowing Skyler will always willingly help someone if she can. It's part of her nature.

"What's the bad news?" Skyler taps her toe against the hardwood floor.

This time, I move over to my woman and bring her into my arms. It's not very professional, but having Skyler here in the first place is unorthodox anyway. "Amy is worried about the potential security risk if the already large audience finds out that Skyler Paige is attending the signing."

Her entire expression falls into one of sadness. "No . . . ," she whispers.

"I'm sorry, Peaches. Amy doesn't think it's safe. The store is hiring more security as it is. You come into the mix, and it could be mania."

She pouts and leans her body against mine, her forehead dipping to my chest. "This isn't fair, Park. I want to go. I've never been to a bookstore signing."

Geneva clears her throat. "What if she goes in disguise? My best friend loves to wear wigs and crazy attire when she goes out, and she buys me the same things. If we change her hair color, put her in a pair of aviators, it could work, no?"

Skyler grins wide, curls her fingers around my waist, and tugs. "Please, pretty please . . ." Her voice dips to that sultry note she uses when she's being playful in the sack. "I'll make it worth your while."

I grind my teeth together. "You are not playing fair."

Skyler spins her fingers in circles around my lower back, sending bolts of excitement through my skin and straight to my cock. I thrust my hips against her without meaning to, and she sighs and giggles.

I groan. "I'll talk to Nate and Rachel about it. Even if you're in a disguise, the public is starting to recognize me and your bodyguards. Who's to say they won't suspect your presence if they see the rest of us?"

Skyler shakes my body. "Parker, I can't live wrapped in cotton or behind gold bars. It's not fair to me, or anyone for that matter. Plus, I'll go in through the back while you and Geneva are led through the front. I'll stand off to the side next to my security team. It will be okay, I just know it."

"That's what every celebrity's famous last words were before they were attacked or gunned down by a lunatic." My heart starts to pound in my chest, and I rub my fist over the tension I'm feeling in my sternum.

She rolls her eyes and pushes out of my hold. "You're being dramatic. The paparazzi don't even know we're here. We've seen neither hide nor hair of them."

I point at her retreating form. "Yet! That's all about to be blown to shit the second one of them catches a whiff of you at the bookstore in downtown London with the book world's most famous author."

Geneva shakes her head. "Not true. That would be Stephen King. James Patterson. J. K. Rowling . . ." She continues rattling off a list of authors.

A heavy sigh leaves my lungs as I plant my hands on my hips. "I'm going to go talk to the Van Dykens. Why don't the two of you figure out what Geneva is going to wear to the event?" I look down at my watch and note it's eleven thirty. "We're leaving in T-minus three hours. Maybe we should order in some food too."

"I can make us lunch," Geneva offers.

Does the woman do everything on her own?

"We'll figure something out." I let out a breath through my clenched teeth and head for the stairs.

Sky grabs Geneva's hand. "Come on. Let's leave him to his brooding."

I grimace as my phone buzzes in my pocket again. I pull it out and note it's a text.

From: Unknown
To: Parker Ellis

WHAT DOES SHE HAVE THAT I DON'T?

I read and reread the text. It doesn't make any sense, as there was no conversation that came before it. Probably an error.

Hitting the "Message" button, I respond:

To: Unknown
From: Parker Ellis

You've got the wrong number.

I click the "Send" button and make my way down two flights of stairs to the front entry, which Rachel and Nate have been guarding. While we've been here, Nate has done intervals walking around the house while Rachel guards the inside, and vice versa.

As Nate's about to exit the front door, I call out, "Hey, Nate, Rach, can we talk? Got a scenario to plan for."

Nate locks the door and checks it's secure before following me into the living room Geneva first brought us to. I stand over by the windows and glance at her garden. So peaceful and serene. Makes me yearn for that type of luxurious respite in my own home. If I had a private space like that, surrounded by trees, barricaded by a nice tall wall so my girl wouldn't be under the microscope, we could lie out in the sun, play Frisbee, get a cat or a dog. Hell, we could get both. Whatever she wants.

70

And if we had a pool, I'd be able to watch my girl walk around in a bikini within the comfort of our own home . . .

"Ellis?" Nate breaks my wandering thoughts.

I cough into my elbow. "Sorry. We've got a situation. We've scheduled Geneva for a book signing at three today. Her agent called and told me there's a line around the block and growing."

Nate grumbles under his breath. The man does not like crowds, and I don't know if that's because he personally doesn't like them, or because a crowd makes it harder to protect his charge.

"The store is hiring more security in the event that something gets out of hand."

"Let me guess . . ." Rachel grins. "Skyler plans on attending."

I point to my nose and then to her. "Bingo."

"Aw, man. That woman has absolutely no sense of self-preservation." Nate runs his hand over his chin.

Rachel licks her lips and crosses her arms. "Maybe because she just wants to live a normal life."

"She should've thought about that before making her career choice," Nate retorts in a deep, growl-like tone.

Rachel scowls. "It's not her fault she's talented. Besides, we have jobs because she is. And frankly, it's our job to keep her safe. I think it's fine. We're solid. This is a bookstore with a bunch of readers, bookish types, not a metal concert with a bunch of meatheads hopped up on X."

"Still, I think we need to be careful. Skyler's going to disguise herself a little, see if we can't fool the readers for as long as we can. If things get out of hand, I want her out of there," I say, trying to run through all the potential scenarios where my girl could get hurt. There really aren't that many. As Rachel stated, these are romance readers, not homicidal maniacs looking to take down a celebrity.

"I'll go now, check it out, scour the space and exits, and bring back some intel." Nate states this to Rachel, not to me.

Rachel adds to the list of things for Nate to look into. "I've got the house. Find the best place to park and make sure the store owner knows who's coming and has a roped-off area that we can hide Skyler away in."

He walks over to his wife, grabs her hand, and squeezes. They just look into one another's eyes, communicating something silently, which I imagine is something like *"I love you. Be back soon. Be safe,"* or maybe all of the above.

Suddenly he lets go of her hand, turns on his combat boots, and disappears out the door.

"Man of few words," I say to fill the awkward silence.

"We're on the job. The lovey-dovey shit does not fly on the job." Her words are a declaration, not open for discussion.

"Good point."

She winks, bringing back the easy levity we normally have. "I'm doing a perimeter check. You've got the inside?"

I can't imagine that someone would be able to scale the gate and get into the house unnoticed, but as I recalled before, this team is hard-core about their security, and that means the woman I love will stay safe and sound at all times. "Yes, ma'am."

She frowns. "Don't call me *ma'am*. It makes me feel old."

I chuckle and salute her instead.

"Now that I like." She grins and takes off out the door.

I shake my head and stroll through the house to find the kitchen. Once there, I go through her cabinets, pantry, and fridge. There isn't peanut butter anywhere, which is weird. Most every American household keeps peanut butter in stock unless someone inside is allergic to peanuts. Except we're not in the States, which means . . . ah, yep. I find the white-and-brown jar labeled "Nutella." Hazelnut. Which, to me, tastes more like dessert and less like a sandwich topping.

Going over to the fridge, I pull out some apples and set those on the counter. I also find some deli meats and cheese. Instead of pulling together sandwiches for the three of us, I make a meat, cheese, and fruit platter that could rival any charcuterie's hors d'oeuvres if I do say so myself.

I find the wine chiller and pull out a crisp New Zealand sauvignon blanc to pair with the meal. Once I've got three glasses filled, I call up to the girls.

The two of them come giggling down the stairs. When they reach the bottom, I open my arms in a "surprise" gesture.

Skyler claps her hands and bounces a bit on her toes before rushing to me and kissing me sweetly on the lips. "You did all this for us."

"I did." I waggle my eyebrows, reminding her that she already owes me one, and this makes two.

"This looks amazing, and I'm utterly famished," Geneva says, sitting at the bar in front of the food.

I pass her a glass, then one to Skyler, and grab one for myself.

"What should we drink to?" Skyler says.

"To finding the words that will write the story as it was meant to be." I pull the elephant we're here to wrangle right out into the open.

"Hear, hear!" Skyler clinks Geneva's glass and then my own.

I do the same before focusing my gaze on Skyler's and drinking in her eyes as I fill my mouth with a fruity taste, not unlike her kisses.

Geneva puts down her glass. "I just want to thank you guys for coming. I mean, I know you're being paid, but today has been more fun than I've had in a long time."

"Oh, Ms. James, the fun has just begun," I promise on a smirk.

She smiles and pops a chunk of apple into her mouth, chewing thoughtfully while looking at Skyler, who's leaning her body against mine. "Spending time with the two of you, I do believe you're right."

6

Geneva's agent way underestimated the number of people waiting to see the author. As we roll up to the front of the bookstore, two security guards come up to the car. The second Geneva exits, the crowd starts screaming, waving books and posters in the air. I scan the street and note that not only has the line gone around the block, it's doubled and looped around itself.

Geneva waves at the crowd as I place my hand on her back and lead her toward the store.

Her cheeks are rosy as she looks up at me. "I can't believe this. I mean, I know the books sell well, but . . ." She loses her wording as the crowd gets louder. "It's incredible."

I grin and push her toward the door, wanting to get her out of the open. I guess being with a celebrity, I'm used to Nate's rule of get the VIP under cover and out of a crowd as quickly as possible.

"You deserve this attention. The books not only are well written, they have a story that connects to people in all walks of life. Your readers find something in your words that speaks to them."

She smiles shyly and looks down at her shoes, almost as if she's pondering what I've said.

The security team follows us in and leads us to the table set up with stacks of Geneva's newest books. There's a six-foot-tall banner next to it with her name on it and a picture of the A-Lister Trilogy couple, once again with faces cut off.

Hmm.

I nudge Geneva's shoulder. "What if you could have the right characters on the cover of your books? Who would be your perfect Simone and Dean?"

She smiles wide. "I told you. Skyler is the basis for Simone, and Dean would be a Henry Cavill type. Brown hair, blue eyes—though you'd work perfectly." She taps at her bottom lip thoughtfully.

"Me?" I jerk my head back.

"Course. In case you haven't noticed, you and Skyler make a beautiful couple. The entire world is going to swoon when you get married and start having babies."

I choke on the lump filling my throat. "Whoa, whoa. Getting a bit ahead of things. Skyler and I are happy, but nowhere near marriage and children."

She walks around the table they've set up for her and shrugs. "Things change, opinions change when you've found the right person to spend your life with."

The bookstore owner comes over to Geneva and shakes her hand, going over the plan. While she's doing so, Skyler enters from the back. I grin and bite down on my lip hard. She's a vision hiding behind long dark curls and a pair of black-rimmed glasses. Her lips are a bubblegum pink I want to bite into like a sugary doughnut.

Nate leads her over to an area that's behind the pop-up banner and a bookcase. She can hang out in her corner, still talk to Geneva and the rest of us, while pretty much hiding in plain sight. I find my way around the bookcase and loop an arm around her from behind. "Brunette . . ." I push aside her fake hair and growl against her neck. "This could be interesting." I kiss my way up the side of her neck until she spins around, looping her arms around mine.

"It's growing on me." She smirks, and I lean down and take her bubblegum-colored lips in a hard, deep kiss. Our tongues tangle, and she presses her body against mine, aligning us from chest to toes. I slant her head and lick deep, tasting as much of her sweetness as I can get, knowing our time hidden away is limited.

Behind us, the sounds of voices and feet on the floor announce the first wave of fans. The rest of the store had to be shut down, but the owner doesn't care. After the readers meet Geneva, they can shop and pay for the books they secured.

I pull away from Skyler begrudgingly and swipe the smudged lipstick under her bottom lip. "Time to work. Oh, but I have an idea I wanted to run past you."

"What's up?" Always so willing, my girl.

"What if I asked you to pose for the cover of Geneva's third book? Would you do it? Do you have any legal or professional conflicts?"

"Did she tell you that's what she wants?"

I shake my head. "No, but part of her connecting with her characters could be seeing them come to life the same way they will on the movie screen. If she could start working on the first movie with the production company, maybe she wouldn't feel so disconnected. I thought if we could get you posing with a model that looks like Dean, it might light a fire under her muse. What do you say?"

She grins wide. "I say hell to the yes! I've never been on a book cover before, but I'd do it for this series and this author. It could also help the higher-ups who are making the movie see me as Simone's character."

I nod. "True. I'll talk to Amy and see what she thinks. Find out if she can get the model who was on the other two covers to come in and pose with you. Though you should double-check with Tracey and make sure you don't have any conflicts."

Skyler pulls out her phone. "Will do that now. Great idea, honey." She lifts up onto her toes and kisses me once more.

"You check in with Tracey, also find out what junket you need to do, and we'll get that set up with Nate and Rachel."

She frowns and runs her toe along the beige floor, her smile slipping.

"Would you go with me? To the uh, press stuff? Usually when I do one, I go for the day and go from room to room and talk about the film. I'm sure it would be totally boring to you, but . . ." She shrugs. "I like being with you, spending time together even when we're working. I don't know; it feels as though maybe . . ."

"This is us. Doing what we need to do to spend quality time together and still be able to do our jobs and fulfill our career obligations."

Her face lights up, and the glow that is solely Skyler comes back, pinkening her cheeks and making her brown eyes sparkle. "Yes!" she gasps. "Exactly."

I grip her by the waist and run my hand down to her heart-shaped ass. I give it a little squeeze as I dip my chin down until I can feel her breath on my lips. "Peaches, of course I'll go with you. If we can swing it while we're here, let's do it."

"I love you, Parker Ellis." Those words are said on a sigh, and I never tire of hearing them.

I nuzzle her nose with mine. "That's good, because I love you, Skyler Lumpkin." I say her name in nothing but a whisper, not wanting anyone to hear. With a quick peck to her lips and a firm squeeze to her ass, I move away from her body, hating the distance, but knowing I need to be on the job more than I need to be kissy-facing it with my woman in a crowded bookstore.

Leaving Skyler to get situated in her cubby space, I head to where Geneva is chatting with a fan.

"Oh my God, you're my favorite author in the whole world. The way you made Dean catch Simone as she fell off the first-floor balcony . . ." The fan's eyes go wild, and she pushes her hand through her hair. "I thought she was going to die, and then I would have been so angry . . ."

Geneva nods and signs the book for the quick talker. "I'm glad it all worked out."

"I can't wait to find out what happens. That ex-girlfriend is still after Dean, and Simone is going crazy thinking she might be pregnant . . . I can't wait!" the fan practically screeches.

"Thank you so much for your support. The third book will come out . . . soon. I think soon."

The next reader comes up with what looks like a scrapbook completely filled with what seems like typed lines from the book, and . . . what the heck? I lean over Geneva's shoulder and see image after image of Skyler, from cut-out magazine advertisements to movie promos, pasted next to Henry Cavill.

Geneva's eyes light up as she turns each page. "She is the perfect Simone."

The reader nods frantically. "Do you think they'll be able to get her? I mean she's done romance before and suspense, and she's just the perfect Simone Shilling. I can't wait for the movies!"

"Maybe. My agent has put in the request for Ms. Paige, but you never know. Keep your fingers crossed, and so will I." Geneva plays it off so coolly.

I place my hand on Geneva's shoulder and lean down to her ear. "Looks like you've got a lot of happy readers here. Not one person has complained about the next book. You're not letting anybody down. Every person here is thrilled to read your stories and share a moment with you. Pretty powerful."

Geneva nods as the next person walks up with her books. "Yes, it is, Mr. Ellis. Feels good too."

"Ms. James, I'm your number-one fan . . . ," says the tenth person in a row.

I chuckle behind my hand and note that the table is getting low on books, but the line is still long. The bookseller is standing off to the side, talking to a couple of her staff, watching the show.

"We're going to need some more books."

"Already?" the owner gasps.

"They're gobbling them up fast."

"Ladies." She turns to the two staff. "Can you get the big boxes in the back and roll them in? We'll just set them behind Ms. James so we can refill the piles without any disruption."

The two staff members move to the back of the store, and I head over to visit Nate.

"How goes it?" I ask. Nate's currently standing like a Secret Service agent guarding the president. His gaze never leaves the crowd to make eye contact with me, but it does scan the space to assess where Skyler is and what she's doing.

Right now, she's chatting with Geneva from behind the pop-up. The two of them laugh as though they are lifelong friends.

Nate's gruff voice fills the air. "It's going well. Even though there are a lot of people, the readers are docile. They wait patiently for their turn; they're not complaining and haven't so much as attempted to approach the back portion of the store." He continues to watch the patrons walk up, say a quick few words to Geneva, get their books signed, and carry on to the cash register.

I inhale fully for what feels like the first time. When Amy sent the warning of the crowd size, the fear for Skyler's safety put a lock around my lungs, to the point where I couldn't breathe easy. Now that I'm here and can verify that the fans are really very sweet and all seem to be extremely civil, I can catch my breath. Of course, they don't know that the most sought-after actress in the world is in a disguise and sitting behind a bookcase twenty feet from where they stand. As long as we keep that under wraps, we shouldn't have a problem.

"Since everything's kosher, I'm going to head to the back and make a few calls." I hook a thumb over my shoulder.

"We've got this under control." Nate's voice is confident and steadfast.

I clap the man on the shoulder and pull my phone out of my jacket as I go. As I pass Skyler, her gaze lifts to mine, and she blows me a kiss. Not wanting to bring attention to her, I just smile a shit-eating grin, head to a quiet back corner while pulling up IG's number on my phone, and hit go.

Annie answers on the first ring. "International Guy, Annie speaking, how may I be of service?"

I roll my eyes and snarl internally, hating that it's not Wendy's sassy voice answering the phone.

"Hi, Annie, this is Parker. I need to speak with Bo if he's in."

"Hello, Mr. Ellis. So good to hear from you. I hope your stay in London is faring well."

I grind down on my molars and force myself to be nice. It's not Annie's fault she isn't Wendy. It's a crazed woman scorned who put our girl in the hospital with a bullet wound to add to her list of things she's survived. I close my eyes and remember that Wendy would nail me to the wall if I so much as thought about treating her temporary replacement poorly. "Very well, thank you, Annie. Is—"

"And Skyler, is she feeling better? I know when I last saw her, she was unhappy."

"She's fine. Thank you for asking. May I speak to Bo, please?"

"Sure. I'll patch you right through, and don't be afraid to call or email requesting things. Wendy informed me this job is not a nine-to-five but more like a twenty-four-seven arrangement, and I'm happy to be your go-to girl." Her voice even sounds sweet as she makes a very kind offer.

"I will let you know. Bo, please?"

"Yes, sir."

I hear a couple of beeps and then my friend's voice. "Tell me Geneva James is as cool in person as her books are?" Bo asks without any form of greeting.

"You've read her books?" I should have guessed that.

He scoffs, "You haven't?"

"Well, I have now. Skyler and I read them together on the plane ride over. I read the first two of the A-Lister Trilogy."

"Can you believe how he caught Simone when she was literally falling from the sky?"

"It was a second-story balcony, not a free fall to earth," I respond dryly.

"Dean is the man. He's cool, rides a motorcycle, and gets a Skyler lookalike. Which reminds me. How are things between you and hot pants?"

"Do. Not. Call. Her. That. *Ever.* You feel me?" My voice comes out in a gravelly, animal-like growl.

Bo laughs loudly, and I have to hold the phone away from my ear for a moment. Bo guffaws once more and says, "What are you going to do about it all the way in London? Hmm? And besides, you're not blind. Your girl has a stellar ass. Four out of five moviegoers agree, according to an online survey I just read."

I groan and press my thumb and finger into my temples. "Put down the gossip rags and keep your mind out of the gutter . . ."

"Can't. Not possible," he quips instantly.

"For a minute or two." I let out an exasperated sigh and lean my elbow into a bookcase to hold myself up. All the late-night sexcapades are wearing me out. We need to sleep tonight. *Sleep.* Not fuck.

"What do you need from me? You sound tired. Ohhhhh, I know why. Because Sky's keeping you up all night with a little brown chicken brown cow . . ."

I want to slam my head—or maybe the phone—into the nearest bookcase. Yeah, the phone. Wendy's not here to get pissed if I ruin another one. Again, a knife prick of sadness wedges its way into my chest. Damn, I thought that pressure and pain would go away when I got Sky back. Turns out, being without anyone I love puts that damn dagger back in its lock within my chest.

"It's bow chicka bow wow—" I say, but he cuts me off again.

"What do you get when you cross a brown chicken with a brown cow . . . brown chicken brown cow . . . ," he sings again, and laughs himself hoarse.

"Jesus, why do I put up with this?"

"Because you love me. Admit it. You. Love. Me. I'm adorable. And, I'm always there for you. Like that time you punched a wall while holding a beer bottle . . ."

"Ugh, don't remind me." I open my palm and am glad to see the skin healing up nicely and only a faint pink raised area where my skin was sliced open and stitched back together. The two broken fingers, however, are still tender when I bend them, though I've kept them taped together to be safe.

"Sorry, bro. All kidding aside. How are you and Sky?"

Just hearing her name has me smiling and seeking out her beautiful face. I catch her across the room shimmying her stellar ass and dancing down the aisle behind her bookcase to a beat I can't hear. "What can I say? I'm in love."

Bo lets out a long whistle. "Thank God. We didn't want to play sides and wanted to wait until you'd had some time before bugging you about it. Did you work it out?"

"Yeah, yeah, man, we did. She didn't cheat, and she understands that she put herself in a very dangerous situation and will not be doing anything so stupid in the future."

"And you?" Because my brother knows I played a role in our breakup. A big one.

"I apologized too. For not trusting her. I'm working on it, but I've come to realize that shit with Kayla, her royally screwing me over, really affected how I perceived my relationship with Sky. And I learned I can't do that. Skyler's nothing like Kayla, and I just have to trust what we have and hold on to it as tight as possible."

"Good. I'm happy for you, brother. Royce is too."

My heart eases into a relaxed rhythm. I'm not sure why, but I guess in the back of my mind I was worried that Bo and Royce might have changed their opinions of Skyler because of what happened with Johan. It's good to know they are trusting me and her, which is a first. They must really like her for me.

"Thank you. Now the reason for my call."

"I'm all ears . . . well, not *all* ears." His voice drops into the seductive tone he uses on his chicklets. "I do have a really large—"

"How would you like to do a book-cover photo shoot with Skyler as the subject and Geneva James as the author?" I cut him off before he starts talking about the size of his johnson.

"Park, you had me at book-cover shoot."

"You're such a fuckin' girl. Now let me tell you what I've got in mind . . ."

***

Two hours flew by, and there was still a line around the block. Geneva demanded to stay until the very last person was seen. Another three hours later, now ten o'clock, I'm leading an exhausted author and superfan to the blacked-out Audi SUV that Nate rented. The three women squeeze into the back as Nate drives, and I take the passenger side.

Skyler sits forward and covers Nate's shoulder. "Thanks for keeping me safe." Sky eases back and grabs Rachel's hand. "Thanks, girl." It's the same thing she says after each outing we take with them.

"We got your back." Rachel nudges Sky's shoulder playfully.

Geneva leans forward and puts her hand on my shoulder. "Thank you, Parker. Today was amazing. Seeing the fans, hearing their love for Simone and Dean, it just . . . it gives me so many ideas on where I could take the story."

I grin wide and glance at Skyler over my shoulder. "Just what we want to hear. How's about tomorrow we sneak out and see some of the sights? Skyler, baby, your choice. Just make sure your team knows."

Skyler rubs her hands together. "Well, there's the London Eye, which is iconic. Buckingham Palace, an obvious go-to. Hello, the guards." Her eyes widen with excitement, and her previous exhaustion slips away as her joy takes over, giving her a second wind.

I just watch her beautiful face as she becomes animated, the hills of her cheeks pinkening with each smile, the dip above her lip as succulent as the day I met her, and the sexy curve of her jawline mouthwatering in its perfection. It all bewitches me. The woman's beauty stuns me silent at the strangest times.

How lucky am I to have this gorgeous woman's heart within my hands?

"There's the Tower of London, Saint Paul's Cathedral, Windsor Castle . . ." Sky cups both of her cheeks with her hands. "There's honestly so much, I wouldn't even know where to start."

Geneva jumps into the fray. "I do. How about since you two are here because of me, I take you around and show you London by a true native."

Skyler holds up her hand, and Geneva pops her a high five. "Works for me. Honey?"

Honey.

I grin and pair my gaze with hers. She smiles softly, and I know she gets it. *Honey.* I missed that one word coming out of her lips more than I missed the sex, and that's saying a lot. I never thought I'd be the sappy fellow who's starry-eyed over his mate, but with Skyler, it's as if I don't even have a choice. The universe has decided for me.

"Yeah, that works for me." My words are filled with emotion as I keep my eyes on my beautiful woman.

"Just give us the rundown of what you're planning, and we'll be ready to take you guys," Rachel adds.

Geneva frowns. "Wouldn't you two rather have the day off?"

Rachel puts her hand over the author's. "Where Skyler goes, we go, unless she's buttoned up safe with Parker, on set, or home."

Geneva looks at Skyler, and a gloomy expression takes over her features. "Are you ever able to go out alone?"

Skyler shakes her head. "I've tried it before. It's not a good idea. When I wasn't in so many blockbuster films, I could go a lot more places unnoticed. Now I can't walk down the street unless I'm in a pretty good disguise."

Geneva pats Skyler's hand. "You poor dear. To not have an ounce of privacy sounds awful."

Skyler's lips flatten into a line as she shrugs. "Nature of the beast. I love my job, and most of my fans are truly kind and considerate, but not all of them. We have to be careful with the ones who can't distinguish reality from the world they see on the movie screen."

"I see. Well, we'll have fun tomorrow, and I've got a fabulous red wig that will look amazing on you."

My girl grins wide. "I've thought about becoming a redhead."

I cringe, and Sky catches the slip.

"Or not."

I answer as a man should unless he fancies standing in front of a female firing squad. "I'd love you with red, black, or even purple hair."

"Good answer, honey. Good answer." Skyler laughs.

Nate lifts his fist, and I fist bump him.

"You're learning." He smiles for the first time all day.

"That I am."

7

"Why aren't you wearing the wig?" Geneva asks as she gets in the car the next day.

Skyler runs her fingers through her long blonde tresses. "Honestly, I had a headache after wearing the brown one all day yesterday. My head needed a break. I've got my guy's Red Sox hat and a nifty pair of aviators. We should be fine."

Nate's lip flattens, and a grimace steals across his face. I know he doesn't like these public escapades out where we don't have a bigger security team with us, but Skyler needs to be able to go out into the world. I can't risk her going back into her shell again. Especially not after she's found her craft and happy place within herself again.

"Don't worry, Nate. I have full faith in your wife's and your abilities to take care of our girl." I try to pump up his ego, but Nate isn't really the type to get off on that shit. Still, a man likes to know that the people he's caring for believe in his abilities.

Nate doesn't say anything, just nods curtly. I can understand the nerves he must have, but he's going to have to get over it. Rachel, on the other hand, is a burst of energy this morning. With a giant *venti* Starbucks cup in her hand and a green straw stuck to her lips, she exudes cheerfulness.

"What's our first stop?" Skyler asks Geneva.

"First stop, the ruins of Saint Dunstan in the East," Geneva exclaims.

Skyler furrows her brow. "I haven't heard of that. What is it?"

Geneva grins. "You'll see."

For another thirty minutes the ladies quietly chat in the backseat as I stare at all the streets and pedestrians. London is really an interesting city. A lot of cobblestone streets mixed in with the norm. Small European cars jetting from place to place are a far cry from the giant SUVs, minivans, and trucks back home. The boxy buildings with their square shapes and stones that cut into the surfaces, the old bridges, and the Thames just make the city feel positively royal. Which I guess makes sense with the most well-known royal family in the world living here.

A few minutes later, Nate finds a parking spot on the street and gets out. Rachel follows him to the passenger side of the car. They let Geneva and then Skyler out. Sky puts my hat on her head, and I wrap my arm around her waist and follow Geneva to what looks like a war-blasted relic.

"What is this place?" Skyler asks, her gaze on the tall stone structure with its cathedral-style windows, which have long since been blasted out. Black burn marks mar the side of the stone facade, and vines crawl up the sides and through the gutted windows and roof.

We enter through a fence and note some people milling about, but none of them pays attention to us.

Sky lifts her glasses off her face and spins in a circle, taking in the ruins. "Was this a church?"

Geneva nods. "During World War II, Germany bombed England in a campaign that we called the Blitz. When the bombing stopped and the war ended, over a million homes and buildings were destroyed, including this one. In 1967, the city decided to turn the ruins into a public garden. It's one of the city's secret gardens, hidden away among the newer buildings around it. Ever since I was brought here as a child, I've been enchanted by it."

Skyler nods and takes my hand so we can walk alone. A moment of privacy for the two of us. Skyler takes off her hat and runs her hand through her golden locks.

"I think we should take a selfie." She smiles. "We don't have a lot of pictures, and I think we need to change that."

I hook her around the waist and hug her to my side. "Whatever makes you happy, Peaches."

We walk over to a section of the building that has an entry with some stone steps leading up into a courtyard and a huge window with a bench under it.

Skyler goes to the bench and sits down, patting the wooden surface for me.

"Hey, guys, I'll take a photo of you," Geneva offers, and Skyler readily hands over her phone.

I sit next to my girl with my arm around her shoulders and a big goofy smile on my face. Skyler snuggles against my side and gives her award-winning pearly-white smile a workout as Geneva takes a couple from Sky's phone and then her own. "For the muse," Geneva says.

Rachel and Nate keep an eye on the property, but every so often I see Nate make his way over to his wife and playfully nudge her side or pinch her ass. Rachel's response is always retaliation, getting him back with a hard ass smack or an attempt to trip him. Still, their attention is focused on the environment even though there really isn't anything to worry about.

Once we've walked through the remains of the old church, Geneva waves us over to the exit. "You guys up for a spot of tea and a biscuit?"

Skyler grins. "I love freshly made English tea and biscuits."

"Then you are in for a real treat!" Geneva gushes as we all gather in the SUV and motor down the road.

The conversation in the car carries us to our next destination, which has Skyler bouncing out of her seat the second she sees the white archway in between two much larger buildings. There's a gold lion perched above the door with two male Asian statues sitting next to it. Under that is a gold sign with the most recognizable name in the tea industry. "Twinings!" Skyler blurts on a rush of air.

Geneva smiles and opens her car door. Before she can even place a foot on the concrete, Nate is helping her out and Rachel is scanning the area.

We're led into the very small store, which smells of rich spices and fresh tea leaves. The store manager, a tall, thin, well-dressed man, comes over to Geneva and shakes her hand. "Ms. James, it is so good to see you again. It has been far too long." He lifts Geneva's hand and kisses the top formally.

"Abbot, thank you for making an exception on such short notice for our little band of renegades." She pats his hand.

"But of course." He lifts his chin and posture to full height before going to the door and turning the lock as well as the "Closed" sign.

Geneva spins out and claps her hands. "I've booked the shop for the next hour and a half for a private tea sampling. This will give you two"—she points to Rachel and Nate—"an experience to enjoy with us."

Nate bows his head a little. "With all due respect, ma'am, I should be guarding the front door and my wife the back door, to ensure we won't receive surprise visitors."

The store manager, who's wearing what seems to be a bespoke suit, runs his hands down his pristine tie and shirt and holds out his hand. "If I may, the doors are locked, and I can assure you that we will go uninterrupted, as is customary during private tastings. I tend to the royal family without issue. An American celebrity and a well-known author will be well cared for and safe in our little sanctuary."

He nods to the window, where a security guard, complete with appropriate weaponry, stands in front of the door.

"There is another in the back. Now, if you will be so kind as to have a seat at the bar. I have already heated the teapots and provided each station with a variety of noshes and nibbles. If you are all ready, I shall get started on the first flavor." He dips forward and with a gentle tone states, "It's the Darjeeling. Only five hundred tins made this year. Come, sit a spell."

The five of us find seats, and Abbot proceeds to lift a teacup. "Take the first cup, which I've already added the leaves to. You will note first the emerald color of the leaves along with the silvery tips. Inhale the scent within the cup, and you may note the floral fragrance unique to a tea that's picked this young."

We all follow along, and the floral notes tickle my senses pleasantly, so I inhale more fully.

Abbot pours hot water in the first cup and proceeds down the line until he reaches Skyler and then me.

"Now inhale the scent and note the floral notes have adjusted slightly when wet. Feel free to sample the tea and pair with a biscuit of your choosing."

"Mmm." Sky sips the tea and wraps her hands around the warm white cup. "So good." She smiles at me. "What do you think?"

I lick a drop of tea off my lips. "Love it. We should get some."

She nods. "Let's buy whatever teas we like today—" she starts to say, but Abbot cuts in.

"Any of the teas you like will be put into a personal takeaway Twinings box courtesy of your host, Ms. James."

Sky turns to Geneva and pokes her arm. "You didn't have to do that!"

"Are you having a good time?" Geneva asks.

"Gen . . ." She says it like the name Jen, having already shortened the author's name into a nickname. "This is an experience I'll never forget."

"Good," she says with a nod. "There's more to come, so drink your tea and we'll try the next."

Abbot goes over to Nate, who's first in the lineup. "The next tea is a double mint tea."

"Like the twins?" I joke, and Sky rolls her eyes. "What? They used to be on gum commercials back when I was a little guy watching Saturday morning cartoons."

Abbot continues his spiel regardless of my joking nature. "It's a mixture of peppermint and spearmint and can be grown anywhere. Give it a good inhale, and the leaves may clear your sinuses."

The five of us breathe in the leaves, and Geneva hums. "I love mint tea."

"It's best used for waking you up or finishing off a meal in the evening," Abbot offers, while pouring the water over each person's leaves, one cup at a time.

I inhale the steam from my cup and can't help but sigh. There's something calming about the scent of mint to me.

"You seem content over there." Skyler runs her hand down my thigh, her touch adding to the contentment I'm feeling.

"This one reminds me of my grandmother. When my brother and I would visit my grandparents in Rhode Island during the summer, she'd sit on her porch swing overlooking her land and drink mint tea. When I was about ten years old, she started sharing her tea. Well, making me a cup, heavily filled with sugar and milk, as my ten-year-old taste buds wouldn't have appreciated the stuff the way she drank it. It was something we used to do together, and I enjoyed it, having something special with my gran."

Skyler rubs her hand up and down my leg, likely for no other reason than making contact physically. "Maybe that's something you can share with your own children or grandchildren one day?"

I smile and lean over close enough to smell the mint on her breath. "Maybe I will. Would you like that for your children?" I say the words not realizing what I'm insinuating until it's too late.

Skyler licks her lips, and I flick my gaze to her pink tongue, wanting to touch it with my own but warring with the need to be civil, especially in mixed company. "As long as I was there to partake of the tradition with you, I'd love it." Her dark gaze lights up, and she grins, not pushing or digging me to commit to something neither of us is ready for right now.

"I think that could be arranged." I cock an eyebrow, feeling brave, but not so brave that I want to make plans for the future right here and now. But I will admit that talking about it, taking the mystery out of it, makes the idea a lot less frightening.

"Good." She crinkles up her nose, pecks me on the lips lightning fast, and puts her used mint cup back in its circular divot.

Abbot drones on about the next tea being a special chai from India, but my thoughts are mired in the future. Sitting on a porch overlooking a plot of land, my grandson at my side, sipping tea with his gramps. The visual disappears as the phone in my pocket buzzes.

I pull it out and see "SoSo" on the display.

Skyler glances at me, and I show her the name, wanting nothing but full disclosure between us.

She smiles. "Go ahead. Talk to her. I know you've been wanting to get in touch."

I get off my stool, tunnel my hand into her hair, and kiss her hard on the lips before clicking the "Go" button and accepting Sophie's call.

"SoSo!"

"*Bonsoir, mon cher*, or should I say *bonjour*? Where is my dear friend these days?"

I chuckle and make my way through the throngs of shelves toward the back of the store where what seems like an endless array of teas in a variety of colors and flavors are packaged and ready for sale. "Actually, SoSo, I'm in your neck of the woods. London to be exact, working a case."

"How lovely. And who is the client this time?"

I scoff. "Like you don't know. Your boyfriend's cousin came to see me."

"Oh *magnifique*. I do so adore Amy. Very bright woman. Excellent at her job."

"Mm-hmm. Speaking of your boyfriend . . . How's that going?"

There's a span of silence, and then I can hear the sound of Sophie's sniffles. Anger flares hotly at my back, and I tighten my free hand into a fist. "If he hurts you, Sophie, I will make him regret the day he was born. And that does not include what Bo and Royce will do to the pip-squeak."

A sob tears through the line. "I broke up with him," she says, her cries getting louder as the misery overtakes her.

"What? Why? Did he cheat? I'll strangle him with my bare hands . . ."

"*Non!* Goodness, *non*. He's a perfect gentleman, or I would not have moved him into my home."

Jesus, they're moving fast. They've been together less time than Skyler and me and have already shacked up. "You moved him into your home? SoSo, what were you thinking?"

"I was thinking, *mon cher*, that I loved him. And I do . . . love him." Her voice comes out small, like the Sophie I first met when she was grieving, not the woman I left and have been friends with since.

"You're confusing me, Sophie. What did he do?"

She sniffs loudly and whimpers.

"Sophie, I swear to God, if you don't tell me right now . . ." I feel a warm hand fall on my back, and I bolt into a spin, surprised at the comforting touch, and realize it's just Skyler. I take a deep breath and grab for my woman's hand, clutching it to my chest over my heart as fear and concern for my friend weave through my blood like poison.

Skyler runs her other hand down my shoulder as I focus on the call. "Sophie, talk to me. What's wrong?"

"He wants to marry me!" she cries out, and I frown, not getting how this information can cause her to be so miserable.

"What is it?" Sky whispers, fear coating her gaze.

I hold the phone over my chest, the speaker muffled against my clothing. "Sophie's boyfriend asked her to marry him, and she broke up with him," I whisper to Sky.

She frowns and shakes her head as if she is also questioning the situation.

"Okay, sweetie, back up. Explain to me why you broke up with Gabriel."

"Are you deaf in the ear? He asked me to marry him." Her crying jag continues while I stare at Skyler stupidly.

"I heard you the first time, SoSo, but I still don't understand why that would have you breaking it off. Was he not good to you?"

Her voice is coated in sadness as she responds, "He was *parfait*."

Perfect.

I lick my lips and rub at the back of my neck. "Sweetheart, you're not making sense. Why did you break it off, then?"

"*Mon cher*, because nothing I love stays. If I give him my heart, he will own it. If he leaves or dies, I will be nothing forevermore."

"Oh no, sweetheart, love isn't like that," I attempt, thinking about how fulfilled I feel with Skyler's steady hand on my heart, her eyes heavy with compassion. Whereas months ago, she was jealous of Sophie, now it seems she's chosen to trust that the relationship I have with Sophie is nothing but friendship, even if it started as something else.

"I loved you, and you left," she states flatly, and my heart breaks.

"Sophie, you know—"

She cuts me off. "I loved my father and he died. My mother too."

"The world isn't like that. You can't be without love in your life." I grind down on my back molars, trying to manage a way to make her see the truth.

"Except I can. If I let him go now, the loss of him will hurt . . . but later, with years of marriage, I'll be destroyed."

I rub at my head furiously. "Fuck, Sophie. You can't do this."

"I can. I have. It's done." Resolute. The same way I was when I cut it off with Skyler. Though there's always room for love to weasel in and make it better again.

"Sweetheart, I want you to think about your life now. Think about how much better it is with Gabriel. Hold on to that feeling and take glory in it. Take as much of it as you can, because, as you have learned recently, life is short. It's better to have him in your life every day that you can have him than not at all. I promise you that."

"How do you know?" Her soft cry tears right into my heart.

"Because in the past few weeks, Skyler and I hit a rough patch. I broke it off with her."

Skyler leans her head against my chest and kisses me over my heart, which I imagine is her way of saying it's okay. That my doing what I did is over now, and she's not holding on to it. I run my hand down her hair and squeeze the back of her neck.

"Oh no, *mon cher*. Are you okay?" Of course. In the middle of Sophie's breakdown, she's worried about me.

I remove my hand from Skyler's head and tap my thumb on her skull so she'll look up. She does, and I gesture to the chair next to where we're standing. She takes the hint and moves out of my hold so I can continue this conversation while pacing, the need to move and plead my argument necessary in order to get my point across.

"Yes, I'm fine now, because I have her back. I got my head out of my ass and realized what I wasn't admitting to myself. I was completely in love with her. During the time we've been together, somehow my life changed for the better. And it's all because of her. Now I'm considering the future, not just worrying about today. I'm thinking about a big house with a porch swing, cats and dogs, children, and grandchildren. Picket fucking fences. And in every one of those thoughts and dreams, Sky's standing right there, holding my hand." I lift up my head and find Skyler, tears running down her face, Geneva's arm around her shoulder. The woman's eyes are also teary.

I purse my lips and shake my head at their sappiness, and Sky just shrugs and wipes at her eyes. I mouth, "I love you," so she knows I see her in this moment, and it's a powerful one for her as much as it is for me.

"What you're s-saying is . . . I need to give Gabriel a chance to stay?"

I close my eyes and take a full breath. "Exactly. SoSo, you do not want to live your life alone, and if you push everyone away because you're scared they're going to leave you at some point, you're not doing you or them any favors. You'll just end up an old maid."

"I do not clean houses. I have staff for that."

Laughter bubbles up my throat and fills the room. "God, I've missed you, SoSo. I want to see you. Soon. Perhaps when we're done with this case, we can stop in Paris."

"Oh, *mon cher*, I would love your visit. Which of the men are with you?"

"Actually, none of them. Skyler's with me on this trip, but Bo is on his way. He'll be here by the end of the week."

"I would love to have any of you for a visit. It would do me some good."

"And SoSo, I didn't love you and leave you."

Sky's gaze shoots to mine as I continue. "I love you still and always will as one of my very best friends, though my life is in Boston and yours is in Paris. Which means we need to be better at checking in with one another. *Oui?*"

"*Oui,*" she agrees, sniffing quietly.

"Will you think about what I said and maybe give this thing with Gabriel a chance? I'm not saying marry the guy, but you don't throw the baby out with the bathwater."

"What baby? I do not have a baby. Is Skyler with child?"

"Ugh. It's an expression, SoSo. And no, Skyler's not pregnant."

Skyler's eyebrows rise up with the shock of hearing her name with the word *pregnant* in the same sentence.

I shake my head and wave my hand. "Just think about what I said."

"*Merci.* I will. I have a meeting to attend and a face to clean up."

"Okay. And I'll call you later this week, talk about meeting up for a day or two. Sound good?"

"Oui. Je t'aime. Bonjour, mon cher." Her voice is shaking when she responds, but I have to let her work this through on her own. I've said what I could, and hopefully it sinks in. Though I swear telling her all of that was like putting a big fucking life-size mirror in front of my own face.

"I love you too, SoSo. Bye."

When I end the call, Skyler rushes to me and throws her arms around me, her face going right against my neck. "Is Sophie okay?"

I nod and run my hand down Skyler's back, appreciating her warmth. "Yeah, she will be. Just a little twisted up. Worrying about losing Gabriel the same way she lost everyone else in her life. I had to remind her that she didn't lose me as her friend, and I think she understands that, but she was tossing everything in her life into a big horrible heap of letdowns and heartbreak. When a person does that, the only thing anyone can do is give it to them straight. I hope I did enough."

"Honey . . . the things you said about us . . ." Her voice shakes with emotion.

"All true." I cup her cheeks and lift her chin with my thumbs. "All. True. You're my future. I know that now, and I'm not going to let the hardships in life ruin what we've got. We're going to enjoy each and every day we're given."

Her corresponding smile is beatific. "We will help her through."

We.

Because that's what we are now.

A couple.

Two people who will brave life hand in hand.

Suddenly the days don't seem so hard, the years not so long, because I have someone to share them with. My dream girl.

Forever and always.

8

By the week's end, we've jetted all around London with Geneva and team. We visited the London Bridge, Big Ben, and Buckingham Palace, and rode the London Eye. Unfortunately Skyler was spotted on that one, and we had to get out of Dodge before the crowd got too big. Skyler didn't seem to care, always willing to sign autographs and take selfies. Nate, however, was about to lose his mind, and Rachel ended up pushing a couple of guys off Sky before pulling out her Taser and warning them to back away or it would be detrimental to their health.

The whole thing could have been a lot worse, but now the press knows we're here, which means we have to be more careful. Since Geneva James was recognized in the photos circling on the entertainment feeds, the paps know where we are and who we're hanging out with. This means playtime outside of the house is limited to highly secure areas, none of which Nate has approved for us.

The ladies, as is their way, are unhappy and feel caged. With two women like Skyler and Geneva plotting against you, all bets are off. Where there's a will, there's a way, and together those two will find it. Hands down. I wouldn't put some seriously sneaky shit past them.

The doorbell rings, and Nate and Geneva head to answer it. Skyler sits in the cushy chair, her cheek in her palm, her elbow supporting the weight of her head in her hand. Her vibe right now . . . bored.

"Howdy, big guy."

I can hear Bo clapping Nate on the shoulder.

"And this gorgeous creature must be Ms. Geneva James."

Aw shit, I better intervene. I jump off the couch next to Sky's chair and head to the entry.

"Bo, glad you could come," I state, but Bo doesn't so much as take his hands out of Geneva's or move his gaze from her face.

"What's doing, brother?" he says, looking at Geneva.

I shake my head and clap him on the shoulder. "I see you've met *the client*. Geneva."

He frowns. "I thought Tannenbaum was the client. Very big distinction."

It is if you're sizing up the woman in front of you as your next potential bed partner, when not two weeks ago did you agree that banging the clients was probably not good for business.

"Uh-huh. Lay off, Casanova," I warn.

Geneva jumps in. "Oh no, don't lay off." She smiles at Bogart, flirting openly.

Dammit all to hell and back. There goes another one. The bass and guitar beat to Queen's "Another One Bites the Dust" flutters through my mind as I watch Bo kiss the top of Geneva's fingers and offer her his panty-melting smile.

Whatever. This is not my bag or my concern. Hell, maybe getting laid by the world's biggest man whore will aid in bringing her out of her writing funk. Couldn't hurt, that's for sure.

Geneva clears her throat. "Would you like a drink?"

"If you're having one," he counters.

"Um, well, I was drinking water. On second thought, yes, I'm going to have one. I think we all need to be shaken up since we've been put under house arrest." Her gaze sends invisible daggers in Nate's direction.

The bodyguard shrugs. "Not sorry, Ms. James. Going to do my rounds. Rachel?" he calls out.

"Got it covered," she hollers from the back of the house, where she's likely checking doors and windows again.

"Nice to see you, Bo. Looking forward to when we get back in Boston and you have to fulfill your end of the bet." He grins wide for the first time all day. The smile is almost menacing, but it makes sense because Rachel still holds all the cards. Bo has to wear a skirt at some undetermined point in the future to fulfill his end of the bet he lost against Nate's wife. Personally, I can't wait. Bo is nothing if not a man of his word. He will live up to his end, I just hope to hell I'm there when it goes down.

Bo tips up his head, jerking his chin in the affirmative. "I'm good for it. She just says when and where, and I'm all over it. Already got the skirt ready." He grins confidently.

"Suuuuure." Nate extends the word in disbelief, heading to the front door.

"About that drink?" Bo levels his gaze on Geneva.

"Right this way." She walks ahead of him, a new sway to her hips that wasn't there before.

Mentally I have to suppress the groan from slipping out of my lips and remind myself, *It's none of your business, Parker.*

Skyler pops up off the chair. "Bo! I'm so glad you're here. We were bored stiff!" She catapults into his arms, and he hugs her tight.

"Missed you too, hot pants. My boy treating you right?" He cups her shoulders and leans back from her hug.

Her cheeks turn pink, and she nods shyly. "Yeah, he is."

Bo kisses her on the forehead, which I try not to growl at because I know it's just Bo's way. He's as tactile as he is wordy with women, friends included. It's his way, and I have to let him form a relationship with Sky if she's going to stay around, because Bogart has proved time and time again, the man is not going anywhere.

"Good," he murmurs against her hair. "Missed you, girl. More than that, missed your energy." He lets go of Sky, and I swoop in to stake my claim, wrapping my arm around her waist and tugging her to my side, where I can feel her warm body align with mine.

Bo continues prattling on. "Without you and Wendy, the office is a real snooze. Royce is making me work on simple, one-off cases that take no time at all. Except I can't complain because they're bringing in the duckets. Though, I'm thrilled you guys called me in." He grins wide, sits on the couch, and stretches his long arms out, his white T-shirt expanding across his muscular chest.

Geneva gulps, gaze glued to my brother's form, while she hands a gin and tonic his way.

Bo smirks and grabs the glass. "What is it, darlin'?"

"Gin and tonic. It's what I was going to have, and I didn't want to interrupt you. I can make you something else if you'd prefer."

He shakes his head. "A woman makes you a drink, you drink it, even if it tastes like ass, because the gesture is more important than the swill. You feel me, sugar?"

She blinks a few times but shakes her head. "No, not at all."

He laughs heartily, and I sit next to my brother.

"It's okay, you will." His tone and words are laced with innuendo, showing he's absolutely planning on taking the next step.

I clap my hands so the three of them focus on me. "Tomorrow, we do the photo shoot. Amy says the model you hired for the Dean role will meet us on the set at ten a.m. Bo, do you have all your equipment?"

He sips on the drink and hums in appreciation.

Geneva blushes and swirls the straw in her drink, her body language 100 percent focused on Bo and his movements.

This is going to be a long night.

"Brought what I needed. Confirmed with Amy that she had it set up with lighting and other tools that are bulky. Wardrobe is there, but it's not like there's going to be much of that . . ." He winks at Skyler.

"Wait a minute." I frown. "What are you talking about? I thought the model was going to wear a suit, white shirt, black tie."

Bo leans back and crosses one foot over his knee. "He will for some of the shoot, but I want to do something a bit hotter. More erotic."

My hands start to sweat, and the collar of my dress shirt feels tight. "What do you mean?"

"I'm going to get Skyler and the model shirtless. See how their chemistry is and take some strategic shots so it can be sexy as fuck."

I stand up abruptly, unable to keep my cool. "Now wait a god-damned minute! That was not part of what we discussed."

Skyler comes over to me and places her hands on my chest. "I've done photo shoots almost completely naked before. This is a book cover; we're creating an optical illusion, not the real thing."

I narrow my gaze over Skyler's shoulder at Bo.

He's smiling like he's loony tunes. I point an accusing finger at him. "You just like riling me up!"

"Every chance I get!" He laughs.

I clench my teeth and work my jaw before cupping Skyler's hips possessively. "You don't have to do this. If you don't like what's happening . . ."

"Honey, I think it's you who doesn't like what's happening. Just relax and trust me." She runs her hand over my heart. "Trust your heart. You know I won't lead it astray."

I close my eyes and breathe slowly for a full minute, counting to ten and back down several times before calm settles over me.

"I trust you," I say to my girl, and kiss her lips, sealing my admission with a physical statement. "It's the ugly bastard I don't trust." I grimace over her shoulder while pulling her body against mine, fully locked in my embrace.

Bo shakes his head and taps his fingers against his glass. "Brother, you make it too damn easy."

***

We show up at nine the next morning so Skyler can get makeup and hair done prior to the shoot at ten. The model hasn't shown up yet, and after watching Skyler get duded up in a man's white business shirt, a black tie hanging from her neck as if she's just taken it off her man, bare tan legs that have been lotioned to the point they seem to shine against the photo lighting, I'm worried there's still no model.

"You want to do some solo shots, Sky?" Bo, wearing a dark pair of jeans and his staple white tee, walks up, a camera in his hand. Once in a while he changes the shirt up from white to black and sometimes even to a dark gray or navy.

She frowns and fluffs her hair in the mirror. "He's not here yet?"

I've checked my phone a million times when I note that Geneva is on hers across the room. She's pacing the floor, and she doesn't look happy.

"Go ahead and do some solo shots, and I'll find out what's going on."

Irritation licks at my heels as I make it over to Geneva, who looks like she's sucking on a lemon. "But we already have Skyler here. There's no way I can ask her to stay longer and do the shoot again. We have a private photographer and everything." She runs her hand over her braided hair. Her blue eyes go dark, and her jaw hardens. "Fine. I understand. Thank you for notifying me."

"What's going on?"

Geneva hangs up her phone and shoves it in the back pocket of her jeans. "He's not coming." Her lip trembles, and tears spring to her pretty blue eyes. "After all of this . . ." She lifts her hand to where Skyler is posing, Bo snapping away.

"Who's not coming?"

"Barron, the model who did the first two covers. Stomach flu. Says he can't risk it. He's too sick. And in a few days, he has another shoot out of the country." Geneva's shoulders slump, and she lets out a shaky breath. "It's ruined."

I glance over at Skyler, who's straddling a stool, her hands keeping the tails of the shirt covering her privates, but her toned thighs are stretched out wide. Her hair falls into her face and she gives the camera the sultriest fucking look, and the tip of my dick buzzes with the need to get near her. My heart starts pounding, and I realize if this shoot doesn't happen, the entire plan of making Geneva see the couple come to life is a big, fat bust.

Until I remember what Geneva said in the bookstore. That she thought I could make a perfect Dean to Skyler's Simone. Well, I've taken photos with my girl before. This is no different.

"I've got an idea. I'll get it in the works, and you tell me what you think."

She sniffs as a tear falls down her cheek. "I'm so sorry, Parker."

"Don't be. I'm going to make it all better. At least I hope so." I head over to where Skyler is shooting and walk right on camera. I tunnel my hand into her hair and tip her chin up and spin her around so that I'm in between her thighs, the camera getting our profiles. "Put your hands on my ass."

She does what I say, and I bring my mouth almost to hers, hovering over her lips. She gasps, and the camera goes wild.

"Now this is what I'm talking about. Skyler. Lift your leg and wrap it around his waist."

She does what Bo says, and for a few minutes, we run our hands over one another and touch noses or cheeks. I run my lips down her neck, creating the illusion that I've seen on book covers in the past.

Bo stops flashing his camera. "Take it off, buddy. I want the tie she's got on around your neck."

I remove my suit jacket, and Geneva jumps in the space to grab my coat. "You guys are amazing together. I've never seen two people that embodied the characters of Simone and Dean more." Her joy is palpable and eases my nerves.

"I'm just glad you're seeing the characters come to life."

Skyler giggles and strips off my dress shirt. "Showtime, honey." She drags me over to a female attendant, who slathers my bare chest with enough oil to create a nice sheen at the dips of my pecs and six-pack.

Bo and a male stagehand bring over a chaise longue that's a deep-red velvet with gold swirls in the wooden trim. It's regal, royal, and about to get oily from our bodies.

"Now unbutton your pants. I want a hint of your ass cheek, Park," Bo calls out, and I do as he says. The second I unbutton them and unzip about an inch, they ride low on my hips.

"Sky, unbutton the shirt and show us what's under it," he commands of my girl.

I jerk my head to Bo and growl. "Fuck you!"

"Dude, she's wearing a black lace bra and panty set that's meant for the cover. Now stop being an asshole and get on top of your woman." His tone brooks zero argument, even though I'd be happy to punch him in his ugly mug for suggesting Sky take off her clothes in front of him.

"Get on top of her," he hollers, his face hidden behind the camera.

For a moment, I lift my hand and give him the bird before I flick my gaze to Sky, who has a come-hither grin and is crooking her finger at me. She separates her leg out to the side, and I see a sexy swath of black fabric at her crotch. Her breasts are pushed up and look so bitable I have to calm the beast's response by thinking of my mother reading stories to the kids at the library.

"Now that, I can do." I grin, my gaze all over her beautiful body.

"Come here, pretty boy, and do your worst!" Sky jokes.

I go to where she's maneuvered herself to lie on the chaise, and hover over her curves. I run my hand down her thigh and up to her hip, where I dig my fingers in. She loops her other leg around my lower half and uses her foot to force me down against her. The camera starts to click, but I can't help kissing my woman. My hearing focuses on nothing but the sound of her breathing and the little mewls that come from her glistening lips as I suck and nibble at each one.

My girl gets lost in the moment too, running her fingernails down my back, softly, almost a teasing gesture. I groan, and she lifts her head back, following the line of the chaise, arching her body and neck in offering. I run my lips down her neck, forgetting where we are.

Suddenly it's just me and Skyler, alone, her body available for the taking. I kiss along every inch of her neck, and cup her ass, bringing her lower half and mine against one another in a beautiful friction we both need.

"Jesus, Peaches, you smell and taste like heaven."

She sighs and shifts her face to the side, her lips opening in a gasp, as I suck at the space just above her breasts.

"Damn, this shit is gold. Gen, what do you think?" I hear Bo's question, but it's muffled, as if it's in a dream far away.

Then another voice enters, and it's all too clear, the bright lights and backdrop coming back, reminding me we're at a photo shoot. Not within the privacy of one of our homes.

"Stunning." I hear Geneva's voice through the lust swirling like mad in my head. "The two of them were meant to be together."

At her words, I cup Skyler's cheek and bring my face as close to hers as I can get, ignoring the camera clicks, cementing this moment as ours. "I would agree. You were meant for me, Sky. Never again. Never again am I going to be without you. Without *this* in my life."

She wraps her arms around my neck and locks her ankles at my lower back. "And you never have to. I'm not ever going to give you a reason to leave me, and I won't hurt you. That's a promise, honey. From me to you."

I kiss her hard, and things start to get a little wild, the two of us forgetting once more where we are and who's watching.

Bo clears his throat as I grind against Skyler's center and she moans. "Um, dude and dudette, you're at a photo shoot. There are six other people watching you two make out. Wanna dial it back a little so we can get the pictures we need for the cover?"

Skyler bursts into laughter, and I follow right along with her. I maneuver back away from my girl and sit back on my haunches. A little space to breathe and let the beast relax is a good idea. I glance over my shoulder. "What's next?"

Bo tips his head. "Actually, I want you to kneel on the floor in front of Skyler. Sky, I want you to place your legs around his waist and back. Cuddle him to your chest, but don't plaster him or it will make his face contort. I want you to close your eyes and nuzzle his hair."

Skyler and I do what he asks, and the camera clicks away. Skyler runs her fingers through my hair, and I sigh against her chest, enjoying the feeling of my woman soothing the fire inside of me. It may be banked, but it's still there, swirling inside, waiting for her to pour on the kerosene and toss the match, rebuilding the flames to an inferno once more. I can wait. Bide my time until we're alone tonight. Right now, it's all about the experience, riding this adventure until it's over. Enjoying each moment as it comes, appreciating any time where I've got my hands on my girl.

"All right, now I want to get a little frisky and push the edge of decency. You two with me, or am I going to have to cheese it up?" Bo's expression is one of challenge.

"What do you got in mind?" I fire off.

"Remove your pants; Sky, remove the shirt. It's all about the underwear now."

Skyler stands and drops her shirt. I bite my tongue but follow my woman, standing up and pushing off my pants, letting them pool at my ankles.

Challenge accepted.

He should know by now that I'd follow my woman anywhere. Especially looking like a goddess in black lace.

"We need some oil over here!" Bo calls out. "Also, wardrobe, I want Skyler in black thigh highs and black stilettos. If you have a pair with red soles, even better. Simone would rock the Louboutins for sure. Bring those sexy stilts out here stat."

I shake my head and put my hands to my waist. Skyler goes off set, and Bo lifts his camera, taking solo shots.

"Move your hands around, bro," he instructs. After he shows me a few movements he desires, I make them my own, moving more naturally.

"Flex your muscles, Park."

I do as he asks but can't help laughing as I do. "You are enjoying this too much."

Bo grins behind the camera. "What can I say? You're a good-looking guy, and these pics will drive the ladies in the romance community wild. I was thinking it would be good to shake them up, get them huffing and puffing over Dean. Geneva reads the responses, and whammo, sexy scene ideas pop onto the page."

I lift my hand back behind my neck and glance off to the side. The camera clicks.

"Not a bad idea."

He snickers. "I know because I had it."

I roll my eyes and then smirk. He walks up until he's only two feet in front of me and clicks away. "You know, bro . . ." He pulls the camera away and checks the screen. "If this International Guy thing doesn't work out for you, you could always pick up a late career in modeling. These are damn good. If I swung that way, I'd totally do you. Look at your body in this photo. Man, it looks sick." He levels the display so I can get a gander at what he sees.

Surprisingly the pictures are damn good. Even in my underwear I don't feel like I look out of shape or old. My abdominals look like cut blocks of cement. My pecs are two large squares to match but not bulky. My shoulders, though, are the best. I didn't realize how much the regular gym visits were doing for my shoulders. They are massive, sinewy muscle and bone, and with a little sheen and the right light, they are definitely picture worthy. For a moment, I let the pride in what I've accomplished in my physical form blanket over my senses. Bo's captured my best features in some great angles, which proves it's true what they say: lighting is everything.

Skyler comes strutting out in a totally different lingerie set. It's red-and-black lace complete with garters and snaps at the silk stockings. Her feet are in the tallest pair of stilettos I've ever seen her wear.

She walks over to me and puts her hands on my chest. "Do you like?"

My mouth waters at the sight, and I run my fingertips over the cups covering her breasts until she gasps. Then I move my featherlight touch down her rib cage, snagging the lace with the slight calluses on my fingers, until I reach the satiny parts. I move my hands over her hips and around to her ass, pressing her body fully against mine. I'm getting used to the camera, which likes to go off when we're not expecting it.

I grip the cheeks of her ass, and Bo leans down to ass level, and I grind my teeth hard, the sound extra loud in my eardrums. Bo's camera focuses on her ass and my hands.

"Dig in, bro."

I close my eyes and try to forget he's there and imagine I'm just copping a hefty feel of my girl's backside.

"Fuck yeah! This is going to be tits," Bo says.

"Tits?" I grunt, irritation flooding the word.

"You know, there's nothing better than a sweet pair of tits. So yeah, tits. As in the pictures are going to be freaking astounding and hot as hell. Now turn your girl around, put your hands over her private areas so nothing peekaboos, and let's get a little dirty."

"You up for this?" I whisper into her hairline as I cup my girl's sex possessively.

Sky gasps and leans back against my body. "As long as you hold me up. These shoes hurt like a mother, and I can barely keep my stance in them."

Laughter fills both of us, and we take erotic photos chuckling like idiots. "God, I love you." I kiss her cheek, and she wraps her own hands over the parts on her body I'm holding, making Bo whoop and holler with pure joy.

"I love you too. Thanks for holding me up."

I tighten my hold, and she bites down on her lip, a whispered moan leaving her mouth.

"Any time, Peaches. Any fucking time." I kiss the spot on her body where her shoulder and neck meet . . . my spot if there ever was one.

"Fucking awesome!" Bo breathes out in awe. The geek in him is coming out full tilt, and there's not a lot we can do except go with it. Usually when that happens, magic follows. And right now, holding my woman seductively while almost naked, her body encased in satin and lace and fuckhot shoes, I can't complain.

9

I wake with my head buzzing as though a thousand angry hornets have taken flight in my dome. Except the rest of me is heavy, weighed down by something warm and soft. I try to blink through the darkness of the room, not recognizing the space, but the body halfway covering mine is *very* familiar. Skyler's peaches-and-cream scent is all over me, as is she. Flashes of last night come back to my mind in a swirl of Technicolor.

Doing shots with Bo, Skyler, and Geneva.

Geneva making us all a homemade dinner.

A game of drunken charades.

More booze consumed.

Skyler's lips on mine as I push her form against the hallway staircase.

Barely making our way into a dark room that smelled of fresh linens.

Skyler down on her knees with me pressed up against the door, her mouth sucking deep.

Me on my knees at the edge of the bed, Skyler's thighs split wide over my shoulders, ankles pressing into my back.

My girl riding me hard, facing me.

Me riding Skyler, facing her.

The headboard pounding against the wall, making my teeth rattle until we both come together in a final burst of energy and collapse.

Damn, as the flashes coalesce, the beast comes to life, wanting in on the action again. Skyler's thigh moves up, rubbing against my not-so-little friend. I groan and stretch, working on the tension in my body. Jesus, I feel like I ran a marathon last night and then someone smacked me upside the head with a baseball bat a few times for shits and giggles.

Skyler sighs against my chest, air puffing out of her mouth prettily as her eyes flutter open. She winces, and her hand flies up to her head.

I run my hand up her thigh to her ass and goose her until she laughs, but the laughter quickly turns into a pained moan as she flops to her back. I roll over and cuddle next to her, the naked pink tip of her breast nudging my nose. Inhaling her scent soothes me, and I attempt to slip back into dreamland, wrapped around my girl, but she's not succumbing to the new arrangement.

Her hands run through my hair, and she wiggles her body away from me. "Honey, I have to pee so bad." The words are pained, which hits my brain, but letting her go is delayed, my hands sluggish due to the little men with jackhammers digging into my mind. Eventually I let her go, and she rolls to the side, her head in her hand before she stands shakily. "What the hell did we drink last night?"

My stomach sours, and I put my forearm over my eyes. "I think the better question is: What *didn't* we drink? I distinctly remember we started with wine and then switched to hard liquor. Scotch, I think."

"Ugh," she murmurs, fumbling for my dress shirt and slipping it on over her bare shoulders, where I can see the faint hint of a hickey I'd given her last night.

That woman, for the love of all things holy, looks just as sexy now, all tousled with sex hair, as she did at the photo shoot yesterday made up like a vixen.

My throat goes dry as I look my fill. "I'm one lucky son of a bitch. Sky . . . don't ever leave me." The tone in my voice is weary, filled with an insecurity I don't often let run free, and nothing but honesty. Pure, undiluted honesty.

She stops at the door and glances over her shoulder. "Keep loving me right, and I never will." She winks and closes the door to what I assume is the bathroom.

God, that woman could ruin me so easily. She holds my heart, my very soul, in the palm of her hand.

I rub at my aching forehead and look around. Seeing the blue walls and airy white lace curtains, I'm reminded that I don't know where the fuck we are. I sit up in bed, and my head protests, the hammering continuing. I need a trough of coffee and a handful of ibuprofen, and maybe even a shot of scotch if we didn't drain all of Scotland of the stuff last night.

The toilet flushes, and what sounds like the faucet in the sink comes on. Skyler exits the bathroom and sits on the edge of the bed, reaching for me. I grab her hand. She grimaces. "I think we're still at Geneva's place."

"Last thing I remember is us drinking a lot with Geneva and Bo, kissing you against the staircase, and fucking the shit out of you."

She grins and leans forward, then kisses me softly. "I remember fucking the shit out of you, mister." She pokes at my chest.

"Be that as it may, we need to put some clothes on and find out what's going on outside of our impromptu love nest."

She snorts. "Love nest. More like a fuck pad. What we did last night, the marks you put all over my body . . ." She lifts up my dress shirt, and her chest has a handful of hickeys on her breasts, the tips a dark red instead of the light pink they normally are, meaning they were treated to some pretty serious suction. Farther down she points out fingerprint marks on her hips.

"Should I be sorry?" I offer a flat mask by way of a facial expression, so she doesn't know how very proud I am of those little reminders of our time together. It's pretty obvious I worked my woman over the way a man should.

Skyler laughs hard and pulls the blanket off my chest. "No way! I think I scarred you." She runs her fingers down the side of my rib cage where some pretty deep red welts exist from what I can only assume were her nails. A couple of giant hickeys mar my chest where she got her Hoover routine on, giving as good as she got.

I grin and finger the purple bruise over my heart. "I'll wear my love bites with pride."

"As will I." She runs her fingers over my abdominal muscles, and they ripple with pleasure. "Besides, last night was a blur." She lets out all the air in her lungs. "All I remember is being naked with you in every position possible."

I don't stop the huge smile that takes over my face.

She shoves at my chest. "You're such a guy!"

I loop my arm around her waist and bring her flat over me. "You sore?" I whisper against her lips, sucking the bottom one in and giving it a little nip.

Skyler's cheeks pinken. "Yeah . . . ," she whispers shyly.

I smack her hard on the ass, knowing it must sting. "Then I've done my job as your man!" I make over-the-top, animalistic-type noises similar to what I imagine a Neanderthal would make, barking out his likes and dislikes.

This has her laughing into my chest until she groans and grips her head.

I grimace. "We've got to find some painkillers."

"Absolutely," she mumbles, pain harsh in her tone.

"All right, up." I smack her delectable ass again until she rolls over me and comes to a shaky standing position. I do the same and put on my white V-neck undershirt and dress slacks. Skyler slips on her underwear, but my shirt goes down to her midthighs, long enough to be decent as a dress. I grab her hand, and the two of us head out the door.

Once out, it becomes clear we are definitely in Geneva's house. The smell of bacon and fried potatoes cooking has me steering us to the stairs, my mouth salivating at the need to fill my belly with as much grease as possible. As we make our way to the top landing, I hear a clacking sound coming from the author's second office to our left. I hold my finger to my lips and make a shushing noise.

Skyler nods, and together we tiptoe over to Geneva's office.

When we get there, the most awesome sight greets us. Geneva, dressed in a burgundy satin teddy, is typing away at her computer. Her hair looks the same as Skyler's, a total mess, only different in color. I press on Skyler's stomach to ease her out of the doorway and leave the author to her work.

Together Skyler and I take the stairs one at a time, rather slowly, both of us a hurting unit if there ever was one.

Once we get to the bottom of the staircase, I follow my nose to the kitchen. At the stove is a bare-chested Bo, wearing nothing but his dark jeans and a brilliant smile. His hair is spiked every which way, proving he too just rolled out of a very active bed.

"Good morning, SkyPark." He uses the name the paparazzi assigned the pair of us.

"Ugh." Skyler moans, maneuvers onto a barstool, and rests her head in her hands, the cuffs of my shirt flopping backward over the sleeves.

Bo holds up a spatula while taking the few feet to a bottle of meds on the opposite counter and handing them over to Sky. "Here, hot pants. Let me get you some water." He sets the bottle in front of her.

"Bless you, my friend."

He chuckles and looks as though he's perfectly fine, no hangover whatsoever, which actually pisses me off. I mean, I know Bo can hold his liquor, but not that well. It was drink for drink between all of us last night.

"How the hell are you so chipper?" I grumble, taking the seat next to Skyler, who pops open the pill bottle, shakes four into her palm, and hands them to me before repeating the process for herself.

She takes the pills and downs half of the water before handing the water bottle to me. I follow her lead, swallowing the pills and drinking the rest of the water.

Bo goes back to his food and flips the bacon over. I practically taste the greasy goodness from the smell alone. My stomach grumbles loudly, and I rub at the empty space. "You went to bed the same time we did . . ."

He turns around with a cocked eyebrow. "Did I?"

"Yeah?" I push back into my memory bank, and I recall Geneva pointing to a room for Skyler and me, while Bo led her into her space, presumably to have the same fun we had.

Bo shakes his head. "Wrong. Geneva had hit a dry spell the past year. I spent the evening making sure every inch of her was filled up." He smirks, and I gag.

"Niiiiice going, bro!" Skyler puts her fist out, and he bumps it.

"Baby, don't encourage him."

She eases her elbow to the bar and puts her head in her hand. "Why not? Geneva is a grown woman; she wanted to get her some lovin'. Look at the guy . . . she couldn't do better." My girl yawns and closes her eyes.

Inside I seethe at what she revealed, heat filling up my chest, making me want to breathe fire.

Skyler opens her eyes and assesses me, then Bo. He has his arms crossed over his bare chest, and he flexes his biceps, making his muscles pop and bulge. "Your woman thinks I'm hot."

Skyler sits up, and her eyes go wide before she points at me and then him. "You both took that out of context." Skyler eases off the stool and wedges her body between my split thighs before wrapping her arms around my waist. "No one is as hot as you. What I meant to say is, your *brother*, Bo, is a good-looking guy and Geneva a beautiful woman. If they want to make friends for the night, why not?"

Sky plants her body against mine and puts her lips to my neck. "You know what I was trying to say."

I inhale her scent fully into my lungs and let the insecurity that crept up instantly go. Skyler's allowed to state her opinions, and I should be man enough to accept that she loves *me*, wants to be with *me*, and finds *me* attractive. I'm her choice. Just because she thinks someone else looks good doesn't mean she wants them. It's just a simple observation.

I breathe through my stupidity and nuzzle her temple, kissing her there. Bo tilts his head, probably waiting for me to fire back at him. This time, I'm not going to give him the satisfaction.

"Damn, woman's changing you," he quips, and tends to the food.

"For the better." I hold my girl close and let her body ease the spot of tension before it can turn into something I'm not proud of.

Skyler lifts her head up and cups my cheek. "I love you."

"I know you do."

"And I think you're the hottest man I've ever known."

"You don't need to say that. I'm man enough to accept that my woman has eyes." I glance over at Bo and note his fit form, muscular back, and large muscles. He works hard for his body, and he does right by it. "You're right. He's a good-looking guy, but don't ever tell him I said that," I whisper.

"I heard that!" Bo hollers over the fan he turned on for the bacon grease. "You think I'm hot." He shimmies his hips to give us an ass-and-back show.

Skyler watches the show and then nudges my chin with her nose until I've got my gaze on her. "You're hotter."

"Did you hear that?" I say as loud as my tired brain will allow.

Bo turns the knob so the fan gets louder. "Nope. Cooking over here!"

"Bastard." I grin and watch Bo make breakfast.

***

Skyler shovels in another bite of eggs and hums around her fork.

"Good?" Bo asks.

She nods but doesn't stop.

"This another one of Momma Sterling's recipes?" I ask.

He shakes his head. "Nah, my mother taught me how to make a southern breakfast when I was young. By the time I was a teenager, I'd perfected all forms of breakfast. Eggs, bacon, pancakes, french toast, biscuits and gravy. You know, the norm." He bites into a hunk of potatoes.

"I assumed you were raised in Boston like Parker and Royce?" Skyler taps her fork onto her plate.

"Nah, born and raised in New Orleans by my mother and sisters. I'm the baby of four kids."

"Four!" Skyler's eyes widen as she stabs the cut potatoes.

Bo chuckles. "Yes, ma'am." His words are slathered in the southern drawl he often hides.

"What do your parents do?" she asks, and I'm surprised he hasn't shut her down yet. Bo doesn't talk much about his family. His doing so means he's accepted Skyler into our inner circle.

"My mother, Elizabeth, is a fashion designer."

"No . . . Oh my God! I never made the connection. Your mother is Liz Montgomery! I've worn one of her dresses to a red carpet event. She's extremely talented."

"Yes, she is." He nods, pride lifting his chest as he straightens his spine. "And my sisters all work for her in the family business. One works as my mother's right-hand seamstress, another in designs, and the last runs the official Liz Montgomery Designs show store in New York City. They're looking to expand across the country and have invited me in . . . but . . ."

My hungover brain buzzes, and the dots of what he just said start to connect. "Bo, you never mentioned that your family wants you to join their business." I can't help the concern in my voice. My filter is not working at all today.

He shrugs and stands up with his half-eaten meal as if the need to escape is more important than the desire to fill his gullet.

"Does Royce know about this?" I continue.

He sighs and shoves the rest of his food into the trash. "No, and I'd appreciate it if you don't tell him."

That has me jerking back and pushing out of my seat. "Why the hell not?"

"Because it's not necessary. I'm not doing it, so it doesn't matter."

I walk over to Bo, the rest of my breakfast left untouched. "Maybe you need to think about this, talk to us about it. We'd never begrudge you what's part of your family obligation . . ."

He turns around, a scowl spreading across his face. "And what about our family? The brotherhood. IG. We did that together. All three of us. Now we've got Wendy on the team, and we're doing better than ever. Hell, last I talked to Royce, he mentioned the idea of us expanding across the nation and hiring a corporate lawyer. Now you want me to think about jumping ship when we're finally seeing our hard work pay off?"

I shake my head and lean against the counter. "No. Not at all, but this is your mom and your sisters. If you want to get involved, I'm sure we could work something out, halve you in a way if that's what you needed. We'd never keep you from something you feel you needed to do."

He grabs the dishcloth and wipes his hands. "That's fine and dandy and all, but my place is with IG. I don't need to be split between my mother's fashion empire and IG. She created the Montgomery name. I helped create the IG name, and I'm proud of what we've accomplished. Right now, sky's the limit for us, and I want to be there for every . . . fucking . . . thing. Is that all right with you?" His tone is firm.

I lift my hands in a gesture of surrender. "Brother, of course. It's IG all the way, but if you need to talk about this or change your mind, I'm here for you. Roy is here for you. If you want to dabble, get your feet wet in the Montgomery business, we'll support you. It's all I'm saying."

Bo lifts his chin, but his jaw is locked tight.

"We cool?" I feel the need to confirm.

His shoulders drop, and he puts out his hand. I move to grab it, and he pulls me in for a full chest-to-chest hug, slapping my back and making the squishy part of my brain scream in agony at the swift, jarring movement.

"We're cool, man." Bo slaps me one more time, and I swear I see stars. Leaning back, I brace myself on the counter.

"More coffee?" he asks.

"Oh yeah."

He chuckles.

"Tell me again how you escaped without a hangover?" I trudge back to my plate and sit down. Skyler has completely cleaned hers and is nibbling on another piece of bacon. Girl is an endless pit after a night of drinking, but I learned that after the first time we got sauced.

"Didn't really sleep. Tired as fuck!" He laughs.

I frown. "But I saw Geneva up in her office, typing like a madwoman."

"Yeah, turns out, whatever you guys have been doing over the past week or so and a night of wild fucking brings out the muse and obliterates writer's block."

"Seriously?" Hope fills my chest, my heart pounding out an excited drumbeat.

He pours a fresh cup of coffee and doctors it just the way I like before setting it in front of me.

"Yeah. The first time, I gave her a couple of solid Os and hit the shower. When I came out, she was at her desk typing. I sat in her office, read one of her books until she came back to me for another go. Did her good, and then she got back up and went to the keyboard. This continued through the night. I fed her food and water in between, and she wrote and then we fucked. Great night. I'm hoping for a nap here in a few and then another go. She's a wildcat in the sack, ooohhh weeeee."

Skyler laughs and I wince. "Too much information, bro. Way too much information."

On that note Geneva walks in, this time wearing a silk robe down to her ankles.

"You hungry, sugar?" Bo asks.

She grins, walks right up to him, and takes his mouth in a searing kiss. It becomes so hot both Skyler and I look away.

"Yeah?" she says softly.

"For food?" He gives her his sexy smile.

"That too."

Bo growls and bites at her neck until she laughs herself silly. When he's done making a seriously gag-worthy public display of affection—the likes of which I'll likely never forget—he lets her go and swats her ass. "Have a seat. I've got a plate warming for you."

Geneva sits down at the table and pushes her hair out of her eyes. "Wow," she mouths to Skyler, and shakes her hand like she's just touched something hot.

"Soooooo . . ." I draw out the word to get her off the topic she was about to go on. "We noted you were writing this morning . . ."

"Goodness, yes, all night actually. I know where the story is going, and I have a grand idea for how it all ends!"

Skyler and I both look at one another, and Skyler reaches out a hand to me. I high-five her, and then we both high-five Geneva, which isn't normally my thing, but it's Skyler's.

"This is incredible news, Gen," Skyler gushes.

The author preens and blushes. "It is. And I can't . . ." Her words fail her, and tears fill her eyes. "I honestly didn't believe that a consultant from the States could help with the issue, but you have. Seeing the two of you together, putting my characters into the love story that exudes from the two of you, just made it all click. Seeing the fans, knowing they haven't forgotten about me or the story . . ." She shakes her head. "It's all been so eye-opening."

Bo sets a plate full of food in front of Geneva. She lifts her hand to Bo's cheek as he leans in to steal a kiss. She pats his scruffy face and smiles. "And a night with a stud like you . . . bloody inspiring."

Bo grins. "See. Told you so." He directs his response to me.

"Where are you planning to take the story, if you don't mind me asking?" I lift my cup and sip my coffee.

Geneva pushes a lock of hair behind her ear. "Well, I've decided to make it a lot hotter. This book will be erotic."

Skyler's mouth drops open. "Oh boy."

"Are you sure that your contemporary-romance readers won't be concerned with the heat level rising?"

She shrugs. "There will have to be a disclaimer for certain, but that is where the couple is going. Their love is intense, erotic, filled with heat, like your photo shoot yesterday. I can no more leave the fire of their love behind closed doors than I can leave the plot hanging. It's time for their love to mature in that way. And plotwise, they will marry."

This has all three of us gasping. "Simone said she would never, not ever, get married in the second book. It was what broke them up at the end," Skyler says, concern in her tone.

She nods. "This is true. She's afraid that things in her relationship with Dean will change for the worse as her family had, and in his first marriage. It colors not only her opinion on the subject, but his too, since he perceives it as a failure. Nevertheless, the story I'm weaving will be one of great emotional growth, sadness, heartache, love, second chances, and Dean and Simone coming to terms with the fact that they don't want to be apart. They need one another to function, or they are only half of the whole. The final commitment is what was missing in the book. Both of them coming to the realization of what they both want. They can't live their lives on borrowed time in between Simone's movies. They must make a final decision and choose love over everything else."

The three of us don't say a word, Geneva's story concept tunneling into each of our minds and finding a personal connection with us, all for different reasons.

I clear my throat. "It sounds—"

"Life changing," Skyler supplies, and I can't agree with her more. "Yes, indeed."

Bo kisses the crown of Geneva's head. "Well, I'm all for the sex out in the open. Let's talk about those scenes. Better yet"—he runs his hands down her arms—"let's reenact them."

Skyler and I stand quickly. Thank God the medicine is doing its job on my headache; it's now at a dull roar instead of a stampeding rumble.

"And I think that means you need to get back to work, and Parker and I to our hotel," Sky announces.

Geneva ignores her food, stands up, and plasters her body to Bo's half-naked form.

"Okay, then. We're off. Let's get our stuff, and I'll call Nate. I could use a hot shower and a nap," I admit tiredly.

"Sign me up," Skyler says, making her way over to the staircase.

"We'll uh, call you . . ." I turn around and find Bo already has Geneva's robe opened, his hand on her breast and his mouth on hers.

Leaving them be, I head up the stairs. As I do, I realize this is probably the last time I'm going to be in this section of Geneva's house. Moving toward the hall I know leads to her bedroom, I slip inside quietly and make my way through until I get to the bathroom.

Opening the first drawer, I find washcloths. The second, toothbrushes, toothpaste, floss, and the like. The third drawer . . . bingo! Makeup. I grab a tube of lipstick, pop the top, and smile.

On the mirror in the corner, I press the peachy-red color against the glass and write her a message that will hopefully have her thinking. I want her to continue to feed what lies within her, and not let anything or anyone make her doubt herself or her talent.

Geneva,
Feed your soul.
Love, Me

Once finished, I put the lipstick back in the drawer and slip out of her room. I grab my phone out of my pocket and hit Nate's number. He answers on the first ring. "Need a pickup?"

"God, yes. The faster the better."

Nate chuckles. "Good thing we're right outside. Came over first thing this morning."

"You deserve a raise." I head for the stairs to get my shoes, my sport coat, and my woman.

"Yeah? Tell it to my boss," he says flatly, but I can hear the humor in his tone.

"Not a problem." I open the door to the guest room and see my girl bending over the bed, her sublime ass on display. I run my hand over her lush cheek, and she squeaks.

"See you in five?" Nate queries.

I run my hand between her thighs and find my girl slick and hot for me. "Uh, make it fifteen . . ."

Skyler moans as I ease two fingers into her heat, her hands flying to brace herself on the bed as I drop the phone. It falls to the ground somewhere, but I couldn't care less. I'm more focused on working my pants down and pulling out my stiff length. "Actually, more like thirty," I call out, and glance over my shoulder to where the phone blinks and the blank screen showing the call has ended comes up.

10

"You are a miracle worker, Mr. Ellis." Amy Tannenbaum's voice on the phone is filled with gratitude. "Geneva said she'd love to say goodbye to the two of you, but she's deep in the writing cave. I think she's going to finish the book in the next couple of weeks. Which, honestly, feels like divine intervention."

I chuckle. "Well, I won't tell you we didn't help, because it was obvious she needed to be recharged and have her mojo reset, but the work is up to her now. We've presented her with the truth. She knows now she's better than what her past publisher put her through. The story is iconic, and the readers are fully committed to her and wherever she takes the story. And perhaps seeing Skyler in the role helped her come to terms with the plot. You never know what's going to pull someone out of a major funk." I think that Bo's night of guilt-free sex probably didn't hurt either.

"The cover photos are incredible. According to Geneva, she wrote two chapters based on the chaise images alone. We'll need both you and Skyler to sign off with your approval to use them."

"No problem. Just email the forms to my assistant, and we'll sign and return them when we get back to Boston. We're heading to Paris today to see a friend before we hightail it back to Boston."

"I love Paris, it's truly the city of love. If you see Sophie and my cousin Gabriel, tell them I said to come visit me in New York City."

"Sure thing. Also, London's been a beautiful experience. We can't thank your client enough for showing us around, sharing her life. I'll have Skyler follow up with her in a couple of weeks. And of course, the next time either of you is in Boston, we'd love to host you for dinner. My family owns a great pub with the best pulled pork around," I gush with pride.

"Sounds lovely. I'm sure when Geneva flies across the pond, she'll want to connect."

"Excellent. Thank you for reaching out to IG. We enjoyed working with you." I grab my folded dress slacks and place them on top of the neat stack in my luggage.

"And I you. I'll have the producers be in touch with Skyler's people. Geneva is dead set on Skyler playing Simone. Funny enough, she actually asked if you'd be interested in auditioning for Dean . . ."

I laugh hard into the phone. "Amy, I'm a lot of things, but an actor is not one of them."

"No burning desire there?" She laughs.

"Not a one. That's all Sky, but she's eager to play the role when the time is right. Positively glowing with the idea. Says it's exactly the kind of romantic drama she's been looking for to challenge her acting chops."

"I'll make sure they're in touch with her agent."

"Great. Have a wonderful week, and let us know if you ever need our help again."

"Will do. And thank you again, Mr. Ellis." She hangs up right as Skyler walks in from the bathroom, holding her toiletries.

She licks her lips and stops in the middle of the room. "I've changed my mind."

I frown. "About going to France and seeing Sophie?"

She shakes her head. "No, I've changed my mind about staying in her house. Can we do a hotel?"

I smile and walk over to where she's worriedly chewing her bottom lip. It's one of her nervous tics, and the last thing I want is for her to be nervous.

"Peaches, we do not have to stay with Sophie. She won't mind at all. If it makes you uncomfortable, we'll stay in a hotel. She's actually in an area where a beautiful hotel is catty-corner from her building. It's fine." I run my hands up and down her arms and dip my head to look into her eyes.

She crinkles up her nose. "Do you think she'll think I'm being stupid?"

I shake my head. "To be honest, Sophie won't care. She doesn't get hung up on the rationale behind decisions like this. Sophie's focused only on the fact that her friend and his girlfriend are coming for a visit. And she needs me right now. Let's focus on why we're stopping in for a couple of days."

She nods. "Okay. Good."

"I'll have Wendy . . . ugh, I mean Annie, book us a room."

This time Skyler burrows her body against mine and wraps her hands around my waist. "You're having a hard time with Wendy being on leave."

I clench my teeth and suck on my tongue, pressing it against the insides of my teeth before I can speak. "I hate it. It doesn't feel right. Do you think Michael is going to get her to change her mind about coming back?"

Skyler snorts and shakes her head. "No way. That woman is devoted to the team. She may be committed a hundred percent to Michael romantically, but she loves you guys too. And she loves her job. Plus, she's the best at it. When you find something you're good at and you love doing it, there's very little that can make you walk away from it. And Wendy's strong."

"Yeah." I run my hand through my hair and wrap my free arm around Sky. We stand and hug for a long time.

"It will be okay. You'll see." She pats my ass and then moves out of my hold. "You almost ready?"

I place my phone charger and toiletry case in my suitcase and zip it up. "Yes, ma'am. Let's go see SoSo. Talk some sense into that woman."

***

Once we've checked into the hotel across the street from Sophie's house, Nate and Rachel walk with us across the way. Shockingly there were no paparazzi at the airport, and none have found us yet. Skyler loops her arm with mine and breathes in the air. "I love Paris. Think we can get some sightseeing in tomorrow?"

"Yeah, I don't see why not."

I knock and wait for the butler to come to the door of Sophie's downtown mini-mansion. He opens the door and greets the four of us with a bow.

"Good to see you, Mr. Ellis."

We crowd into the entryway. Sophie appears at the top of the first level of stairs and rushes down them. Once she reaches the bottom step, she's dashing into my arms.

"Mon cher!" She hugs me hard, her face alight with joy as she pulls back and air-kisses one cheek and then the other. Turning, she pulls Skyler into a hug, *"Ma chérie, bonjour!"* She repeats the two-kiss greeting.

Skyler hugs her back, and the rigidity in my girl's body relaxes. Any bout of nerves she had at seeing the woman I'd been with in the past is gone. Sophie has that ease about her. It's one of the things I adore about her.

"Come, come in, all." She holds out her hand to Nate and then Rachel. "I am Sophie Rolland. It's good to make your acquaintance."

"Nate and Rachel Van Dyken." Nate shakes her hand and points to his wife. "Security team for Ms. Paige."

"Ah, *oui*, I imagine you have to be very careful, *non?*" She glances at Skyler, understanding in her gaze.

"Yes. The business I'm in requires it," Skyler offers.

"The more, the marriage." Sophie smiles sweetly, butchering an American saying along the way.

All of us chuckle. "SoSo, it's the more, the merrier," I say.

She pouts and taps her lips. "I shall endeavor to remember this one. Come, all. I have espressos and a snack before we head to dinner. I've made a reservation at Buddha-Bar. It is quite fantastic. The lighting is often low, with a red-and-purple tint. In the center of the space is an enormous copper-colored statue of the teacher himself. You'll love it!"

Sky's eyes light up. "I've been wanting to go there for ages! It's on the other side of the Seine and a ways down from the Louvre. Right?"

"*Oui.*" Sophie's eyes turn glassy as she sighs. "Parker took me to a special dinner at the Louvre when they did a never-before showing of an American artist. We had dinner in the exhibit. It was amazing."

I remember the time fondly, checking out the Georgia O'Keeffe paintings, chatting with Sophie about art and life. It was the best date I'd ever had until I took Skyler out and about for a day in New York. "We had a good time." I smile and glance at Sky to find she's not smiling at all. Her jaw is tight, and she separates herself from our little group, walking over to the window, where she pulls back the heavy curtain and stares out at the view.

Sophie winces when she notes that Sky has removed herself from the conversation. I knew this would be awkward. Sophie and I have a history. Skyler is my future. Both are my present—Sophie as a dear friend and Skyler as my woman. There are going to be bumps in the road to us being close, but it's important to me that we find a happy medium.

"I'll get the espressos going," Sophie states, and walks out of the room.

I head over to Skyler and wrap my hand around her waist, leaning my chin on her shoulder. "You okay?"

Skyler hums. "Mm-hmm."

"I know this is awkward, but I really want to get past that to the point where the two you can be friends. Sophie is important to me, as are you. I want the two women besides my mother and Wendy to connect. Do you think that's going to be possible?"

Skyler sighs and spins around, wrapping her arms around me. She glances into the empty room, making sure Sophie hasn't returned. "I'm not going to lie and say it's not hard that you two have a past as a couple."

I shake my head. "We weren't a couple. We had a physical relationship for a couple of weeks. That's it. You and I have been together for twenty times longer." I nuzzle my nose with hers. "It's important to note that you are who I've chosen. You are my future. And Sophie in that capacity is my past. Both of us have gotten over this. I hope you can too."

She nods. "I will. It's just sometimes I remember that she's had you in that way."

"No. Sophie never had me the way you do. She had my body for a very short time. You own my heart and my soul. And besides . . ." I kiss her lips softly. "I love you. I'm *in love* with you, and that's not going to change."

She grins, wraps her hands around my head, and kisses me hard. "I'll let it go."

"That's my girl." I tap her chin and kiss her again as Sophie comes back into the room.

"Oh goodness. I can leave and come back in a while."

"No, Sophie, it's okay. Just can't keep my hands and lips off my girl."

Sophie brings her hands to her chest. "I'm so happy for the two of you."

And what a perfect lead-in to why we're here in the first place. "You know, you have that too, with Gabriel. Have you talked to him?"

Sophie's smile slips, and she clears her voice. "He's staying in the same hotel you're in. He will not remove his clothing from our closet. Says he will leave them there until I accept him back in our bed. Stubborn fool."

"Sounds to me like he's a man in love. Doing whatever it takes to win his girl back. The question is: Are you going to let him? Are you going to take a chance on him as he's taking one on you?"

Sophie sits primly on the couch and serves the espresso. "I do not know. I have been thinking of nothing but what you shared." Her hand shakes as she lifts one of the small cups toward Skyler. Sky takes it and sits next to her. A woman hurting is like a beacon to Skyler's compassionate side.

"SoSo, do you love Gabriel?"

"*Oui*. So much." Her eyes fill with tears, but she straightens her spine and takes a deep breath as if she's pushing the emotional turmoil away with the force of her will.

Skyler puts her hand on Sophie's knee. "It's okay to be scared. Giving up yourself, committing to one person is life changing. And when it's someone you've fallen in love with, it means more."

Sophie pats Skyler's hand. "I want to try, but I don't know how to fix what I have already broken."

Skyler frowns, her entire body seeming to take on Sophie's sadness as if it were her own. "What do you think, honey?" she asks me.

I lean forward and clasp my hands together. "I think we should call Gabriel and invite him to dinner."

"Just invite him like that? Out of nowhere?" Sophie scoffs.

I chuckle. "No. Say you have some surprise guests and would like to make our threesome a foursome. Have him meet us at Buddha-Bar for dinner. Then we take it from there."

Sophie rubs her hands together. "And what if he cannot attend at such short notice?"

"SoSo, I hate to say this, but sweetheart, you are clueless. A man asks you to marry him. Refuses to remove his clothing and personal items from your home, and books a room in the hotel across the street so he can be near you? Sophie, he's absolutely going to drop everything to be available when you call. Believe me. This I know as fact."

"How can you be so sure?" Her voice softens and shudders with her breathing.

"Trust me. I know what a man is willing to do for love. He'll answer."

***

Buddha-Bar has a dark and mysterious vibe when we enter. The owner meets us at the street-side door and shuffles us through the waiting patrons up to a roped-off section that's above the main eating area.

I turn to Nate, whose face is a grim mask of uneasiness as he and Rachel follow Skyler into the belly of the restaurant.

"You do that?" I comment about our immediate entry into the restaurant.

"No. It was already done when I called. Ms. Rolland must have taken care of it."

And what do you know, when we get to the private area, a man I vaguely recognize stands abruptly, straightens his suit jacket, and holds out a chair. He's got thick dark-blond hair, a chiseled jaw, and a pair of black-rimmed glasses perched on his face over blue eyes. The man looks to be around five to ten years older than Sophie, but he's well groomed and attractive. They are definitely yin and yang, the dark and light of each other.

Sophie smiles shyly, reminding me of the woman I met several months ago. The one who lacked confidence and serious sex appeal in her wardrobe. Neither of those two things is a problem any longer, but her sweetness has returned in full force. In the months since I've been to Paris, Sophie has changed for the better. She's stronger, direct, and no longer responds like a wallflower, though I can tell this man brings out something demure in her.

"*Bonsoir*, Gabriel."

Gabriel has eyes only for Sophie; he doesn't so much as glance at us as he cups her around the neck and hip, bringing her into his embrace. "*J'ai rêvé de ton appel.*" He whispers something else into her ear, then boldly kisses her on the neck before doing the two-kiss greeting that is standard in France.

If my memory serves, he said something to the tune of "I dreamed of your call."

"Please speak English, as our guests are Americans."

"How do you do?" he says with a thick French accent while holding out his hand to me, and tilts his head as if in recognition. "I am Gabriel Jeroux."

I smile and shake the man's hand. "Parker Ellis, and my girlfriend, Skyler Paige."

His eyes don't so much as widen at Skyler's name. Either he can hide the fact that he just met one of the most famous celebrities in the business, or he hasn't made the connection yet. I continue, "We've met before, briefly. You're a scientist at Rolland Group."

"*Oui.* That is how I met my Sophie." He places his hand on her chair. "Please everyone, do sit down."

As we sit, Gabriel glances at Nate and Rachel, who flank the private booth, arms crossed, or in Rachel's case, behind her back.

"Do you want me to secure chairs for your friends? I'm not sure why they are standing there as though they are guards."

Skyler chuckles. "They won't sit even if we invite them to. They're my bodyguards."

A waitress comes up and discusses the evening's drinks and chef specialties. We set about ordering wine, cocktails, and appetizers right away, so we can get it out of the way.

"Skyler, is it?" Gabriel asks, and Sky nods. "What is it you do?"

Sophie and I both laugh hard.

"This is so refreshing. You know, I like you already, Gabriel." Skyler beams, giving him one of her megawatt smiles.

He pats his chest, making sure his tie is in place. "I shall thank you for the compliment."

Sophie puts her hand on Gabriel's thigh, and he looks at it and then at her as she speaks. "Skyler is a very well-known actress."

He blinks a few times. "Oh? Anything I might have seen?"

This time I'm laughing. "You really don't recognize her, do you?" I lean back and put my arm around Skyler's chair.

Gabriel shakes his head. "I'm sorry, no." He frowns, his cheeks pinkening with what I assume is embarrassment. "Though, I'm sure that does not mean you are not good. I do not get out to the movies much, or rather, not at all. My time is spent at the lab and with Sophie when possible."

Skyler grabs my hand that I have around her chair. "It's okay. It's nice not to be recognized."

"Do you get recognized a lot?"

She grins. "You could say I get my fair share," she responds, with an out-and-out downplay of her success and status. "Tell me about what you do at Rolland Group?"

Gabriel's eyes come alight with excitement. "I aid my love in creating unique scents, as somewhat of a perfume chemist." He nods to Skyler. "Yours, however, is not a mixture I recognize. It's like peaches . . . and . . ."

"Cream," I add, bringing my nose to her neck and inhaling fully. A powerful shiver of arousal ripples through my body. "My favorite smell on earth."

Gabriel leans forward toward Sky. "Is it a perfume?" He grabs her wrist and lifts it up to his nose. "May I?"

Skyler giggles. "Sure. Though no, it's not perfume. I think it's just a combination of my bodywash, shampoo, and lotion."

"And your natural essence. My nose can detect the subtle differences in each application or beauty product," Gabriel announces.

"Gabriel's olfactory receptors are the best in the business. Many competitors have tried to steal him from me, but alas for them, he stays." Sophie beams with pride at the man who's focused only on her.

"I stay for you, *mon amour*," he declares with zero humor. "I live for you."

Skyler eases her body next to mine. "She's gonna give him the green light, right?" she whispers conspiratorially.

I hold up my fingers to shush her lips and point at them. Sophie and Gabriel are holding hands, facing one another, her long dark hair falling down her shoulders, hiding some of her face from our view. Still I hold my breath, waiting . . . hoping.

"Gabriel . . ." Her voice is shaky, which in this situation is a good sign.

He cuts in. "I just want to be with you always, *mon amour*. Can I please come home?"

Her chin trembles and she nods. "*Oui*, I have been so alone without you."

Skyler watches the couple and wipes at her eyes. I feel my throat tightening and my heart pumping. Skyler and I were in a similar space only a couple of weeks ago. Just proves where there is love, there is always a way.

"You're never going to be alone. You have me. All of me. Until you take your last breath," he promises.

"*Je t'aime*, Gabriel." Sophie cups Gabriel's cheek and kisses him.

Skyler squeezes my hand and brings it up to her lips, so she can kiss the top. She presses my hand to her cheek, her gaze not leaving the romantic display in front of us.

"Does that mean you'll marry me, *mon amour*?" Gabriel's focus is entirely on Sophie.

She pulls back and laughs. "One thing at a time. Let us work on this phase and not rush it."

Gabriel smiles. "If that is your wish, I shall wait for you forever, if I must."

Sophie cups both of his cheeks, kisses him sweetly, and then pulls back. Her gaze goes to our side of the table, where Skyler and I are dead silent watching the show.

"Where are those drinks, anyway?" she inquires, a blush creeping from her neck to her cheeks.

Sky and I laugh, trying to break up the tension so they don't feel as though their entire moment was on display, even if it was.

Carefully I reach out my hand under the table and grab Sophie's. She holds mine, and I squeeze it. "Proud of you."

She grins and silently squeezes my hand, then lets it go.

SKYLER

Parker swings my hand up and back as we walk around the Saint Germain area in Paris. Rachel and Nate are trailing us, but so far we haven't seen a hint of the paparazzi. It's like we've fallen off their radar, which I gotta admit is *awesome*!

"What about there?" Parker points at a boutique filled with women's clothing.

I crinkle up my nose and shake my head. "Nah, not feeling clothes shopping."

"Huh. That's unique."

"Not really. I'm not much for clothes shopping, but I love accessories." I swing his arm some more and step over the small ledge to cross the street. We walk along Rue Dauphine, not far from the Notre-Dame Cathedral. The sun is shining, and there's a chill in the air that has me holding my woven sweater tighter against my neck. "I could use a scarf."

As we pass by the Hôtel d'Aubusson and come to an area filled with brasseries and more stores, I notice a stand full of scarves at the front of a small, artsy-looking shop.

I stop in front of the store and finger the pretty lengths of fabric, appreciating how different each one is. Parker lets go of my hand and scans the window.

"I'm going to get a scarf for me, oooh, and Wendy, Tracey, and maybe your mom." I turn around and wait until Rachel locks gazes with me. "You want a memento scarf?"

Rachel looks down at her black cargo pants, tough-girl boots complete with studs on the heels, and black leather bomber jacket, then back up at me. She grins. "Don't think it would go with my outfit."

I twist my lips to the side and take a gander. "Nope, you're right."

She smiles but makes herself scarce, walking around the perimeter as I remove a couple of scarves and unfold them so I can see the design unencumbered.

"I'm going to go check out something inside." Parker grabs the handle of the door and heads inside.

"Cool. I'll be there in a sec." I put one brilliant red, blue, and brown scarf around my neck, knowing it will be perfect for Parker's mother's complexion. Next, I pick out a bright canary-yellow, white, and black one for Wendy. That girl loves to match wild patterns and colors, and I'm certain she can do something with this. I pick out a lovely pink-and-black one for Tracey, one she can wear with her stylish black peacoat back in NYC. Then I find a cool orange, purple, and royal-blue one that will go with my jeans and sweater, and tuck that around my neck too before heading inside.

The store has a wide variety of paintings, sculptures, trinkets, and other wares that I imagine tourists go crazy for, except it all looks hand-crafted, not just bought in bulk to reach the masses.

I find Parker in the back of the store pointing at some lengths of leather. Each piece is different. Some have a snap at the end or a buckle, and come in a variety of widths.

"Whatcha looking at?"

He grins. "Remember how I told you that I needed to get my mantra tattooed on my wrist?" His blue eyes gleam with mirth.

I chuckle and loop my hands around his waist from behind and look down at the lengths of leather. "Yeah."

"Well, I was obviously joking . . ."

"Uh-huh."

"Though the idea of wearing something with my mantra sounds fitting."

I purse my lips and finger one of the lengths of leather that look like bracelets. The item seems about nine inches long with a snap on the end. It's a burnt sienna color with three brassy grommets on each end and a blank space in the center. It's just under half an inch wide.

Behind the counter a little old man is working on a machine making a bunch of noise. He then comes back to Parker, blowing on a strap of leather in his hand and rubbing it across his fingers. He lays the bracelet down on the counter, and my heart stops.

In the center of the leather are three words:

TRUST YOUR HEART

"Whoa!" I gasp and run my fingers over the imprinted leather. "He just made this for you? It's incredible."

Parker smiles wide, grabs the bracelet, puts it around his wrist, and snaps it into place. It's so hip and cool and . . . *everything*. "You put my words on your body, honey?" I hold his hand and look down at the most amazing gesture he's ever made besides telling me he loves me.

"Yes, I did." His tone is proud and filled with love.

I frown. "Well, I want one too! With my mantra on it, but I want . . . ohhhhh!" My gaze falls onto a strip of leather the same width as his, but it's black instead of his sienna color. On each end are cut flowers and leaves as though they've been etched into the leather and are a light tan against the stark darkness of the black on top. It's a beautiful mix of colors. "Excuse me, sir. May I have this one with a different phrase on it?"

"*Oui.* As you wish."

"I'd like mine to say in all capitals: 'live your truth.'"

He nods, grabs a new leather bracelet from under the counter, and goes to his machine.

"Oh, and when you're done, I want to buy these four scarves too!" I pull the scarves off my neck, set them on the counter. and bounce from side to side, my excitement rushing through my system like ants dancing in my pants.

Parker hooks his arm around my shoulders and brings me into his side. "You know, this is positively romantic."

I grin and lift up my chin as he looks down at me. "I'm going to wear mine all the time."

He kisses me soundly on the mouth and then pulls back. I swear, when he kisses me like this, stares into my eyes so deeply, I feel as if we're the only two people in the whole world. I fall more in love with him each and every time he stares at me with awe in his gaze.

"Me too. Then, when we're apart, I'll have a reminder of my love for you, hanging right on my wrist."

"You know the guys are going to give you mad shit about this." I chuckle.

He closes his pretty blue eyes for a moment. "I know. You're worth it."

"It is done." The man behind the counter breaks up our little snug-fest and lays the length of leather out for my inspection.

"It's beautiful." I run my fingers over the words that have come to mean everything to me.

LIVE YOUR TRUTH

Parker snaps the bracelet on my wrist and runs his thumb over it. He lifts my hand and kisses the words over my wrist. "It's even prettier on the wearer."

I nudge his shoulder and laugh. "Smooth talker."

He chuckles.

The Frenchman rings me up, and soon Parker and I are holding hands and walking back down the lanes of the Saint Germain district. I lead Parker down a street I know well and to my favorite place to eat in all of France. Well, my favorite pizzeria.

Parker's eyebrows rise near his hairline as he takes in Pizzeria Pepone. It's a tiny little hole in the wall that can only seat maybe fifteen people on one side. On the other side, the chef is spinning dough in the air and cooking up the pies and pastas made fresh to order.

"Skyler!" The owner opens his arms, and I let go of Parker in order to hug the man. He pulls back from the hug and smiles. "You have come back."

"Told you, every time I'm in France, I'm stopping in for my pizza fix."

He ushers us to a prime table where we can still watch people walk by on the street.

"You come here often?" Park whispers in my ear.

I nod and bite into my bottom lip. "When I'm in Paris, yeah. Best pizza in Europe."

Parker holds my chair out for me before seating himself. "You know, you're the perfect woman." His words send butterflies flapping their wings inside my stomach.

"Perfect?" I return dryly.

"Well, perfect for me."

I can feel the blush rush across my skin in a heated wave. "I guess I'll have to accept that, since you're perfect for me."

My phone buzzes in my back pocket, and I pull it out and note it's a text. Glancing down at the screen, I frown.

From: Unknown
To: Skyler Paige

I thought we were friends. Friends tell each other everything.

"What is it?" Parker asks while the owner sets down my favorite wine. It's a burgundy they've had available every time I've been here, which, over the years, has been at least a dozen times.

I shake my head, and an uncomfortable feeling sets up root where Parker's butterflies had been. "I don't know. It's weird. Look." I hand him the phone and he scans it and frowns.

"Unknown caller. Definitely not someone you programmed. Do you think it's a mistake?"

"Guess it could be. Probably." I run my hand through my hair.

He taps the top of the phone. "It's strange. A week ago, I received a text from an unknown caller too."

An uneasy feeling prickles at the back of my neck, but I push it aside. "Hmm."

Parker stands up. "Pour the wine and order me whatever pizza you're having. I'm gonna give your phone to Nate and have him investigate."

"Don't you think that's going overboard a little? It's one text."

"Two if you count my unknown-caller text."

"You're reaching . . ."

"Maybe, but better safe than sorry, right?"

I shrug. "Whatever you say, pretty boy. Just hurry up and get your ass back. I want to toast to our last night in Paris before we go home."

He leans over and runs two fingers down the side of my face until he gets to my chin. I lift it up, and he kisses me briefly before heading about ten feet over to where Rachel and Nate have already ordered food, sitting at the table right near the exit, where they can see everything.

While I watch, Parker hands the phone to Nate and says a few things, and then his own phone must have rung because he pulls it out of his pocket and lifts it to his ear. His face lights up with happiness, and I wonder who he's talking to.

The owner comes over, and I order us two margherita pizzas, which are amazing here.

Parker smiles as he returns and takes his seat. God, I love seeing him in a tight-fitting pair of jeans and a chunky sweater. He's *GQ*, the boy next door, the successful businessman, and confident lover all in one. I could lick up the side of his neck, wiggle my hand between his hot skin and the zipper of his pants, and go to town on him right here and be hard-pressed to feel bad about the public indecency of it. The man just sets me on fire with desire.

"Yeah, Roy, got it. Cool. Two weeks at home, though. Yes." The word comes out in a happy hiss. "I don't know if she's traveling, I'll find out, but if she's heading to New York, I may follow her there and take the laptop with me."

I grin as he finishes his call and sets his phone on the table.

"You've got two weeks?"

He smiles. "That's right. And depending on what you have, I thought we could spend a week in Boston and then a week in New York. I know you said you have some junkets in the Big Apple."

"I do. That would work perfect, actually."

"Then it's settled. Besides, Ma has a homemade meal at home planned for us when we get back."

"She does?" I croak.

"Yeah, Peaches. Oh, and Pops wants you to sign a few things he can auction off at this charity thing he and my ma are doing at her local library. If you don't mind."

"Course not. I'd be happy to help. And donate too."

"Great! Oh, and Royce and Bo want to challenge you to a game of pool at Lucky's. They're still pissed you beat them last time. And . . . if you wouldn't mind, I'd like to stop at Wendy and Michael's place. See how she's doing in person." He rattles off the laundry list of things we need to attend to when we get home.

Home.

A foreign phrase ever since my parents died. My penthouse in New York City is comfortable and the inside is definitely me, but it's not a home. It's a place I stay when I'm not filming. Being with Parker, his friends, his family, Boston . . . that all feels like a real home.

Parker smiles, and it shoots right through my chest and burrows deep in my heart, warming me there. I take his hand on top of the table and interlace our fingers, our bracelets looking wicked cool under the soft lighting in the restaurant. Sitting here, holding my man's hand, planning to go back to Boston and have a family dinner, do a charity auction for his mother's job, it all seems so right, so . . . normal.

I lift up my glass of burgundy, and Parker follows.

"What should we drink to?" he asks.

"Going home."

He clinks his glass with mine and sips, his gaze on nothing but me. "To going home."

The end . . . for now.

BERLIN: INTERNATIONAL GUY BOOK 8

To the team at Ullstein Verlag,
Berlin is for you.

Thank you for sharing your beautiful country with me.
From castles of long ago
and rooms filled with thousands of seashells,
to tasty German beer
and the historic Berlin Wall . . .

I'll never forget my time with you.

SKYLER

A tingle slides up my spine before warm lips press down on the base of my neck. That featherlight feeling wisps across my shoulder until, in that whisper of time between sleep and wakefulness, teeth dig into the rounded ball of my shoulder, hitting a spot that makes me giggle.

"It's time to get up, Peaches." Parker snuffles against my neck and shoulder, nibbling as he goes along toward the other side of my body, lest it feel neglected.

I love that about him. His need for symmetry. Balance in all things.

Actually there are so many things I love about him, like being woken up by lips and soft touches instead of the blaring screech of an alarm clock. My man wakes with the sun, unless we've tied one on the night before. It's as if the sunlight enters the room, falls upon his handsome face, and gently caresses him awake, the same way he does to me. Except my guy is smart. He has coffee ready and gentle words to go with his onslaught to bring me out of slumber.

"There's coffee . . . ," he prompts.

See?

Best. Man. Ever.

With a sudden burst of energy, I roll over and wrap my arms and legs around him, bringing him down upon me. He's warm and smells of coffee and mint. He must have already brushed his teeth.

"Hmm." I sigh into his all-encompassing heat. I've always wondered how men can be so warm all the damn time. It's like they're supercharged heaters, ready to go at a moment's notice.

"You've got to get up. I've already allowed you to sleep an extra twenty minutes, and I really want to get to Wendy's house. It's been too long since I've seen her, and I gotta admit, it's weighing on me." He sits up, and I follow him.

I nod into his neck. "Me too. I know we've talked to her every couple of days, but you're right, seeing is believing. I'll be fast getting ready."

He kisses my cheek, cups my face, and gives me a proper good-morning kiss. I swoon as my heart beats double time and butterflies do their flutter gig in my belly.

Every time.

I'm constantly amazed at having this man in my life. Just the way he looks at me as though I'm solid gold topped with rubies and diamonds is enough to make a girl cry. Add in the fact that I never make my own coffee when I'm with him, plus he lets me use the shower first so that I get the hot water, unless of course we're saving time and sharing one, makes him the perfect man for me. We're still growing and learning one another's quirks, but every day is better than the last the longer I'm with him.

I deepen the kiss and let the blanket fall down between us, exposing my breasts against his bare chest.

"Sky . . . ," he half warns as I push him to his back so that I can straddle him. He makes a half-hearted attempt at tug-of-war but lets me take over, and I press my naked body against his pajama-clad lower half. I run my tongue up his neck and back down. He grips my ass and grinds his hardening length against my core.

"How about we save time and shower together, today? Hmm?" I bite down on the flat disk of his light-brown nipple.

He hisses through his teeth. "You do not play fair."

I grin, knowing he's going to cave. His dick is as hard as a bat between us and ready to go. I rub my lower half along his, working my clit over his length until I know I'm ready for hard and fast up against the shower wall.

He clenches my ass cheeks and lifts us both up in one go. His shoulder hasn't given him any trouble since we've been back, and his fingers are finally healed. No more punching walls for my man. That's for sure.

I wrap my legs around his toned waist and lock my arms around his neck. "I love mornings with you." I clench my thighs tighter so that his hardness gets a little extra friction.

He hugs my body closer as he gets to the bathroom and holds me with one arm wrapped tight around my back as he flips on the hot water. Once done, he pushes his cotton pants down, fixes the water to the right temperature, and brings us both under the spray.

Hot pinpricks hit my back as I adjust to the water temperature. I feel Parker's lips on my neck and dip my head back. Steam billows all around us as he presses me against the tile wall, one hand under my ass, the other on my jaw, forcing my face to his so he can devour my mouth. I've come to expect some of Parker's moves sexually. Before he enters me, he likes to take my mouth, licking deep, biting on my lips until I cry out. And that's when he goes for either a smooth or a hard, deep thrust; it totally depends on his mood. Apparent urgency pushing his "beast," he enters me with a firm lunge. I moan and squeeze my legs, pointing my toes, letting the feeling of being joined move through me in pleasurable waves of ecstasy.

He drags his lips down my neck, nibbling as he goes until he can reach one of my breasts. He sucks it hard, alternating between biting and flicking the tender peak mercilessly. He knows how sensitive my breasts are, and he uses that to his advantage as much as he can . . . thank God!

"Honey . . . ," I say while digging my nails into his back, likely leaving little crescent moon indents behind. "More. Please, more."

He grins against my breast, sucks it hard before letting it go with an audible plop. "You want me to ride you hard, baby? Make sure you feel me between your legs . . . ?" He nuzzles my neck and up to my ear. "All day long. Hmm. Would you like that?" He eases his length out and slams back in until my teeth rattle and my sex contracts, tightening and holding on, getting ready for one helluva pounding.

"Yeah . . . ," I gasp as he does it again, though this time he runs one hand up my back so he can cradle my head against the shower tile.

"Just remember, you asked for it." He bites down on my shoulder and uses the slickness of the wall to aid in moving me up and down, on and off his cock like I'm a racehorse jockey bouncing away down the track on a speeding horse. Only he's the horse.

Pleasure roars in my veins as the bulbous head of his cock pushes along each nerve, his pelvic bone crushing my clit with each thrust in.

The heat of the enclosed space tingles against my skin as an over-powering sense of peace, happiness, and pure love fills every one of my pores.

"God, I love you," he grinds through clenched teeth. "And I love fucking you. Damn it! I'm never gonna get enough." He pierces his words with a brutally deep thrust, sending me into a long, drawn-out orgasm the likes of which women talk about but never really experience. Only Parker delivers. Every. Single. Time.

"Love you. Love you. Love you." I chant the two-word phrase over and over as he rides me to his own finish, gushing inside of me and outside with a single powerful breath and a warrior's cry that bounces off the walls of the small space. He digs his fingers into my skin, hold-ing me tight, gripping me to him as though he may never let me go.

"Jesus, you undo me, Skyler."

I grin lazily as he pants against my skin and kisses his way up my neck until he reaches my lips, where he seals his love for me with a kiss. It sounds cheesy, but when he does it, it's almost as if he's thanking me for being with him, for loving him.

"Shower time with you rocks!" I smile as he laughs against my lips and lifts me up, disconnecting us. A small burst of pain shimmers within my sex as he disengages and helps me to my feet, then leads me back under the spray.

As I wash my hair I take inventory of my body. Thighs are definitely burning. Shoulders tired but could be worse. Parker squirts some of my shower gel into his palms, rubs them together, and proceeds to kneel down and cup one leg at a time, washing each one meticulously. As he runs his hands over the muscles, they're all sore. Two days of nothing but sleeping, eating, and making love will do that to a woman. Not that I have a single complaint. Nope.

Parker runs a soapy hand between my legs, and I hiss at the twinge of discomfort. He rubs his fingers between my thighs, cleaning me of our lovemaking. "Sore?" He grins maniacally as if that was his intent all along.

"Yeah. Proud of yourself?"

He smirks, applies more soap, and runs his hands up my stomach and over each of my breasts, cleaning them and stirring my desire once more. Except when he gets to my nipples a bite of pain reminds me just how much attention he's given the twins in the last two days—hell, in the past several weeks if you count Montreal, London, Paris, and our time in Boston.

"Hurt?" He tweaks each tip and I try not to wince, but I can't hold back.

He purses his lips, dips down, and kisses each berry-red tip softly. "I'm sorry," he says to each breast, *not* to me.

I brace my hand on his forehead and shove him back. "Get off, maniac."

He chuckles and gets his own soap while I shampoo and condition my hair.

"Did you tell Nate and Rachel they need to be ready by nine?" he asks.

I nod and rinse out the conditioner. "Yeah, Nate was happy about it because he did a drive by the apartment last night and didn't like the herd of paparazzi camped out."

Parker frowns. "As much as I hate to say it, this apartment is not safe for you. You can't be alone here. Ever."

"Yeah, I've started to realize that fact, as much as I don't want to."

I bite down on my bottom lip and think about the surprise I've been holding on to. While he was on his laptop yesterday, I was signing legal documents for the new place I leased in Boston. I would have bought the thing, but I still don't know how he's going to respond, and I'm not sure about the location. It may be too much, too soon.

There's also the glimmer I saw of the life that Parker might want when he mentioned his grandparents and how much he loved visiting them. I get the feeling that he wants a real home of his own, with land, a porch, dogs, cats, kids. The place I leased is not going to be that. Though if this relationship continues where I think it's headed, it would be better to pick out a home like that together. A place we both fall in love with.

Parker turns off the water and grabs two fluffy towels as I push back the dreams for the future, not wanting to get my hopes up. Parker and I have only been together several months, and some of it has been rocky. We need the time to just be a couple. Live in the same city. Experience friends, family, and everything in between along with our careers. Together, as a couple, we need to be able to balance it all and find out where our love fits in too.

The only saving grace? I know I own his heart and he owns mine. Everything else we'll figure out.

"Yeah, the paparazzi are getting bolder. We'll discuss it more later. Nate has some ideas." I wave my hand, trying to get him off the subject. Once he finds out about the surprise, this may not be an issue, at least for a while. "Let's get moving. I want to see Wendy."

He smiles wide, and the tension that marred his brow disappears as he thinks about his redheaded assistant.

"And the best part . . ." He waggles his eyebrows.

I wrap the towel around my body and tuck the side into my armpit. "Is?"

He gifts me a brilliant, giant grin. "Bo is meeting us there. And he's supposed to be wearing a skirt!"

"No way!" I chuckle and slick back my long wet tresses.

He nods and rubs the towel down his ripped chest, catching stray droplets as he goes. My guy is standing naked in front of the mirror, not self-conscious in the least, moving his hands through his hair. I scan his sexy form, noting the long, lean slabs of toned muscle. Parker Ellis takes damn good care of himself, and I'm the lucky woman who gets to take advantage of all that hard work.

Yum.

"Totally. He's showing up in a skirt. Rachel told him today was the day, and since they're escorting us to Wendy's, it's the perfect time."

I think back to when my bodyguard bested Bo on the mechanical bull, outlasting his time. "Serves him right that he has to go to Wendy's. She'll get a kick out of it."

"Yeah, as long as Michael doesn't end up kicking Bo's ass while we're there, we'll all be good."

I shrug and start brushing my hair, working out any tangles as I do so. "At least the skirt won't be a hindrance. He'll get a nice shot at Bo!"

Parker laughs and applies some sunscreen moisturizer on his face. "This is true."

I watch Parker get ready and realize how nice it is to just share space with a person. Get ready together, talk about your friends, plan things. It's not something I had before but something I'd fight to keep. Maybe that's the part of love people don't really talk about. The beauty of just being a team.

I pad over to where Parker is standing with razor in hand, cleaning up his face. Usually he does the shave deal before he gets in the shower, but I kind of messed that order up by coming on to him. I don't think he cares.

When I get to his back, I press my body against him and kiss the center of his spine, ease my arms around his waist, and set my cheek against his warm skin.

"I like this. You and me. Doing normal and kicking its ass."

His body bounces a little as if he's laughing before he turns around and lifts my chin. I look up and find he's still got shaving cream on his face and neck, but his eyes are burning with an intensity I've only seen when he looks at me. "Me too." He leans down and kisses me, getting shaving cream all over my face, but I ignore it, wrap my arms around his neck, and kiss the heck out of him.

1

Wendy and Michael live off the beaten path in a private, gated community about thirty minutes outside of Boston proper. I've been dying to go to their house. I can easily imagine sex swings hanging from the rafters like chandeliers, dotted throughout, and floggers lying on the tables in case the mood strikes at a given moment. As serious as Michael was about the collar issue in Montreal, I wonder if he treats Wendy like a sex slave.

Oh my God, what if he makes her walk around the house naked?

Sweat beads up on my upper lip, and I tug at my dress shirt and unbutton the top. No, he wouldn't let her be naked around her guy colleagues. He's very territorial, and besides, Bo is coming. He has a hate spot for Bo, not a soft spot.

Still, as much as I'm intrigued, I'm rather nervous. I haven't seen Wendy in what feels like forever, and I don't know how to react. The soft side of me wants to fall at her knees and beg her to come back. Explain that Annie is nice and efficient at her job, but she's not a badass or a hacker extraordinaire. Plus, her awkwardness annoys me.

I wipe my brow and upper lip with my handkerchief and shove it back into my pocket and stare out the window.

Nate breaks into my strange worries. "Oh, Sky, that thing you requested . . ." Using the rearview mirror, he glances first at me and then focuses on Skyler. "It's um, yeah, it's ready for this evening."

"Really? Cool!" Skyler crosses her legs, and those long tanned limbs make an appearance through the split in her maxi dress.

I place my hand on her bare knee, wanting not only to touch her and ground myself from the nerves prickling within about seeing Wendy, but also to get her attention.

"What do you have brewing?" I squeeze her knee and focus on my girl.

Skyler bites down on her plump bottom lip, covers my hand with her own, and turns to face me so I can see her brilliant brown eyes sparkle in the daylight. She's effervescent in her beauty. Like a ray of sunshine, warming me from the outside in with a single look.

"It's for me to know, and you to find out!" she teases.

I quirk my head closer. "Are you keeping a secret from me, Peaches?"

She bobs her head up and down. "Yep. And I'm hoping you'll like it, even though it's more for me than for you, but it's still for you . . . you know?" Her brows pinch together as if whatever she's keeping from me is wearing on her conscience or she just sucks at keeping secrets.

I bring her hand to my lips and kiss her knuckles. "Why don't you just tell me, and then I'll let you know if I like it or not?" I attempt with my smoothest voice.

She shakes her head. "Nope. No way. Nohow. I've been keeping this secret for weeks, and it's finally ready. I'm equally excited and nervous about it. Just promise me that today, when I can show you the secret, you'll have an open mind. Okay?"

I kiss her fingers again. "Anything for you." I hold her gaze with my own until her cheeks pink up in a pretty blush.

"Whoa. There's rich, and then there's überrich. Holy freakin' A." Rachel gasps in awe at the sight of the black double gates, complete with a security guard at an outpost.

"Can I help you folks?" the guard asks, gun belt displayed with a big, fat holstered whopper of a .45.

"Yeah, we're here to see Michael Pritchard and family. Rachel and Nathan Van Dyken, Skyler Paige, and Parker Ellis," Nate answers.

The man evaluates the clipboard and nods, making check marks. "A Bogart Montgomery and a Royce Sterling were supposed to be with you?"

Nate shakes his head. "Coming separately."

"All right, you've got clearance. Just go in, and at the triple fork in the road, take the road to the left. When you come to another fork, take the left again. The Pritchard estate is at the end of the second fork to the left."

Nate salutes the guard, and the gate opens wide. As Nate drives slowly down the road, we're treated to acres and acres of rolling green hills, giant pine trees, a full-on lake, and giant mansions dotting the hills in different directions.

"Jesus . . . I had no idea this is where they live." I gawk at the luxury homes.

"What does Michael do anyway?" Skyler looks out the window, mouth agape, eyes wide.

"Advertising is what Wendy said when she first came on, but I never got into the details, and she was lying through her teeth, so I don't really know." I scan the rich landscapes. There's no way a person could score a home with an estate like this for under $20 or $30 million. It's beyond lush and dripping with privacy. Plus, it's an easy commute to downtown Boston, which is highly desirable.

After what feels like a ten-minute drive through the massive swaths of land, we come up to a giant home, the type Jay-Z and Beyoncé would probably live in, not my fiery, hacking personal assistant with a punk rock edge.

"This is bizarre . . . ," Sky whispers, getting out of the car.

The four of us look around and see only the tips of some of the other houses, way off in the distance. Each mansion must be on its own fifteen-acre lot or more. "I didn't even know this area existed," I say.

"Me neither. I wonder if anything is for sale." Sky scans the area, and my heart starts to pound.

Will she really consider moving out of NYC to Boston to be closer to me? I know we've both hinted at wanting to be near one another, and after having been without her, I'm in no hurry for us to live separate lives again.

I lift my hand to my forehead to block out the sun. No way in hell I could afford one of these properties . . . but she could. Probably wouldn't even put a dent in her bank account. And if that were the case, what would I have to offer?

The door beyond the car opens, and Wendy is led down the handful of steps to the gravel drive by her guy. Her red hair looks magnificent under the sun's rays. I grin wide and beat feet over to her to take her into my arms.

"Minxy . . ." I inhale her coconut-scented hair. "I've missed you, girl." I look over at Michael, who's hugging Skyler and shaking the hands of both Rachel and Nate.

I lean back as Wendy wipes under her teary eyes.

"How are you feeling? You look fantastic!" I lie, noting the dark circles under her eyes and lack of color to her skin tone.

She clears her throat. "Good. Better with you guys here. I'm so glad you came." Her voice cracks, but she swallows and shakes it off before looking around. "Hey, where're Bo and Royce?"

"Coming separ—" I start to say, when I see a gleaming silver Porsche 911 fly up the drive and come to a complete stop, as if on a dime, directly behind the blacked-out Range Rover Nate uses when Sky's in Boston.

"Holy shit, he did it." I gasp at the beautiful sex on wheels.

Royce pops out of the vehicle and pats the top. "Like my new leading lady?"

"You dog! I can't believe you bought her." I shake his hand, and he pulls me in for the standard chest bump and back slap. "You've been dragging ass on this purchase for over a year . . . Why now?"

He shrugs and comes around to where Bo is sitting in the front seat, not having left the car.

"It was just time. No more waiting for things to happen in life. If I want something, I'm going to go out and get it my damned self." He runs his hands down his dress shirt. He looks incredible as usual in a full suit but no tie. Seems we both went for business with a hint of casual for this outing.

"Hear, hear!" Wendy fist pumps and then winces. I hook my arm around her waist and pat her shoulder.

"You okay?"

"Fine, fine." She waves a hand in annoyance. "Bo, get out of the car."

Bo closes his eyes, and then the door opens. A black motorcycle boot hits the gravel with a crunch. I notice the bare slip of ankle and shin visible under the door and remember what I'm about to see.

"Come on, you big baby!" I holler, hoping to add to his discomfort. "A bet's a bet."

"What's going on?" Michael comes over to Wendy's side and holds out his hand, which she takes, leaving my side and sliding against her man's.

"Bogey lost a bet against Rachel. Come on, Bo, be a man!" I cry out, and he huffs, pushes the door all the way open, and stands abruptly.

The seven of us stare at Bo but do not say a word. He's wearing huge black motorcycle boots, his standard leather jacket, and a white tee underneath, which is average for the guy. It's the green-and-black plaid kilt that falls from his hips that has all of our attention. It comes to just above the knee and has a thin yellow line threaded through the plaid. At the top is a thick belt with what looks to be a pouch of some sort hanging dead center over where I imagine his junk would be.

Bo crosses his massive arms over one another and stands like a Scottish biker, ready to ride his hog through the northern hillsides of Europe.

"What?" he grates through clenched teeth.

And that's when we all lose it. Seven different variations of laughter break through the silence and fill the air with humor. From Wendy's giggling into Michael's shirt, to Royce's rumbling laugh behind his hand, to Skyler's high-pitched giggle, and more. We all lose it.

Rachel struts her tiny toned body, dressed all in black—this time leather pants, a tank, and her bomber jacket—around Bo's form in a slow circle. She crosses one arm over the other, her hand lifting to her chin as she inspects his kilt. "Well, friend, I do believe you have met the parameters of our bet. We are even." She clocks him on the back good-naturedly.

He grins and struts in a circle, clearly feeling more confident. "You know, that isn't the best part . . ."

Rachel stops in front of her husband, who puts his hand on her shoulder. "Which would be?" she asks.

Bo flings his body around, bends over, and flaps the kilt back and up, mooning the seven of us with his white ass. "What's underneath, bitches!" He laughs at his own joke.

Skyler loses it, running over and smacking his bare ass as hard as she can, then bringing her hand up to her chest in pain saying, "Owie, owie."

Bo screeches as she runs back to me and hides behind my body, laughing hysterically. Michael slowly walks over to Skyler and puts out his fist. She bumps it, giggling like crazy.

"Good show. I was too busy trying to cover my woman's eyes before they melted out of her head." He grins.

Bo rubs at his sore cheek. "Damn, Sky, you've got an arm on you, girl."

She peeks over my shoulder, her body pressed up against the back of mine. "I did a sports romance movie once. They hired a professional baseball player to teach us how to play. I got pretty good, if I do say so myself."

He pouts. "Park, you better watch out. Your girl there has a stinger of a hand."

I chuckle. "You think I don't know that?" I cock a brow as Sky puts her arms around me from behind, locking her hands together at my chest.

Bo's brows go up. "Brother, you've been holding out on me. Tell me everything."

I roll my eyes and turn to Michael and Wendy. "Thank you for having us out. I'm looking forward to sitting down and catching up."

Wendy nods but heads over to Royce and hugs him. He pulls back and cups her cheeks, then turns her face this way and that. "You look tired, girl."

She smiles flatly. "Yeah, well, it's not as easy to sleep as I thought it would be."

I unlock Sky's hands from me and head over to Michael. "What's she talkin' about?"

"Nightmares. But she made me promise not to dwell on it. She wants to have a good time, and I like seeing her smile. Let's just say I'm glad you're home for a while. She needs the support right now."

I nod and watch as our girl hugs Bo. He wraps his arms around her slowly as if she's made of porcelain. "Tink . . . you okay?" he says loud enough for me to hear.

She nods against his chest and smiles, but it doesn't reach her eyes.

"Come on, everybody. Mick's made brunch, so let's eat." She eases up to her man, and he leads her up the stairs, supporting her body in case she needs it.

God, I wish she didn't need it.

Upon entering, I'm struck how the house is nothing like what you would expect someone like Wendy to live in. A chill condo with old-school music records and obscure movie posters hanging on the walls, yes. Maybe even a converted warehouse turned funky home, sure. Definitely not an estate home you'd expect from a politician. This home is old money. If anything, it reminds me more of a museum than a home.

"Wow." Skyler glances up the grand staircase at all the paintings lining the walls. "This place is . . . uh, massive."

Wendy chuckles. "Yeah, for the first year I lived here, I didn't even see every room. The second day, I actually got lost and had to call Mick to come find me." She socks her man in the shoulder playfully.

I scan the art and recognize a real Picasso and Monet hanging among some other fine pieces that would go for hundreds of thousands if not millions. "You really have quite the eye for art." I'm trying to take in all that is a painting by Claude Monet I've not seen before.

Michael glances at the painting and inhales fully. "My grandfather and his grandfather before him were collectors of the finer things. I grew up in this home when my grandfather passed it down to my parents. Both have since left this earth and passed it down to me. One day, I will pass it to my children . . ." He doesn't complete the sentence, as if the words have gotten lodged in his throat.

I place my hand on his shoulder and squeeze while my own heart pounds out a sorrowful beat.

He would have already had a child on the way if that wack-job in Montreal hadn't taken it away. A bolt of anger pierces my chest, and I grind down on my teeth, attempting to hold it back. This pain and anger is not mine to own. It didn't happen to me, even though it breaks my fucking heart in two.

I whisper low enough that I hope only he can hear. "I'm sorry."

Surprisingly he puts his hand on mine and squeezes back. "Thank you. We're dealing."

I nod solemnly as Sky comes over and grabs my free hand. "Everything okay?" She must note the stiffness in my demeanor and the sadness in both our eyes.

"Just talking art."

Sky places her other hand on my chest and glances at the art. "Park loves art and museums. I'm looking forward to seeing the rest of the place."

Wendy pops over, a bit of a spring back in her step I hadn't seen when she approached us outside. Looks like just having us here is helping her attitude. "That would take all day. We'll just show you the cool bits, but Mick promised me I could have a full glass of white wine now that I'm almost completely weaned off my meds. And I've been a good girl. Haven't I, baby?" Her tone is pleading but also laced with a hint of innuendo.

He smirks and cocks an eyebrow. "Yes, Cherry. I did promise you one glass with your friends. I shall make good on my promise now. Is everyone ready for drink service and hors d'oeuvres in the parlor?"

"You have a parlor?" Sky asks, awe in each word.

Wendy grins and loops her arm with Mick's before leading the way.

"This place is insane," Sky whispers in my ear.

"Absolutely." I glance over my shoulder at Royce and Bo, who are bringing up the rear of our group and scanning the center of the entryway. The ceiling must be twenty-five feet up with a giant dangling glass chandelier hanging over our heads. No sex swing, though, and I'm beginning to think I'm going to be let down based on just the entryway's grandiose decor. I'm still holding out hope for a red room like in *Fifty Shades of Grey*.

Rachel and Nate decide to take off now that they have assessed the safety of the property and excuse themselves.

Once we get into the parlor, a bartender greets the group, standing behind what looks to be a full bar of solid, sealed mahogany, which spans the entire corner of the room in a beautiful setup complete with bottles of varying colors and sizes sitting on matching shelves with glass behind them.

"What can I get for each of you? We have a white and a red wine that Mr. Pritchard has chosen, as well as a full bar at your service."

Royce orders a whiskey neat. Sky and Wendy go for the white wine, Michael for the red, and Bo and I for a gin and tonic.

After each of us gets a drink, we follow Wendy and Mick through the sprawling, oversize rooms: one for billiards, a library, what looks like a home office, a bathroom, and a ginormous kitchen with staff bustling around. Then we move through a dining room to a back living room that leads to what seems like a sunroom facing a beautiful garden. The room is set up with a large dining table already prepared with finger foods galore.

"Please, have a seat, enjoy some spanakopita, quiche, egg rolls, and mushroom caps before the brunch is served." Michael gestures to the food and leaves us, probably to check on the entrées.

We each sit down, Skyler to my right, Wendy to my left. Across from us are Royce and Bo, with Michael's empty seat likely the one at the head of the table. There are two additional place settings for Rachel and Nate, but we weren't sure if they were welcome at the time.

"Now I feel bad that we told Rachel and Nate to go on ahead," Sky murmurs, a hint of sadness in her voice.

I nuzzle my girl's temple, loving her kind heart. "They enjoy time alone. The duo are with you twenty-four seven. This gives them some time to be a couple. Go see a movie, have a meal alone. You know, normal married-people stuff."

She pouts. "I guess that's true."

"It is. Trust me." I hug her around the shoulders and rub her bicep until I feel the tension abate.

"'K," she says easily, then wiggles in her seat, scanning the eats before choosing a mushroom cap. Her eyes light up with glee. At first,

I think it's from the food. My girl loves to eat. Hates to work out, but loves her food.

"Oh! Wendy, I've got something for you." Skyler puts the food on her plate, wipes off her fingers on a napkin, and rustles through her big bag hanging over the edge of the chair. She pulls out a tissue-wrapped present and hands it to me so I can pass it to Wendy.

Wendy blinks rapidly and looks down at the pink wrapping and big yellow bow, flipping it over and over. "For what?"

Sky leans her elbow on the table to turn fully toward Wendy. "When Parker and I left London, we stopped in Paris to see Sophie. Park took me sightseeing and shopping, and we got you a little something to let you know we were thinking about you."

Wendy's gaze lifts to mine and then back to Sky's. "Um, I don't know what to say." Her voice sounds raspy and uneven.

Sky frowns. "There's nothing to say, silly. It's just a little travel present. Open it up!"

Wendy does so and fingers the silk scarf with bright-yellow streaks and black-and-white patterns that will definitely look sharp on her. She sniffs and wipes at her nose with her napkin.

I put my hand on Wendy's neck until she lifts her teary gaze to mine. "Hey . . ."

"It's beautiful . . . Uh, I-I don't know how to thank you enough. I love it." Her words are muffled through her teary response as she lifts the scarf to her chest as though it's the most precious gift she's ever received.

I run my thumb across her chin and dip closer into her line of sight so I can meet her eyes. "Minxy, what's the matter?"

She shrugs and then winces.

"Don't do that, your wound," I chastise. "Just tell us what's wrong."

She shakes her head as Michael comes up behind her, dips down, and kisses her cheek before speaking against her skin. "Cherry, it's normal for a female to buy her friend a present. Just say thank you. That's all you need to do." He kisses her again.

"But I've never been given a present from a friend before. I've never had a girlfriend before." Wendy swallows, and the tears fall as she lifts up the scarf lovingly. "It's the very best scarf I've ever had. I'll wear it all the time. Thank you, Skyler and Parker."

My heart hurts, and I rub my chest and shake my head. "Oh no, it was all Sky—" I start, until Sky pinches me on the thigh and glares when I cut my gaze to hers.

"You're welcome, Wen." She uses the little nickname she's given Wendy. "We missed you and wanted you to know we were thinking about you."

Bo jumps in. "Then where's my present?" he mumbles, and Royce pushes him so hard he almost falls off the chair, the legs teetering over the Oriental rug below our feet.

Skyler rolls her eyes and Wendy laughs, then Sky lifts up her wineglass. "So glad we're home and you're on the mend. I know the guys can't wait to get you back in the office."

Royce's voice is a deep rumble. "I will drink to that for sure."

"Hell yes." Bo nods. "Bring back my Tink. That blonde is chilly cold and doesn't so much as smile at my jokes. Plus, she dresses all stuck-up. There's absolutely zero to look at."

I lean my head back and groan at the absolutely horrid comment.

"What? She's all buttoned up and professional. So boring. Ugh." Bo makes a gag sound before taking a pull on his gin and tonic.

"Don't listen to him, minxy." I narrow a warning glare at Bo.

"Like I ever do. Except the part about you guys missing me. You really do? I know Annie is doing a good job. I call every day . . ."

"Three times a day, girl. You do not need to call and check up on me." Royce sighs.

Wendy pouts. "But you were all alone, and I needed to know you guys were okay."

I place my hand on the upper part of Wendy's back. "Wendy, no one will ever replace you. Your job is there waiting for you when you're healed up and better."

She smiles wide, and Michael runs a hand across her neck before he finally takes a seat after setting a bottle of champagne in an ice bucket at the side of the table. "She's dying to come back to work, but I'm forcing her to take the full eight weeks. She needs this time to mentally and physically prepare for being back in the office. The doctor concurs. Right, my love?"

She sags in her seat. "Yes. And it's totally lame. I'm fine."

Michael's jaw tightens, and his gaze is ablaze when it reaches mine. He subtly shakes his head, silently communicating to me that Wendy is not fine. Not at all.

2

"What's next on the IG agenda for you boys?" Wendy asks. She sips her white wine slowly as if it's straight nectar from the gods. Most likely because she's being limited to one glass by her guy.

Royce rubs a hand over his bald head, then cups his chin, leaning on the table. "All three of us are headed to Berlin to work with a car company."

"Berlin babes. I cannot wait." Bo groans, running his hand down his white T-shirt as he eases back in his chair. The brother has to be overfull. He put more food away than both Roy and me combined. It's as if the man hadn't eaten in a week.

Roy sighs and scrapes his hand over his neatly trimmed black goatee.

Wendy smiles. "Oh, Germany. That sounds like fun."

I shrug and push my plate back. "I'd rather have a long span in the office."

Skyler puts her hand on my thigh and eases it up and down in a supportive gesture. "At least you have another week or so off."

"Except we plan on heading to New York next week."

Wendy frowns, and I watch as Sky's smile falls as well. Looking thoughtful, my girl says, "Actually, I think we might just stay in Boston. Besides, I need to get with Wendy about wedding stuff."

Wendy's face lights up as if a spotlight was just turned on from within. "Really?"

Sky makes a face. "I wouldn't be a very good maid of honor if I didn't help the bride with the nitty-gritty."

Wendy smiles wide. "That would be so cool. Thank you, Sky."

"Course. It's what friends are for. We'll set up some time later this week, if you're up to it."

"Oh, I'll be up to it. The only thing Mick is allowing me to work on is the wedding. From bed with a phone and a laptop at the ready." She crunches up her nose at her fiancé, who simply takes the hit and ignores it.

"Speaking of work . . ." Royce stands from his chair, lays his napkin over his plate, and comes around to our side of the table. "We need to get back." He opens his arms to Wendy. "I sure miss the hell out of you, girl."

Wendy stands and puts her arms around Royce's waist when he brings her slight form against his chest. He holds her for a full minute, then dips his head down to her level, their foreheads almost touching. "Now you be good. Do what the doctor orders. Listen to Michael, as long as he's not trying to talk you out of leaving us. Then ignore every word. You hear?"

She grins and nods. "I hear."

"Well, all right." He pats her back. "I'll check in on you in a couple of days. No more calls." He gazes into her eyes like a big brother chastising his baby sister. Which, as things have progressed, he kind of is.

She frowns and then grins. "I promise not to call *you*."

He purses his lips and kisses her on the forehead. "Get better."

Wendy nods. "Will do."

Bo comes up from behind, and this time Michael stands, practically guarding Wendy. Royce can hold her, kiss her on the forehead, but Bo so much as approaches and Mick's readying for battle.

I chuckle behind my hand and loop an arm around Skyler's chair. She snorts but sips on her second glass of wine. The alcohol has made her cheeks rosy and her smiles easier and more forthcoming. I love a tipsy Skyler. I love getting *into* a tipsy Skyler even more.

"What? I'm not going to maul her. Relax, Tarzan," Bo says to Michael, then opens his arms for Wendy to embrace him.

She does, but as he puts his hands around her back, he slides them down, going for her ass.

"You touch my ass and I break your fingers."

Bo stops his play instantly.

Mick growls and eases Wendy out of Bo's hold. "She won't have to. I'll have already removed them one at a time with a cigar cutter," he threatens, but it sounds more like a promise.

Bo lifts his hands in a gesture of surrender. "Fine, fine. Bunch of sourpusses. For real, though, Tink, you need anything, we're only a call away, yeah?"

"Got it." She snuggles against Mick as the two men head out of the room.

I cup my hand around my mouth and call out, "Good luck finding the exit!"

Royce laughs. "Yeah, yeah. I got this."

"Are you two done?" Michael gestures to the empty plates.

I slap my belly. "So done. Wonderful meal, Michael, thank you."

"I believe you've earned the right to call me Mick."

Wendy's brows rise up on her forehead, and she tries to cover her response by looping an arm through Skyler's elbow. "Do you want to see the stuff I've already got slated for the wedding?"

"Heck yes!"

"Would you like a top off of your drink?" Mick asks me.

"Sure thing." I follow Mick back through the house toward the parlor. "This house has been in your family a long time. Do you like living here?"

Mick slows his gait. "Yes and no. Sometimes I want Wendy and me to find a place and start from scratch, although this home is all I have of my family. I come from a long line of only children, and both of my parents and all my grandparents are gone. No family other than Wendy. Being able to give her this was important to me. And she seems happy here."

We make it to the parlor, and Mick has the bartender refill our drinks.

"I think Wendy would be happy anywhere you are. How is she really doing, by the way? You mentioned nightmares?"

Mick closes his eyes and takes a full breath before opening them again and gesturing to the leather chairs in front of a window overlooking his estate. He glances over his shoulder at the open doorway, likely to make sure Wendy is not coming in.

"Every night. She screams out. One hand reaches for her chest, the other, her pelvis."

"Fuck." His words hit me like a truck going fifty and slamming right into me.

His lips twist into a snarl, and one of his hands forms a white fist. "If we'd only known. I would have kept her home. Made sure she was safe at all times . . ."

"Mick, you can't wrap her in cotton and wool and expect her not to resent you."

He runs his hand through his light hair. "Then what would you have done?"

I shake my head. "There's nothing you could have done that would have brought a different outcome. Believe me"—I pound the center of my chest—"I've tried to figure it out, and it keeps coming back to the fact that there are crazy people in the world. That woman was ill."

He huffs. "And because of that, my unborn child is dead."

Knife. Straight through the heart.

I swallow down the dryness in my throat. "Is she seeking help? Are you?"

He shakes his head curtly.

"Man, this shit can fester."

He inhales and sips his drink. "I have a plan."

"And that is?"

Please don't say "make her quit." Please don't say "make her quit."

"I'm going to get her pregnant as soon as she's healthy and we're married."

I tip my head and look down at the ice cubes swirling in my glass and the tonic bubbles popping. "Is that really a good idea? I mean, substitution isn't always the answer."

He raises his fist up but then seems to catch himself and lets it go. He grips the bullnose edge of the chair instead. "No, it's not. Though through this experience, Wendy and I found that we both want a family. Soon. We need to have something between us that we can love and share. Something that's ours together, and because of our loss, we realized how badly we both want a child. Many children actually."

I lick my lips and nod. "As long as you're doing it for the right reasons, I'm happy for you. For you both."

Mick sips his drink, and his cool gaze settles on mine. "I've come to understand how much you, the IG team, and your extended families mean to my Cherry. As much as I want to be everything she needs, I'm man enough to admit my woman's heart and ability to love are vast. She desires the family environment the three of you have built. And I want to give my mate everything her heart desires."

I dip my head in reverence. "It's good of you. We love her. Like a sister, and as long as she wants, she'll always have a place on our team and with our family. She and Sky get along famously."

"I'd like to attempt more dinners and events like today. Get to know all of you better."

"Even Bo?" I snicker and grin.

He glances out the window, a disdainful expression on his face. "If I must."

"You realize he's truly just joking with Wendy. The innuendo, the flirting—it's harmless. He wouldn't ever go past that, even when he pretends he's going to. Wendy has become important to him. And frankly, Bo doesn't let women get close. Especially not women he's interested in romantically. The fact that he cares for her proves he's not interested in her that way."

"Be that as it may, his sense of humor is insufferable."

"And that's why he does it. He loves getting a rise out of you and Wendy both. Trick is, don't play into it and he'll stop." I shrug and lean back, getting more comfortable in the leather chair.

"Hmm. I shall take your assessment under advisement."

"All joking aside, what does her doctor say about her nightmares?" I lower my voice, keeping with the confidential nature of his concerns.

He lets out a long, tired breath. "He prescribed sleeping pills she refuses to take. Says she doesn't want to have drugged sleep."

"Anything else?"

"Time. A therapist."

"Maybe if you went to the therapist with her, she'd go?" I shrug. "Would you do that?"

His head snaps forward. "I'd do anything for her."

"Then maybe suggest it. See if it helps. Couldn't hurt. And we'll make more effort to visit, but you're going to need to get her out of the house. She needs to see there's life beyond what she went through and the loss the two of you sustained."

The women enter the room giggling like schoolgirls, Wendy's sadness completely erased by the time spent with Skyler. I know how she feels—my girl does that for me regularly.

"Honey, you have got to see the dress Wendy picked out. It's ah-maze-ing!" She draws out the last word.

"I'd rather see it on her on her wedding day. I like surprises. Remember?"

Her eyes widen at the word *surprise*, telling me she picked up on the fact that I'm still waiting to find out what surprise she has in store for me.

At the sound of crunching gravel, I look out the window and see the blacked-out Range Rover. I stand, buttoning my suit jacket. "Looks like our ride is here."

Wendy pouts. "No. I was having so much fun."

Mick goes over to her, brings her into his arms, and kisses her forehead. "Yes, and you look like you're about to drop where you stand. I think a nap is in order."

She frowns and looks up at him. "Will you take one with me?"

He dips down and kisses her softly, just a simple peck that, for some reason, fills me with such light. Seeing him dote on her, how much he genuinely loves and needs this woman, eases my worry. She's got a bit of a hard road to recovery ahead, especially mentally, but with Michael by her side and the rest of us to support her, she'll be just fine.

I clasp Sky's hand and tug her to my side. She comes willingly. "Ready to go, Peaches?"

"Peaches and Cherry. What is it with you men?" Wendy laughs.

"My girl smells like peaches and cream." I nuzzle at her neck and make sloppy eating sounds to get her laughing.

"Ha!" Wendy laughs, pointing at us. "Mick calls me Cherry because he took mine."

Both Skyler and I stop and stare, stupefied at how to respond.

Mick closes his eyes, drops his head, and sighs. "Baby . . . ," he says tiredly.

"What?" She frowns.

He lifts his head and taps her lips. "Too much information. Not everyone needs to know everything about us." He shakes his head and wraps her in his embrace. "Come on, let's walk our friends out."

"Our?" she says, hope filling her tone.

"Yes, Cherry, our friends."

"Righteous. I knew you'd fall in love with my guys."

He groans. "I'm *your* guy. Those are your friends."

She wiggles her hips and runs her hand over his back as we walk to the front door. "I could call them my boyfriends."

"Sure. Over my dead body," he says flatly and with a seriousness I couldn't muster up if I tried. Maybe he is being serious. The guy is one level over territorial, clinging to obsessive, but who am I to judge. They're happy. That's all that matters.

Wendy and Skyler laugh heartily as we open the door, and Nate and Rachel pop out of the car.

My phone buzzes in my pocket, signaling I have a new text. I stop and read the message before getting in the car.

From: Unknown
To: Parker Ellis

GLAD YOU'RE HOME SAFE. MISSED YOU.

I read and reread the words. *What the fuck?* This has to be someone pranking me. One of the guys or maybe an old friend?

We say our goodbyes and wave off Wendy and Mick. Once Skyler and Rachel are back in the car, I stop Nate at the driver's side. He closes the door, obviously keyed in to the fact that I need a moment privately.

I gesture to a spot about ten feet away and show him my phone.

"Did you get anything off Skyler's phone?"

"While you were gone, I got word from a tech guru buddy of mine. He says the number is traced back to a burner phone. He can't locate it because there's no specific service, and whoever has it turns the thing completely off and doesn't call between texts, so we can't trace it."

"Have you gotten any more texts on her old phone?"

"Yeah. Got my buddy on them too, but he's at a stalemate." He pulls out Sky's old phone and places his back to the car as he shows me the string of new messages.

From: Unknown
To: Skyler Paige

WHY ARE YOU IGNORING ME?

From: Unknown
To: Skyler Paige

I THOUGHT YOU WERE DIFFERENT

From: Unknown
To: Skyler Paige

YOU'RE JUST LIKE ALL THE REST

From: Unknown
To: Skyler Paige

You think you're better than everyone else? Because you're famous? You're not and I'll prove it.

"Fucking hell." I read them over again. "This sounds like a stalker or maybe a superfan gone bad."

Nate nods. "I thought so too. I have a call out to Tracey, her agent, to get some additional intel. See if there's anything she may have received by phone or in Skyler's fan mail. I know she has a service that deals with her mail and another for her website. I'm going to have her web team tell us if anything weird has come through her contact sheets. I should have more tomorrow."

I cringe but nod anyway and try to plaster a happy face back on for Sky's benefit. "Notify me the second you find or hear anything? How the individual got our personal cell phone numbers is baffling."

"Or they're a really good hacker."

I smile. "I know one person that good, and she's about to take a nap." I hook a thumb up to the mansion behind us.

"Yeah, well, maybe when she's feeling better we can get her opinion on all of this. See if she can help."

I nod and look back up at the giant house before popping back into the car.

Skyler reaches over and puts her hand on my thigh. "Everything okay?"

"Yeah, just talking to Nate, following up on some things. Now . . . about my surprise."

Skyler smiles wide. "Nate, is it ready now?"

He nods. "It is. You want to head there?"

"Absolutely!" She shimmies in her seat, dancing in the car. "Put on some funky music, white boy! I'm in the mood to move."

And that third glass of wine I saw her grab is making an appearance. "Did you have a good time?" I hook my arm around her shoulders and bring her against my side.

"Totally. I love hanging out with your friends, honey."

I breathe in the peaches-and-cream scent wafting up from her hair. "They're your friends now too. You can count on them."

She grins. "True! I like having people we can both hang out with who are fun." She sighs happily. "Makes life worth living, you know? Working as hard as we do. Being able to share time and space with great people makes it all worth it."

I kiss her temple until she lifts her head and gives me her lips. She tastes of white wine and the strawberries she was snacking on at the end of our meal.

"Mmm," I hum against her mouth, licking her bottom lip and nibbling it before repeating the process with her top lip. Her fingers dig into my thigh and slide up higher, cupping my hardening length. My entire being is focused on her hand and that part of my body getting a pleasurable stroking. I allow it for a couple of minutes until my balls tingle and I know if we keep this up, I'm going to want to mount her in the car, bodyguards be damned. With all the strength I can manage, I cover her hand with my own, her palm still working my length over my slacks.

I groan into her mouth and pull her hand away. She leaves the kiss breathlessly, her eyes a wild mixture of brown and yellow flecks, looking like a dusting of caramel fluttering through those chocolate depths. She bites down on her bottom lip and gives me the most wounded, needy look I've ever seen.

I groan against her hairline. "You're not playing fair, baby."

She grins, realizing the predicament she's putting me in. "Okay, I'll stop. For now."

I suck in a full breath of air, trying to think of anything that will calm the beast down.

All too soon we're stopping in front of a very recognizable building. "You brought me to work? Is my surprise at work?"

She smiles huge. "Kinda but not really. Just come on."

Rachel holds the door for Sky, and the two Van Dykens are flanking us as I button my coat over my hard cock—trying to be subtle about the jollies my girl was giving me in the car—when out of nowhere a horde of photographers bum-rushes us.

I hook my arm around Skyler's waist as Rachel and Nate shield both of us, pushing the paparazzi back.

"Sitting ducks," Nate grumbles. "We need to use the garage entrance next time," he mutters, one arm looped in Skyler's elbow as he leads the way.

Once we get in the building, it's fine, because it's private property and security is everywhere. You have to have a badge and appointment to enter, unless you live here. I know the top five floors cater to the rich businesspeople who want to live in the city they work in. The security team hustles us through; they know I'm allowed to be here, and Nate, Rachel, and Sky all have full clearance.

When we make it to the elevator, Nate presses the button for the top floor, using his thumb.

"Uh, Nate. Those are the housing floors. The one you're pressing is the penthouse actually."

He smirks and crosses his massive arms over one another, ignoring my comment.

"What's going on, Sky?" I turn to her, and she's practically jumping out of her skin with excitement. This could be one of three things. She had too much to drink. She's horny as fuck, which I basically confirmed in the car with her mini–hand job routine, or she's about to lay a fat shocker on me.

Finally the doors open on the top floor, right into an apartment. Nate walks in with Rachel on his heels. "Wait here, we're going to check the place out."

When they leave I turn to Sky. "What is this?"

She bites her bottom lip, grips her maxi dress, and swishes it from side to side as though she's nervous. "It's my new place. I leased it for six months."

I open my mouth and glance around at the fully furnished large apartment. There is an entire wall of windows across a span of at least thirty feet from where I stand at the elevator. I move in and notice there's an entryway table. On it is a candid photo of Skyler and me at her house in New York City.

The farther I go in, the more I notice the furniture is similar to Skyler's penthouse. Comfortable, fluffy, and using rich fabrics with tons of throw pillows and blankets for cuddling on the large sectional.

"You bought the penthouse apartment in the same building as the IG offices?" I open my arms wide and spin around, trying to take it all in.

"Leased with the option to buy," she whispers tentatively.

I spin around to face her. "Are you freakin' kidding me?!"

3

"Does that mean you're happy or pissed off, because right now, honey, I'm so nervous and split right open wide, I can't tell the difference." Her voice trembles, but she lifts her chin, showing her strength of character.

I rush to her, grasp her cheeks in my hands, and kiss the holy hell out of her. Except it's not enough. Never. Enough.

I lift her up by her ass until she wraps her legs around my waist, then I lead her to the couch I can see in my peripheral vision. Once there, I sit back with her straddling my lap. She grinds her crotch against mine, turns her head to the side, and delves her tongue deep. Our tongues tangle like mad until I'm squeezing her ass and pressing my hard-as-stone cock against her over and over.

"Whoa, whoa! Okay now. Guess you didn't care if the pad was safe or not," Rachel says from somewhere behind me. I can't tell because Sky is grinding her sexy body against mine and I'm losing my mind. Rachel's voice continues, "We'll be on our way. Our apartment is one floor down. Should we expect you to need us today?"

Sky doesn't remove her lips from mine when she mumbles, "Nuh-uh."

I pull back, needing the air and wanting to answer her team. "We're fine." I lick my lips and taste her sweetness on my tongue, a taste that sends a bolt of arousal straight through my body to my hips, where I arc against her until she mewls.

She giggles as I wave them off. "We're good," I say. "We'll call if we need you, but I think tonight we'll stay in."

"Got it. Have fun, you two!" Rachel teases as Sky slams her lips over mine once again.

"You happy, honey?" she says while placing a line of kisses down the column of my neck. Gooseflesh and heat erupt all over my skin, and I'm wondering how quickly I can get this suit off, or maybe I'll just fuck her fully clothed, riding my cock to completion. Then we can take it slow. Yeah, I like that plan.

I can only tilt my head back and let her devour me. "So. Fucking. Happy." I groan as her hand goes to my belt and undoes the leather from the clasp, unbuttoning my slacks along the way.

"Want to be closer to you." She eases back and pushes her hair out of her face. "Is it too much, too soon?" Her hand stills on my hard cock, and I want to cry out in pain, but instead, I focus on the words she's saying and the meaning behind them.

I shake my head and cup her cheeks. "Having you close, in my town, in the same building as my workplace . . ." I let out a huge breath. "It means the world to me. But what about New York?"

My dick throbs in retribution for asking a question right now.

She licks her lips and runs her fingers through my hair until I bite into my lip, holding back the moan that wants to slip out. "New York doesn't have you in it."

A spear of desire at her words has my cock weeping at the tip with the need to get inside of her.

Still, I bite down on my lust and grind my teeth. "Boston doesn't always either," I remind her, honesty in my tone she can't deny.

"Not always, no. Except this is home to you and becoming home to me." She unbuttons my dress shirt, one button at a time, as she speaks. "Your family, your business, your life are here. I can do my job anywhere and fly where I need to be for work." She opens the shirt and places her warm hands against my bare chest. It's like a brand, and I hiss through my teeth.

"The rest of the time, I want to be close to you." She leans forward and flicks her tongue against my nipple.

I cup her chin, bring her face to mine, and kiss her hard and fast. "Are you sure? It's a big step."

"Moving in together is an even bigger step. For now, I want us to be able to spend as many nights as possible together. And you were worried about my safety. This building is completely safe." Her nimble fingers move to my crotch, where she works the zipper open. "Nate and Rachel looked at a lot of them, but I wanted this one. They approved it based on the security in the lobby and garage, as well as the thumbprint activation on the elevator."

Speaking of thumbs . . . she swipes hers along the wet cloth of my boxer briefs, teasing me with what her thumb can do, when I know her mouth or her wet slit can do even better.

Her words break into my sensual thoughts. "Which reminds me . . . you'll have to get your thumbprint on file so you can come and go as you please. The guys and Wendy too. And your mom and dad."

I groan and gasp when she wiggles her hand in between the fabric of my underwear and my flesh and wraps an eager fist around my length to give it a good tug.

"Jesus." I bite down and palm her ass, looking for the end of her gauzy dress.

Eventually she helps, scooping the thing up and over her head until she's sitting on my lap in a strapless nude bra, which does everything for her plump tits, and a pair of nude lace panties. Instead of having her stand and remove the lace, I just tear the sides by piercing my thumbs through the flimsy fabric. Once I've got hold of each end of her shredded undies, I hold on to one edge of the fabric at her lower back, my other hand at her front, bringing the wedge of lace tight against her sex until she yelps.

"Parker . . . honey." She gasps as I maneuver the fabric back and forth over her wet slit, dragging it up and across her pebbled clit. "Need you. Need you. Oh God." She lets her head fall back until her hair tickles my hand behind her as I work her over. "Please . . . ," she begs.

I lean forward and bite down on the fleshy part of her tit. "I. Love. When. You. Beg." I bite harder, then ease the bite with my tongue.

"I know." She gasps as I pull the fabric tighter, her hips moving with mine to add more friction. My girl is a wildcat in the sack, all feelings and need, never insecurity and unease.

Her breath is coming in pants, and just when I know she's going to come, I pull the fabric away, center my cock, and lunge up into her depths. She cries out, the walls of her sex locking down and fluttering in orgasm as I penetrate her deep.

I clench my teeth so hard, pain batters at my jaw joint as I try not to come instantly. When she's breathing easier and back to herself, that's when I go hard at her. As I'm thrusting up and working her body on top of mine, eventually she starts to participate, my greedy girl wanting more, always more.

I hum as she bounces on my cock, her fingers holding on to the back of the couch for leverage, her breath sawing out of her lungs as she works her body up and down with each plunge.

"You're a goddess . . ." I gasp as my cock swells, my balls drawing up tight with every hammering downstroke she gives.

"It's so good. It's sooooo gooooood." Her mouth slams down on mine as she cries out, her body locking in place.

With a fiery animalistic need, I flip her over onto her back, her hair flying, her tits bouncing out of her bra. I lift one of her legs, holding it up and out, opening her wide as I take her hard, my desire fueling me to go deeper, pump my hips harder. I want to make her scream until her voice is hoarse.

Her other leg locks around my ass where my slacks have slid down in a bundle between us, the space restricting my movements until I'm grinding my teeth, working her until I see nothing but black. Hear nothing but the sound of her second orgasm barreling through her chest and out her lungs in a cry so loud I fear the windows might shake.

My lower back goes tight, my ass cheeks clench, and my thighs brace as I plow deep and stop on a mighty thrust. A shudder rips through me as my cock releases everything in me in powerful bursts that mimic a bomb going off at the head of my dick with each spasm. It continues until I'm spent, my bones no longer capable of holding me up. I flop onto her body in a heap, my breath dragging out as though I've been holding it for years. She wraps her legs and her arms around me in a Skyler cocoon, not caring that I'm probably too heavy.

I never want to leave.

This woman has become my ultimate happy place.

Eventually I know I need to give her a little space, but instead of getting off her, I ease to the side and bring her with me so that we're side by side, still connected.

"I take it you like the place?" she whispers against my lips.

"Hmm. I like the place a lot."

"And just think about how good it will be when you actually see some of it."

Together our bodies start to shake and tremble with laughter. My slacks are caught around my knees, my underwear pushing up against the underside of my junk that's now starting to slip out of her.

"We better move or you're going to ruin your new couch."

"It has stain protector," she says on a yawn, closing her eyes as I maneuver her leg down between us, hopefully catching anything slippery that wants to escape before I can locate a cloth of some sort.

Pushing against the cushion, I ease up, and she snuggles her naked body on the pillow.

"Why is it we fuck on couches so much?" I yank up my underwear and pants, zipping them in place as I go.

She yawns again. "We like couches. It's our thing."

And as I stare down at the most beautiful woman I've ever known, the one who makes me insane with need and desire, I smile. "Yeah, baby. It's our thing. You snooze." I grab a throw blanket and toss it over her naked body.

I spin around in a circle and evaluate my surroundings. Skyler leased an apartment in Boston. For me.

No . . . for us.

***

Two days later, back in the office, I'm staring out the window, tapping my pen against my lips, remembering all the scandalous things I did to Skyler before I left her upstairs this morning.

I sigh as I hear a tap on my door.

"Come in." I smile as Annie enters holding two white bags.

"Good afternoon, Mr. Ellis." She holds up the bags. "I got deli sandwiches and some chips in the event that maybe we could have a working lunch, go over some of the travel plans for the Berlin trip?" She smiles wide as I take in her outfit. Standard pencil skirt, this time paired with a flowing purple top with long chiffon sleeves that go to a point past her wrists. Reminds me of a Renaissance maiden from a Shakespearean play. Not exactly something I'd imagine her wearing. Skyler rocking it with a pair of jeans and suede boots I can see, but on Annie, not so much. At least she always looks nice and professional. Exactly what this office needs.

I sigh and open my hand to the chair across from my desk. Wendy would want me to make an effort with the girl, and during my meeting with Royce yesterday, I learned he believes we should consider keeping Annie on for our bookkeeping needs. Not to mention he's also talking about hiring a lawyer. Apparently our corporation is growing beyond leaps and bounds, and we're not keeping up with the legalities as much as we should. The company needs to be protected at all costs.

"That's very nice of you, Annie, but perfectly unnecessary."

She offers me a beaming smile, a blush crawling up her neck to her cheeks as she sets down the two paper bags and pulls out a sandwich wrapped in white plastic. "I got your favorite."

I frown. "How would you know my favorite?"

She blinks for a couple of seconds, then shakes her head. "Oh, it was in the lunch file Wendy keeps. She has notes about what all of you like. I worked off of that."

"Wow. Efficient."

"I try." She's just about to hand me the sandwich when I hear a few taps before the door opens and my ultrahot girlfriend prances in, a ball of nothing but sunshine. Her golden hair is in a flirty ponytail, swinging to and fro as she struts. She's wearing a pair of skintight skinny jeans that accentuate all her attributes, a tank top, and five different necklaces of varying sizes and lengths, along with a silk paisley-print overshirt with fringe. She has three different silver rings on one hand and two on her other. The "Live Your Truth" leather bracelet is coupled with a few other beaded ones that also look handmade.

I stare at her as though I am a suffocating man who's just gotten a full breath of fresh air. The navy tank she's got on is low enough to give a hint of her awesome bosom, and my mouth waters. Sandwich be damned, I'd much prefer to take a bite out of her. I gnaw down on my knuckle as she holds up a bag.

"I made us lunch, honey!" She comes over to my side of the desk, where I pull her onto my lap in a flourish of flapping silk and female giggles.

"Oomph!" She cracks up, nuzzles my nose, and kisses me quickly.

I gaze down at her, taking in her fresh face and sweet berry-colored lips, until I remember and she realizes we're not alone.

Sky tilts her head and hooks her arm around my neck, adjusting her seating position. "Hiya, Annie! How are you settling in?"

The woman across my desk is standing still, a wrapped sandwich in her hand. "Good. Thank you, Ms. Paige."

Sky waves her hand in front of us. "Call me Skyler, or Sky."

Annie's eyes light up at the personal offer. "Thank you, Sky. I had brought Mr. Ellis lunch, so we could go over the Berlin trip, but I can save it for tomorrow or something. No worries." She puts the sandwich back into the bag.

"Why don't you give mine to Bo, Annie? He can go over the particulars with you while I have lunch with my girlfriend." I squeeze Skyler's hip and inhale the sweet smell of Italian food coming from the bag Sky set at my feet.

Annie's smile falls, but she replaces it with a fake one. "Okay. I'll do that."

Skyler points a finger toward Annie's chest. "I have that same blouse! So comfy, right? And it looks great on you!" She gushes the way only my woman can. *Exuberance* should be Skyler's middle name, not Paige.

Annie's real smile comes back, like an ugly duckling who's told she's pretty for the first time. "You do?" Her voice rises in what I can only assume is glee. "I'm wearing something that *Skyler Paige* owns! Oh. My. Goodness. I'm going to call my mom and tell her! She'll just die!"

Skyler laughs. "Pishposh."

I glance at Skyler. "Pishposh," I murmur dryly. "Someone's been talking to my mother again."

Sky grins a cat-that-ate-the-canary smile. "If you want, I can totally sign something for you and your mom. Then you can surprise her with it!"

Her eyes widen to the size of dinner plates. "You are . . . one of a kind," Annie says in awe.

"Nah. I just know how it is. Moms are really important. We need to make them feel special as often as we can." Skyler pulls out my pad of paper from under a stack of files, at the same time rubbing her fine ass against my soon-to-be-hardening cock.

Jesus, one touch from her and the beast is jumping to attention. Teenagers get wood less often than I do, for the love of all things holy.

"What's your mom's name?" Sky grabs a pen from my holder and bites the cap off . . . with her *teeth*.

I groan and tilt my head back, pressing my thumb and forefinger against my temples.

Do not get hard. Do not get hard.

"Trudy."

Skyler pushes her tongue against the side of her cheek, and I swear all I can think about is my dick prodding her mouth in a similar fashion.

Back to my chanting.

Do not get hard. Do not get hard.

I bite into my bottom lip and wait it out while Skyler creates two messages, one for Annie and the other for her mother.

Skyler rips the sheets from the pad. "There you go. Now you're going to get best-daughter-ever status!"

Annie takes hold of the pages and looks at them once, twice, and then a third time. She runs her fingers over the signatures with reverence before looking back up at us. Her voice shakes when she responds. "Thank you. Thank you so much. I knew you were amazing."

"Aw, that's sweet. Now if you'll excuse us . . ." Skyler nuzzles my cheek openly. "I've got a lunch date with this hot guy."

Annie's eyebrows rise up. "Oh my. Yes. Of course. Alone time." She grabs the two bags and hustles out of the room, signed sheets in her other hand. "Do let me know if there's anything I can do for either of you," she says upon parting.

"Where were we . . ." I lock my arms around my girl's waist and plaster her front against my own.

"She's nice, don't you think?" Skyler hums against my cheek.

"Mm-hmm. Very nice. So, what did you bring me that's making my mouth water and my eyes want to weep with joy?"

Skyler grins and pulls back so she can see my entire face. In the light from the window, she's incredibly pretty. Her tanned skin glows, and her brown eyes show every fleck of gold magnificently. "I made you homemade lasagna and french bread with a salad."

I cock an eyebrow. "You made all that since I left you sated and snoozing this morning?"

She nods her head. "Yep. Nate and Rachel took me to the grocery store, and I stocked up."

"You stocked up. I thought maybe you might change your mind and head to New York this week before I head out to Berlin with the guys and you go out for your press junkets."

"Nope. I decided I'd rather get to know my new city. Nate's already picked out the Range Rover he wants suited up. And shocker . . . it looks exactly like the one we've been renting." She rolls her eyes playfully.

"If it works, it works." I grin. "How did the store run go?"

Her smile slips off her face. "At first it was fine, and then a woman recognized me, and she flipped out. When I say flipped out, it wasn't that want-to-hug-me-get-my-autograph type of flip out. She literally started screaming at the top of her lungs. Then she passed out. Right in the middle of the frozen foods section." Sky's shoulders fall, and she sighs, getting up from my lap. "It sucks. You know, I love my job. There is no other job in the world for me, but sometimes . . . sometimes it just sucks to be famous."

I lean forward as she pulls the Tupperware containers out of the bag she brought and sets one down in front of me and then one across from me.

"What did you guys do?" I ask, taking the roll of silverware and cloth napkin from her hand.

"Rachel went and got help, and an ambulance was called. The woman just fainted, but because she fell in a grocery store, it was this superbig deal. Next time I'll go somewhere else and wear a disguise." Another sigh passes her lips as she sits across from me and opens the lid on her dish.

Steam puffs out of the container, and the scent of garlic and cheese hits my nose with a one-two punch of hunger. My stomach growls and rumbles.

Sky points her fork at my Tupperware. "Dig in while it's hot."

I open the lid and set aside the utensils. "Peaches, it's going to take some time to find the places you can go without worrying about people reacting. You know that, right?"

She nods but purses her lips. "I guess because I've been locked in our little bubble of normal this past week, I got used to it." She puffs air out of her mouth aimed at her forehead, where the longer layers of hair move and shift. "I don't know why it's too much to ask to not be recognized or left alone. I should be used to it by now, but I'm not. I'd love to be able to just pick out my own freakin' veggies without being bothered for an autograph or a selfie or for a person to tell me how much they love me or my movies. It's heaven and hell at the same time, you know?"

I put my hand over hers across the desk. "No, I don't know fully, but when we're together and the paparazzi come out of nowhere, I think I get a hint of what you deal with. I'm sorry, baby."

She shrugs and runs her hand through her ponytail. "It's fine. I'm being dramatic, but you should have seen that lady. One minute she's holding two packages of frozen berries, the next her eyes are rolling back in her head and she's going down like a bowling pin."

I laugh hard, which has Skyler giggling around her pasta too. "At least we can laugh about it since she wasn't hurt."

"True. Thank you, honey."

"For what? You're the one who brought lunch. Which is excellent, by the way." I spoon up another bite of cheesy goodness.

"Thank you for being you. For getting it. For letting me vent."

"You can always count on me, Sky."

She tips her head to the side, focuses her gaze to mine, and stops my heart with her words. "I'm so happy you knocked on my door that day."

"Me too. I thank the big guy upstairs every day for it. Now eat up, I've got work to do so I can get home to my girlfriend."

"Oh? I imagine she's not the type that will wait around all day too." She chomps off a hunk of bread too big for her mouth.

"Nah, my girl doesn't have to wait. I rush through my day just to get to the best part: the minute when she opens the door and I get to see her smile."

Sky wipes her mouth primly and then nails me with a zinger. "Man, I should have brought some wine for that hunk of cheese you just served up!"

I toss my napkin at her giggling face, and she throws hers back at me.

Laughter and love. Nothing could be better than this.

4

First class fills up as the guys and I get settled in our seats. Royce takes the window seat since he knows I don't care to look out at the ground below. I treat airplanes like floating trains or buses. No need to look out—just let the motion lull me to sleep, score the two to three meals that I didn't have to cook, and catch up on either work, reading, or whatever movies have just come out. The plane ride to Berlin, Germany, is going to take about ten hours, and since it's overnight, we should be able to get on European time pretty quick.

Bo takes the aisle seat across from mine and stretches out his long legs. Royce hands me his suit jacket, which I hand to the flight attendant along with my own. We're meeting the client right after we land. The three of us agreed that we'd make this trip a week or less. We have a slate of clients lined up, and the next one is in Washington, DC. I was hoping to escape that one, but since I've taken more free time off than the guys recently, I need to be on point. Which sucks, because I really want to spend more time showing Skyler around Boston. Of course, that's if she's even in town.

The flight attendant takes our drink order, and I go straight for the good stuff, ordering a whiskey. I want to sleep on this plane ride. Skyler kept me up all night with her feminine attributes. Ever since she got her own pad in Boston, she's been a horndog. We've christened almost every surface to "create memories" in her new space and make it ours, not just hers. I could have cared less. All I cared about was getting into my woman as often as possible. So essentially, her plan worked for me . . . in a big way.

I grin as the attendant hands us each our drink and moves on to cater to other passengers.

"How was Sky when you were leaving?" Roy asks, sipping from his own whiskey neat.

"Fine. Except I gotta say, I had no idea she was going to lease an apartment like that."

Royce smiles softly and points at me with one finger, the other four holding his whiskey tumbler. "You don't think you're worth a fine woman like her?"

I shrug and mull over his question. "Truth?"

"Always, brother, always."

"Not in the beginning, no. Hell, not even in the middle of our relationship, but a lot has changed the last couple of months. Especially after the breakup and the time we spent in London and Paris. It's as if the two of us together makes sense now. It might not be easy; dating a celebrity of her caliber wouldn't be easy on anyone. There's a lot of security issues and real-life concerns that can get in the way, but we've been talking them through and keeping communication open at all times."

Roy nods, listening intently.

"When she leased the place in the same building as IG"—I shake my head—"it's as if something broke open in me."

"Acceptance?" he suggests.

"Yeah." I sip on my drink and let the fiery liquid warm my throat and gut. "She may be everything I could ever have wanted in a woman, but with her moving here, taking time to get to know you guys, my family, it hit me."

"What did?" His coal-black eyes focus on me and nothing else. Not the people moving around us, finding their seats, or the guy repeatedly taking something out of the upper cabinet and slamming it closed.

"Maybe I'm what she's been looking for all along. To her I'm everything she wanted in a man . . ."

Royce cocks a questioning brow.

"Okay, perhaps without the trust issue."

He grins. "All right. I didn't want to say it, but you got there on your own." His words are followed by a soulful chuckle. "If what I'm hearing is correct, you two have worked out your differences regarding your exes and, of course, Sophie?"

I sigh and press my head back into the leather headrest. "Honestly, I think so. I can't say that things won't come up. I'm never going to be okay with Johan in her life just as she wouldn't be okay if Kayla suddenly showed up. Sophie, though, that's a deal breaker and she knows it. SoSo is my friend, and on this last trip, I believe Sky was able to see how much our relationship is based on friendship, not romantic love."

Royce sucks in a breath through his teeth. "I don't know how you did it. I've never known a woman who was cool with her man being friends with a woman he'd taken to bed in the past."

I chuckle and push my seat back to get more comfortable. "Maybe it's because we don't live on the same continent?"

He points at me again. "Now you're talking. That I understand."

Together we both chuckle as my phone goes off in my pocket, signaling I've received an email. I pull it out and note the familiar email address.

From: Paul Ellis
To: Parker Ellis
Subject: Berlin or Bust

P-Drive,

*Just spoke with Ma! I know, long time, no
talk. Sorry about that. I've been in deep
cover for a while but finally got my wings.
At least for a while. I'm in Europe and was
going to head home in a few days. Ma said
you were heading to Berlin today. I'll be in
Frankfurt tomorrow and can fly to Berlin and
meet up with you. It's been too long, bro.
Too. Damn. Long. Miss your ugly mug.*

Shoot me your coordinates when you can.

*Give Royce a chin lift for me. Tell Bo he still
owes me twenty bucks for that last round of
fantasy football he lost.*

*Try to make some time for your big brother,
okay? We need to talk. There are things to say.*

The more attractive Ellis,

Paul

P.S. Are you really banging Skyler Paige?

"Holy shit on a shingle," I gasp, rereading the message from my
brother. I haven't seen the guy in two years or spoken to him in over
six months.

"What's up?" Bo narrows his gaze at me, and Royce leans over my
phone while I read my brother's message for a third time.

I have to hold back the approaching tears. Honestly, I figured the next message we'd hear about Paul was that he'd died in battle. He's never gone six months without making contact. Ma must be overly emotional herself, and fuck all, I can't call her to check in since the captain just announced they're readying the plane for takeoff.

"Shee-it. Paul reached out?" Royce rumbles over my shoulder, and I nod and hand him the phone. He takes the device and reads the message before handing it to Bo.

Bo scans it and scowls. "That fucker owes *me* twenty bucks. He can suck it!"

I chuckle when the guy stuck sitting next to Bo grumbles and turns to the side as if he's trying to avoid being associated with my friend and his loudmouth profanity.

"Damn, when was the last time you heard from Paul?" Roy asks as Bo hands me back the phone and leans over the arm of his seat to be part of our conversation.

"Six months. Maybe a little more."

"At least you know he's okay. I worry about the guy," Bo offers, before sucking back a pull from his beer.

I shake my head and sigh, letting out the worry I didn't know I'd been holding for my brother until this moment. "Shit . . ." I run my hand over my hair. "He's okay. Got something to tell me and plans to come home. Ma and Pops will be freaked. Overjoyed."

"Yeah, wonder what he's got to tell you?" Royce says.

I take a sip of my whiskey and then finish the lot, needing the liquid burn. "Whatever it is, I don't care. As long as he's safe and not dead in a war-torn country, I'm good with anything."

Royce nods a few times. "I heard that. Glad your boy is coming home, though." He puts out a fist for me between us. I place my own fist on top of his and knock it, then he knocks mine.

"Happy Paul's coming home." Bo leans back and stretches his legs back out, shifting his head to the side so he can stare at me. A serious expression crosses his features. "But it's *he* who owes *me* twenty bucks, and I'm collectin'."

Laughter billows out among the three of us, and I ease back, raising my hand holding an empty glass until the attendant sees it and nods.

"Thanks, guys."

"For what?" Royce rumbles.

"For just being there."

"Shoot, that's the easy part. Family's there for the good, the bad, and the fugly. Right, Bogey?"

Bo snarls at the nickname, sucks back his beer until there's nothing but the dregs, and nods. "Word."

I inhale long and deep. "Family: it comes in all kinds."

***

The OhM Motors corporate offices are set in the heart of Berlin. They also have offices and manufacturing plants in their partnering countries of the US, France, Japan, and India. When the three of us arrive, we're as refreshed as we can be, having brushed our teeth on the airplane and washed our faces with the hot cloths they pass out before arrival. Even Bo has on a leather blazer with black jeans, his standard motorcycle boots, and a nicer V-neck T-shirt than his normal wear.

Bo is Bo, and regardless of his attire, he's a valued member of this team. The guy wears what he feels puts his best self forward. Who am I to judge what that means? At the complete opposite end of the spectrum, Royce is in a perfectly fitted black Tom Ford suit and a pink pinstriped dress shirt with silver button cuff links, looking like a million dollars. Me, I'm somewhere in the middle wearing a navy Hugo Boss suit with a white dress shirt, green-and-teal striped tie, and my brown Ferragamos.

This job, though only a week, is paying a quarter mill for our full services—hence the entire team's presence. Except of course our redheaded Moneypenny back home. I send myself a mental reminder to let her know we arrived safe and check in on her. Not that she doesn't already have our credit cards tracked. Heck, the girl might have even slipped trackers in our wallets when we weren't looking.

The woman is paranoid.

Then again, if I look at things from her perspective, she was shot on the job by a freakazoid. We're her only family outside of Mick. She's a little overprotective, and frankly, I don't give two shits. It isn't hurting me or my guys, and if something did go wrong, we'd have some backup.

Royce holds open the door for the OhM offices in the downtown of the former East Berlin. Immediately we're greeted by a receptionist and taken straight through the building to a set of double doors. The receptionist knocks, says something in German, and then opens the door.

"You three may go in. Mrs. Schmidt is expecting you."

Monika Schmidt is a tall, statuesque blonde with blue eyes and striking features. The woman reminds me of my mother's favorite model, Claudia Schiffer, with similar high cheekbones, a long face, and perfectly bow-shaped, naturally pouty lips. Except this woman does not look like a runway model; she looks ready to pull off a takedown in a courtroom battle. Her suit is a dark gray with black stitching. The skirt is a severe pencil shape with a kick pleat in the back. It fits her like a glove. Her white-blonde hair is pulled back in a tight bun at the nape of her neck. Her makeup is simple, no frills, but doesn't take away from her natural beauty.

"Monika Schmidt. Welcome to OhM Motors," she states with a German accent but with perfect English pronunciation. "I am happy to welcome you and get right to work."

Okay. No going around the board once, collecting your two hundred bucks—just go straight to building hotels on Boardwalk and Park Place. A better Monopoly player you won't find.

I shake the hand she holds out. "Mrs. Schmidt. Thank you for having us. We're eager to find out more about your company and the launch of your business worldwide."

Once she's shaken Bo's and Royce's hands, she gestures to a conference table by the side of her desk. No comfy seating here. It's all about the work.

After we've each gotten settled in a seat, she picks up a remote and presses a button. A large projector screen comes down from the ceiling. The lights go out and a video pops up.

"I would like for you to watch the two videos we had made by two separate but equally well-known marketing firms about our product and the launch of the company. I would like to hear your thoughts on these first."

"Okay, shoot." I wave at the screen.

She nods and starts the videos.

The first is of a sexy woman in a cocktail dress oohing and aahing over one of the breakout vehicles the company is going to launch.

I understand from the reading material that there are six cars they're launching at the same time. Though these cars are unique. The entire company creates only hybrid, environmentally friendly, high-performance vehicles. Much like Tesla back in the States, but this brand caters to the hybrid gas and electric option where the gas charges the battery and the car can go more miles with fewer emissions and less gas.

A man takes the woman's hand and kisses her, then proceeds to waltz her around the car as if they're in a ballroom. I cringe and yawn at the image. The jet lag is already starting to hit. Bo plucks at his goatee, watching the screen intently. Royce is watching the couple dancing, and then it skips to the woman being pregnant and the guy dancing her around the car again. This one has Royce lifting his upper lip in a curl as if he's smelling something stanky. The last image is of the man dancing around the car with his daughter on his feet and the woman with a toddler on her hip. The OhM Motors logo appears on the screen followed by the tagline "Dance your way into the future."

"Any commentary?"

The three of us look at each other, and I hold up my hand. "Let's see the next one before we comment."

Monika's lips twitch as she presses the "Play" button for the next.

The screen comes to life again, showing one of the OhM crossovers on a racetrack. Next to it are a Mercedes, an Audi, a BMW, a Porsche, and a Lexus, each in its version of a crossover. The green flag goes up, and I roll my eyes as the six cars fly around the track. Of course, the OhM crossover wins in the end. Then out of each car exits a thirty- or forty-year-old woman. The OhM logo pops on the screen and ends with the tagline "Don't settle for second place. Race through life in style."

I have to blink my eyes a bunch of times to rid my mind of the extreme boredom those two videos caused.

Monika presses a button and crosses her arms over one another. "Thoughts?"

"Those were awful," Bo states flatly.

"I wouldn't buy the car," Royce rumbles.

I turn to Monika in my chair. "We mean no disrespect to the efforts of your marketing firms. However, after viewing the two companies' offerings, I now understand more clearly why you called us."

"Well, I've been told you are the best at unique situations."

"Is that so? By who?"

"Alexis Stanton. We use her technology. She impressed upon me how you solved a problem for her and could likely solve mine. You see, I have exactly one month to do an entire new campaign and distribute it to our four partners in France, the US, Japan, and India. These videos are not going to launch a new brand of vehicle that needs to sell well in a global market. I'd like to hear some of your initial ideas."

I pull out my briefcase and remove four files I had Annie assemble after the three of us did our research on OhM Motors. I pass them out to each guy and one to Monika.

"First, let's talk about what we didn't like about the videos," I state to the group.

"Too narrowly focused. The first one promotes a man and woman in cocktail attire, which immediately makes people think of money. Then, you show their family growing, so you've basically promoted the new vehicles as a family car for the rich," Royce remarks thoughtfully.

Bo jumps in. "The second used a racetrack. Immediately, I think of men and sports. Then you bring out a bunch of women who seem as if they're in the building-a-family stage of their lives. What about the men or single individuals wanting a new car?"

"My concerns are those but also the fact that the car was almost secondary to the people," I say. "We need to make the car part of the larger picture. I get that they were trying to make it sound like a car that can move through your future, but in my opinion, they went about it in the wrong way."

Monika taps her lips with the back of her pen. "And how would you change these concepts?"

"Open the file. Let's talk about the features we want to impress on all buyers. Not just one demographic. What is special about the OhM vehicle?" I ask the group.

"Environmentally friendly. With every car being a hybrid, the user not expending as many emissions and using less fuel," Royce tosses out. "Plus, that makes the car economically friendly because you're not paying for as much gas. So, you're saving money and the environment."

I point at him. "Exactly. Saving money and the environment. Bo?"

He twirls his pen around in his hand. "Each of the six vehicles coming out is high performance. That appeals to the male demographic whether you're a motorhead, a college kid, a jock, a father, a businessman, or a grandfather. It's no secret that men tend to like fast, well-oiled machines. It's possible one could joke it's in our genetic makeup."

"Your cars have high performance. Check. And I was also looking at the fact that each car is based on size. You've got the motorbike, the two-seater, the truck, the sedan, the crossover, and the full SUV. There's a play on numbers here. One, two, three if you put a dog in the truck, four for the sedan, five for the crossover, and six for the full-sized SUV. Which means . . ." I drag out my thoughts.

"There's something for everyone . . . ," Monika states, scribbling on her pad of paper.

"Bingo. What you want to do with your campaign is show all of those things so that you can hit all the demographics out of the gate. If you want to do a series of smaller campaigns for each car to promote to a specific demographic, that would be good. For now, though, if you're going to come out with a new car in today's market where your competitors are, US-based cars versus the luxury European and the environmentally friendly Teslas, you're going to have to appeal to everyone."

She nods and continues to write. "All good. How do you propose we do that?"

"Well, the three of us have been bouncing ideas off one another, but I'd like to see the cars in person. Get a feel for what we're selling. Take them for a drive. Then, I think I'm going to make some calls to a friend of mine."

"Who?" Bo asks instantly.

"Pritchard."

"Great," Bo states dryly.

Royce's eyes widen, but he nods in agreement. "The guy has his stuff on lock."

"Exactly. And we're in a crunch. If they're going to have a fully developed campaign in a month, we're going to need to shoot this week and prepare print materials, set up commercials, car showings, user groups, etc. He's someone we know who would bend over backward to help us, and he has the right contacts."

Last week when we visited a second time with Mick and Wendy, I found out that Michael not only owns one of the largest advertising firms in the US, he owns publishing firms, printers, model agencies, basically anything involving marketing and advertising, all the way down to the small outfits that print business cards.

The dude has some serious issues with control and privacy. He likes to have ownership from seed to bloom on a project, which is why he's a multimillionaire a hundred times over. Not that we had any clue that level of success was hiding under his suits. All he ever presented was the controlling and loving boyfriend to my assistant. Now that I'm getting to know the guy even more, he's showing an entirely new side. One that's starting to branch out and trust other individuals in his life aside from his woman. Still, he has a long row to hoe with the team, but we're getting him there. Well, Royce and I are.

"Michael Pritchard?" Monika's eyes light up. "We offered him the project, but he turned it down."

I frown and lean back in my chair, pulling my ankle up to cross over my knee. "Really? Any particular reason why?"

She inhales and lets it out as if she's centering herself. "Michael and I were in a relationship once upon a time. It was long ago, but he's not the type of man who mixes business with pleasure."

Mic. Drop.

Shit just got far more interesting.

"Reeeeaaaally?" Bo says with a sarcasm that can't be missed.

She shrugs. "It is not a problem. I am married. He is to be wedded the last I heard. Still, we didn't leave things on good terms. I doubt he'll assist you. The Michael I know rarely changes his mind."

I grin wide. "Oh, he'll change his mind."

"You think so?" She tilts her head, and her dark-blue-eyed gaze pierces through mine, searching and hopefully finding nothing but pure confidence oozing from my eyes.

"Yep. We have an ace in the hole with our friend Mick."

Royce shakes his head. "You're going to go there, aren't you, Park? Right after we smoothed things over? You're going to talk to Wendy."

I smile wide. "Only if he says no first."

Bo cackles as he rocks back and forth in his seat. "Ask Mom if Dad says no? I like it."

"If I have to, but I don't think I will. Mick and I have come to an understanding as of late." I face off with my two brothers. "You'll see."

5

"Absolutely not! Ellis, do not go there. You don't know what you're wading into here, and I'm not about to put my relationship with the love of my life on the line for a one-off business deal for IG." Mick's tone brooks no arguments, but I push on.

"Mick, if anything, helping IG would go a long way toward making Wendy happy." And it would. I know Wendy has a vested interest in IG and us. We're like her big brothers now. Her man working with us on a project would thrill her to no end; I'm certain of it. And what makes Wendy happy makes everyone happy, most especially Mick.

"You do not understand the history there . . ."

I wade in, bringing up what the client said in our meeting. "Monika mentioned that you'd declined the invitation and that you'd had a connection in the past . . ."

Mick's voice rises when he responds. "That woman *destroyed* me once. I will not let her get her claws into me again."

I close my eyes and rub my temples while pressing the phone to my ear. *Shit. This is not going how I'd hoped.* "You wouldn't have to. You've got Wendy, remember. Besides, she's married and has no hard feelings . . ."

"Of course she wouldn't. I broke it off with her," he seethes through the line.

"Look, this is a big contract for IG and an opportunity for your company to get involved at the initial phase of a universal car company launch. What they're doing here, it's new, hip, and unprecedented, but we need *your* help to get it off the ground. *I* need your help."

"Parker . . ." Mick sighs and then clears his throat. "You don't understand."

"What don't I understand? Tell me, and I'll fix it. Whatever complication there was or however bad you left it, believe me, I'm good at fixing things. It's what I do. Fix people's problems."

"You can't fix what she did. The circles Monika, Wendy, and I play in are not part of your world."

I grimace and pace the length of my hotel room. "I'm assuming by that comment you're referring to the BDSM lifestyle?"

"In a sense, yes. There are lines you don't cross. She crossed them. It took me years to trust another sub again. It wasn't until I found Wendy that I became reborn, chose to live again."

"Mick, I had a woman in my past fuck me over royally. It prevented me from trusting a woman again for a long damn time. Not until Sky. And even then, I almost ruined what we have due to the demons of my past. The best advice I can give is not to push it under the rug, but to air that shit out in the open. Work it over with Wendy, with me. I'm your friend. There isn't anything I wouldn't do to help you. Especially now, after what Wendy's gone through." I grind my teeth and take a deep breath in order to get out what I need to say.

"I hurt every day for her, man. Every. Fuckin'. Day. I wish things were different, but pushing it aside and not allowing everyone to grieve doesn't work in the long run. It makes it to where you can't help out a buddy when he needs your experience."

A little dose of Catholic guilt my mother taught me has Mick sighing heavily. For ten long seconds I hear nothing but silence.

"I need to talk to Wendy. Give her a heads-up about Monika. I'll let her decide if I can help you or not."

"That's great, man! Wonderful. Thank you." Wendy will talk him into it if nothing else. It's IG, and she's 100 percent a member of the team. She'll have my back.

"Don't thank me yet, I still have to approach Cherry about it. There's no telling how she'll react."

"Regardless, I just appreciate that you're willing to consider helping out. You know, you could just tell me what happened, soften the shock of talking about it." I sit down on the soft bed and lift my leg, crossing my ankle over my knee and holding it there.

"Fuck," Mick practically snarls. "It was a long time ago. I was in my early twenties, right out of college, already running my company and making more money than I thought was possible. Even with my family inheritance, I wanted to build my own empire. Everything blew up globally, so much so I ended up in Germany, opening another branch of my offices there. That's where I met Monika. Initially she came to work for me. Her intelligence turned me on first. Of course, it didn't hurt that she had a great pair of legs. Well, you've met her."

I grin. "Yeah, I did. Very pretty. Not Wendy, though."

Mick laughs hard through the line. "No one in the world is like Wendy. I compare all human beings to her. She's true to herself and others at all times. There's a freedom in Wendy that enchants me. I want to hold it in my hand, make it mine forever. And I will . . . only because she's going to let me, not because I demand it."

His words have my thoughts wandering to Skyler. My world has become so different now that she's in it fully. Our commitment to one another has never been more solid, and I'd go a long way to protect it, the same way I imagine Michael feels about whatever he needs to tell Wendy about Monika.

"Wendy's one of a kind. I can understand how you would want to protect her from any and all things. Though you can't keep her from your past or prevent it from popping up every so often. I learned that lesson the hard way with Sky. I'm sure Wendy updated you on Johan."

He sighs. "Yeah, that was a few nights of my woman losing her mind over what was happening between you and Sky. She's relieved it all worked out. I am too. I like Skyler. She reminds me of Wendy in the sense that she loves deep. You can see the way she feels about a person through her eyes. The way she looks at them is very telling."

I smile and lean forward over my legs. "Yeah, but let's get back to Monika. You were about to tell me why you have such an adverse reaction to working with the woman."

The sound of Michael moving around his home office paints a clear picture. I can easily see him pouring himself a drink from his crystal decanters, sitting at his huge mahogany desk, and staring out over the lush landscape of his Boston mansion.

"We were together for five years. She was my submissive. And in the lifestyle, it's common practice to attend private clubs where we occasionally engage in consensual acts with other member couples. Monika was adventurous. At home and work she was prim and proper, a loving, doting girlfriend and submissive. At the club, she was a pain slut. Preferred to practice her kink with many partners. There was one in particular, the owner, who'd taken a liking to her. If a submissive consents to sharing, the final permission rests with the Dominant. I had become uncomfortable with sharing. Learned that I don't prefer it, nor will I push my sub past her limitations just because I have her at my mercy."

Oh, sweet baby Jesus. This is not the type of conversation I thought we'd be having. Something inside of me is screaming *too much information, too much information*, but I've already gone down the rabbit hole, and there's no hope of finding that exit anytime soon.

"Mm-hmm. That sounds reasonable." I say the words, thinking I have no freakin' clue if what he's discussing is reasonable in that world.

"The thing about BDSM and D/s relationships that is crucial is trust. More than anything, trust is essential, or the types of physical and mental play will not be pleasurable for either party. I didn't want to hurt Monika in the way she preferred, which happened to be one that made her bleed. I do not mar the skin of the woman I love in a way that won't heal quickly or requires bandages of any kind. What I didn't know was, behind my back, she started seeing the owner of the club, who would hurt her the way she liked. Then she'd lie to me, sneak back to the club when I was away on business, betraying me repeatedly. Until she betrayed me in a way she couldn't defend."

"Holy shit. Mick, I'm sorry, brother. I can only say, I feel you. I *feel* you."

"I suspect you do or you wouldn't have had the trouble you had with Skyler. However, Monika took it a step further than emotional and physical betrayal. She became pregnant and attempted to pawn it off as mine. The math on conception never added up. I had been gone for three weeks during the time she would have conceived."

"Christ." I growl and stand up, needing to pace the room, anger boiling in my stomach. Hell, and I thought Kayla was bad. At least she didn't try to lie about being pregnant with my child.

"When the baby was born, I had it tested. It wasn't mine. Not that I expected it to be."

I let all the air out of my lungs along with my anger on his behalf. "Mick . . . that was messed up. You know Wendy would never do anything like that to you."

His laughter bursts through the line. "Hence the reason I put a ring on it, but more importantly, a collar."

"Collar is a bigger deal than the ring, huh? I could kind of see that when she had her mini-meltdown at the hospital over the fact they cut it off. The ring she didn't even blink at."

"In our world, our lifestyle, the collar means I claimed her. The fact that she agrees to wear it every day means she's giving herself to me, body and soul. A ring is just another public, mainstream symbol, though I'm not going to lie and say I'm not after that legal certificate. I'm going to hang that piece of paper on my wall with pride. Look at it every day, knowing that there is one person on this earth who is truly mine, and in reverse, who I belong to. Understand?"

My throat is clogged, and words are hard to find, the emotion of his speech hitting me right where it counts. "Yeah, man. I do. So, you going to tell her and fly out to Germany to help me with this thing?"

He sucks in a loud breath. "Yes. I am. I find that speaking to you made the situation feel a little lighter. Though I can't promise that, if or when I come, seeing her again won't bring the ugly feelings back to the forefront."

If I were there by his side, I'd clap him on the shoulder and give him a hard squeeze in support. Since I can't do that, I have to use my words. "And I'll be there for you. As your friend. As someone who cares about you and Wendy having your happily ever after."

Silence greets me for a few seconds until Mick's now-raspy voice cuts through it. "I see why she loves you."

"Who? Skyler?"

He chuckles. "No. Wendy. You're genuine, and you mean what you say. It's rare in a person, even more so in a businessman."

"Yeah, well, I prefer to do business how I live my life . . . by trusting my heart. Sounds cheesy—" I start to explain, but Mick cuts me off.

"And that is why you will always be successful. I'm going to let you go so I can have a chat with my dearest. She's probably made her house nurse nuts by now, watching endless hours of *Days of Our Lives* and reality TV."

"Yikes."

"Indeed. Thank you for your call, Parker. I will be in touch."

"Hey . . ."

"Yes?"

"Tell her I miss her and mean it."

Another couple of seconds of dead air fills the space before I hear his voice respond in a calm and succinct tone. "As you wish."

I hang up, toss my phone on the bed, and run my fingers through my hair a few times. I'm a ball of energy and uncertainty after hearing about Mick's unfortunate past. Shit, what did I just ask this guy to do? Meet up with his ex who treated him like shit. Lied. Betrayed him. Lied some more.

I pace the room faster, my strides long and quick. *I'm an asshole.* I'm a complete . . . asshole. Fuck!

My phone buzzes from where I threw it. Maybe it's one of the guys wanting to go out to eat and have a drink. Many drinks. Multiple drinks would be good right about now. More than anything I need to get my mind off Mick, Wendy, and Monika and get my thoughts on coming up with a brilliant campaign to present to the team.

I grab the phone and pull up my texts. I snicker at seeing my brother's name in my display.

To: Parker Ellis
From: Pretty Paul

In Berlin. At Reingold on Novalisstrasse 11. Meet me for a drink bro.

Yes! I fist pump the air and smile wide. My bro is in town. Hell to the yes! I cannot wait to see him. With a quick scan of a map on my phone, I find I can get to the place by cab pretty quick.

To: Pretty Paul
From: Parker Ellis

Be there in twenty.

As I jet around the room, grabbing my blazer, wallet, and hotel key card, my phone buzzes again.

To: Parker Ellis
From: Pretty Paul

Come alone. Want to talk bro to bro.

I frown. Not that I was planning to tell Royce and Bo to come along, but in the past, he would want to see the guys. Likes them as much as I do. This switch in his request is odd; then again, I haven't seen my brother in two years. Maybe he just wants quiet time with me to catch up about the family.

Instead of responding, I take a moment to check my hair and smooth the unruly curls on top that need to be cut. I should have had it done when I was back in Boston, but I spent all of my time playing house with Sky and catching up on all things IG. Not a bad way to pass the time. Which reminds me I need to call my girl.

I head down the elevator and out of the hotel lobby, where I hail a cab. A black Audi pulls up, and I hop in. "Novalisstrasse 11, Reingold, please," I tell him in my best pronunciation of the street name as possible. He must get it because he nods and pulls out into the evening traffic. Knowing I've got about fifteen minutes, I pull my phone back out of my pocket and press on Skyler's pretty face in my favorites list.

"Get this!" Skyler says upon answering, no hello, just right into what she wants to tell me.

"What, baby?" I smile at hearing the sound of her voice. Something so simple and yet immensely comforting at the same time.

"Wendy wants to have bright yellow and hints of green and white for her wedding colors! Isn't that weird? And awesome! She's going to have standard daisies, you know, the ones with the white petals and yellow centers, along with carnations sprinkled throughout and big, fat yellow gerbera daisies. It's going to look rad."

I chuckle at the exuberance in her tone. "Rad?" I shake my head and look out at the eastern part of Berlin as it goes by.

"So rad! Anyway, how are you doing? The guys, everyone okay?"

I close my eyes and breathe in deep. Having someone to ask how I'm doing, whether or not I'm okay, and genuinely wanting to know . . . that's what it's all about. A flash of Sky's naked sexy body enters my mind. Well, not what it's *all* about. I get why Mick would want to legally tie himself and Wendy together for life.

"Knowing that there is one person on this earth who is truly mine, and in reverse, who I belong to. Understand?"

Mick's words spin through my mind like a gerbil on a plastic wheel, round and round, no end.

"Yeah, Peaches, I'm okay. The guys are fine. You'll never believe who contacted me, though."

"Who?" Her voice changes to one of concern.

"My brother, Paul. He's in Berlin. I'm heading to meet him now."

She gasps. "Oh my God! That's amazing, honey. I know you were worried about him."

"Except it was strange, the email coming out of nowhere. He'd usually just call. Also, he's mentioned a couple of times that he needs to talk to me about something."

"Hmm, could it be that he's leaving the military? Maybe he needs a place to stay. If that's the case, perhaps he can stay in your apartment and you can stay here. Whatever would make him most comfortable. Or he can stay here in one of my extra rooms." She offers up her new home without ever having met my brother.

"I love you. Have I told you that today?"

"No, but I never tire of hearing it. I love you too. Why do you sound sad?"

I let out a long sigh. "It's been a weird day. Not really feeling like talking about it. How about you? What are you up to? Better yet— where are you?"

"In New York. Right now, I'm with Tracey at the Marriott Marquis on Broadway where the media is set up. We're just finishing up a quick lunch before we go for round two with the press for the movie. And check this . . ."

"What?" I ask, my own excitement ramping up at the sound of her happiness.

"Our book cover was revealed today! The third book in the series is already a bestseller, and it doesn't come out for another two months! Geneva is through the roof with excitement!"

I smile wide and press the phone closer to my ear. I want to hear nothing but my girl's joy. "That's great, baby."

"It so is, and guess what else!" she practically screams with delight.

"What?" I chuckle, loving every second of her.

"I'm going in for an audition for the part of Simone Shilling in the A-Lister Trilogy! Though I think it's going to be a saga because Geneva told her agent, Amy, and Amy told Tracey that the third book is going to be long. Which means a two-parter in the movie world. That could mean four back-to-back movies! And guess what else!"

The laughter leaves my chest in a mighty guffaw. "Tell me. I'm all ears, Peaches."

"They are going to film on the East Coast! That means I'll be in New York for filming! Except Geneva told them she was looking for more of a local down-home feel for the bar that Dean's character works in, and I told them about Lucky's! The production team is checking it out to see if it would work! *Can. You. Believe. This?!* They will pay your dad a whack-load of cash to let them film when needed, and they can do it during the morning when he's closed anyway! He'll make extra cash hand over fist!"

"Hand over fist. Baby, who taught you that!" I tease.

"Did you hear *anything* I said!" Her voice rises in playful irritation.

"Yes, yes, I did. Sounds awesome. I'm really happy. For you and for me."

"I'd hoped you would be. I'm on cloud nine. How's the car project?"

I dip my head from side to side and purse my lips even though she can't see it. "It's . . . good. We've got our work cut out for us but not anything we can't handle."

The cab pulls up in front of a rusted-out door that has "Reingold Bar" in black writing against a white-lit background. Looks like a hole-in-the-wall mixed in between other businesses and apartments.

"Peaches, I'm here. I'm going to let you go. Have fun promoting your movie. I'll call you again tomorrow, around lunchtime for you. We're six hours ahead, so text me if you're wanting to touch base late, in case I'm sleeping." I pay the driver and hop out of the cab to stand on the sidewalk.

"Okay, honey. I love you," she murmurs in my ear, sweet and sexy like she does when she wakes in the morning.

"I love you, Sky. So fuckin' much."

"Dream of me, honey."

"I always do," I say, because it's true. She fills my thoughts during the day and my dreams at night.

She makes a smack sound into the phone, which I'm assuming is her air-kissing me, before the line goes dead.

"My crazy girl," I mumble, and shake my head, checking out the establishment and pulling on the wrought iron handle. Once I'm inside, it's a whole new world. The place is dark, lit up by the soft glow of back lighting and red tubes of light. Some of the walls have copper plating, which has a glowing effect from the stream of lights at the bottom and sides of the wall. Leather and wood abound, and iron tables with high stools are intricately spaced for maximum capacity. As it is, the place is crowded, and it's still pretty early in the evening.

I scan the darkness, squinting to focus my gaze on any bulky, six-foot-two guys likely in army fatigues or some form of commando-like gear. My eyes land on a broad back; a mostly shaved head, but you can still see some dark-brown shading; a strong, chiseled jaw; camo pants and boots; and a black long-sleeved thermal shirt.

The familiar form turns his head from talking to the dude on his right, and his dark-brown gaze comes to me. I stand stock-still and take in all that is my brother. Alive and well. Here. Twenty feet in front of me. Paul maneuvers his big body off the stool at the bar and opens his arms wide.

"P-Drive! Get your ass over here!" he bites out, and I rush to him in a handful of fast strides and slam into him with enough force he has to take a step back to brace us when I embrace him hard. I hold him so tight my arms might leave imprints on his skin.

"Fuck. Fuck. Fuck," I chant against his head as a tidal wave of emotion shreds through me like wildfire. He smells of leather and sunblock and something so uniquely my brother it makes my throat itch and my nose tingle.

He claps me on the back and holds me tight. He pulls back enough to cup my cheeks and shake my jaw a little. "Missed your goddamned face, Park. My brother. My baby fuckin' brother. In the flesh." He pulls me back in, and I take full advantage, hugging him so hard I want to imprint this moment on my soul.

"Two years, Paul. Two years too long." My voice shakes, and I clear my throat, trying not to let the tears fall, but my eyes fill up anyway.

He nods and claps my back a bunch more times, almost trying to smack the relief right out of me. "I know. I know. Come on, have a beer with me."

I grip his giant bicep just to keep the physical connection and realize the guy is hard as steel and huge. Like he's made working out his profession or something. He'd probably give Nate a run for his gym money. "Damn, bro. Work out much?"

He shoots me a wicked grin. "Best shape of my life. Not much to do besides working out when you're waiting on orders in a shit-hole undercover location."

"This is true." I raise my arm to get the bartender's attention. "Beer. Whatever you recommend that's local."

Paul chuckles. "Still after the local tastes when it comes to beer. Bet it makes Pops proud."

I shrug. "He likes new recommendations, and I drink free at his bar. It's the least I can do."

Paul jerks his head back. "Way I see it, you bought that bar, you deserve to drink free."

"Nah. He raised us, took care of us and Mom. The guy deserves to be his own boss."

Paul sucks in a breath through his teeth before clapping me on the back. "Sure glad to see you, Park."

I smile as wide as my heart feels. "Me too. Why all of a sudden are you back? You are back for a while, right?"

He nods. "Done my tenure, served my twelve years. I'm up to reenlist for another four at least. Thinking this might be the end of the road for me in spec ops. Maybe in service at all."

"No shit?" I don't mask the shock in my voice.

My whole life all my brother wanted to be was a soldier. A special operative, best-of-the-best type of soldier. He's done that and beyond. And from all the medals I know he has, he's damn good at it too.

"I wouldn't shit you; you're my favorite turd." This is the same thing he used to say to me when we were kids, and like then, he proceeds to sock me in the arm. A starburst of pain spears out from the point where his knuckles hit and spreads like hot lava oozing from a volcano across my shoulder and arm.

"Dammit!" I shove him back and rub at my wounded arm and pride. I should have seen it coming. "Why are you thinking of quitting?"

He picks up his beer right as the bartender sets down a chilled pint glass in front of me. We both take sips, and I let the hoppy goodness coat my nerves and excitement on seeing my brother for the first time in two years alive and sitting right next to me.

He tips his head over his shoulder to look at me, his dark gaze serious all of a sudden. "Thinking of settling down."

If I weren't holding my glass over the bar I would have dropped it on the floor. "You've met a woman. Ma is going to shit her pants. Between me getting with Skyler and you finding a nice girl to bring home—I'm assuming she's a nice girl . . ." I take a sip and blather on. "Ma's going to be going to church twice a week to thank the good Lord for her boys finally growing up and settling down."

Paul doesn't say anything, just stares at me, his dark eyes broody. An uncertainty settles in his expression when he says, "You see, that's why I needed to talk to you. I'm not going to be bringing home a nice girl to our folks. I'm going to be bringing home a nice *guy*. My boyfriend. Dennis Romoaldo."

6

"I'm sorry, say that last part again. I don't think I heard you right."

Paul scowls. "You fuckin' heard me, Park. You didn't *want* to hear me."

I stare at him, blinking stupidly for a good full minute. He's patient, though, I'll give him that. Doesn't so much as move a muscle as I process what he just said. Must be all that special ops training shit they taught him.

My brother is gay.

"You're gay?"

This time Paul grumbles, "Gay, bi, whatever you want to call it."

"You're bi?" I say even louder, then realize that I'm spouting his personal business out in the open, and loudly, so I lean closer and whisper more conspiratorially, "You're bisexual?"

He turns his head and nods. "Yeah, I am. I like women and men. Had both. Like both. Get off on both. Right now, I get off hard-core on a man named Dennis. Met him a year ago in South America. Been seeing him on and off since then, when I could get away. Now I'm seeing him full-time. As a matter of fact, he's here. Right now. Across the bar."

Paul waves to a dude with a light-ish complexion, thick dark hair, and brown eyes. He's rockin' what seems to be a navy sport coat with tan patches on the elbows. Sitting on the bridge of a nicely shaped nose is a pair of trendy black glasses. He smiles wide, giving me the impression that it's natural, especially when he waves back at my brother. Still, he doesn't get up and come over right this second, which I'm grateful for.

I suck in a long breath and let it out slowly. "Okay, so, you're bi." I shrug my shoulders and let this new information about my brother simmer.

Paul stares at my face in a way I can tell he's looking for any subtle nuances, and then he tightens his jaw. "I can understand if you're not cool with it. Not sure Mom and Dad are going to be, but it's who I am, and you know I'm not about hiding . . . well, unless it's from the enemy." An offhand joke, probably to lighten the load he just dumped on me.

I place my hand on his shoulder. "Bro, there's nothing for me to be cool about."

His lips flatten into a thin line as he grips his drink so hard his knuckles turn white. "I can understand how you might want to avoid this, not think about it, whatever." He starts to make excuses. "I'm sorry if this changes your opinion of me. I'm still your brother and a man, but this relationship is not going away."

With my heart pounding and hurting like mad, I wave my hands in front of us. "Whoa, whoa, whoa. Back that train up. How could you think this would bother me? Paul, you're my brother. You're my fucking *hero*. I've worshiped the ground you've walked on for decades. I couldn't give a rat's ass who you get your jollies off with."

His body goes ramrod straight for a few moments before he speaks. "Really? You don't . . ." He licks his lips and focuses his gaze on his drink. "You don't see me differently?"

"Uh, no. What the fuck century are you in? I'm living in the twenty-first century, where a man or woman can be with whoever the hell they want to be with. As long as you're not lusting after my mate, I could care less."

Paul tilts his head to the sky, rolls his shoulders, and turns to me with his arms open. Before I can respond he pulls me against his brick wall of a chest and slaps me on the back hard enough I cough.

"Thank fuck, thank fuck," he whispers, and shakes his head. "You were all I worried about."

I pull away and tilt my head, feeling a bit put out. "Why would you think I would be so closed-minded? That hurts, man."

"Nah it's just, so many in my circle are not so easy. The guy I've been partnered up with in the field . . ."

"Kenny?"

He nods. "Yeah. He, uh, he didn't take it so well. Caught me and Dennis, in a lock . . . you, uh, know what I'm talking about."

I grin and nod.

"Then he told me, via spit on my boots, how he felt about my orientation and asked to be given a new partner."

Bile swirls in my belly as anger ripples up my spine. "Douchebag."

He shrugs. "Nah, he was cool until he wasn't anymore. You never know how people are going to respond, and I . . . Fuck, P-Drive, I just couldn't bear it if you thought less of me, as a man, as your brother. Kenny, I write off; you, you're my blood. My family. What you think means more."

"Is that why you didn't want the guys coming tonight?"

He nods. "In part, yeah, and because I wanted to tell you in private, introduce you to Dennis before I bring him home to Mom and Dad."

The idea of our parents sitting down with Paul and Dennis, him busting out with the fact that the guy is his boyfriend, paints a hilarious picture in my mind. I start to chuckle, and then it turns into an out-and-out guffaw.

Paul sips his drink and grins. "You suck."

That has me howling with laughter and unable to catch my breath. "Apparently not as well as you!"

Paul smirks and punches me in the arm playfully, but a good-spirited punch from GI Joe himself sears me to the bone.

"Ouch! Fuck, man. Keep your sledgehammers on lockdown. I need those arms. Crap!" I rub at the sore space.

Paul stops smiling and turns toward me. "You're really cool with this?"

I smile so he can see for himself that I am. "Yes. It doesn't matter to me who you want to be with romantically. Just as long as you keep your big paws off my Sky, we'll be just fine."

"Oh yeah! That's right. Baby bro is bangin' Hollywood's hottest star. Dude, I've been out of the country, out of touch, and even I know how lucky you are to score an in with that beauty. Is this like a regular thing, or a hookup? Give me the four one one."

Thinking of Sky has me grinning like a lunatic. "She's everything, bro. The first thing I think of when I wake, the last thing I think about when I go to bed. I'm balls to the wall in love with her. And she just got a pad in Boston. Another step forward in our relationship."

"Holy hell. My brother's been roped in by a beautiful blonde actress. You picking out diamonds yet?"

I sip my beer and shake my head. "Nah, we're taking it day by day. It's hard with both of us traveling and her being in the public eye. Makes things a bit more difficult. You'll see when you meet her in Boston."

"Looking forward to it." He holds up his glass, and I knock it with my own and take a swallow.

Paul looks down and then over at the other side of the bar. "You ready to meet Dennis?"

"You ready to introduce your guy to family? Is it that serious?"

He smiles so wide his cheeks pinken. "Yeah. I am. Something between us that I've never felt with anyone else. Knocked me on my ass the very first time, and I haven't been able to catch my breath since."

"It's called love, brother. Sounds like you're in love with the guy."

Paul's gaze goes over to the man patiently sipping his beer and playing with his phone. He looks up and catches Paul's gaze and grins. The two only have eyes for one another. "Yeah, you're right. I'm in love with him. Never thought I could be in love with a guy, but . . ." He lifts his shoulder and then lets it fall. "Guess the world works in mysterious ways."

I clap him on the back. "Yes, it does. Go get him and bring him over so I can meet the man who's captured my big bro's heart."

Paul smiles, removes his big body from the stool, cups my neck, and pulls me forward so he can kiss the crown of my head. "Missed you so much. Nuthin' better than having my brother close. Love you, Park."

I close my eyes and breathe in my brother, safe and sound in a bar in Berlin of all places. I lift my head, cup his cheek, then smack it. "Love you too, Paulie. Now go get your guy."

He winks cheekily and saunters his big body over to the end of the bar, an unmistakable spring in his step. I watch while Dennis has his gaze glued to my brother and vice versa. Paul is using his big form and swagger to maximum effect. All the women at the surrounding tables turn and watch him as he strides ahead with one goal in mind. His man.

While my brother sits in the chair next to Dennis and hooks an arm around the smaller man, I think about the fact that Paul was genuinely worried about telling me he was gay. Technically bi, or whatever. The particulars don't matter to me. If my brother is happy in his life, has someone to love and love him in return, I'm going to support him. Now that I have Skyler, I don't know how I lived without her. If my brother has that connection with Dennis, I'll be the first to congratulate them.

I am pissed off about what he said about his old partner, Kenny, spitting on him. That shit hits me where it hurts. If I could have five minutes in a room with the douchecanoe, I'd light the bastard up for being a bigot and a stain on society. Not only is my brother brave by risking his life every day as a soldier, but it had to take an enormous amount of bravery to come out to me. He'll have to summon up that bravery again when he goes back home and introduces his boyfriend to Mom and Dad.

Do I think they'll ridicule him or be angry with his choices? No. It's not how we were raised, thankfully. I know that's not necessarily the norm, but I'd like to believe that society is changing. Who one takes to their bed or shares their life with is a personal preference. It's not something that any one person has a right to truly have an opinion on one way or the other. My parents will welcome Dennis into their open arms. Though I can say that Ma will give Paulie a ration of shit about going on thirty-two without progeny on the horizon. Now that he's with a man, she's going to have to change tactics, which will mean she'll start in on Sky and me.

Suddenly I get a flash of a future where Skyler's belly is swollen with my child, the two of us sitting on a porch overlooking some type of land or lush view . . . The crazy thing is, I can totally see it. In the future. Not today, or tomorrow. Probably not even a year from now.

I wonder if Sky thinks about having kids with me. When we talked about my grandmother and her tradition, she seemed keen on the concept of the two of us having kids down the road, but we haven't really had an out-and-out discussion about it.

Would she want one soon, say in the next couple of years, or down the road?

I'll be thirty in a month. She's a few years younger with more time and a career that is currently in the stratosphere. She'd be crazy to step back, even a little, in order to have a family. At least for now. Still, it warrants a chat just so the two of us are on the same page. I can totally see myself with a couple of kids. Especially with Skyler's big brown eyes and unconditional kindness.

My phone buzzes as I notice my brother across the way with a fresh round of drinks, leading his significant other toward me.

I look at the display and grind my teeth.

To: Parker Ellis
From: Unknown

DISTANCE MAKES THE HEART GROW FONDER. I MISS YOU.

"Fuck!" I growl as my brother walks up, his jaw tight.

"What's got you looking like you're about to punch someone?" He looks left and right, scanning the environment with an operator's ability, meaning he probably can tell you what every single person is wearing and doing in this establishment right now. "I got your six."

I let out a huff and a laugh at the same time. "It's fine. No harm, no foul. But damn it's good to have you back."

"Yeah, well, it's good to be back. I've got someone I want you to meet, little bro." He hands me a fresh drink and, once I've taken it, eases his arm around the man who's shorter than him by at least three inches. He has a nice form and is quite the smart dresser. The blazer I noticed is coupled with a pair of dark jeans and camel-colored suede loafers, sans socks. "This is my man, Dennis Romoaldo."

Dennis pushes his black frames higher up on the bridge of his nose and smiles softly. "Hello, Parker. I'm delighted to meet you. Paulo tells me so much about you and his family. He is very proud of all you have accomplished at your young age." He rolls his words around with a unique accent.

I frown and lean closer. "I detect an accent. If you don't mind me asking, where are you from?"

Dennis brightens, and his entire face seems to glow. "I do not mind at all. I am from Rio de Janeiro, Brazil. The most beautiful city in all the world," he gushes with obvious patriotism.

I nudge my brother. "Brazilian, eh?" I waggle my eyebrows in good fun.

Paul takes in his guy from his face down to his shoes and back. "You don't know the half of it, little bro."

Laughter bubbles up and out of my mouth as I turn toward the chairs. "Have a seat between us, Dennis, so I can get to know you better."

He smirks at my brother, pulls out the chair, and takes his seat like a gentleman. Paul sits on his right, and I take his left.

"All right, first and foremost, I gotta know how you guys met."

Paul traces a circle on the glossy bar top. "I was stationed in Brazil for a time. We actually met through a mutual friend. It, uh, turned into a night of debauchery. Denny was acting coy with me all night at a bar our friend had taken us to. He was already there along with a hot broad named Andrea. At first, I was feeling out the chick . . ." He laughs heartily. ". . . until the lot of us got smashed. I didn't have to be back on assignment for another seventy-two hours, and the girl was forward. Invited me and our mutual friend and Dennis back to her pad. Things got a little freaky from there. Turned out Denny and I had more fun together, and the two of them went at it like wild animals. We've been seeing each other on and off since. Right, baby?"

I stare at the poised man and watch as his cheeks turn a fine crimson. Paul puts his arm behind Dennis's chair and runs his hand up and down his back casually, as though he doesn't even realize he's doing it. Probably trying to make Dennis feel comfortable after he relayed a pretty private story.

"Yes, *pistola*. However, you could have shared that we met through a friend in Brazil. That would have been . . . less invasive." The words he chooses are almost formal and have a proper connotation to them as opposed to casual.

"You speak very good English, Dennis. Did you learn in school?"

He nods. "Yes, as well as with a private tutor. My family's business is in international imports. In order to do good business and provide superb service, we must speak English fluently."

"Well, you've got it down pat, my man." I clap him on the back, and that simple gesture of comradery has my brother grinning and Dennis smiling shyly and looking down and over to Paul.

"Told you he'd love you." He rubs Dennis's neck.

I hold up my hand. "Whoa, whoa, whoa. Wait a minute there, sparky. He has not mentioned who his favorite baseball team is yet. Love is reserved for true—"

"I love the Red Sox and the Patriots." Dennis rushes out the words before I can even finish my statement.

Paul chuckles, and I jerk my head over to him. "You taught him to say that."

"Yeah." He laughs.

"Doesn't matter. Still counts." I open my arms. "Welcome to the family, Dennis."

***

Later that night, back at the hotel, I'm forwarding the most recent text I received from "Unknown" to Nate. Within moments of it being sent, my phone rings.

The display reads "Nate Van Dyken."

"Yo!" I answer.

"I'm at a dead end with my resources. I don't like to say this, but the texter is smart. Uses a different burner phone after every couple of texts." He sighs loudly through the line. "Parker, I want to call in Wendy."

I suck in a breath through my teeth, knowing that I already asked her man to help me with the job. "Man, you know she's healing."

"Understood. And I respect it. Except, according to Skyler, she's chipper as a squirrel. Worse. She's bored. Blowing up Skyler's phone about wedding stuff because she's got nothing better to do. Rachel's had to field a few calls. She likes Wendy. Very much. What Rach doesn't like is distraction from her charge. It makes her itchy and brazen. Parker, you do not want to deal with my wife when she's brazen."

I swallow down the concern and fear to focus on what Nate is saying. "Where are you guys now?"

"Skyler and Rachel are getting shit-faced."

I blink at the empty room a few times, then kick off my shoes and unbutton my shirt. "W-what?" I choke out on a laugh.

"You heard me. Work is done. We're actually at our apartment. The two of them ate half a large pizza while they slammed copious amounts of tequila in margarita format. Now they're doing straight shots of Patrón while playing the card game War." I can hear whoops, hollering, and laughter in the background. Nate continues, "Whenever they have a war, the loser takes a shot. Needless to say, their numbers have matched up more than a few times."

"Yikes." I tug my shirttail out of my pants and toe off my socks before heading to the bathroom.

"You're telling me . . ." His voice dips down to a deeper timbre and a more serious note. "Not to worry. We're keeping her in the spare room tonight where I can watch them both. Keep them safe. Don't want her alone, even if she needs to meet with the porcelain throne in the process. I've got your girl."

I smile and lean against the mirror. "Can I talk to her for a sec?" Even knowing she's right there makes me desire her voice in my ear if nothing else.

"Yeah, but seriously, are you against me talking to Wendy?"

I put my phone on speaker and reread the text.

DISTANCE MAKES THE HEART GROW FONDER. I MISS YOU.

A shiver races through my body. I take the phone off speaker. "No, fuck . . ." I run my hand through my hair a few times trying to decide.

Skyler needs to be safe. "Just go in easy. Maybe take her out to lunch and discuss the issue. See what her thoughts are out the gate. She'll jump on it if she thinks she can help. Don't push. Did you hear back from Tracey?"

"Yeah, and you're not going to like it. Wanted to wait until we could meet face-to-face to discuss—"

"Fuck face-to-face. If you've got something to say that involves Sky, you need to tell me now."

"It's nothing too intense, but I have some suspicions."

"Which are?"

He breathes through the line and moves away from the noise I was hearing in the background. "Tracey mentioned that Skyler had at least ten to twenty superfans who have regularly mailed, sent gifts, etc. Skyler's team doesn't respond to any of them. The nature of the texts is passive and then aggressive. I've been analyzing the texts Sky's gotten, and they go from friendly with the 'I thought we were friends' and get angrier. As though Skyler is not responding to more than just the texts. The texts say, 'Why are you always ignoring me?' then, 'You think you're better than everyone,' but then something changed."

"What?"

"You and Skyler got the same text."

An uneasiness sets up in my gut. "What do you think that means?"

"I'm no expert, but somehow Sky's back in the texter's good graces. Rather suddenly. Then again, the two of you are apart. Is it that the texter misses you both or that this person knows you both miss one another?" Nate surmises rather succinctly.

"It could be either, or both. A person never can tell when they're dealing with a clearly troubled mind."

"And yet the individual has both of your cell phones but hasn't contacted you personally."

The word *personally* pings around in my head.

"Shit," I hiss.

"What? What aren't you telling me?"

"Fuck." I sigh and pull at my hair. "I received a letter at my office. It was weird, and I didn't put the two together until now. It said something about 'her being me' or 'she is me.' No. Wait . . ." I reach back into my memory bank, scanning that day until the moment when I opened the envelope. It was one of those yellow ones. Typed on front. *Confidential* stamp. "It said, 'I am her. She is me.' Yes, that's what it said. 'I am her. She is me,'" I repeat.

"Parker, that's extremely dissociated. When I was in the military, we dealt with individuals with dissociative behavior. They can be extremely unpredictable, and their motives can change on a dime. Reading between the lines of what this person wrote, he or she basically implied that they and Skyler are the same person. Except the notes afterward have been fluctuating between passive and angry and now sweet." He growls. "This situation just got worse. I need to get all of that mail from Tracey and review it. See if I can match any of the word style and tone to the texts and note you received. I want a copy of that note. Do you still have it?"

"Yeah, I left it back in the office. I'll call Annie and have her fax it over."

"Okay, thanks. I'll schedule a meet with Wendy."

My heart sinks, but I've come to know Nate very well. He will not take advantage of a woman in pain. If she's doing well, he'll bring it up. If she's not, he'll move on.

"Can I speak with Sky?"

I can hear the voices in the background get louder again. He must be walking back into the room where they're partying.

"Skyler, Parker is on the phone."

"Woo-hoo! My sexy man, my sexy man. Woo-hoo, gonna talk to my sexy boy fran." She makes the last word rhyme with *man*.

I chuckle and wait. "Is she there?"

"No, she's doing her sexy-man dance," Nate replies dryly.

"Get it, girl. You go. Shake that ass!" Rachel whoops in the background.

"Sky, he's on the phone right now," Nate adds.

"Oh yeah! Awesome!" Finally I'm greeted with a breathless "Hi, honey . . ."

The sound goes straight to the beast, waking it up from its slumber. I adjust my package and smile at the sound of her slurred, sexy tone.

"Hey, Peaches. I heard you're doing shots and playing cards."

"I'm so winning!" she screeches, and then lowers her voice. "I'm totally winning, babe. I'm winning Rach at cards."

I can hear a sound that vaguely resembles a person sticking out their tongue and blowing hard, so it makes a blubbering, wet, rude noise.

"Stick your tongue back in your mouth, whore!" She laughs. "Rach gets out all the naughty words when she drinks." Sky hiccups and then sighs. "I miss you lots and lots, and I want to fuck you right now . . . ," she murmurs.

"Mmm. I want to fuck you right now too, honey, but we'll save that for when I come home. Are you going to be in Boston next week? I'm going to stay on at least another three days after the week is up for the new campaign."

"Oh no, boo-hoo, booooo that sucks! I hate that. Booo!" she hisses, and then laughs herself silly.

"I know, but the job is a big one, and I'm hoping Mick will come out and help. I'll tell you about all that later."

"Mmm . . . I'm tired," she mumbles drunkenly.

"Yeah, I'll bet. You talk to Nate. He'll make sure you get some good sleep. I love you, baby."

"I love you lots and lots. Like . . . honey . . . I love you a lot."

I chuckle and shake my head, wishing I could enjoy drunken Skyler for longer, but I can't because we're an ocean apart. "Go, have fun and take a nap if you need to. It's really late here. I need to catch some shut-eye before my meeting tomorrow, but I have so much to tell you."

"Okay . . . Dream of me lots and lots."

"Lots and lots." I laugh. "I promise."

"Okay. That's good. I love you."

"Good night, Peaches."

And right as I'm about to hang up, I hear a noisy smacking for a bunch of kisses and then an "Oooh gross. That's Nate's phone! Nasty . . ." in the background, and then dead air.

I pull off the rest of my clothes and turn on the shower spray. "My girl loves me lots and lots." I snicker and get under the spray, a smile on my face.

7

The restaurant is freezing cold as I enter, and I button up my suit coat against the frigid air conditioning. I scan the layout and find Bo and Royce sitting in a window seat overlooking Berlin. The street is teeming with passersby and cyclists making their way to work.

The two men look up and watch as I head to them, pull out my chair, and grab an empty coffee cup already on the table. I shake the empty mug at the waiter, and he nods.

"Hey, guys, how goes it this morning?"

Royce lifts up his phone and waves it around. "Wendy . . . damn that girl." He scowls. "Can't keep her nose out of work. Check this."

I set my elbows on the table as the waiter fills my coffee cup. "What's she up to now?"

"She's getting on a plane this morning. To Berlin. Apparently private jet. Alongside her beau."

I raise my eyebrows in disbelief. "You're kidding. Did the doctor clear her travel?"

He nods. "Yep. Says she's fit enough to travel as long as she takes it easy. Apparently, she's healing incredibly fast for a woman who sustained a gunshot to the chest and a collapsed lung. What's it been now?"

"A little over five weeks since the injury." I count back, refreshing my memory. An extra few days in Montreal. Home a week or so. In London two weeks, back home for another two weeks.

"That doesn't sound smart of her. How did she get Mick to agree to come to Berlin?" Bo says.

I drop my head and glare at my coffee. "Yeah, that would be me. I called him yesterday. Asked for his help with the campaign. We need him on this if it's going to be a success and announced properly. The guy's a genius."

Bo eases back in his chair and taps the table with two fingers. "Except for the fact that he has history with the client. A history that none of us knew about . . ."

I crinkle my nose as if I've just smelled something funky and look away.

"Or should I say, something Roy and I don't know about?"

"Look, the guy told me some things about his past with the client. It's not my business to share. Just know that I feel like shit asking for his help, and now that Wendy's coming too . . ." I shake my head and rub the back of my neck.

Roy claps me on the forearm. "Brother, don't take on worry that isn't yours. If they're coming to Berlin, it's because she's well enough and he wants to help. He's becoming a friend, and I like the guy. He loves Wendy to distraction, and our girl deserves that."

Bo grimaces. "Not that she couldn't get that from another man who would lovingly dote on her."

Royce frowns. "You gonna put a ring on it?"

Bo's eyes widen substantially, and he gives a quick shake of his head in return.

"Then shut the hell up." Royce groans. "Tired of the barbs between the two of you anyway. Wendy needs some peace right now and to feel a part of something. Don't push her away by being a dumbass. Ya hear?"

Bo rolls his eyes and crosses his arms. "Whatever. Do you think his past relationship with Monika is going to be a problem?"

All I can do at this moment is shrug. "I hadn't really thought that far ahead. Though I believe Michael is a professional first and an emotional man second. He'll take care of Wendy's needs privately but tend to business as usual. Of that I have no doubt."

Royce nods. "Agreed. Now we just need to come up with the perfect campaign."

I grin. After last night's revelation with my brother, a new concept came to me in my sleep. "I think I've got that on lock."

Bo uncrosses his arms and sips at his water. "What's brewing?"

"Okay, imagine that we've got soldiers from the US, France, Germany, Japan, India—all the partner locations. Women and men. We show them in their uniforms or something respectfully similar that we can use on camera and in ads. The thread will be that they're soldiers, brave, and putting their lives on the line for the greater good. Then we'll show them in street clothes, with their families getting into a car, a single guy on the back of the bike or in the truck with his dog, a businessman in the coupe, etc. We'll showcase the environmentally friendly side by having the cars driving through different landscapes, by trees, near the beach, the mountains, the autobahn . . . with a narrator talking about low emissions."

Royce nods. "All right, all right, I'm feelin' this . . . Keep goin'."

I grin. "Then we'll use the tagline . . . 'Brave the ride.' Which will relate to the bravery of these soldiers, putting their lives on the line, now safe and sound, living life, getting into a new universal vehicle in different parts of the world."

Bo springs forward and claps, a smile stretching wide across his face. "I love it."

"Damn, brother, you must have had some serious think tank shit goin' last night," Royce applauds, picking up his steaming cup and lifting it to his lips.

"Actually, I met Paul last night at a bar."

Bo lifts his head back. "Ah, that's where the soldier angle came from. How is he doing anyway, and why didn't you call us to meet you?" Bo tilts his head, his dark gaze searing straight through me.

I adjust my red Ermenegildo Zegna woven box print tie that I've paired with a light-blue dress shirt, my tan blazer, and navy dress slacks. On my feet are my favorite brown Ferragamos. I purse my lips, lift my cup, and take a sip of the hot liquid, needing the caffeine boost to lay out the details of last night's confession session. Paul told me to bring the guys up to date so things won't be strange when we all get back and they meet Dennis for the first time.

I clear my throat. "Well, in regard to seeing Paul, he had something private he wanted to share with me."

Royce's and Bo's faces both show an expression of concern as they stay silent, waiting for me to continue.

"Uh, as it turns out, Paul met me at the bar to inform me about a life choice he's made."

Royce grins, and his cheeks turn a shade rosy. "Is he bringing home someone special? Oooh boy, Momma Ellis will be so happy."

I tilt my head. "You could say that, yes."

Bo slaps the table. "The little devil. Where'd he meet the woman? Hell, with Paul's good looks and hero status, I'll just bet he's bringing home some hot little spicy thing from another country. Asian, maybe? Petite, long black hair, big dark eyes. Hmmm . . ." Bo leans his head back and stares at the ceiling. "Maybe a statuesque German . . . ooh, I know. An *Italian*." Bo shakes his fingers in the air as though they've been burned. "I love Italian women. So passionate in the sack," he says reverently, as though he's recalling a time when he bedded one.

"Actually, you're wrong. He met someone in Brazil."

Bo's eyes glitter like cut diamonds. "Oooh . . . Brazilians are *muy calientes*," he gushes.

"That's Spanish, dumbass. Brazilians speak Portuguese." I sigh and ease back, pressing my thumb and finger into my suddenly pounding temples.

"Doesn't matter. A woman speaks another language in my ear while I fuck her . . . pure bliss." Bo kisses his fingers dramatically and flings his hand in the air.

"It's not a woman!" I fire off in a blunder of words.

Royce rubs at his chin. "Excuse me? I thought I just heard you say it wasn't a woman. What isn't a woman?"

"Paul's mate. It's a man. A guy named Dennis. I met him last night. He's cool. Proper and rather sweet, which I wouldn't have expected my brother to dig on, but whatever floats his boat." I shrug and sip at my coffee, allowing the two men to come to their own conclusions.

Bo leans forward and whispers, "Paul's gay?"

"Bi, actually."

"Wow. I did not expect that. He's always had a gaggle of chicklets to choose from when he rolls into town." He lets the words fall off, and then his face splits into a wide grin. "With beefcake soldier Paul off the market . . . that just means more for me."

Royce turns his head to Bo and, quicker than lightning, punches him in the arm.

"Thank you," I say to Roy.

He shakes his head. "Brother has sex on the brain twenty-four seven. I swear to God, one day it's going to bite you on the ass."

Bo grins. "If that's the case, let it be a busty brunette digging her teeth into my white ass."

"Mother hell," Royce rumbles, and runs a hand over his bald, shiny dome. "The boy will never learn."

His words have me chuckling. "Seriously, though, guys, Paul is gonna fly home and meet up with Mom and Dad. When we get back, he'll still be there. He's thinking of leaving the service. He's done twelve years, saved all his wages by not having a home outside of the bases. I think he's going to take some time for himself, maybe spend that with his boyfriend, Dennis."

"Tell me more about this Dennis fellow. He really cool?" Royce asks, lifting up his cup to the waiter, who grabs a pot of steaming coffee and brings it to the table, refilling all of our cups.

"Do you want breakfast?" the waiter asks.

I nod, my stomach grumbling.

Before I can tell him what I'd like to eat, he exits through a set of double swinging doors.

"Okay, anyway, Dennis seems like a nice guy. Timid, reserved, polite. Says he likes the Red Sox and the Pats, though."

Bo snickers. "I'll bet Paul told him to say that to win you and Pops over."

I grin. "Totally. We didn't spend much time together as they'd traveled all day and were tired. I'm hoping to hook up with them when I get home. Have him meet Sky, if she's back from New York."

"I'm glad that you and Sky worked everything out, brother." Bo reaches across the table and grips my forearm. "Was worried about the two of you, but I know she makes you happy . . ."

"Thanks, man."

"And who wouldn't be happy getting to bed Skyler Paige every night. Damn, your woman is smokin' hot . . ."

I reach across the table and grip his hand, his thumb pressed back in a way that if I keep pushing it will break.

"Dude!" Bo laughs heartily. "Okay, okay, I'm sorry," he says, but continues to laugh.

"I'm only backing off because you're right . . ." I smile playfully and let go of his hand. "Skyler is smokin' hot."

Royce chuckles loudly as the waiter comes back with a tray. He sets three bowls of what looks to be cornflakes mixed with dried fruit and granola or nuts in front of us. Then he puts down a pitcher of milk, a mixed bread basket with a variety of small containers that seem to hold butter and jellies, and a tray filled with cold cuts.

The three of us scan the strange breakfast, and my stomach growls again, announcing its dissatisfaction. At this point, I don't care what we eat as long as it gets in my belly. Now.

"Danke," I tell the waiter, who offers a slip of a smile before leaving us once more.

"Apparently we're having cereal and meat for breakfast." Bo cringes.

"Just eat it. It's food. Don't be an ingrate. They have different customs than our standard eggs and bacon or pancakes slathered in syrup. Besides, when was the last time you put something healthy in your gullet?" Royce flaps his napkin over his lap and grabs a roll and an orange-colored jelly.

Bo plucks a dried piece of fruit out of his bowl and pops it into his mouth. "You mean that half a slab of cow I ate last night covered in béarnaise with a baked potato sans veggies wasn't healthy? Blasphemy!"

"Not for your heart. Eat your cereal and like it. Give your body something it craves." Royce starts eating, and when Bo lifts his head to no doubt make an offhanded sexual retort, Roy pokes his fork toward Bo's face. "Don't even think about it."

Bo bites at the fork jovially. "Jeez, you guys are prickly this morning."

I pour a large dose of milk over my squirrel breakfast and tuck in. Within five bites I swear my molars are revolting and about to disintegrate into dust if I grind down any more on these rocks they call nuts in this cereal. I push the squirrel bait back and grab a soft roll. "When did you say Wendy and Mick will be here?"

"This evening. Gives us some time to flesh out the new concept with Monika, get her buy-in, and start making some preliminary plans." Royce bites down on a chunk of roll.

I nod through my own bite as Bo hoovers through his cereal.

Once we finish, Royce signs the bill, charging the breakfast to our rooms, and we all stand and head for the exit. Outside, we note that Monika has sent a driver with a sign with two words on it.

INTERNATIONAL GUY

I smile. "Looks like our ride is here."

Bo slaps me on the back. "I am lovin' this star treatment." He lightly smacks my face. "Keep bringing in these top-dollar clients, bro. A guy can get used to this."

I grin, taking in the beauty that is a spanking new OhM Bolt six-seater in gunmetal gray.

"Yes, he can."

***

"*Ich liebe es* . . . I love it!" Monika gifts us with her smile, showing a full line of white even teeth. Her blonde hair is sleek and down around her shoulders today, another fierce, perfectly fitted suit on her graceful form. "We will have to see about uniforms. I'm not sure each branch of the military will be okay with displaying their official uniforms on a television commercial or ad campaign for a car."

"Agreed. I'm sure we can work something out. Michael will have some ideas."

Her dark-blonde eyebrows rise up questioningly on her forehead. "Mr. Pritchard. So, he is going to assist in the project after all?"

I inhale long and slow, determining how I want to share this information. "Yes, Michael is a friend of ours. In fact his fiancée works for International Guy."

Her head tilts back. "Ah, I see."

"We want the very best to ensure the campaign goes off without a hitch."

"That is wise. Though I'm not sure we can avoid a hitch as it were. Michael and I still have unfinished personal business . . ." Her voice lilts and her eyes sparkle with awareness when she says Mick's name. Reading her body language, I can tell there is more than professional interest involved in her reply.

"As it were, it shouldn't be a problem as he is bringing his fiancée with him."

She blinks a few times, and her mouth drops open. "His woman is coming here?"

I grin. "Like I said, she's a member of the IG team. I have asked for her fiancé's assistance; it makes sense for them both to come . . . does it not?"

Her expression becomes guarded, and she eases back in her chair, then stands abruptly. With poise and purpose, she moves over to her desk, not meeting my gaze. "Yes, it makes perfect sense. I shall welcome them both to our team. Please do let me know what you have planned, as we are short on time and I worry that we will not be ready for the reveal at the time the partners and investors have agreed upon."

"Don't you worry, this team will do what it takes to perform nothing short of a miracle to make this project successful. It's not just your company's reputation on the line, it's ours as well."

Her lips tip in a purely disingenuous smile. "You are welcome to use the conference room I set up, and the two assistants are ready to move mountains as requested."

"Thank you." I stand up, and Bo and Royce follow.

"Gentlemen. I will catch up with you later."

Royce firms his jaw and leads the way out of the room. When both he and Bo go through the door, I stop and wave the guys off. "I'll be there in just a sec."

They nod and carry on down the hall to the room Monika set up. I close the door and walk back to her desk.

"Yes, Mr. Ellis?" Monika sighs and crosses her shaking hands over one another on her desk.

"Is there going to be a problem bringing Michael and Wendy on the project based on your history?"

She purses her lips. "I'm not sure what you mean."

Michael's words come back to haunt me.

"The thing about BDSM and D/s relationships that is crucial is trust."

"She became pregnant and attempted to pawn it off as mine."

Remembering them makes my blood boil, but she is the client. We're here to do a job and nothing more. Michael wouldn't be coming if he didn't think it was worth the potential emotional turmoil.

She tried to pawn off a child on him that wasn't his. Why would she do that? To save the relationship? If he couldn't give her what she wanted, why did she want him in the first place? Money? Maybe. He's definitely a good-looking guy.

Don't get involved any more than you need to be, Parker. Let it go.

My heart pumps in my chest, tooting a horn like a steam engine.

Trust your heart.

I rub my finger across the band of leather with Skyler's words to me burned into it. Sometimes you have to take a leap of faith for a friend, no matter what that could mean. It reminds me of a famous Malcolm X quote: "A man who stands for nothing will fall for anything." My father used to repeat that quote all the time when I was growing up. It stuck with me and has never been more relevant than right now. It's up to me to stick up for my friend, the risks be damned.

"Michael told me what happened between you two. It's not pretty. I understand you parted ways on unseemly terms. Now I'll repeat: Is having Michael and Wendy on this project going to be a problem? If so, my team will pack up and fly home, because our loyalties lie with them. International Guy will promise to do our best work, but we need complete compliance and a harmonious work environment to do it. Can you be certain that your past will not cause a problem?"

Monika's chin trembles, but she holds it together. "It is my fondest wish to have this project seen through to its fruition. And if, in that time, I have the opportunity to resolve some past transgressions with a good man, I would like to take that time. However, I do believe we can all work through this project professionally."

I suck on the inside of my bottom lip and evaluate the sincerity in her eyes and posture. She seems . . .

Defeated.

I imagine having your past come back to bite you in the ass will do that to a person. I know if Kayla showed up unannounced, begging for my forgiveness, I'd want to throw her to the wolves. The wolves being my mother first, Skyler second, and Momma Sterling third. Those three women together would whip that woman to shreds. Though Kayla is stupid, last I heard she was married to some ambulance-chasing lawyer hack in Chicago. Not that I care. The woman deserves every last bit of crap life can dole out to her. Still, a part of me hopes she sees the gossip mags and the pictures of Skyler and me together. Such a perfect revenge.

Shit, as I'm thinking of revenge, it dawns on me that Wendy likely knows about Monika and Mick's past. Knowing my fiery minx, she is not going to let sleeping dogs lie. She's ferocious in her protectiveness of those she cares about, and that's just with three guys she works with and considers friends. Her mate . . .

I wince. I almost feel sorry for Monika. Almost.

Silently I say a small prayer that Mick does not introduce Wendy to Monika.

"Okay, I'm going to go back to work. Figure out the phases of the print, internet, and video campaign. Can you send in your web developers first? We should get them working on revamping all of the cars' pages with new imagery and phrasing that suit the new direction."

She picks up her phone and nods. "Anything else?"

"Besides you leaving the past in the past? Nope." If shit hits the fan, we're out. Simple as that. International Guy does not risk its team members and friends over money in our pockets. It's not how we do business. It will never be how we do business.

"Agreed," she mutters through a tight jaw.

"I believe we understand each other. We'll have something for you to look at later in the afternoon."

Monika nods curtly.

"Then I believe we're done here." I smile and walk out of her office, knowing that I trusted my heart even when it could have risked our company a huge profit. The guys will understand. Money is not the end-all, be-all.

Money is meant to help one get the things one wants, aid in enriching one's life, not control it.

8

"Wow, honey, your brother is . . ." Skyler gasps. "Really *freakin'* good looking. Why didn't I know this?" She bites down on her lip as she studies the image I texted her earlier. The FaceTime app gives me a clear view of my girl looking at the photo of me and my brother. I also sent her one of my brother and Dennis.

Bo cracks up laughing across the room, obviously having heard her exclamation. He's sitting at the conference table while I'm tucked in the corner where a couple of leather couches and a small bar are set up.

"Shut up!" I holler over the phone.

Skyler smiles, and it makes my heart fill with need.

The need to hold her.

The need to feel her body pressed against mine.

The need to just be where she is.

It's a powerful thing, love. The feeling swoops in and destroys all reason, controlling your every thought.

"And this guy is his boyfriend?" She taps the screen.

"Yeah." I rub at my tired eyes.

"He's cute. A little conservative looking for a big bad soldier, don'cha think?" She taps her lips and bites at her finger.

I groan, briefly imagining that finger in my mouth or *her* mouth around something of mine, something much larger and sensitive.

"I don't know, I guess. Love's weird. You and I know that all too well." I grin, and she responds by blowing me a kiss.

"When is he coming to Boston? I want to host him and Dennis at my house if possible. Have a nice dinner. I'll cook."

"You'll cook?" My woman does cook well, though she hates going to the grocery store, so I'm surprised she'd offer.

"I, uh, hired a service to do my grocery shopping. So instead of picking items out while rolling through the store, I do it online." She shrugs. "Guess it's kinda the same thing."

"Peaches . . ." I sigh, knowing her fame gets to her.

She pushes her long layers out of her face. "It's okay. I figure eventually I'll find a little place I can shop at where I'll get to know everyone there and the newness of having a celebrity around will wear off. My friends in the industry say they find little places like this all the time. Kind of like Lucky's. No one bothers me when we visit there."

"Probably because my father would lose his cool if anyone bothered you. Plus, it's mostly a local crawl for blue-collar men. Many of them likely don't even know who you are, and the other half are just happy to have a sexy blonde grace their environment every so often."

She smiles. "Maybe. Anyway, I'm looking forward to meeting Paul. How's the campaign going?"

"Kickin' ass and takin' names! Boom!" Bo leans over my shoulder. "Hiya, Sky. We gonna see your fine ass back in Boston?"

I grind down on my teeth. "Watch it, brother."

Bo rolls his eyes as Skyler laughs.

"Yep. Finishing up the junket this week. I'll probably be back a day or two before you guys since you've extended it through Wednesday."

"Right on. See you at Lucky's, girl."

"You got it, Bo. Don't let my man take work so serious he forgets to laugh!"

Bo makes a crude sound with his mouth. "Never!"

Royce walks up and hands me a file. "Hey, girl. How's it shakin'?"

Sky wiggles in her chair. "Pretty darn good, if I do say so myself. How about you?"

Royce chuckles. "All right. It's all good." He taps my shoulder. "Michael's on his way up."

"Peaches, I gotta go. Call you later tonight before bed." I waggle my eyebrows, and she giggles like a schoolgirl.

"It's a date."

"Love you."

"Love you too!" She air-kisses the screen and ends the call.

I button up my sports coat and head to the conference room door, where I'm met by Monika holding a set of images of the cars she printed out. Down the hall behind her is a mob of people approaching. All in fine, richly made suits in varying shades of black, gray, navy, and tan. If I didn't know any better and we were in the US, I'd assume the company was being invaded by the FBI. At the front is Michael, leading the pack of people. By his side, holding the crook of his arm, is my Moneypenny.

"Wendy . . ." I say her name on a breathy gasp and head down the hall.

She grins wide, lets go of her man, and skip jumps over to me, where I meet her in the center of the long hallway. I open my arms, and she plows into my embrace, smelling of coconuts and happiness. I grin. "You look incredible!"

Wendy tilts her head back, her longer red hair slicked back like one of those Robert Palmer girls that my dad was in love with. Her lips are a bright, shiny bubble-gum pink, and her suit for the most part is . . . boring. I hold her at arm's length and take in her navy suit lacking any interesting color or adornment. The only difference with this one and the everyday suits women wear in offices is that hers happens to be super short, edging on the side of a miniskirt. Otherwise, it's not something I'd ever expect my loud and proud assistant to don. "What are you wearing?" I can't help but ask.

She grins and leans toward my ear as if to whisper a secret. "It's my power play suit. I'm going to catch the evil sub off guard by looking like one of her own kind, then swoop in and take a bite right out of the heartless tart." She squeezes my biceps. "It's good to see you, boss man. I can't wait to dig into this case and get my feet wet again."

Mick comes up behind his woman's back and loops an arm around her waist, leaning against her back. "Cherry, you're going to take it easy or I'm going to lock you in the hotel room with one of my goons to prevent you from leaving."

Wendy pouts. "The doctor gave me the okay," she reminds him.

While Wendy speaks, Monika has made her way to our little huddle. The rest of the people Mick brought are holding back, quietly waiting to be introduced.

Wendy and Michael must care very little that the client—Mick's ex—is standing behind me, because they continue candidly with their spat.

"Yes, well, it may be necessary to secure a new doctor who can listen to reason . . . ," Mick growls under his breath.

"You mean *bribed* to your way of thinking." She rolls her eyes. "He means bribed," she specifies to me for her own benefit, then turns around and prods at his chest with one long delicate finger. Yikes, I hate when women do that. It hurts like hell.

"Just wait until you get me pregnant again, big guy. You're going to be all kinds of crazy when it comes to dealing with doctors and midwives . . ."

He laughs. "No, because I've already interviewed nurses and midwives. We will have our own in-house nurse and midwife to help you tend to your pregnancy. No accidents this time. Whole hog, remember?"

Her eyes widen, and she loops an arm around his waist, kissing his neck sweetly. A pink ring of lipstick sticks to his skin, but Mick is so cool, the guy ignores it.

Royce clears his throat from behind me, and I turn to see that he and Bo are there waiting while the three of us, mostly Wendy and Mick, banter. Roy steps forward. "Michael, hello. Wendy, get yo' small booty over here and give me a hug, woman."

Wendy grins and beats feet over to Roy, who embraces her in a bear hug. "Good to see you, girl."

"It's good to be seen." She moves out of his arms and into Bo's.

"Hey Tink, lookin'"—Bo frowns, assessing her suit—"uh . . . professional."

She slaps his chest. "Just hug me and don't ask."

He does, closing his eyes and breathing her in before exhaling, as though a large weight has been removed from his shoulders. I know we all feel the relief of having her back after being so close to losing her.

"Enough, Montgomery. Wendy . . . ," Mick calls out to his fiancée.

She grins and pushes back but not before smacking Bo's face a little. "You look good . . . for a total man whore."

He grins and puts his hand over his heart. "She said I look good. See, Tink, you like me. You love me. You wanna get down with me," he teases, and Mick bristles.

At that point Monika finally steps up. "Michael . . . it has been a long time. Thank you for coming." She holds out her hand to Mick, who takes it briefly in one hand, wrapping his other around Wendy's neck. The lock dangles on its new white-gold band that loops at the base of her neck like a choker.

Wendy puts her hand out. "I'm Wendy, his fiancée." She tips her head to Michael.

Monika offers a hint of a smile and a weak handshake but nothing more. "And the people with you?" She frowns, not understanding their presence. Which I understand, because I don't know either.

"Experts pulled from a few of my European offices." He turns around. "We've got social marketing, commercial marketing, internet and search engine optimization, TV, radio, modeling and casting, content development, and so on. It's my understanding that the turn-around on this project is short. Many hands will be needed."

"You're a lifesaver, Mick." I move to take his hand in a fierce shake, gratitude coating my tone.

His lips quirk, but that's all I'm going to get from the currently stoic man. Usually he's a tad more personable with me, but business is business, and this particular company happens to be run by his ex-submissive. One who broke his heart and his trust.

Monika stands taller, lifting her chin. "Yes, Michael, I am in your debt . . ."

"No, your debt will be to my accounts payable. My services and team are expensive. Top dollar," Michael states flatly with zero kindness.

"Oh of course. OhM Motors will take care of any expense."

Michael puts his arm around Wendy. "Great. Where should we set up?"

I step back a few paces and put my arm out toward the conference room I exited down at the end of the hall. "The door on the left."

"And I assume IG has their concept and theme ready, Parker?" Mick asks.

"Absolutely. We just need the team that will make it come to fruition." I smile.

"Excellent. Lead the way."

I turn on my heel and head toward the conference room. As I glance back, Wendy is sending evil dagger glares at Monika as she passes. Which answers the question of whether or not he's discussed the full scenario from his past with Wendy. That would be a big, fat *yes*.

This ought to be an interesting few days.

New goal: prevent Wendy and Monika from being alone while getting this new campaign off the ground.

***

"No way . . ." Royce shakes his head the next day. "You've got to be crazy, Pritchard," he mutters. "I'm not doing it. My mother would kill me!"

"Hell yes! Count me in." Bo shimmies his lower half. "I'm excellent at making the ladies swoon." He rolls his hips in a shoddy impersonation of Elvis. "Thank you, thank you very much."

"What's going on here?" I sit down and groan, then tip my head back against the leather couch in the conference room. We ended the previous evening at midnight, then ate crappy bar food and finally went to bed at two in the morning. I need more sleep and less work. We've been at it for five hours and gotten so much done on the campaign my head is spinning and pounding out a tired rhythm.

I check my watch as Mick drones on about how he fully expects all three of us to perform accordingly. Jesus, it's actually afternoon. My stomach rumbles right on cue, demanding sustenance. I don't catch the full details of what he's talking about but nod anyway. "Yeah, okay. Whatever you need, Mick," I respond, without knowing what I'm agreeing to.

Mick is no joke. He's a fiercely intelligent businessman who knows exactly how to move the pieces of a project of this size. I just wish I hadn't drunk so much and had slept more.

One of the TV experts comes over to me and shows me a handful of head shots. "We can't get a guy rugged enough for the truck pic. We want to use an American soldier for this one and, of course, a German shepherd." He places six head shots on the mirrored coffee table in front of me. "What do you think about these men?"

I scan the faces while Michael lays out some plan he has for the end of the TV shoot.

Too *GQ*. Too skinny. Too beefy. I tap on each face and push it to the side. Who would have ever thought I'd be in a position to pick through mug shots . . . I mean head shots . . . of models for a commercial. Unfortunately after I've gone through the next batch, I touch one face. "He'd be good as the husband for the family-car one. Put that guy in a polo and jeans with a woman who looks like a female soldier."

The man's shoulders drop. "You've pushed out every image we've chosen for the soldiers."

"Probably because those are all models." Then an idea forms, and I pull out my phone and scroll through my received calls until I get the one I want.

"P-Drive, how's it hangin'?"

I grin at my brother's familiar rumble and adjust the beast. "A little to the left. Hey, I've got a problem with this project I'm doing, and I want to run something past you, if you've got the time."

"Brother, I've got nothing but time on my hands. Denny and I are just sitting by the hotel pool taking a load off and having a beer. Lay it on me."

I stand up and maneuver through the bodies in the conference room and step up to the window where I can stare out at half of Berlin. Fuckhot German cars race down streets teeming with a mixture of contemporary buildings, remnants of war-torn, crumbling relics, and some incredible structures that survived the bombings.

"I'm having a problem with casting soldiers for the commercial. They're not talking parts, but the modelesque faces and trim physiques I'm seeing don't convey *real* soldiers. Men and women who've been through hell fighting for their country, protecting civilians from tyrants and war."

"Okay, this probably has something to do with just seeing your own soldier brother after so long. That shit eats at you, which is completely normal, Park. I've been gone a long time. Wasn't easy on me, and I know it wasn't on my family. Never knowing where I was, when I was coming back, if I was safe . . . alive. Hell, it had to be hard. Part of why I'm planning on retiring from it."

I mull over his words. "I guess. I just feel as though choosing a seasoned model or actor lacks sincerity and reality, you know?"

He sucks in a breath, making a whistling sound. "Then why don't you just sign real soldiers? Tons are on leave or retired. Many that won't have a problem being part of an international campaign. I have friends in branches all over the world. How many do you need?"

Instantly an image of my brother jumping into the cab of the two-and-a-half seater with a giant dog has me smiling like a loon. "Including you, five, and I'd prefer two of them be women, and all ethnicities preferred. I'll text you the details of what we're looking for. Will you do it? I'd love to see my brother's face on camera, hopping into a truck, an American flag waving in the background. What do you say?"

"Two things."

"Name 'em."

"Does the job pay? And can I bring my boyfriend?" Humor fills his response.

I start laughing hard, bending at the waist as his simple request hits my gut. "Fuck yeah, it pays! Of course you can bring Dennis. Give us a chance to introduce him to the fellas too. Is it going to be a problem, though, having you on camera? You know, for your top-secret special ops assignments?"

"Nah, brother. For one, no one knows what I do, where I do it, or what I'm assigned to. They send me when it's in and out, rescue, retrieval, recovery, and other shit I can't talk about. Doesn't matter if someone sees my face on a job, because if they do, they won't be breathin' for long. Feel me?"

My mouth goes dry, and I nod slowly, then shake my head. Fuck no, I don't feel him. From what I'm getting, my brother just admitted that he does some seriously scary shit that ends lives. I do not need to know any more about that.

"I'll, uh, just make some calls after I get your text," Paul says.

Once I end the call I walk over to one of the assistants. "Need commercial model specs placed in a list and texted to this number as soon as possible."

Michael walks up next to me, holding some schematics he's run through on the internet distribution and press releases. "We need a car show."

My shoulders sink. "How fast can you put one together?"

"It's being done now. Contacted some European clubs and am getting the details together now. We'll have it up and running to open the weekend that the cars go live."

I nod. "I've got an issue with the models."

Mick frowns. "And that issue would be?"

"None of them look like soldiers."

"Probably because they're models and not soldiers," Mick notes resolutely.

"I'm having my brother call in some friends, see if we can't highlight real soldiers in the commercials."

Mick smiles devilishly. "I want their approval to use their name, rank, and branch of military. If we're going to tug on the heartstrings of worldwide viewers, we need names with faces." Mick claps me on the back. "Great idea."

I smirk, glad my concern actually adds to the concept.

"And we'll see the three of you tomorrow for hair, makeup, and wardrobe," Mick throws over his shoulder as he moves through the room.

"Wa-wait a minute. What are you talking about? Hair and makeup. The three of us?"

Michael turns around, crosses his arms, and levels a dark stare. "The addition to the campaign. For the tagline. 'Brave the ride.'" He blinks as though his words should ring some bells.

Ring-a-ding-ding. Nothing happens.

"Nope. Not sure what you're talking about."

He sighs. "Parker, you agreed to shooting the three of you and performing the tagline for the cameras. Monika and I believe having the three of you on the screen would be an excellent addition, and more than that . . ." He steps forward, leans into my headspace, and whispers, "It's a perfect payback for dropping everything, seeing my ex, and coming to your rescue."

I close my eyes. Fuck me.

"So, you're putting us on camera."

He smiles.

"Tomorrow? Do I even want to know what we're going to be doing?" All kinds of crazy ideas of the three of us in fatigues, pretending to be soldiers, fill my imagination. I guess that wouldn't be half bad.

His smile turns into a wicked-evil grin. "The three of you will be standing in front of a long mirror with three sinks, like in a locker room. You'll have just gotten out of the shower, your chests on full display with towels wrapped around your waists. Royce told me you have a penchant for leaving your clients little messages on mirrors."

"Oh, sweet hell . . ."

He keeps talking. "I thought to myself . . ." He brings his fingers up to his face and rests his chin on them. "What would be a grand gesture to the client, to the world, and of course, something that will make the three of you increasingly uncomfortable . . . ? For *my* pleasure, of course." He grins wickedly. "Then it came to me. Three naked-ish men, about to shave their faces, standing in front of a mirror with a can of shaving cream. Each of you will write one word of the campaign tagline on the mirror in front of you." He holds his hands out in front of him about a foot and glances to the sky, where he creates an empty box. "Brave." Another box a space over. "The." Yet another air box. "Ride." He grins maniacally. "Snazzy, right?"

I clench my teeth, grinding down on my molars. "Fine. If that's what it will take to pay you back . . ."

Mick tips his head. "Oh no, no, no. You see, my woman is all over me to have a genuine bachelor party, one I have decided you will now be planning. Seems my Cherry doesn't want me to miss out on the normal things in life. I've explained all I want is her, but alas, what the woman wants, she gets. Add that to your calendar. Since the wedding is soon, you'll need to get to work. I'll provide you with a list of invites, but I expect IG to be there."

I chuckle and shake my head. "You dirty dog. Fine. Whatever it takes to get back into the good graces of Michael Pritchard, I'm game for."

Mick smirks as Wendy comes up and loops her arm around his waist. "I'm hungry." Her gaze slips over to Monika's across the room, who's not-so-surreptitiously staring at the duo. "Take me somewhere *off-site.*"

"As you wish, my love."

She grins. "I do wish! Park, you hungry?"

"Actually, I am . . ."

Mick shakes his head once. Okay, that invite has just been rescinded.

"I'm gonna wait until the guys are done and get something with them. Maybe call Sky."

"Oh, she's doing good. Spoke to her this morning." Wendy wiggles her shoulders. "Her maid of honor dress is to die for. Pale yellow. Sleek. Sexy as shit with her golden hair."

I smile. Any mention of my woman and I can't keep back the dopey grin. "What about me?"

"We'll get you and Michael set on tuxes when we get home."

I step up to her side and ease her away from Michael but stay within hearing distance. "You know, Wendy, if you want to call it off, bail at any time, as the man giving you away, it's part of my job to supply you with an escape route . . ."

Mick growls and removes her from my grasp. "Not funny, Ellis."

"So funny." I choke back a laugh.

He narrows his gaze at me.

I hold up my hand, separating my thumb and forefinger an inch. "A little funny."

"Cherry, I believe you said you were hungry." He cocks an eyebrow and focuses on Wendy.

"Famished." She lowers her voice and runs her hand along his light-blue satin tie.

"Then let's get you fed. We'll be back."

"I'll miss you," I joke, and Mick's jaw tightens.

Bo comes up and hooks me around the neck. "It's almost too easy with him."

"It is." I start cracking up. "You hungry?"

"My stomach has eaten its way through my insides and is gnawing on my backbone," he delivers with no voice inflection.

I can't suppress my laughter. "Gross."

"Had you laughing."

I pat his shoulder. "You're always there to make a brother laugh."

"I take on that duty the same way I worship a woman . . . like it's my job," he says, deadpan.

"You're remarkable . . ." I deliver this in a way that should be an insult.

"That's what she said." He grins.

I shake my head and push Bo toward the other side of the room, where Royce is. I make eye contact, and Roy lifts his head, puts down his papers, and buttons his jacket before meeting up with us. "Time for some grub, I hope?"

"As long as we can keep this one under control." I point a thumb at Bo.

"What? You know you love me. You guys would be bored to tears if I weren't in your life, keeping you on your toes, laughing your cares away."

Royce claps the back of Bo's neck, and I nudge Bo's shoulder roughly.

"You're right. I guess we'll keep you." I rib him again.

"Damn straight." Bo frowns.

"How's about we get you a nice tall—" Royce begins.

"Chicklet?" Bo's eyes widen with unrepressed glee.

"Beer." Royce chuckles, that deep rumble like thunder cresting over a mountaintop.

Bo's face falls. "Second best, but it will do."

The three of us shuffle out of the building and into the waiting OhM vehicle. "Take us somewhere we can get a cold beer and an American-style burger, friend," I tell the driver.

"I've got just the place."

9

"This is insane." I cross my arms over my freezing-cold chest. "It's so frigid in here my nipples are going to crack like ice and fall off my chest. Does it have to be so cold?" I rub at my arms, which are covered in gooseflesh.

"I don't know what you're all griping about. I'm fine." Royce stands with his big feet apart, a white terry-cloth towel wrapped around his trim waist, the hem falling just above the knee. The guy is huge, and his skin, which a makeup artist is currently rubbing with oil, is a rich ebony color, a dark contrast to the sparkling-white towel. He smirks before winking at me. His abdomen is like one of those old-school washboards that people used to use to launder their clothes. Jesus, the man is cut. I mean, I'm no slouch, but I'm man enough to note my brother is toned as fuck.

"Well, I'm not standing here being rubbed by a pretty brunette, now am I?" I gesture to the makeup artist, and she grins.

"There are benefits to my job. This is one of them." She grins and slathers more oil down Royce's bare back. "Don't worry, you're next." She offers a saucy wink.

Bo saunters over in his own towel looking like a goateed tough guy with a muscular build and a lean waist. "Oooh, when is it my turn to be rubbed? Better yet, can we do it lying down?" His suggestive tone leaves nothing to the imagination.

I grit my teeth and just barely refrain from wringing his neck. "Ever heard of sexual harassment, Bo? That shit applies to clients too."

The woman oiling Roy stops what she's doing, looks Bo up and down, and apparently likes what she sees because her response says it all. "You. Me. After work. Maybe instead of me oiling you, I'll let you rub me down."

Bo puts his hand over his heart. "Woman, you're speakin' my language."

She snort-laughs. "Not hard to guess, player."

"Takes one to know one," he fires back, and she smiles wide.

Once she's done with Royce she hands me the bottle of oil. "I think your friend needs a little help with his back. Maybe the two of you can help each other. I need to find the soldiers." She smirks and saunters off, her hips swaying back and forth.

Bo watches her walk away. "Da-yum. I can't wait to take a bite out of that to-night. Mmm." He grunts.

Pouring some oil on my hands, I rub it over my arms and down my own chest. Bo mimics my movements, and we begrudgingly oil one another's bare backs with zero finesse.

"Ah, there're my models!" Mick, followed by Monika, shows up in a pristine black pinstriped suit and another satin tie, only this one is yellow. I'd bet Wendy bought him that tie since it's her favorite color. "They're perfect for this piece, don't you think, Monika?" He gestures to the three of us standing in nothing but towels and jockstrap-type undergarments. They want the little dip in our butt cheeks to be hinted at in the towel, so we can't wear our regular underwear.

"This sucks. You know that, right?" I state flatly to Mick, making sure he understands how I'm not impressed.

He responds with a Cheshire cat grin. "Yes, I do. Do you have anything you want to contribute, Monika?" Mick addresses our client, and she gazes up at him adoringly, a brightness in her eyes I hadn't seen before.

"Everything is just right when you're here," she says in a sexy timbre that would lead one to believe her response is twofold.

Before I can say anything, Wendy comes up behind the two. She chuckles, putting her arm through Mick's on his opposite side. "Funny, I tell him that all the time."

"Cherry . . ." He tips her chin up and kisses her softly on the lips.

"Cherry?" Monika says with disdain. "He used to call me Buttercup."

"Whoa . . . ," Bo says.

"Aw shee-it." Royce sighs.

"Not a good idea . . . ," I warn.

"Excuse me!" Wendy spins around to face Monika. "We doing this? Right now? Right here? Because I've got a lot of choice words to say about you." Something in her tone tells me her words are more of a promise than a threat.

Bo's eyes widen, and he covers his mouth with his hand. I step back a foot in order to avoid being part of any takedown that may occur.

Royce wades in. "Girl . . ."

I put my hand out and shake my head. "Not our deal, brother," I remind him, knowing that this is between Mick, Wendy, and Monika. "We should, uh, go . . . somewhere. Anywhere."

"The hell you will," Wendy blurts to us, then quirks her head with all the sass I know she has inside of her and directs her irritation Monika's way. "Let's get this out and done with right now . . . *Buttercup*." She enunciates the nickname with malice in her voice.

"My love, really, this isn't the time, or the place," Mick attempts. Ah, poor guy. He means well, but for the short time I've known Wendy, she's not been the type of woman you prevent from saying her piece. I've learned to ride it out.

Wendy's face contorts into an expression of disgust. "I don't think so, Mick. This ends here." She brings her attention back to Monika and points at her.

Why do women always do the pointing thing? I'll have to ask Sky.

"You may have had a history with my man, but you *don't* have a future with him. That would be me." She waves her hand to the top of Mick's hair down his frame and toward his feet. "All of this could have been yours. Fortunately, you screwed up, and now it's all mine."

"I'm sorry, Michael." Monika practically whimpers her apology.

Wendy's head jerks with rage. "Did I say you could speak? I wasn't finished."

Monika's lips flatten into a thin white line.

"You"—she points at Monika again—"betrayed his trust, lied your skanky ass off, and didn't deserve to wear his collar." She fingers the padlock at her neck. "Or his engagement ring." She holds up her hand, where the huge diamond Michael bought her refracts the light brilliantly. "Me, I love him more than life itself. I don't need to be pleasured by another man, because he gives me *everything* I need."

Monika frowns and swallows slowly, her neck muscles moving with the effort, her hands in fists at her sides. My guess is she's at war with wanting to respond to what Wendy is saying, being professional, and realizing that Wendy's right.

Wendy continues to lay it out for her. "I can see that you're sad you lost him. It makes sense. If I were in your shoes, not that I'd ever be stupid enough to be in your ugly shoes, but if I were, I'd want nothing more than to get him back. So, I get it. I get that you want to say you're sorry, make amends, remind him of the good times you've had. Except I'm here to say, honey, don't bother. What you don't know and I'm here to tell you is what Mick and I have is fucking *legendary*. What you had was forgettable." Wendy shrugs. "Sad, but true. Now, we have a campaign to finish with my team here. Can I trust that you're going to keep your comments to yourself and leave the past where it should be . . . dead and buried?"

Bo whistles under his breath. "Ouch. Harsh, Tink."

Michael puts an arm around Wendy's neck and fingers her lock, tugging on it. Her eyes sparkle like silver glitter when he does.

"Yes." Monika licks her lips nervously. "I just want to say I am sorry for how we left things. My actions back then are not who I am now."

Mick clears his throat. "And I'm sure your husband appreciates the difference." Mick's voice is in monotone, absolutely no feeling whatsoever.

"We're separated," Monika adds.

Wendy's entire body goes rigid, but Michael is quick to pick up on her discomfort. He rubs her clavicle with his thumb as he responds. "That's too bad. Thank you for the apology, but as you can see, it worked out for the best for me. I've got the woman of my dreams wearing my collar, my ring, and we're planning a family. We'll finish up the TV specials over the next couple of days, and we'll be out of your hair. My team will be able to finish anything else at their own offices, and we can all follow up via conferencing and emails." Michael's gaze meets us where we're attempting to shrink ourselves down and away from their conversation.

"Continue on, men. Wendy and I are going to check on the other sets." And on that note, Mick and Wendy present us with their suit-clad backs and coolly walk away, arm in arm, a united force.

Monika's shoulders drop in defeat. "I'm, um, sorry you had to witness that. It was unprofessional and—"

"We understand. How about we go over the scene so we can get out of these towels and back into our suits," I offer, trying to change the subject.

She nods in a numb way as though she's back in the past, not really paying attention to what's happening around her right now.

"Speak for yourself brother, I'm perfectly fine in my skivvies any time of the day," Bo adds, lightening up the tension that Mick and Wendy left in their wake.

Royce shakes his head and nudges Bo to his spot in front of the counter. We each have our own sink, a can of shaving cream, and a razor in front of us.

Monika lifts her chin and straightens her spine before walking over to the camera operators and crew. Bright lights as blinding as the sun flicker on and glow all around us. Instantly my skin starts to warm. Thank God!

"All right, turn toward the mirrors. We're going to scan each of you a few times with the camera. Then we'll have you each lift his can to the mirror. We'll scan the space again. Then one at a time, you will each write your word on the mirror. Got it?"

The three of us respond with our own versions of yes.

"Ready, quiet on set!" the director of the commercial calls out, and everything goes dead silent. "Action!"

The camera guys scan each of us from their angles and stop.

"Next, shaving can up . . . and I want you each to assess your skin, your face, move your body in small movements. Do what feels natural."

We follow their instructions and smile at our reflections, tipping our chins, assessing our level of hair growth, etc. until he calls out to stop.

"All right, Royce, you're up first. Action."

Roy shakes his shaving cream can and squirts out the letters onto the mirror until you can see the word "BRAVE" in all caps.

"Bo, you're up . . . ," the director mentions, and Bo follows with his own shake and squirt of the word "THE" along the mirror's surface.

"Parker . . ."

I shake my can, smile, and write the word "RIDE" in all caps to match the guys'.

"Okay, we'll have the mirrors cleaned and we'll do it again."

All three of us groan and moan like babies.

***

Eventually the director lets us leave and calls a wrap to our scene. Once we're dressed, I lead the guys over to the other set, where I can see Paul is already in a pair of camouflage fatigues. They aren't standard issue and they certainly aren't his real ones, but it sucker punches me in the gut seeing him in them. Reminds me that I'm lucky to have my brother back in one piece.

"P-Drive." He pulls me into his arms and claps my back hard. "We're almost ready to shoot." He waves over to Dennis, who is sitting in a chair off to the side and out of the way of where they're filming.

Behind Paul is a badass silver truck OhM Motors is calling the 2.5 Amp. All of the cars have a flashy name that relates to the electric nature of the cars' hybrid ability. To the right of this set, I see a tall, lanky fella in a uniform with the French Armed Forces color scheme standing in front of the 1 Volt, which is the motorcycle. On the opposite side is a woman wearing the German Army's duds with the black, red, and yellow flag stitched on the bicep. She's holding a baby on her hip, and her husband is opening the door while the camera follows them. She puts the baby into the sedan, which is called the 4 Watt.

"Dennis, come over here," I call out. "I want you to meet my brothers." Dennis strides over in a smart pair of navy dress slacks and a white polo. He's got a blue, white, and yellow scarf wrapped around his neck, a brown leather watch, and matching shoes. Black-rimmed glasses are perched on his nose, and his dark—almost black—hair is swept back in a neat, gentlemanly style.

"Parker, thank you for allowing me to come today. This is quite exhilarating seeing all of this behind the scenes."

"Guys, this Dennis Romoaldo, Paulie's man."

Dennis holds out his hand to Royce first, who takes it.

"That's Royce Sterling, my business partner, and Bogart Montgomery, our other partner." Dennis takes Bo's hand next before easing toward Paul.

Instantly Paul rubs the man's back as if he's soothing him.

Dennis smiles sweetly. "I've heard so much about you all. You are brothers from other mothers according to my Paulo. *Sim?*"

Bo and Royce both chuckle. "Yeah, you could say that," Roy answers. "Parker tells us you're from Brazil."

Dennis beams, his chest puffing up with pride as his cheeks flush a brighter shade of rose. "Yes. Rio is my home and the headquarters of my family's business."

"Oh? What do you do?" Bo inquires.

"My family is in international imports and trading. While I'm in Boston meeting Paulo's family, he's going to help me look at potential locations for a new warehouse as well as a shipyard in Boston Harbor. See what's available."

At that bit of information my ears perk up. "You're expanding and thinking of doing so in Boston?" I grin so wide my brother notices it instantly.

"No promises, Park. Denny has to do what's best for his business and himself . . ."

"And if his boyfriend just happens to live in a harbor town that is awesome for East Coast shipping . . . ," I gush, letting them put two and two together themselves.

Paul laughs. "Don't think I haven't thought about it, but I'm not pushing him. He's also looking at Texas and California."

"California is expensive," Royce adds thoughtfully. He keeps track of trends in business, especially when it pertains to capital. "Some of the most expensive yards are on the Californian coast."

Dennis nods. "That's what our research is finding too. There's also potential for Oregon and Washington."

"Those are better options monetarily, though it could make the ground shipping less profitable depending on your needs," Royce chips in.

"Exactly. Not as good as *Boston*," I grit through my teeth, narrowing my eyes at Roy. Hello, I just got my brother back, I'm not eager for him to fly all over the place with his mate just yet.

Bo chuckles and loops an arm around my shoulders. "Our boy here just wants his brother to be in Boston. He's going to push for it hard-core. Be prepared," he warns Dennis.

I scowl at him and shrug off his comradery. "Whatever. We don't need to discuss it now. Let's do the shoot and go out and have some food and drink on IG tonight."

Paul grins and squeezes Dennis's nape. "How's that sound? You good to go out with all the guys tonight?"

Dennis preens under Paul's attention. Honestly I'd never pictured my brother with a guy before, but he's rather attentive and sweet about the way he communicates with Dennis.

"I would love to spend time with the guys." Dennis's cheeks flush pink again.

Royce claps. "Okay, it's settled. I'm going to go check on the finance side of things with Michael. Bo, you want to give your input on the photos and ads?"

Bo nods.

"I'll make sure the rest of the commercials are working and moving in the direction we decided," I pitch in.

Paul hooks a thumb over his shoulder. "I should probably get back to my spot."

Right when he says that, a German shepherd puppy races through the set. *"Nein! Halt!"* shouts a crew member in German while running after the wayward dog.

"Uh, did I just see a cute, fluffy *puppy* run by?" I frown and scan the big space.

Bo smiles wide. "Hell yes. I want in on that action. I love dogs!" Bo spins around and chases after the guy who's chasing the dog through the sets, the puppy's long pink tongue lolling out the side of its mouth.

"That is not a giant, full-grown, badass dog. That is a cuddly puppy." I sigh and roll my eyes. "Gotta go deal with this. Dinner tonight. I'll invite Wendy and Mick too. She'll find us a place."

"Sounds good. Catch you on the flip," Royce says, and knocks fists with me.

I wave to my brother and Dennis and head for the two dumbasses chasing a puppy.

***

The music is thumping while I watch Bo grind all over the makeup artist he invited to meet up with us after we had dinner. The one thing about Bo is he'll have his fun, but with family and close friend time, he doesn't involve his chicklets. He keeps his playboy life mostly separate from his friends and family. He's never brought a woman to Lucky's. I figure when that day happens it will be the woman he's fallen ass over dick in love with.

Royce sets down a fresh, cold pint in front of me, a whiskey neat for Mick, and another gin and tonic for Wendy. He sips his own whiskey and shakes his head at the display before us. "Well, the brother has definitely got the moves. I should get up there and show him how a real man gets down and dirty with a woman." He smirks.

I grin. "Dude, I freakin' dare you. Twenty bucks says you can't get his girl to turn around and grind with you."

Royce sets down his whiskey after taking a generous swallow. "Shoot, brother. Watch and learn." He eases from his chair and saunters his way over to the dance floor.

"This place is awesome, Wendy. Great find." I smile in gratitude.

And it is. Earlier in the evening it was pumped full of food and dinner goers, but the second the clock hit ten it started to transform into a club environment. The dinner lights went low and neon lights took over, along with the addition of a DJ in the back mixing his beats. It's a combination of American hip-hop hits and rock, so our crew knows all the songs.

"Yeah, one of the TV crew guys recommended it." Wendy stands up, and Mick loops her waist.

"Where you going, love?" Mick squeezes her hip.

"Restroom."

He's about to get up and escort her when Dennis stands up. "I'll go over there with you." His gaze meets Mick's. "Keep an eye out, stretch my legs."

Wendy rolls her eyes. "You've got to get past this issue of yours of me not being within your sight." She levels him with an endearing smile and caress of his face.

"Never." He says the one word and nothing else.

"Ugh . . . men. Come on, Dennis, let's vent about how stupid men are."

Mick swats her ass as she's about to loop her elbow with Dennis's.

"I love men," Dennis responds earnestly. "Especially a man in uniform." He smiles shyly at my brother. "Explain this vent to me?" He frowns taking Wendy's arm.

She shakes her head. "You have got a lot to learn about playing hard to get. Don't worry. I'll teach you."

Paul's brows go up. "She is a fiery one, your fiancée." He gestures to Mick.

"That she is." He leans back but watches her ass as she goes.

"Everything okay between the two of you after the debacle today?" I nudge his shoulder, but he doesn't take his eyes off Wendy.

"It was . . . *difficult* to see Monika, but not because I miss her. Mostly because I truly wanted the best for her. I don't think she's happy, and that saddens me." He purses his lips and then lifts his whiskey.

I nod. "She had the opportunity to be happy with you. She passed on it. Now you've got a firecracker lighting up your world. You came out aces. Still, she chose her path. It was the wrong one. That's on her."

Mick slowly sips his drink, his gaze set on the hallway where the bathrooms are.

"You're dying to go follow her, aren't you?"

Mick's shoulders fall, and he drops his head toward his chest momentarily. "Christ, yes." His hand shakes where he holds the glass, and he focuses back on the spot she walked through.

"You talk to anybody about this fear you've got going?" I ask cautiously, no judgment in my tone.

He sighs. "Yeah. We're both seeing a counselor together and apart. Almost losing her, actually losing the baby . . ." He swallows and sets down his glass. "It's taken its toll. She's all I've got in this world that matters. Though planning the wedding, being open to another pregnancy, is helping. We're talking a lot about the future, what we want, and how we want it to look."

I clap him on the shoulder and squeeze. "It's good, brother. All good coming your way. And it's healthy to be sad and need to work things through. I've been doing the same with Skyler. Talking about it. Trying to get past the guilt . . ." I admit the hurt in my soul over what happened to Wendy.

Mick turns his light gaze to meet my own. "Why do you feel guilty? You had nothing to do with it. Do you think . . ." He blinks several times, staring into my eyes. "Aw fuck, man. Are you blaming yourself?"

A whoosh of fresh guilt and pain sears my senses, and my mouth dries up. I try to swallow against the sudden empty feeling filling me and reach for my beer, sucking back more than I should in one go.

Mick frowns. "Parker, neither Wendy nor I blame you or anyone on the team for what happened. That woman was ill. She's paying for her crimes; my lawyer is seeing to it. Justice is being served. Wendy is mostly healed, and being here . . ." He leans closer. "I've not seen her this happy since your last visit. She lights up around the team. Do I like that three men have such a hold on her heart? No, I don't, because I'm a jealous bastard. Do I trust her? With my life. Do I trust you? Yes. Royce? Absolutely. Bo likes to push limits. I don't appreciate his personality and will continue to push back. I've accepted that in order to have Wendy's love in my life, I have to allow her to love others too."

I smile huge, put my arm around the guy's shoulders, and give him a manly half embrace. "We love your woman, and each one of us would die before she got hurt again. If it had been in my control . . . I would have taken that bullet."

Mick flattens his lips and places a hand at the crook of my neck and shoulder. "I do know that, and I thank you. Please let the guilt go. Let's all focus on the good in front of us." He tightens his hold on my neck. "But don't you dare give my woman an out on our wedding day. I'll come after her with guns blazing. There is nothing that will keep me from making her mine in every possible way. You got it?"

I laugh hard until he squeezes my neck a little more forcefully. "Dude, I got it! I was just joshing you. Besides, she wouldn't take the out."

Mick lets go, fluffs his sports coat back into place, and flattens his tie of any creases. "Be that as it may, I will not take any chances. She means too much."

I sip my beer and turn toward him. "Thank you," I say randomly, but the gratitude is real and full of emotion. I owe him a lot. More than he realizes.

He narrows his gaze. "For what?"

"Coming here. Saving our asses. Dealing with shit you didn't want to deal with to help out a friend. Take your pick."

Mick nods, inhales deeply, and watches the doorway Wendy slipped through. His eyes brighten suddenly, and he smiles as Wendy appears next to Dennis, walking our way. "Just keep my girl happy when she's on your time, and we'll call it even. Except, you still have to host my bachelor party."

I grin. "Not a problem. I've already enlisted Bo, Royce, and Paul's help."

Mick crosses his arms. "Great. I can just imagine what Curly, Moe, and Larry will come up with."

"Hey . . ." I clap his back again. "We've got your back."

Wendy struts our way, wiggling her hips and smiling. She points to Royce and Bo on the dance floor. "Are you two catching this? It's a Bo and Royce dance-off." She scrambles for something in her purse and pulls out her phone. "This is going to be epic. Gotta catch this on film. Blackmail material for later . . . woot woot!"

I follow her gaze and find Royce grinding down on the pretty makeup artist. She's got her hands all over his body, up and down his sides. Though Bo is no slouch either. He's at her back, hands hooked on her hips so she's in a manwich, smiling like the kitty that just got served a fresh bowl of cream.

"Damn, I owe Roy twenty bucks."

10

The screen across the open auditorium-style conference room lights up with the image of a man tossing his toddler in the air. His pretty wife comes up to his side, wearing fatigues with the German flag patch on the arm. As they walk, her uniform turns into a flowing dress. He opens the door of the 4 Watt sedan, and they settle the baby into the car. That image changes to a man, my brother, in a set of camouflage fatigues. He's got dirt and grass smudges on him. As he walks up toward the 2.5 Amp, he's wiping off the grass and dirt as though he's shedding his skin. The fatigues turn into a pair of Levi's and a T-shirt with the American flag emblazoned on the front. Right as he's about to get in his truck, he leans down and picks up a German shepherd puppy that licks his now-clean face. He smiles wide for the camera, puts the dog in the front seat, and enters the truck. Next, we see an image of a man in a French military uniform running down the street. The uniform turns into a pair of black dress slacks, a leather jacket, and a scarf around his neck as he straddles the 1 Volt and zooms off down a Paris street, the Seine and the Eiffel Tower in his rearview mirrors.

A couple of more images fly through the commercial of the other cars driving through mountains, along a beach, through snow and fields, words on the screen flashing the cars' environmentally friendly nature, before the scene lands on the three of us in front of the mirrors.

They've got us wiggling our towel-clad booties. Bo's singing into his shaving can, I'm smiling wide, and Royce is laughing before the music gets louder, and then the announcer's voice comes through.

"At OhM Motors, we're taking you through every phase of your life in a series of vehicles that don't corrupt life but add to it. All you have to do is . . ."

Then it shows the three of us writing the words "BRAVE THE RIDE" on the mirrors right as the announcer says the same tagline.

The last image is all of the cars lined up in different colors and the tagline . . . "For every phase of life . . . brave the ride. OhM Motors."

When the screen goes blank, the fifty or so employees sitting in the theater-style chairs start clapping wildly. The lights around us come back on, and Mick and I, alongside Monika, approach the front of the room.

Monika speaks to the crowd in German and then hands the microphone to me.

"Thank you all for watching. We hope your enthusiasm spreads across the globe. We truly believe the Brave the Ride campaign will take OhM Motors and the new line of cars blazing into the future. We showed you a mix of the military forces in this sample so you can see a glimpse of what each tailored commercial will look like. Each one will have soldiers and uniforms from their own military branch and country. Monika will present the German commercial and the additional marketing plans to the board in a couple of weeks before the launch. International Guy is happy to have been part of such a cutting-edge release. And now, I'm going to give the mic to the CEO of MP Advertising, who will give you additional details about the launch."

The crowd claps as I hand the mic to Michael.

"*Danke*, everyone. We are thrilled with how the commercial came out, the concept and theme all contributed by International Guy. Thank you, gentlemen."

I bow with my hands in prayer position at my chest.

Audrey Carlan

"The campaign will launch with the commercial translated into fifteen different languages, going live in twenty countries. A car show will launch the line with the aficionados and get some media press the week of release. We have the website ready to go live at the push of a button, again, translatable in fifteen different languages, available worldwide. We've secured a few television spots where Monika will present the vehicles on late-night and morning talk shows, etc. A list of those will be provided. Newspapers across the world will have your cars announced in their transportation sections. This is a very costly campaign, but one I assure you will be successful. Thank you all for your contributions over the last week. We've accomplished so much, and none of this could have been possible without your talent and hard work. Now it's your turn to 'brave the ride.' We wish you all the best of luck."

The crowd stands up and claps loudly. He hands the microphone to Monika and shakes her hand, then turns, and the two of us shake hands before he continues down the line of his top executives, then to Bo, Royce, and other personnel who have come to the front.

Monika comes up behind him and taps him on his back. I scan the space and notice Wendy across the room talking to another member of Mick's team.

"Michael, uh, may I speak with you privately?" She firms her spine and lifts her jaw as though she's ready to battle.

His smile flattens into a grimace. "No, you may not. My work here is done—"

"Michael, you can't leave without us talking about the past. There was so much love between us, and I know, if given the chance, I could make you happy again . . ." Her tone is pleading, and I'm at war with the desire to whistle loudly to get Wendy's attention and/or break it up myself.

Turns out, I don't have to because, as she tries to reach for him, he steps back a couple of paces, running into me. I stop his exit but stand up next to him in male comradery.

"Monika, God willing, this is the last time you will ever see me. I came here for Parker, Wendy's employer and best friend. I'm not here for you. I don't even think about you."

"But we have so much history . . ."

He grates through clenched teeth, "And that's all it is. *History*. I would appreciate it if you'd stop embarrassing yourself, and *me*, by hanging on to something that is long dead."

"You loved me once . . . ," she counters.

"Goddamn it! I didn't know what love was back then," he blurts out on a growl. "I know what it is now because of the goddess who wears my ring and my collar. I bow down to her every night at the same time she kneels at my feet. Submissive. Open. Loving. Giving me everything I could ever want or need and waiting for me to give it in return. And I do. With my entire fucking soul. We never had that. You never gave yourself to me wholly. Trusted in me to give you the world."

"Michael, I still love you . . ."

His entire body goes ramrod straight, and he sneers. "You don't know what love and trust are. I'm done. We're done. This. Is. Over. Let it go. Let me go."

"I don't know how." She tries to grab for his lapels, and I ease in front of her and lightly lead her back.

"No more. From here we all go our separate ways. Your campaign is done. It's what you wanted."

"Go back to your husband, Monika," Mick states flatly. "Do the right thing. Commit fully to someone who loves you in return, because it's not me, nor will it ever be."

At this point Wendy bounces up, smiling wide, her cheeks flushed with excitement. "That. Was. Awesome!" She flings her arms around Mick, not knowing what just transpired. He wraps his arms around her, lifts her up off her feet, closes his eyes, and buries his head against her neck, where he kisses her several times on the collar and skin.

"You ready to go home, my love? You've got a date with Skyler and the guys' mothers and sisters for a full spa day to tend to."

She beams and nods. "Heck yes. And I get to have champagne!" she gushes.

He frowns, sets her back on her feet, and places his hand over her abdomen. "And what if you're already pregnant?"

"I won't know that for sure for another two weeks. Just because we're trying doesn't mean it's taken. I get to drink until that stick turns pink, Mick. You promised!"

He chuckles, his eyes staring into hers. I chance a glance at Monika, and her lip is quivering and her eyes filling with tears. Then an expression comes across her face. I recognize it like the back of my own hand. It's defeat. She sniffs, firms her stance, and turns to me, her face now a mask of professionalism.

"Parker, I want to thank you for coming, bringing MP Advertising in, and making a remarkable campaign. I will be proud to present it to the partners and the world in the coming weeks." She holds out her hand for me to shake.

I take her hand in mine. "I'm glad things worked out well . . ." I turn my head to look at Wendy and Mick still speaking in hushed tones, completely lost in one another. "For all involved. I think, given a little time, you'll understand that too."

She licks her lips and swallows slowly. "Perhaps I will. For now, I will mourn the loss of what could have been and learn from it."

I smile and squeeze her hand. "That's all any of us can do. Take care of yourself. Let us know if you should want any further assistance with the launch. We can be available by phone, email, and video conferencing if the need arises."

"Have a safe trip home, Mr. Ellis."

***

Lucky's is full of patrons as the three of us mosey in the doors. At a huge table in the center is my family. Paul, Dennis, Ma, Pops, Rachel, Nate, and running at full speed, my dream girl, Skyler. She launches into my arms, and I catch her by the ass and upper back. Her legs wrap around my waist, and her lips land on mine. She kisses me hard once, twice, and then pulls back, her cheeks flushed, her hair a wild halo of golden waves, and her berry lips glistening.

"I missed you so much! And I have tons to tell you!" Before I can respond, she peppers my entire face with kisses.

I crack up until she loosens her legs and slides down my body. "Hi, Peaches." I kiss her much more softly than she kissed me, and her peaches-and-cream scent wraps around me like a fuzzy blanket. I dip my nose into the crevice where her neck and shoulder meet and let the peace it brings fill my tired body and mind.

She holds me for a full minute as I become grounded once again, my legs firmly planted to the floor as I connect with her. Bursts of electricity shoot through my limbs, and I charge up in her presence. God, what this woman does to me is unlike anything I ever could have dreamed of feeling while in a relationship.

I tunnel my hand into her silky hair and caress her cheek and her bottom lip with my thumb. "Can I say hi to Ma and Pops, or do you need to tell me everything right now?" I grin but wait for her reply.

She wiggles where I hold her loosely by the back of the head and hip. She tips her head from left to right, her lower lip caught by upper teeth. "I guess you can since it involves them. Hurry, though."

I ease my arm around her shoulders and move over to the table. She slips out of my embrace, and I hold her chair out for her to sit before going over to my dad and hugging him. He claps me hard on the back several times.

"Good to have you home, son."

"It's good to be back."

I move into my mother's arms, and she squeezes me tightly. "Both of my boys in the same place at the same time. I'm in heaven."

I kiss her cheek and let her hold me for a little while until she lets go and bosses my dad. "Randy, get some drinks for these boys. They look parched."

"Woman. I know these boys like I know my own reflection. Just hold your horses." He bristles but heads to the bar. When he gets closer he turns around. "You could help . . ."

Her face contorts, and I can see the sass is about to come out. "Help? I gave them life. That's my golden ticket forever!" she fires off, but bustles over to his side.

I chuckle, take Paul's outstretched hand in a shake, and nod to Dennis, who's sitting primly next to him, taking in our crazy group.

"Everything go okay with the introduction?" I gesture my head to our folks at the bar.

Paul smiles wide and puts his arm around Dennis. "Right as rain, bro, right as rain. All is good in the Ellis household. Mom's just happy I'm home and healthy. Plus, she thinks Dennis here is 'super cute'—her words, not mine. I think it was a bit of a shock, but they're rolling with it, which I'm grateful for."

I grin and fist-bump him. "Good to hear. It will get even more comfortable as time goes by."

Paul nods, lifts his beer, and takes a swallow. "Absolutely." He hugs Dennis tighter. "Because I don't see anything changing anytime soon."

Dennis beams under my brother's praise.

Nate clears his throat from behind me. I turn and shake his hand. He gives me the half hug, after which I lean over and kiss Rachel on the cheek. "Good to see you guys too. Was missing my shadows for a while there."

Rachel grins and punches me in the arm.

"Ouch! You've been lifting more weights or what?" I joke.

"As opposed to any other time?" she says, deadpan.

"Good point." I ease past her to sit next to my woman. "Hi, baby. Now what's this news you've got?" I dovetail our fingers together, just happy to sit close and touch her after ten days without her.

"Well, first of all, the new movie, they're going to do some filming here in Boston. Isn't that awesome!"

"It is. Means you'll be away less. I like the sound of that for sure." I dip my head and kiss her neck, wanting her scent all over me. I've gone too long without it. At least it feels that way. I sigh against her skin and kiss her there. She runs her fingernails through my scalp, and I close my eyes, humming with the pleasure her touch brings.

"Honey, you're tired."

"Yeah, didn't sleep much on the plane. Was trying to knock out some work. Royce says we need an attorney, been trying to locate one in the area, put feelers out, but nothing has come of it. Mick says he's got one he uses who he found out is moving back to Boston. With the workload we've already got and the next client we're set to meet with next week, we need a full-time attorney."

She frowns. "What's your next case?"

"Washington, DC. Pharmaceutical company. Something having to do with moving legislation on a specific bill. Before we sign on, we need an attorney who can not only protect us, but lobby on the Hill on the client's behalf."

"Sounds complicated."

"It is."

She cups my cheek and kisses me. "Well, for now, let's get you filled with food, booze, and family." She leans in and lowers her voice. "And then later, I'll let you fill me with you."

"Have I told you lately I fuckin' love you?"

"Not in the last twenty-four hours."

"I fuckin' love you, baby."

She smiles huge. "I love you too."

"Ah, I love you; no, I love you more, kissy face, kissy face . . ." Bo mimics air kisses. "You two make me want to hurl." He fake gags.

"You're just jealous because you don't have a woman to welcome you home."

"Oh, I do . . . two in fact, ready and waiting at their apartment. Twins."

This makes the rest of us gag, and Royce and I wad up the napkins and pelt him with them. "Gross. Keep your kinky stories to yourself, bro."

Bo raises his hands. "What? What'd I say?" He grins maniacally, knowing exactly what he said and having gotten the exact reaction he wanted. Our own personal bar clown.

Pops and Ma come back holding trays of drinks, mostly beers and whiskey. Nate and Rachel accept the waters they set in front of them and a single glass of white wine for Skyler.

"Bogart, son, you should never risk dating sisters. Nothing but trouble will come your way," my dad warns.

My mom nods in agreement and puts a hand to a hip. "Besides, you'll never find the one if you're always playing the field."

"Who says I'm trying to find the one?" Bo grins sheepishly.

Paul hooks his arm around Dennis, who cuddles against Paul's massive side.

Mom huffs at Bo's comment. "Bogart, every man needs a special someone . . ." She glances at Paul and Dennis. "A good mate in their lives. No one should be alone. Humans are not meant to live their lives alone. My fondest hope is for you to find the right person for you."

Royce and I sit back and just let my mom spread her wisdom.

Bo plays along. "How will I know when she's the right one?"

Oooh, this is dangerous territory. If you allow Momma Cathy an inch into your dating world, she'll take more than a mile. She'll take the entire Eastern Seaboard.

"Well, the right woman for you should set your heart on fire. You should be unable to stop thinking about her. You should dream about her. Imagine a future with her eyes in those of your children."

"What if I don't want children?" he pipes up, completely serious.

"Fuck . . ." I groan and slump against Sky.

"Shee-it, brother, now you've gone and done it."

My mother bristles where she stands. The concept of one of her boys, even one of her adopted sons, not wanting to have children is incomprehensible. Her mothering heart can't handle such a blow. She clutches at her chest. "My goodness, Bogart. Bite your tongue, or the good Lord will make you sterile."

He grins. "That could actually improve things . . . with no risk of pregnancy . . ."

My mother places her hands together and whispers up at the ceiling. I catch bits and pieces.

"He knows not what he says, Lord," she mumbles, and I crack up. I can't help it. Jet lag is overtaking my mind as the full beer I've sucked back in what feels like two seconds swirls pleasantly in my gut.

Skyler wraps her hand over my mouth. "He's really tired," she says apologetically while I laugh through her fingers.

"All I'm sayin', Momma Ellis, is that I don't think I want children, and the odds of me settling down are slim to none. Hell, falling in love is a complete no-go. It's never happened to me before, and it's never going to." He sucks back a long swallow of his beer and eases his chair back so he's teetering on the back legs alone. "I'm happy. The women I date know the score. Everyone wins."

My mother shakes her head. "You mark my words, Bogart Montgomery, son of mine by choice: one day a woman is going to knock you on your ass, and you won't know what hit you."

He grins and slams the chair back down and smirks. "If that day happens, you'll be the first person I come to for advice."

His statement seems to appease my mother for the moment. "And I'll be here for you. Ready to smack some sense into you. Now who's ready for some pasta? The cook has made an amazing Bolognese with fat rigatoni, a parmesan garlic bread, and a hearty salad."

I shake my head as my mouth waters and my stomach grumbles. "In the same sentence my mother can put a man in his place and fill his stomach. I love my family!" I raise up the last of my beer, and everyone around me does the same.

"To an amazing family."

Everyone at the table clinks their glasses into one another's, and I sit back, my girl in my arms, beer in my belly, and the people I care about spending quality time with together. Life couldn't get any better.

Right as I think that, my phone buzzes in my pocket. Except when I go to grab it, I realize my phone is in my breast pocket. It was Skyler's buzzing.

She chuckles and pulls it out in front of her.

The background display shows a picture of us in London sitting on that bench in the old church. She looks stunning with the sun sprinkling in through the trees, casting light across her beautiful face. Me, I look like a guy who's got the whole world in his arms, probably because I did . . . I do.

A prideful sensation puffs out my chest, and I take in the scents and sounds of my father's familiar bar, which lull me into a deeper pool of relaxation. Being at this table with my family all around me, laughing, imbibing, and the woman I love filling my soul with her simple presence, the case closed, client happy—there isn't much more I could ask for.

"Just a text," she murmurs, and clicks on the button to open it. I look away, wanting her to have her privacy, until I feel her entire body tense against mine.

I glance down at my girl's face, which has gone completely white. "What's wrong?"

SKYLER

Fear rips through my nerve endings and heats my blood as I stare down at the strange text.

"Park . . ." I gasp his name as my hands start to quake. "It's from . . . th-the p-person. It has to b-be," I stutter, and hold up the phone for Parker to see the message.

To: Skyler Paige
From: Unknown

Glad you're home. I can't wait to see you. Soon.

Parker's jaw firms, and a muscle in his cheek throbs visibly when he sees who it's from. He snatches the phone and reads the message. The fear I felt before turns into a moment of mild panic. My heart starts pounding a teeth-rattling beat in my head as anxiety slithers down my spine like a cold, wet snake. I glance around from table to table, scanning faces, body language, seeing if anyone is on the phone. Trying to see if I can figure out who it might be.

Could the person be watching me now?

Is he here? Listening, learning everything there is to know about me?

A tremble works its way through my body, and Parker's arm tightens around my shoulders.

Solid. Strong. Impenetrable.

He leans against me and puts his lips to my temple. "Nothing is going to happen to you, I swear it on my life, Skyler. I'm not sure how this number was traced, but we'll get to the bottom of it. Rachel and Nate are here. The guys are all here. Ma and Pops are right there." He nudges my head so that I'm looking at the familiar faces. "My brother could drop a potential threat in less than half a second. He's trained for it. I'm certain he's already assessed every single human being in this room. It's part of his makeup. That shit is in his DNA. If there were a threat in any way, shape, or form, he'd already have handled it. Okay?" I stay silent as he continues. "We're in a public restaurant. You. Are. Safe. You hear me?"

I nod against his lips, but he has more to say.

"I'd never let anything happen to you. Whoever this is will be found. I promise you, baby. Now I'm going to let you go for a moment and discuss this with Nate. Okay?" I glance up and watch as Parker makes eye contact with Nate, giving him a chin lift.

Nate eases out of his chair and comes to sit right next to us. "You okay, Sky?" he asks in a low tone.

I shake my head because I'm not okay. No. Way. I'm *freaked out*. Big-time. Parker hands him the phone. Nate scans the words, and I watch as his face becomes hard and expressionless. I'm certain by the stillness that he's working hard to control his anger on my behalf. Pretty much the same way Parker looks right now.

"I've got a call in to Wendy. She agreed to meet with me tomorrow. I think we should do it together." His voice is stern and direct.

Parker nods.

"I want to come." I toss my hat in the ring but am greeted by two unhappy faces, one I hope to stare into the rest of my life, the other the man I've hired to protect me.

"Skyler, I don't think it's a good idea—" Parker tries, but before he can go into a long, drawn-out excuse, I cut him off.

"No. This involves me. I want to know what's going on. It's the only way I'm going to feel safe. Period. Nate, I'm sorry to do this, but I shouldn't have to remind you that you work for me."

He clears his throat and wipes at his scruffy face. "No reminder necessary. What you say goes."

Parker growls. "Skyler . . . you don't need to be worrying about this. We've got it covered."

I scowl. "Do you? Do you really? Because from where I'm sitting, we've gotten yet another message, on a brand-new phone number no less, and we're no closer to finding out who it is since you took my other phone back in London. What was that, a month or so ago?"

Parker closes his eyes and rubs at his temples with his thumb and forefinger.

"Fine. We'll discuss what we know when we get home. We're enlisting Wendy's help because whoever this is, is getting to your personal information." He focuses his attention on Nate. "Did Tracey send over the fan mail?"

He nods. "Yeah, I've got the ones that make Rach and me uncomfortable ready for your review." He grunts. "I mean, for the two of you to review."

"Thank you. For including me and for being on top of this. I appreciate you, Nate. You know that. You and Rachel are a huge part of my life now. You're like my family. We need to figure this out together. As a team."

His jaw tightens, and I swear it's as if he were chewing on rocks. "Your safety is our number-one priority. Which is why, now that I see that text, I think we need to share this information with the police."

I jerk my head back. "The police?"

Unfortunately I say it so loud the entire table stops talking and drinking and looks at me.

"What's this about the police, sunshine?" Cathy asks, a mother's concern coming to the forefront.

Ugh. The last thing I want to do is involve Parker's family, especially his parents. "Oh, nothing. Nothing. Just talking shop. Talking about the portion of the movie that's going to be shot in Lucky's!" I say, changing the subject.

Nate's lips flatten, and he leans back in his chair, crossing his arms over one another. His muscles bulge in the lighting of the pub against the hem of his tight-fitting tee.

"Oh yes! Our Skyler got us a deal with a real movie company!" Cathy spills to the group. "At some time in the next month or so, we're going to have a crew set up to do some filming of Skyler's movie." She smiles at me, her face filled with pride. I can't express in words how that gaze acts as a soothing balm over my distress. She reminds me so much of my own mother. Not in looks or words but in actions. My mother would mother hen this group, treat them all like her very own baby chicks. And my, oh my, she would have loved Parker. Not only is he handsome, compassionate, and kind, his love for me can be seen like a beacon sprouting from his chest. I can feel it in every look, each subtle touch of his hand, and in his smile.

Cathy continues telling her story, and I try to take my eyes off of my man long enough to catch it all.

"And the best part: every time they show the character in his bar, he'll be shot in Lucky's, so we'll get to reap the profit of this agreement for the next couple of years!" She hoots and waves a bar towel in the air with glee.

The crowd at the table claps, and raucous cheers are heard from those who are not part of the worried party of three huddling over a crappy text on a stupid phone.

I straighten my shoulders. "I'm done talking about this. Tonight is about friendship, food, and family. The most important *f*s there are. Our problem will still be here in the morning when we can discuss it at length and come up with a plan . . . together. Not just between you two." I point an accusing finger at Parker and Nate.

Parker pulls me against his side, hugging me close to his body. I snuggle in because he's warm and it feels good, but more than that, it feels safe. Like home.

Nate stands, his face devoid of emotion as he moves away from the table. "I'm going to walk the premises," he whispers to me, and then to nods to Rach, signaling that she's on me alone.

She returns his gestures.

Parker dips his head down to me and kisses my temple, then brings his lips against the shell of my ear. Tingles of pleasure and arousal zip through my body, replacing the earlier dread and uncertainty I was holding on to.

"You know, there's one more *f*-word you forgot to add."

I frown. "Hmm?"

"*Fuck*. Tonight is about friendship, food, family . . . and *fucking*. You're not going to sleep tonight without one helluva a welcome-home fuck."

I press my lips together, then lean my head back onto his shoulder so he can bring his lips closer to mine. "Maybe I wasn't planning on fucking tonight."

His eyebrows rise up on his forehead.

"Maybe I was planning on making love with you. That's an *l* word or an *m-l* word if you put them together. Making love."

He nuzzles his nose against mine. "Oh, I'll make love to you all right . . . right after I fuck you to kingdom come. Does that sound okay for this evening's plans?"

Images appear of him taking me against the headboard, diagonal across my king-size bed, on the floor, bent over the couch—the possibilities are endless. A soft whimper escapes through my lips, and he kisses it away, delving his tongue in deep and thoroughly, unlike our fast-and-hard kisses when he entered the bar. This kiss is deep, wet, and a promise of things to come. When he pulls back, he nips my bottom lip.

"I think that means you're on board with the plans." He grins sexily.

"I'll be the naked one waiting." I stand up abruptly, and all the eyes lift to mine. "I'm really tired. It was good to meet you, Paul and Dennis. I hope to have you over for dinner soon. Royce, Bo, I'll see you tomorrow. Cathy, Randy, thank you for having me. Rachel?"

She gets up and gets close to my side. She pops her phone open and speaks quietly into it, probably getting Nate to bring the car around.

I turn around to Parker, who has stood up and is speechless at my sudden need to flee. I cup his cheeks and kiss him hard on the mouth.

"Hurry home, honey," I say with as much lascivious intent as possible.

"Oh, I will. You can count on that." His tone is thick with arousal, his normally light eyes now a desire-filled, stunning dark blue.

I wink. "Remember, I'll be waiting."

The end . . . for now.

WASHINGTON, DC: INTERNATIONAL GUY BOOK 9

To Lauren Plude and her rescue pup, Sophia.

Lauren, you took a chance on me and International Guy;
I endeavor to be worthy of that commitment.
Your love for Sophia and unique stories cannot be matched.
I'm thrilled you're my publishing editor.
I feel like I hit the jackpot!
Thank you for being you.

And thank you to Sophia
for the inspiration found within this installment.
Much love and slobbery doggy nuzzles and kisses.

AUTHOR'S NOTE

In this installment of *International Guy*, I delve into some rather serious topics, including politics, animal cruelty, sexual assault, abortion, ethical misconduct, and animal rescue. Basically, I lost my mind. *(Grin.)* In all honesty, I did a lot of research in order to write this novella and provide the reader with the most accurate information possible, along with using some creative liberty, as this is a fictional tale.

Animal cruelty that is permitted in testing products for human use, including but not limited to the beauty industry, is a problem in our country. In truth, I was shocked by the horrid things I found in my research. Some of those scenarios and situations inspired the graphic nature of what has been written herein.

If you'd like to know more about animal rights and rescue, check out the Rescue Freedom Project: https://rescuefreedomproject.org/.

If you are a victim of sexual assault or want to know more about how to help, check out RAINN: https://www.rainn.org/. If you need help right now, please call 1-800-656-HOPE.

I hope you enjoy this installment of *International Guy* and that it encourages you to do your own research and take action on what matters to you.

What scenario would have you breaking all the rules to follow your own moral compass?

Live your truth,
Audrey

SKYLER

I hate running. I hate running. I hate running.

The standard chant flows through my mind as Nate and Rachel run alongside me, both flanking my body at a protective distance.

"We going for another mile or two?" Nate says with a grin, sweat running down the sides of his face and into the short, neat reddish-brown beard he's taken to growing recently.

Rachel firms her lips into a grim line. "I can take it." She hammers out a burst of energy so that Nate and I have to pick up the pace to catch up.

The building for my penthouse is in sight. "Are you two nuts?" I jog inelegantly and then come to a screeching halt, bending at the waist and resting my hands on my quivering, noodle-like quads. "Seriously, you two are trying to kill me." I lift my hand and mimic a duck face talking. "Oh, let's take a leisurely stroll, Sky. Jog a little. The weather's great. It will be nice to work out outside. Uh-huh." With extreme effort, I press my hand to my chest and attempt to control my breathing. Sweat trickles down my spine, and I flex my back and rub at the spot with my shirt.

Nate sets his hands on his waist. "A fit body is a healthy body."

"And a healthy body is a tired body!" I say with a pout. "I'm pretty sure you're trying to kill me. Death by running. Next time, chase me with a knife, will ya? I'm sure you'd get your extra mile in." I turn on my Nike-sheathed toes and start walking fast to get ahead of the two hard bodies and their relentless workouts.

Rachel is unable to contain her giggling, which makes me glare and flip her off as I bolt at a fast trot toward the building where I now live in Boston.

"You said you wanted to be in fighting shape for the A-Lister Trilogy. I do believe that was you!" Rachel calls out, laughing, the two of them not more than five to ten feet from me at any given time.

"Grrr!" I see the coffee shop, Grounds, next to the building where my penthouse and the IG offices are right up ahead. Most of the time, the owner is working the counter along with the same barista. I've gotten to know them, given them both selfies and autographs so the newness of a celebrity living in the building next to their coffee shop has worn off. They've been really good about not making a big deal about seeing me either. Plus, they've allowed me to have a tab, which works for the times that my security team is trying to kill me and I don't have any money on me.

Looking back at them, I open the door to Grounds and slam right into a firm chest. Iced tea splashes all over me and down my workout shirt, capris, and zip-up hoodie. "Shit!" I jump back and shake the ice from my shirt.

"I'm so, so sorry!" I cry out, then scramble to the ground to pick up the ice. "I'll buy you a new one, right away. I wasn't looking where I was going," I mumble while grabbing at slippery pieces of scattered ice.

"Skyler?" a voice says with familiarity.

I glance up at the tall man and look into the green eyes of someone I recognize but can't place. I frown and stand up, ice freezing my palms even as it melts.

"I'm sorry . . ." I shake my head and toss the ice into a nearby trash can.

Right behind me, Nate and Rachel come in. As the familiar person reaches to take my arm, Nate grabs the man's forearm and pulls it behind his back and up between his shoulder blades in a move that would make Bruce Lee proud.

"Aaaahhhh! Let me go!" the man screeches, his body arching into the air in obvious pain.

I wave my hands. "No, no, no, Nate! I ran into him. And he's . . . I know him. Please, drop him."

"Let me go!" He shoulders Nate back, and eventually Nate lets him go but moves to stand in front of me, arms crossed, a total menace.

"Skyler and I are old friends." The guy rolls his shoulder and rubs at his now sore hand and arm.

"This true, Sky?" Nate grumbles deep in his throat, sounding a bit animalistic, his eyes never leaving the man in front of us.

I bite into my lip and take in every one of the stranger's facial features. Kind green eyes. Pointed nose. High cheekbones. Shaven jaw. A normal if unremarkable short haircut. Jeans and a polo. A regular guy if I ever saw one.

"I'm sorry, I don't recall when we met." I frown while mentally digging into my mind.

The man winces, his face taking on a hurt expression. "We're *the same*, remember? You and me. Worked on that commercial together." His brows furrow. "Yum yum, in my tum tum. Fun fun in the bun bun. Frosted Mini-Buns!" he sings jovially.

"Oh my goodness! The Mini-Buns cereal commercial! That was . . . wow, seventeen . . . eighteen years ago? I was eight!"

He smiles. "I was ten." His response is said with bravado, as though his being two years older than me when I filmed a commercial seventeen years ago is something to be puffed up about.

"Uh, yeah." I nod my head. "What's your uh . . . I'm sorry, I don't remember your name."

The smile he's sporting slips away, and his jaw firms. "Well, now that you're so famous, it's probably hard to remember old friends. It's Ben. Benny Singleton."

Benny Singleton. Ugh. Now I remember. My mother told me to stay away from him because the boy was always trying to kiss me in between takes. No eight-year-old girl wants to have a boy kiss her. Especially a gawky one who always smelled like maple syrup.

"Right, I totally remember now." I playfully conk at my head. "Acting. You know how it is. Play so many parts you forget the real names of people."

He purses his lips. "I guess."

"Well, let me refresh your drink," I offer with a smile, pointing toward the busy coffee counter.

He glances over my shoulder. "As long as your boyfriend keeps his big paws to himself. You know, he could have really hurt me." He rubs at his arm and hand.

I snicker under my breath, which causes Benny to frown.

"Sorry." I place my hand on his bicep in a friendly manner until he looks at the hand longingly, his green gaze darkening at the single touch. I snatch my hand away quickly. "He's not my boyfriend."

Benny's corresponding smile is wide, revealing relief and maybe even anticipation.

"Bodyguard," Nate grates through clenched teeth as he follows us up to the counter.

"Oh. That's good." He grins at me and licks his lips, his gaze moving to my mouth. "Real good."

I suck in a huge breath, turn to the counter, and greet the barista. "Hey, Freddy, how goes it?"

"Can't complain. The sky is blue, the coffee is hot, and the muffins are fresh baked. Unless you'd rather have tea . . ." He scans my sodden shirt and smirks. "Although I imagine you've had your fill today."

I slump over, leaning on the high counter. "Ran into an old friend, spilled his drink everywhere. I'm sorry. There's a huge wet spot." I look over my shoulder and note Rachel is mopping it up with napkins. "Though it seems Rachel is cleaning it up for me. Can I get my usual,

Nate's cup of black nothingness, Rachel's Americano with room for cream, and whatever my friend here just ordered? Oh, and two blueberry muffins."

Benny's eyes light up when I say the word *friend*. Ugh. I really need to take lessons on how not to encourage unwanted attention.

"Sky . . . ," Nate warns when I add the muffins.

I turn around, my ponytail flying like a whip behind me. "I'm hungry."

"Then eat something with protein in it," he states flatly.

"You're going to make me a protein drink when I get back, aren't you?"

He narrows his gaze. "Yeah, I am, but that was supposed to go with your Egg Beater omelet. Not your blueberry-muffin, high-carb, high-fat, high-sugar treat."

I turn back around to Freddy. "Make that two blueberry muffins *and* a banana nut!"

Nate groans from behind me.

"It has nuts in it. Nuts count as protein." I gift him my best crooked smile.

"Yeah, a high-fat protein. Now you're going to have to give me six extra air squats. And you may have to hold ten-pound dumbbells while you're at it."

I squint, pinch my lips together, and step up right to Nate's furry, playfully scowling face. "You wouldn't dare."

He squints. "Try me. I'm not afraid of you. Remember who fired her personal trainer." He reminds me of the requirement Parker made when we sealed the deal on our relationship. No sweat equity with a man I'd had sex with. Since Nate's with me 24-7 anyway, it makes sense for him to train me.

"I hate you," I hiss with mock agitation.

"You love me. More than that, you're going to love how hard your ass will be when you step on the set of the next movie," he fires back with a snarky grin.

"Shut up!" I stick my tongue out at him and realize that Nate and I are going on and on while Benny and Freddy watch. "Sorry, guys. Add it to my tab, Freddy?"

"Sure thing, Sky."

Benny follows me over to the counter as the owner hands me the tea. I shift it over to Benny, hoping he'll take the tea and leave. No dice.

He sucks on the straw loudly as the rest of our drinks come out along with my bag of goodies. My belly growls, and I walk over to an empty table and sit down. Benny follows. Nate joins Rachel at a table across from me. He starts to hand her the Americano. "Milk, baby?"

She nods.

Nate opens her drink and takes it over to a table set up with creamers, napkins, and other café needs. He pours in a small dose of milk, stirs it, and brings it back before settling his big body into the chair.

"Those two together?" Benny dips his head in the direction of their table.

I nod. "Yeah, they're married and my security team." I pull out a blueberry muffin, unwrap the side, and take a giant bite, locking eyes with Nate. "Mmm . . . so goofff," I say through a mouth of carb heaven.

Nate smiles and shakes his head.

I am so going to pay for this, but it tastes so damn good.

As I'm chewing, I feel the air in the café ignite with electricity. I glance up, and my heart starts beating fast, and butterflies take flight in my stomach. Parker, in a gray suit, white dress shirt, and navy tie, is standing at the front of the café. He looks good enough to eat. I chew the mouthful of muffin as his eyes scan the place and settle on me. Once he sees me, he grins that devilish smile and saunters over to us.

The entire room shrinks down to nothing but my man. The pants cling to his muscular thighs, and the dress shirt stretches across the broad expanse of his chest. I lick my lips and lift my head up as he approaches.

"If he's not your boyfriend, maybe you and I can . . ." Benny starts to speak, but I can barely focus on what he's saying, I'm so intent on greeting my man.

"Hi, baby . . ." Parker reaches us, leans down to me, grasps my chin, and kisses me soundly on the mouth, nibbling on my bottom lip before pulling away. "Mmm. Blueberry and peaches. My favorite." He winks before noticing the man sitting at my table. "Hi. Who are you?"

"Friend of Skyler's. Benny."

I want to tell Parker that Benny is not, in fact, my friend, but there will be time for that later. "Honey, I ran into Benny. Literally. Spilled his tea all over me." Parker's gaze runs down the front of my sodden shirt and back up to my face as I continue. "Then we realized that we'd been in a commercial together as kids. Can you believe that?"

Parker purses his lips and cocks an eyebrow. "Small world. Where are you from? Benny, is it?"

"Y-yeah. Um, not from around here, actually. Was in New York for a while. Now I'm here. I work in this building." He points to the wall that's shared with the building I live in and where the IG offices are located.

Park tips his head. "Really? I work in this building as well. Have never seen you."

"Just started a few weeks ago," Benny answers.

"Hmm." Parker notes the bag of goodies and reaches for it with a smile.

"Yes, there's a blueberry muffin in there for you. *And* a banana nut for Bo." I glance at Nate and smile before focusing back on my guy. "Royce says he doesn't do muffins or carbs for breakfast."

Nate gives me a silent slow clap.

I make an ugly face at him, and he and Rachel laugh while sipping their drinks.

"Thanks, baby. I'll walk you back home."

I stand up, realizing this is Parker's way of giving me an out. The moment I stand, he loops his arm around my hip and runs his hand down to cup my ass. "Getting even tighter." He squeezes my glute firmly. "Nate, you're workin' my woman too hard. You know I like a little junk in the trunk."

"See!" I point at Nate, and he shakes his head. "My man likes my ass just the way it is."

"Let me remind you for the hundredth time: you were the one who wanted me to train you!" Nate responds with a note of exasperation.

"Uh, well, I can see that you've got some things to do." Benny stands up. "It was nice seeing you, Skyler. Now that we're in the same place, I hope to see you around."

"Mm-hmm. Take care of yourself." I snuggle against Parker's chest as Benny finally leaves. "Ugh."

"Guessing that was *not* one of your friends?" Parker kisses my forehead.

"No. We did a commercial together seventeen years ago, and he acted like we've known each other forever."

Just when the words leave my mouth, I feel Parker tense up. He narrows his gaze and lifts his chin at Nate.

Nate shrugs. "I didn't get any strange vibes from the guy, but it wouldn't hurt to look into him. I'll add his name to the list."

This has me jerking my head back. "You think Benny is the weirdo sending me texts?"

Parker cups my cheeks. "I don't know, but he did mention living in New York City, and now all of a sudden he lives here. Acts like he's a better friend than you believe him to be?"

"That's true. He did act overly familiar, but a lot of times people do that when they think they know someone."

"Can't hurt to look into him," Nate repeats.

I shrug. "Whatever you guys say. I need to finish my muffin and coffee and get a shower, and then you two need to show me the goods you've been hiding on my texter."

Parker loops his arm back around my waist and leads me out of the coffee shop and toward the entrance to our building. "It's not that we've been hiding anything from you. We just thought—"

"You were protecting me. I get it, honey, and I'm not mad. I know you love me and want to keep me safe."

He stops on the sidewalk and turns me to face him. His blue eyes look gray in the morning light. "I'd do anything to keep you safe. You're my world."

I lift up onto my tippy-toes and kiss him. "I know, but keeping me in the dark isn't working anymore. Did you find out if Wendy can meet us?"

He nods. "Yeah, she says we should come over for dinner. Is that fine? I have a lunch meeting today with Andre, my headhunter, and a prospective new hire."

"Oh, for the lawyer position?"

"Yeah." He fingers his jacket and tie. "Do I look okay? Apparently, this person is a Harvard grad who then transferred to Georgetown University on a full scholarship and passed the bar exam with an outstanding score. She's been working on Capitol Hill for the past few years but suddenly wants to move to Boston."

"Honey, you look perfect. I'm sure you're going to knock her socks off."

He smiles and leads me into the building, through security, and into an elevator. "How about you guys let me off at my floor, and you can clean up and change. Then we can discuss the issue in my office before lunch. Sound good?"

Nate and Rachel, following us this whole time, both agree, and I nod as the car rises. Just as the elevator dings on the IG office floor,

Parker kisses me swiftly and moves to leave. Annie is standing at the door, holding a bundle of mail in one arm.

"Hello, everyone," she says sweetly.

"Hey, Annie," I say. "Sorry, you got the car with the stinky bunch! We just got done with our run. We're also going up."

She waves her free hand. "No problem. I'll just take it for a ride. Taking these to the mail room." She gestures to the stack in her other arm. "Are you happy to be in Boston?"

"Yes! So happy. You know, I've only been here a short time, but coming home to Parker just feels right."

Annie smiles wide as the elevator rises. "I'll bet."

"Do you have someone special?" I nudge her shoulder with my own.

Her cheeks pinken, and she fiddles with the mail. "Maybe. It's new, and I don't want to jinx it."

"I can totally understand. Just don't be afraid to have fun. Live a little." I waggle my eyebrows at her, and she chuckles, dipping her head so her blonde hair falls around her face, covering her laughter.

The elevator dings at my floor. Rachel and Nate get out, even though their floor is one below mine. They never hit the button for their floor before they come into mine and do a walk-through to confirm it's all clear.

As I exit the elevator, I suddenly get an idea and turn around to the skittish and rather shy woman. "You know, we should have lunch sometime."

Annie's blue gaze seems to widen. "Really?"

"Totally. You're working with my man. We should be friends, don't you think?"

"I'd love that," she says, then gasps. "Oh my, my mom is going to keel over in shock."

I chuckle and shake my head. "I'm just a normal woman in her twenties who doesn't have a lot of friends in the area. I'd like it if we could be friends."

Her shy smile turns bright. "Me too, Skyler. Me too."

"Then it's settled. We'll confirm something this week."

"Okay. I'd like that very much." She beams, waves, and lets the elevator doors close.

I gesture to my place with a wave of my arm. "All right, you two, do your worst. I'll wait here, bored out of my mind, while you do your search."

1

Nate stacks the sixty or so letters he found most suspicious from Skyler's fan mail into five specific piles. "These five individuals have the most consistent history of sending mail. I figured we should start with the ones that have had a commitment to Skyler long-term."

Skyler and I each grab a stack and head to the couch. For a solid ten minutes, the two of us sit side by side and go through each letter in our respective piles.

"Wow. I had no idea people got this involved. I mean, in the back of my mind I knew, and obviously I've had a wide fan base for a while, but this is outrageous." She gasps. "This person has not only sent me fan mail since I was a teen, telling me how much he loved me, but he sent birthday cards every year, congrats notes on making a certain role, and even a sympathy card when my folks died." She shakes her head. "How can a person be so involved in my life when they've never met me? I just don't get it." She sighs.

I place my hand on her thigh and rub her quad soothingly. "Peaches, they think they know you. Believe it with their entire being. The roles you play, the people you present to the world on the big screen, are friends to them. People they look up to, admire. Add in the fact that you're fuckin' gorgeous and sweet as pie, and you've got a hard-core fan.

I get it. I'm smitten." I lean toward her, she lifts her chin up so that I can reach those sweet lips easier, and I give her a gentle kiss.

Her shoulders sag as she curves her spine along the back of the couch. "I don't think this person is creepy. Just likes me a lot."

Nate nods. "Yeah, I agree. Park?"

I jut my chin and grab the next set of letters. Within moments, something catches my eye. A stack of white envelopes. No return address, but "CONFIDENTIAL" stamped on the front of each. The letter I received had the same word stamped on the front. It could be a coincidence; a lot of people stamp or write that on something they want only the intended person to read. I open the first letter. It's typed, and the date at the top is ten years ago. Sky would have been around fifteen.

I scan the letter:

> *Sky,*
>
> *Bittersweet Dreams was excellent. I saw the movie three times in the theater. You made the perfect runaway. Sometimes I wish I could run away like you did in that movie. You were so brave. If I ran, I'd be caught. Then the She-Devil would beat me black and blue like the last time I tried to leave. Anyway, it would have been so nice to sit with you and watch the movie. I would have held your hand through all the scary parts. Then you wouldn't be alone.*
>
> *As long as we have each other, we're never alone, right?*
>
> *Your real BF*

"There's a conversational tone about this letter that tweaks my spidey sense." I hand the letter to Nate, and he barely scans it before handing it to Sky. He's already read them all since he picked the ones that made him uncomfortable.

I grab the next typed letter.

Sky,

I wish you lived here. I really need you right now.
Everything sucks. High school is awful. People just don't
get what it's like to be different. You do, though. I knew
it when I saw you in Journal of a High Schooler and
you played the girl that got bullied and picked on. I sure
know what that's like. If you were here, we could hang
out, watch other actors mess up their lines in movies, get
ice cream. I'd show you the best time, I promise. Then
they'd all see what we were to each other.

  Your real BF

I hand over this letter to Skyler and scan the next three in a row.

Sky,

I miss you. It seems like forever since you were on the
screen entertaining me. I read that you got hurt on set,
which pushed production back. You should have called
me. I would have been there for you every second, hold-
ing your hand, making you laugh, whatever it took to
get you better. Instead I'm stuck here with the She-Devil,
waiting on the queen hand and foot and taking business
classes. She's so horrible. I wish I were with you. You'd
make it better. We could take care of each other. Think
about it. I'll always be here for you.

  Your real BF

Sky,

I saw you today. Just a glimpse, but you looked right at
me and waved. I wanted to rush to you, get through all

*the security and tell them that we know each other, but
then that stupid witch agent of yours got in the way and
pushed you inside to do your Today show piece. I recorded
it. Watched it a hundred times. You're so beautiful. Still,
I'm angry that we couldn't spend time together. It was hard
getting away from the She-Devil. I had to lie a lot, but it
was worth it to see you waving at me. I'll always love you.*

Your real BF

Sky,

*Why are you with that scumbag! I can't believe you would
date him. He's beneath you. Please break it off with him.
Now. I am not happy about this. Not happy at all. I have
a mind to do something about it. Johan. What kind of
a name is that anyway? He's using you. Open your eyes.
Get rid of the snake. He disgusts me.*

YOUR REAL BF

"Jesus. These read like this person is in your day-to-day life. It's bizarre. The individual is having a completely one-sided relationship with you. And this last one, where you'd obviously started dating Johan, really pissed him off. Look at how the typed font goes to capital letters like he's yelling at you that he's your real boyfriend."

Sky bites down on her lip and frowns. "Except the person never leaves a return address or uses a name. It's as if a part of him knows it's unwanted correspondence, and yet it's still so familiar. As if I *should know* who it is."

I nod and scan the next letter.

Sky,

*My heart is breaking for you. I tried to come to the
funeral. I really did. The She-Devil would never allow*

it. I'm so sorry. You needed me, and I wasn't there. Worse, that horrible, ugly man was. Holding you when I should have been your shoulder to cry on. Me. Your BF. I would give anything to be with you, Sky. You know that. You know how much I love and care about you. I know your parents were good people. Always smiling in all the pictures of them with you. Always there on set like good parents should be. Please know that they will always be with you. Like me. I'm always here for you. Always, beautiful girl. I will find a way to get closer. Be there for you. I promise.

Your real BF

Painstakingly I go through the rest. It seems as though there are at least one to two a year. All typed. All with *confidential* marked on the front.

"Well, there's no return address on any of these. Just the postmark that matches wherever Sky was living at the time," I mutter, and run my hand through my hair. Skyler eases her hand up and down my back, and I close my eyes, enjoying her touch for a moment.

"It seems as though the guy moved with her. Where she went, he went," Nate adds.

"Yeah. And what about this She-Devil part? That started young, so it can't be a girlfriend; it has to be a guardian, a mother figure of some sort. The person repeatedly makes reference to not being able to get away. Being beaten. How could a grown man not get away? I get it when he was younger, but after he turned eighteen . . ." I shake my head.

Nate frowns. "Another mystery."

He hands over another stack, and I paw through them. There are threatening ones that probably should have been reported to the authorities, but nothing that seems concrete. "My money is on BF being our suspect." I toss the stack I was looking at onto the table.

"Why wasn't this person found a long time ago? I mean, Tracey handles my security and my fan mail. She obviously thought these ones were odd or she wouldn't have kept them all these years."

I hook my arm around Sky's shoulder. "I don't know, baby. Maybe she just got busy, didn't really think they were a major threat. Most of them seem innocent enough. It's when you put the whole picture together that the pattern of disturbance becomes visible. We're probably missing tons of letters in between. Even from BF there're gaps of six months to a year or so between letters. A person who thinks they're your boyfriend would definitely reach out more. Don't you think?"

She shrugs. "I don't know. I guess."

There's a knock on my door, and it opens to reveal Annie poking her head in. "Am I interrupting?" She smiles.

I shake my head and stand, buttoning my suit jacket. "No, we're done here."

She enters on black leather spiked heels, wearing a pencil skirt with a blue silk blouse that caps her small shoulders. If she weren't so thin and gangly looking, she'd be a beautiful woman. Her pointed facial features make her look cold unless she's smiling.

"Oh my God!" Skyler points down at Annie's feet. "I have those exact shoes! Aren't they comfortable? They cost a mint, but they're so awesome. I can totally run in them!"

Annie looks down at her shoes and blushes. "You have these same ones?" She smiles.

Skyler nods. "Uh-huh. And they look smokin' hot on you, girl. Don't they, honey?"

I turn my head toward Sky. "What?"

"Don't those heels look hot on Annie?"

I glance at the heels and evaluate them from the side. "Sure. Hot to trot." I offer a flat, closed-lip smile and look down again. If she'd eat a bit more, gain a good fifteen pounds, her legs would fill out, and then they'd look a whole helluva lot better, but I keep that last bit to myself. Skyler would not be pleased, and I wouldn't want to hurt my receptionist's feelings.

Annie's face is beet red when I finally look at her.

"Thank you, Parker. That's nice of you to say." She looks down and away.

Great, now I've embarrassed her.

Skyler stands up and puts her arm around Annie's waist. She nudges her shoulder conspiratorially. "You got a date tonight where those shoes will be appreciated by a certain special someone? Hmm? Huh?" She bumps shoulders again.

"Sky . . . ," I warn. "Workplace," I remind her.

She laughs. "Not my workplace. I can ask whatever inappropriate questions I want. Besides . . ." She hugs Annie to her side. "We're friends, and friends talk about our men. Right, Annie?" Sky grins and looks at Annie.

A huge smile lights up Annie's entire face. "Right, Sky. Friends. Friends do that."

My girl waggles her brows. "See. Told you. Friday we'll do lunch, yeah?" she asks Annie, and I groan. Of course, she's going to make friends with the receptionist the same way she did with Wendy.

"I'd have to check Mr. Ellis's schedule . . ."

"Not him." Sky points to me and waves. "I see him all the time. You. Me. Lunch. Friday. Cool?"

"Cool." Annie wraps her mouth around the word as if she's testing it out. "Yes. That would be *cool*, Skyler."

"All right. Well, my man has to go see a dude about a lawyer." She drops her arm from around Annie's waist and trots over to me, wraps her arms around my neck, and kisses me hard. "I love you, honey. Have a good meeting."

I tunnel my fingers into the long tendrils of hair at her nape and slant my head, kissing her much deeper than I would normally with an audience in the workplace. Before I can pull away, Nate's clearing his throat. I smile as I ease back. "I love you too." I run my hand over her silky hair, committing it to memory so I can revisit it throughout the day. Wanting a little more, I dip my head to the crook of her neck and inhale her peaches-and-cream scent, letting it fill me with the peace and serenity I've come to associate with it. I kiss her neck softly.

She hums in the back of her throat. God, I love that sound. It goes straight from her mouth, fills the air, and travels like a caress over my dick. "The beast" approves a hundred times over and is starting to make it known just how much he likes it by making my slacks a bit tight.

I grit my teeth and push my girl's hips away from touching distance. She smirks and winks, knowing exactly what her close proximity is doing to me. "Dinner at Wendy and Mick's. Rach and Nate too for the powwow."

"Got it on my calendar; I'll meet you there."

"You're, um, seeing Wendy?" Annie's voice sounds shaky, nervous.

I turn Skyler and grab her hand, lifting it to my mouth for a kiss.

"Yeah, dinner, you know," Skyler says conversationally.

Annie frowns. "Oh, I just thought maybe you were going to talk about when she was coming back. You'll, um, give me plenty of notice, right? I mean, not that you have to since I'm a temporary employee, but I've, uh, gotten to love it here, and I'd like to maybe say goodbye or—"

I wave my hand in the air. "Annie, Wendy is planning to come back. Very soon. However, we are in the process of discussing continuing your employment as our receptionist. Wendy is needed by us in a variety of capacities. We're discussing making her our chief information officer and keeping you on as our personal assistant. Would that be something you'd be interested in on a permanent basis?"

"You want me? Really?" Her eyes are a blaze of blue fire, her gaze intense and focused on mine. "I never thought or hoped . . ."

I smile softly and lower my voice. "You've done an excellent job here. The team is very happy with your work, and we're growing by leaps and bounds. I'll run it past the team and have an official letter of intent with the offer drawn up by the end of the week, detailing the process of officially becoming a member of IG."

She licks her lips, and her eyes tear up. Not exactly what I thought would take place, but at least she seems happy about the job opportunity . . . I think.

"I want to be here for you guys more than anything. We're a team. It feels so right," she whispers, as if awed.

I suck in a breath between my teeth. "Yeah, okay . . . Well, put a meeting with me and the guys on your schedule for Friday. I have to go meet with Andre and the prospective new lawyer."

It's as if my words snap her into motion. "Yes, of course. That's why I came in, to remind you of your appointment. You don't want to be late for an important meeting. Good luck, Parker. I hope she's the right fit for our team." She smiles widely, and her cheeks pinken to a rosy hue.

Odd girl. Smart. Efficient. Fast learner, but odd when it comes to social interaction. Hopefully, over time, she'll get over it.

"I'll walk you to the elevator." Sky grabs my hand.

Nate stands, ready to follow.

Sky holds out her hand and shakes her head. "Not going anywhere, Tarzan. Just walking my man to the elevator and will be right back to view more letters."

Annie points to the table. "What is all that?"

"Crazy fan mail," Skyler blurts out.

Annie frowns. "There's a lot of it."

Skyler laughs. "That's nothing. I get thousands of letters a year."

"Thousands . . ." Her eyes widen as she looks at the stacks of letters.

Sky nods. "Yep. People are so weird."

Annie crosses her arms over her chest and glares at the stack of mail. "Well, if you need help with anything, I'm here for you," she offers sweetly. "This looks like a lot of work."

I grab Sky's hand and tug her toward the door. "I think we've got it under control. Thanks, Annie."

***

The swank restaurant near downtown Boston is nestled down a side street of brownstones. As I enter, Andre waves from a courtyard section completely encased in brick walls, lush greenery, and a water feature. It exudes calm and relaxation, except everyone sitting is in some form of business attire. The place is known as a hot spot for busy professionals lunching out. You can speak frankly because the tables are separated far enough apart that the trickling water drowns out any additional sound, and the waitstaff are fast with the service.

As I approach, Andre stands, as does a very tall African American woman. I can see only her back. She's wearing a navy sheath dress with a kick pleat at the back of the narrow skirt and a gold belt with matching gold Christian Louboutin stilettos attached to a smokin' hot pair of long, shapely legs.

I peel my eyes away from her legs when she turns around, and I'm struck dumb by her hazel eyes. A very familiar pair of hazel eyes, the prettiest I've ever seen. Her lips are full and stained with a peachy shine. Those lips stretch into a wide smile, revealing gleaming, even white teeth. Her espresso-colored hair is flat ironed and cut just at the clavicle in a blunt style that suits her oval-shaped face and high cheekbones beautifully. Her fawn-colored skin is smooth and attractive. The woman could be Vanessa Williams's daughter with her features. She's a striking woman, and for a moment, I'm stunned stupid. Speechless.

"Parker, it's . . ." Her words leave her.

"Kendra Banks, I . . . wow . . . I can't believe I'm seeing you again. I can't believe you're the same Kendra I went to college with."

She blinks and glances down. "Yes, well, I wasn't planning on returning to Boston. *Ever.* Plans changed. Now I'm here."

I open my mouth and close it again. This is when Andre, my headhunter, finally interrupts the awkward greeting.

"So, then you two know one another. Great!"

I lick my lips and step closer to a woman I truly didn't think would ever enter my world again. I grip her bicep lightly and set my cheek to hers. I inhale her lemon-and-citrus scent as I close my eyes and let the memories of years gone by rush to the surface. "I'm happy to see you, Kendra," I whisper in her ear, and squeeze her arm.

She sucks in a harsh breath and swallows as she nods. "You were always Switzerland."

I pull back while running my hand down her arm until I've got her hand in mine. The last time I held her hand, I was telling her not to go. Not to leave. She didn't listen.

"Someone has to be."

She tightens her jaw. "I can't imagine other people in your life will be as pleased as you are at seeing me again. If our paths cross, that is."

I frown. "Did Andre not tell you?"

Andre perks up at hearing his name. "Tell her what?"

"Royce and Bo are not silent partners; we run the business together."

She twists her head toward me. "Then this meeting is useless. They'd never agree to work with me."

"Sit down, both of you; people are starting to stare," Andre urges.

We take our seats and say nothing more until the waiter takes our drink orders. Seeing Kendra again, I order a beer. She must feel just as shaken, because she orders a glass of white wine. Andre orders iced tea.

"What is this about the meeting being useless?" Andre continues once the waiter leaves to get our drinks.

Kendra places her napkin primly in her lap, sitting ramrod straight in her chair. "I had a personal relationship with a member of the International Guy team. Let's just say it didn't end badly . . . but not well."

I tilt my head and lean back. "Depends on who you ask." I smile and wink at her, letting her know there are no hard feelings between the two of us. "Are you really considering a job working with IG? We need a lawyer stat. One we can trust not to screw us over and who has our best interests at heart, especially as it pertains to corporate law. You'd be a perfect candidate. You've got the skills, the background, and you have a personal stake in keeping us happy."

Her gaze reaches mine, looking far greener at the moment. "I guess that depends on who you ask." She repeats my words.

I grin wide. "Royce isn't here."

"No, no, he is not." She looks away, her expression turning to one of regret for a scant moment before it's gone, and her eyes flash in my direction. "You prepared to deal with his wrath if you hire me?"

I laugh out loud. "He trusts me to put IG's interests above our own. It's just business, right? Besides, what the two of you had ended amicably enough. Right?"

Her expression flits to one of surprise. "Is that what he told you?"

I nod, frowning. "Yeah."

"Then, if you're interested in making me an offer, I'm very interested in hearing it."

2

The mansion door flies open, and a blur of white and gold rushes down the steps before my girl is flying into my arms. I catch her by the waist and swing her around; her exuberance at seeing me melts my heart. "Hey, baby!"

She lands her mouth on mine in a heated kiss. I take the kiss deeper and slip her a little tongue action. She moans into my mouth before pulling away and licking her lips. "Guess what!" She smacks my chest, excitement rushing her words.

"What, Peaches?"

Skyler smiles. "Not only is the *A-Lister* series going to shoot the bar scenes in Lucky's, they are going to shoot most of the movies in Boston! Which means"—she wiggles wildly in my arms—"I'm not going to have to leave much for the next two years! Not only is the series three parts, but they're stretching it out for maximum money-making potential and making the last movie a two-parter like they did with the Twilight Saga!"

I smile wide and kiss her silky lips hard. "That's awesome, Sky."

"And guess what else!" The dancing keeps going as I hook my arm around her and start walking her up the steps to Mick and Wendy's mansion. Wendy is patiently waiting at the top, leaning against the doorframe. Her cap of flaming-red hair is bright and shiny, glinting in the light from the huge chandelier inside the door. She wiggles her fingers at me, grinning.

"What?" I chuckle and lead my woman up the concrete stairs.

"They've cast Rick Pettington as my costar!"

This stops me before my foot touches the next step. "Rick the Prick?"

She turns with one foot on the step above and frowns. "I thought you liked him. You gave him tips on how to be sexy in a scene and everything. I figured you'd be happy." She pouts.

I lift my hand and tunnel it into her hair at her nape. "Sky, I'm never going to be happy a man is playing your love interest in a romantic movie. Doesn't matter who it is or if he were my best friend. Another man kissing and touching you is a fact of life that I have to swallow down on the regular; doesn't mean I gotta be happy about it."

Her shoulders drop, and her spine curves toward me along with her arms. Behind her, Wendy is laughing behind her hand.

"But you know Rick thinks of me like a sister. I thought you'd be"—she shrugs—"excited about this news."

"Baby, you love your job. I'm excited you're happy. You being happy is all that matters to me. Your costars can be cool, and treat you with respect, which I expect to happen always, or else . . ." I leave that bit unspoken. She knows what the *or else* means without me having to say a word more. I tug her body flat against mine with her standing on the stair above, putting us at eye level. "I'm never going to like you pretending to be in a relationship with another man. I love you too much. You're mine. I'll never tell you to not accept a role or to not do your job. It's who you are. It's a beautiful part of you. I'm proud of the work you do and talent you have and will support you always. Asking me to like a man kissing my woman?" I shake my head. "Baby, you gotta look at it from my perspective."

She kisses me softly. "Well, at least I get to be here all the time for the foreseeable future!"

"Now that part I absolutely love." I run my hands down to her ass and give it a playful squeeze combined with a lip nip.

She laughs but kisses me back.

"Uh, guys . . . still waiting. Are you ever going to come into the house?" Wendy calls out, reminding us she's standing there.

"Oops!" Sky laughs. My girl is always laughing with me, and I'll go a long way to hear that laughter as often as possible. She's had enough strife in her world to last a lifetime.

I turn Skyler around and push at her booty to get her moving.

She dashes up the stairs as I come to the top and open my arms for my second-best girl. Wendy grins and comes right into my embrace, placing her face flat against my chest. Her coconutty scent mixes with Sky's own fruity smell, filling me with familiarity and comfort.

"How's it going, minxy?"

She nods against my chest. "Good. Now that we're home and away from that witch Monika, it's all good. We're well into final wedding plans, and"—she leans back and looks into my face—"we've been trying to get pregnant. I'm off all the meds, no more pain, just a few tweaks here and there, but nothing I can't handle with a glass of wine and a good night's sleep. Both of which I'm getting in spades."

I loop my arm around hers and walk her into the house. I kiss her forehead. "Keep me posted," I whisper, knowing she's sharing something incredibly private.

"Okay, I will. I'm just really excited and nervous about it. I hope it happens soon. We want to have our own family so bad." She worries her bottom lip, and I stop before we enter the receiving room.

I frown and whisper in her ear, "Stop worrying. You've got lots of time. Take it all day by day. The moment you stop fretting is when it will happen."

Wendy nods sharply. "Good advice. I'm just going to roll with it."

I squeeze her shoulder and kiss the crown of her head as we enter the formal room that oozes old money, from the artwork to the large antique mahogany furniture and vibrant gem-toned fabrics with gold accents everywhere.

Mick is already waiting with a drink in hand.

"Ellis, I've made you a gin and tonic, but I've got cold IPA at the ready if you'd prefer." He holds out a cocktail glass.

I let Wendy go as he hands me the drink. His eyes go from hers to mine and back to hers. "Something you two want to share?" He smirks.

She shakes her head. "Nope. Just Park reminding me to 'go with the flow' and let nature do its thing."

Mick cocks a brow. "I see you've been sharing . . ."

She lifts one shoulder and presses her lips together. "Not much. Besides, I have to talk to someone."

Mick's gaze narrows, and he curves an arm around her waist, bringing her body flat against his chest. "I'm your someone. You talk to me."

She rolls her eyes and pushes away. "Not when it involves you, silly."

He brings her back against his chest with an iron grip.

I chuckle under my breath as Sky wraps her arms around my waist, leaning her chin on my chest.

"Especially when it involves me." He kisses her sweetly.

She stares at him directly. "You're insufferable sometimes."

"You love it."

Wendy smiles huge. "I totally do." She kisses him hard once before spinning out of his arms and addressing Nate and Rachel, who are sitting on the couch.

"Well, now that you're all here, do you want to chat before dinner or after?"

"I think it would be wise to get the work stuff out of the way first, then enjoy our personal time. Yeah?" I suggest.

Sky nods. "Yeah. Did Park or Nate tell you why we wanted to talk?"

Wendy's eyebrows furrow. "No, just that you had a security issue that would take up some tech time on my part."

Skyler blurts out, "I have a stalker."

Mick's arm wraps around Wendy at the same time that Wendy's mouth drops open and her blue eyes turn a fiery deep blue. "Say again?"

"How about we sit down?" I point to the comfortable couches.

"How's about you tell me what the hell is going on and why the word *stalker* just came out of my best girlfriend's mouth?" Wendy's voice is low and demanding.

"Cherry, let's have a seat. I'll make you a stronger drink."

"Yes, yes, you will." She stomps over to the couch and sits down on the edge of the arm.

Skyler and I take positions on the couch across from Nate and Rach.

"Hi, guys," I say.

"Hey," Rachel replies at the same time Nate offers a chin lift.

Mick crosses the room to his bar setup and sets out six tumblers. He grabs a crystal decanter sitting on a matching tray and pours two fingers of amber liquid into each tumbler before bringing the entire tray over to the coffee table. He sets the tray down, picks up one glass, and hands it to Wendy. She immediately slams the two fingers of what I assume to be whiskey in one go. Then she promptly picks up another. "For sipping."

I grin, recalling the first time she did that in a hotel in Canada when I was losing my mind over Skyler. Wistfully I let those thoughts go and grab for a tumbler to hand to Sky. "Whiskey?" I ask Mick, and he nods. Once Sky's taken hers, I accept one for myself. Mick chooses his when both Rachel and Nate shake their heads. They're on the job, which means they don't drink. Ever.

"All right, someone tell me what's going on," Wendy demands.

We start by giving her the lowdown on the texts. Nate printed them out, complete with time stamps and the phone numbers they were sent from. One set for Skyler's texts and one for mine. Then he presents her with copies of the three individuals' letters we narrowed down from the fan mail. Still, all three are anonymous. The only saving grace is two of the three have the same postmark, meaning every letter was mailed from the same location. One is New York, the other some small town in Alabama.

Wendy skims through the papers. "The letters are strange. Some downright upsetting. I'm sorry, Sky."

Skyler reaches for my hand, and I hold on to it, letting her know I'm here for her.

"The texts worry me," Wendy says. "They're all over the place and change from friendly to possessive to angry. Parker's texts less so. The letters seem as though they were written by a male who's obsessed with Skyler as a love interest. A companion. The texts almost sound like they were written by a girl. You see the phrasing: 'I thought we were friends. You think you're better than everyone else.' But the last two are most disconcerting. Whoever sent those texts is watching you. They know when you're coming and going. Look at the word choices. 'Glad you're home. Distance makes the heart grow fonder.'" She shakes her head. "And Skyler's gotten a lot more texts than Parker and more often. Which, to me, is almost a jealous behavior. Didn't you say there was a note you received, Park?"

Nate shuffles through the files in his hand and gives her the original letter, which is encased in a clear plastic bag.

Wendy reads the letter out loud. "I am her. She is me."

On that, I suck back a generous swallow of the whiskey. It's smooth and warm going down. Must be a good year. As with anything Mick owns, it's probably top-notch.

Wendy taps her lips with her finger while staring at the letter. "It's like she's proving that Skyler and she are the same somehow. But why would she need to make that clear to Parker? Then the first text he receives is a comparison. Maybe the person who's texting Skyler is after Parker? This person could be after Parker and messing with Skyler to get to him."

"He did receive the note first and then the first text. Skyler's came after," Nate says.

"Could it be two different people, possibly working together to freak you both out?" Wendy suggests.

I shrug and run my hand through my hair. "Could be, I guess. They sound similar, all grammatically correct, no quick text. No emojis. Except the first one Skyler receives talks about them being friends. The letters she's received from fans have been overly friendly. They all believe they have a form of friendship or relationship with Sky."

Wendy bites her lips and nods. "I'm gonna do some poking around. Work these phone numbers, see if I can't trace them back to actual cell phone purchases. Maybe narrow down the location where the person is buying their phones. It's not much, but it's a start."

"What do you think about bringing the authorities in?" Nate inquires.

"What do we really have?" I ask. "There's nothing threatening in them. Just because we're uncomfortable doesn't mean whoever this person is has broken the law. It's a bunch of texts and a note. Even the fan mail spans years with no security breaches or harm having come to Sky," I add.

"True. You can't do anything without the threat of physical violence," Mick states.

"Either way, I'm gonna look into it. And of course, if a person tries to mess with you, they've got He-Man"—she hooks a thumb toward Nate, then Rachel—"and She-Ra to contend with. If it were me, I wouldn't make an approach. Then again, I'm not stupid. Though nothing in these texts or the way the sender is evading identification says the person is stupid either. Just keep your eyes open and be careful." Wendy finishes her second whiskey.

"Well, if we're done with the ugly portion of our evening, I think it's time to retire to the dining room. Our chef has prepared a feast for the *six* of us." Mick stresses the word *six* and glances at Rachel and Nate.

Rachel's brows seem to jump up into her hairline. "Uh, I thought we would just come back after you've had your meal with friends," she says, looking at Skyler, then at me.

Wendy stands, grabs Rachel's hand, and pulls her up. "You are our friends. Now come on. I don't want to ruin Chef Fancy Pants' plan to feed the whole group. Chef Tony is Italian and loves to have many mouths to feed and bellies to fill. Another reason we need to have a house full of babies. Come on." She hooks her elbow with Rachel's. Nate and Sky follow close behind. As I'm bringing up the rear, Mick stops me with a hand to my bicep.

I stop abruptly, and he lets go but waits until the group is out of the room.

"Should I be worried about Wendy's involvement in this issue?"

I take a full, deep breath and rub at the back of my neck. "Honestly, Mick, I don't know. I'm uncomfortable with a lot of things in Skyler's world, but it comes with the territory. She has Nate and Rachel with her at all times when she's not with me. Heck, most of the time, they're with us too. No one's going to know Wendy is looking into things, but if you don't like it, I'm not sure what you can do to change it. Wendy's the best we've got when it comes to detailed searches. If anyone can find something on these letters or the texts, it's going to be her. Nate and I are at a complete loss. We exhausted all possible avenues before coming to her."

His jaw seems to clench before my eyes as he nods curtly. "Open communication. At all times. This is not just you, Wendy, and Nate. You understand? If my woman is in on this, I'm in on this."

"Full disclosure. Done," I promise right away. I'd want the same respect if the situation were reversed.

"Then we understand each other perfectly. Hope you're hungry. I understand Tony went family style with dinner tonight."

I grin widely. "Is there any other way?"

A small hint of a smile appears across Mick's lips. "Apparently not."

***

"I'm up to my eyeballs in paperwork, brother. This shit is too much. I can't handle the money, manage our investments, wrangle Bo, and pretend to be a lawyer." Royce's deep voice over the phone has an extra element of grating I don't remember it having normally.

Skyler tosses her sweater on the back of her couch as I meander through her penthouse and into her bedroom. I walk into the closet to hang my jacket and stop dead in my tracks at the entire right side, which is filled with suits. Men's suits. Polos. Dress shirts. T-shirts. Jeans. Slacks. Even a flat surface that has expensive ties in a variety of wildly colorful and cool-as-shit designs, all spread out along a handmade wooden tie holder thingamajig. I blink a few times and refocus on the call as my eyes take in the other three-fourths of the closet, loaded with Skyler's clothes and gowns, many of which still have tags.

"Brother, I get you. *I get you.* And I'm on it. I actually met with Andre today and a lawyer who would be perfect for us—"

"Great! Fucking hire the man." His voice is tired and determined.

"It's a woman, actually, and—"

"I don't care who it is. Is the person qualified?"

"Very." I sigh.

"Educated? Credentials up to snuff?" he adds.

"And then some. But—"

He butts in again. "Is she experienced?"

I clench my teeth. "Yeah, worked on Capitol Hill, specializes in corporate law but also dabbled in legislation, which would be ideal for the case we're starting next week with Pure Beauty Pharmaceuticals."

"Hire her," he states flat out.

"Royce, I don't think you understand . . ."

"I understand you've got a qualified, educated, experienced female. Is she dog ugly or something? Have you slept with her?"

I cringe. "No! And no! Jesus. She's beautiful. Classy."

"Awesome. Then the only issue we'll have is Bo wanting to bang her."

Actually, Bo is the least of my worries when it comes to Kendra Banks.

"There are things you don't know. Also, I had a chat with Annie today regarding permanent employment. She was happy. Well, at least I think she was. I can't get a good read on that girl."

Booming laughter greets me. "Probably because the last few times you've been in the office, you were there with Skyler. That woman is your perfect distraction."

I grin. He is not wrong. "Be that as it may, she's interested in full time. I didn't talk with Wendy about our idea for her being the chief information officer because I thought you'd want to do that together. Same with Annie and the new lawyer."

"Fuck it. Bo doesn't care. You already know that. Wendy he'll want to be in on just because he loves her and loves poking fun at her. Annie, he could care less. Hiring a lawyer, he wants no part of. If you say this woman is qualified, just take the plunge. We'll get to know one another later. Do you get along with her?"

I finger the store tags dangling from all the clothes hanging in Sky's closet. "Yeah, totally. It's just—"

"You found your surprise!" Skyler squeals from the entrance to the closet. "Man! I was going to blindfold you and everything." She pouts.

"Looks like you got yo' girl to deal with. Send my love. In the meantime, Park, I trust you. Save my ass. I do not have time to drag this out. We need help now. The sooner the better. Now that's all I'm going to say. Have a good night. Peace." It's the last thing he says before he hangs up.

I tip my head back and rub at my temples with my thumb and forefinger.

A pair of arms slide up my chest and loop around my neck. "Honey, I thought you'd like the surprise. Makes it easier for you to stay whenever you want without having to stop across town for your clothes."

I let out a long breath and pull my girl into my arms. "Good surprise, baby. I love it. How did you get my sizes?"

She grins and pulls back. "Had Wendy look up all your clothing purchases for the past year. Figured out your style preferences and then called my personal shopper. She picked it all and sent it over. It should all fit perfectly. If it doesn't, she'll take it back and charge my account."

"It's awesome, Peaches. I'll have money wired over to pay for it."

She frowns. "No, honey. This is a gift. From me to you. I want you to feel at home here. This is just one step, don't you think?"

I know if I force the issue, especially the money part, she's going to shut down. And honestly, I'm tired. Bone tired. Instead, I snuggle her neck. "Thank you, baby. I love it. Very thoughtful. Now all I need are my Sox tees and we'll be set."

She backs up, waggles her eyebrows, and leaves my arms to flounce over to a set of drawers. She opens the top drawer. "Underwear." The second. "Socks." The third. "PJ pants. And in the last drawer . . . Sox gear!" She grins wide.

"You just proved what I already knew," I say with nothing but admiration and love.

She smiles wide and comes back into my arms clutching a Sox T-shirt. "Which is what?"

"You're the perfect woman, and all mine."

3

"Jesus!"

"Oh my God, honey . . . ," leaves Sky's lips on a breathy gasp.

"Get there," I growl, powering into her with long, hard thrusts. I grit my teeth as desire ripples down my spine to pool at my lower back.

I suck a pink-tipped nipple into my mouth. Skyler arches into it, serving up her body on what must be pure instinct. Once I've swirled my tongue around the slippery, erect tip, I bite down on the sensitive flesh. That's all it takes to have my girl crying out and her body tensing under mine.

"Fuck yes!" I slide my hands up her back, curl them around her shoulders from underneath, and clamp down, while her thighs press tighter against my rib cage.

"Parker, I'm coming!" She cries out again, her body giving me the lockdown at three points. Legs. Arms. Pussy. Pure heaven.

"Fuck yeah, you are." I use my leverage on her shoulders to go to town, pounding deep and grinding down on her pelvis until she mewls with my efforts. Which sends a calling card straight to my dick that has me shooting off in pure fucking bliss. My mind is obliterated as I groan, "Yes!"

Once the aftershocks settle down to a dull simmer, I burrow my head against her neck, tasting her while the last of my arousal coats her insides.

"Mmm," she murmurs, and sighs as I kiss every inch of skin I can put my mouth on.

"Love you, Peaches."

She runs her fingers over my hair, holding me to her, heart to heart. "I love you, honey. Now that you've had a good night's sleep and a raucous round of morning sex, are you going to tell me what's wrong?"

I frown against her neck, then lift my upper body so that I can stare into her beautiful brown eyes. "You think something's wrong after I slept the sleep of the dead with you in my arms and woke up with your sweet mouth all over my dick, for which I returned the favor by putting my mouth *all over you*. Tasting one of your orgasms, felt the second one even sweeter, and then got mine? Baby . . . you are looking at one happy fucking guy."

Skyler chuckles, and I watch while her laughter spreads unbelievable beauty across her features. Christ, I'm a lucky man. And to think I could have lost her with the shit I pulled in Montreal. Fuck!

My girl runs her fingers through my hair and assesses me. "Honey, you were stressing about more than our stalker/superfan issue. What's going on? Does it have anything to do with the meeting you had yesterday with the lawyer?"

Damn, she's good.

I sigh, disconnect with her, and roll over onto my back. She cuddles into my side and waits patiently, content to hold out until I'm ready to tell her what's on my mind.

"Turns out I know the lawyer personally."

Sky runs her hand up and down my bare chest and abs. "Meaning this is someone you know intimately?"

"Well, not sexually. She was Royce's ex-girlfriend back when we were in Harvard. Thought they'd go the distance too. He dated her for a full two years. Was totally into her. Then, when we were graduating, they ended it and she went off to law school in DC. He didn't say much about the breakup, just that she wanted to focus on her career and he wanted to focus on International Guy. Why they couldn't do both together, I don't know."

"Hmm, so you're worried about hiring her?"

I nod. "Yeah, and I wasn't sure I was going to, but then I spoke to Roy last night, and he's done taking on the lion's share of the legal shit for the company. It's too much alongside what he's doing, and we need a full-time person."

Skyler shrugs. "Then find someone else."

Again, I let out a long sigh. "Problem is, we don't have a lot of time. This next case needs a corporate lawyer on point. It's big money. Huge. Not to mention it's a pharmaceutical company that wants us to get into their legislative dealings. Kendra has experience doing that. Lots of it, actually. She'd be a real asset on this project. Plus, Roy told me to hire her."

Sky lifts her head up to pair her gaze with mine. "He did? Well, then there's no issue. Apparently, they left things in a good place."

I shake my head and run my hand through her messy golden locks. "Not exactly. I didn't even get to tell him who the interviewee was before he told me to hire her. And even though I really want to hire her, I feel like I'm doing it for the wrong reason."

She narrows her gaze. "She's got all the skills and qualifications you need, plus she can do this big case right now?"

"Yeah."

"You said there was another reason?"

I grin.

"Oh no. You're sticking your nose somewhere it shouldn't be, aren't you?" She frowns.

I tug my girl over and onto my chest so that I can not only feel her warmth skin to skin, but I can hold her the way I want to. "Back when we were in college, there was nothing separating those two. She was it."

"It?" Sky sets her hands on my chest and then places her chin on top of them.

"It. The one. His one and only."

Sky's lips flatten. "Then what happened? Why didn't she just go to law school at Harvard and stay in the area, so she could be with her man?"

I shake my head. "See, that's the thing. I don't know. Roy was super tight-lipped about it. I think Bo knows, because when it all went down, both of them were surly about it. Me, I was dealing with my own shit with Kayla and her fucking Greg. I was in no place to handle the breakup between Roy and Kendra when I was dealing with my own breakup and betrayal by a best friend and my fiancée. During that time, the guys and I barely got our shit together enough to start the business after graduation. The three of us just pushed all the personal baggage to the side and focused all of our attention on building the business and making a real go of it. Thank God it worked out, but . . ." I let my words fall off.

"You feel bad you didn't dig into it more?" Sky surmises.

"Yeah, baby. I feel like a shit friend. And when I saw Kendra today, I realized how much I missed her. She was a true friend. Like a sister I never had. I loved her. Trusted her to take care of my boy. Something happened, and out of nowhere, she was gone. The timing was just after Kayla's shit. As in within a couple of weeks. I was still sucking back the booze to wash away my sorrow. Bo and Roy were taking care of me. Then Bo was taking care of both of us."

"And Roy never told you what happened?"

I think back to a night of shit whiskey shots between the three of us while playing pool at Lucky's. My father didn't own the business yet, but we were regulars. "I remember asking him, and he said something about wanting different things. When I pushed the issue, he said she cut things off with him and told him she was leaving."

"Poor Roy."

"Yeah, I knew he'd already bought her the engagement ring and was waiting for the perfect time. He'd said he was going to pop the question on graduation night. Make it the best night of his life. She broke things off a week before. Then we all walked, and she left the state for DC. Far as I know, she's been there ever since."

Skyler's expression is so sad, I lift my head and kiss her pouty frown.

"That sucks. She was his one and she bailed. I don't think I'm going to like her." My girl, loyal to her core.

"I'm certain you will like her, though she has this edge to her now. A bit of armor. Like she's hiding her true self behind a wall where her emotions are guarded. She is still beautiful, maybe even more so now that she's filled in from a twenty-two-year-old to an almost thirty-year-old. Roy's gonna shit when he sees her, and after the crap that went down with Rochelle Renner in San Francisco, he admitted he's ready to settle down. Even made a comment about how lucky we are because we've found each other and are moving forward with our lives. He wants that, and I don't know, seeing her again—maybe the reason he hasn't found it is because he's supposed to be with Kendra."

Skyler's eyebrows rise up into her hairline. "Are you playing match-maker . . . with Royce?" Her mouth drops open, and she smiles huge. "I want in."

I move to deny her claim, but she presses two fingers over my lips.

"Honey, I want in. If this is the woman for him, his long-lost love, we have to get them together!" She sits up on me, and her center makes contact with the beast.

The beast perks up, ready to go for round two. She must feel the hardness between her thighs because one eyebrow cocks and she rubs her hips back and forth teasingly. "You gonna let me in?" She smiles, puts two fingers into her mouth, licks them seductively, and then presses them on the small landing strip at the apex of her legs.

"Fuck." I stare at those two digits twirling around that hot bundle of nerves, wishing they were my tongue instead.

"You gonna let me in?" She sighs and circles her hips along with her fingers, then moans.

"You gonna let *me* in?" I grab for her hips, wanting to lift her up and place her on my now rock-hard cock.

She grins salaciously but is no less beautiful for it. Her other hand comes up to my lips, and I suck two fingers into my mouth, running my tongue between them the way I want to between her legs. She removes those fingers and then brings them to her nipple, where she swirls them on the pink tip before pinching it until it turns a berry red.

"Jesus!" I grind my teeth. "Let. Me. In." I attempt to move her hips again, but she locks on to my hips with her thighs. I could overpower her if I really wanted to, but this game is fuckhot, and I want to see where it goes.

"You let me in on the matchmaking and you can do whatever you want to me," she taunts, her hands still a busy blur between her thighs and on her breast.

Hell, I don't know what I want to do first. Suck that ripe titty, make the other one just as dark by teasing the fuck out of it, plunge three fingers deep into her wet heat, or thrust home and watch while she bounces on my cock.

So many choices.

"Hmm . . . deal," I tell her, already planning to give in because, if I'm going to get Kendra and Royce back together, or at the very least see if the two of them are still compatible in a forever capacity, I'm going to need all the help I can get.

Her grin is huge. I return it. "Now give me that hand." I grab for the wrist that's attached to the hand working her sex and bring those fingers between my lips. Her sweet-and-salty taste hits my tongue, and suddenly I'm ravenous. I lick her fingers clean, grip her around the waist, and push my legs hard into the mattress until I'm taking the two of us back to the headboard with her in my lap. I lift her up and thrust her down on my now raging cock.

"Oh my!" she calls out, but I cover her mouth with my own until we're a mess of gyrating bodies, throaty moans, and rutting, animal-like cries. We take one another to the peak of ecstasy, our orgasms rushing through our bodies like freight trains.

We settle back down in a sweaty heap of limbs, Sky still in my lap, the beast firmly wedged inside of her, and her face in my neck. I pet her back, enjoying the heaving of her body as, with each breath, her breasts tickle my chest.

"You good?" I smile into the empty room, appreciating our hearts beating in a synchronized rhythm in our chests.

"So good." She sighs into my neck, her breath hot against my skin. "I love making deals with you."

I grin and wrap my arms around her bare body. "Especially when they involve naked compensation."

She nods and weakly taps my chest. "Yes. Especially then. Everyone wins."

"Yeah, baby, everyone wins."

***

"You did *what?*" Bo stands in front of my desk, one hand on a denim-clad hip, his motorcycle jacket still on, the other arm curled around his bike helmet.

"I hired Kendra Banks, Esquire, as our new in-house counsel."

Bo's face pinches into an expression of disgust. "I heard what you said; I'm not quite believing my ears. Tell me what you meant to say was that you hired another lawyer who happens to have the same exact name as Roy's ex from eight years ago?"

I shake my head and place the file of docs I've just signed back into the tray for Annie to pick up. "You heard me right. I met with Andre. Kendra was the best candidate for the job."

"Doesn't the bitch live in DC?" he growls.

Bitch? Whoa. Did not expect that level of anger to come from Bo's lips.

"No, she's moved back to Boston. I didn't ask why, only confirmed that she would be here for the foreseeable future because we didn't want to hire someone only to get used to them and have them bail on us."

Bo starts to pace. "I cannot believe this. And Roy approved this shit?"

"He told me to hire the best candidate. Andre did a thorough search. She's the only one who has not only corporate law experience, but legislative experience. Meaning, she will be on point for the Pure Beauty Pharmaceuticals case. Which, may I remind you, is a half-million-dollar case for us!"

Bo clenches his teeth and locks his jaw. "I don't give one flying fuck how much money they're paying us. That bitch cannot work here!"

"It's too late, I've already hired her. She'll be here within the hour."

His brown eyes practically bug out of his head. "You've gone too far with this shit, Park. Too fuckin' far. Do you remember what it was like when she left him?"

I shake my head and stand up, a tingle of dread putting pressure against my temples. "No. I was dealing with my shit over Kayla. Roy didn't tell me jack shit. Made it sound like it ended amicably."

Bo flaps his free hand in the air. "Who the hell breaks up a two-year relationship—one in which one of them bought a diamond ring—with nothing but sweet goodbyes? Are you kidding me? You are not that dumb."

I let out a long, bloated breath and rub at the back of my neck. "Roy was losing his shit about the legal stuff. I tried to tell him who the candidate was. He didn't care. He told me to hire her. I hired her. You told me you didn't care. So. I. Hired. Her! Fuckin' A!" Irritation mixed with a hint of regret pushes its way to the top of my psyche.

Bo shakes his head, goes over to the door, and grabs the handle. As he turns it, he pierces me with a deadly gaze. "You are going to regret this."

When he opens the door, Kendra and Annie are standing in front of him, blocking his way.

"Fuck me!" he roars, looking Kendra up and down not once, but twice, from her pristine white tailored suit with red piping to her sexy red slingback heels. She looks like a fierce, expensive, take-no-prisoners professional. "Couldn't you be fat . . . and as ugly as your soul?"

Kendra's lips compress into a flat, emotionless line. "It's nice to see you too, Bogart. I see that not a lot has changed with your fiery temper."

He points a finger in her face. "I'm watching you. I don't know what this is, or why you chose now to come back when everything is aces, but I got your number, woman. I got your fuckin' number."

"How comforting. I'll consider myself warned by that thinly veiled threat." Her gaze comes to mine. "Good morning, Parker."

"'Good morning, Parker.' Unbelievable!" Bo growls and then pushes his way past Kendra and Annie and out the door.

"That will be all, Annie, thank you. Kendra, please come in."

Kendra enters my office, shuts the door, and takes a seat in front of my desk.

"That did not go as planned. I'm sorry," I state with a note of frustration.

She shakes her head. "No need to apologize. I anticipated backlash from one or both of your partners. Though I knew Bo would be unhappy at my presence, I didn't think he'd be livid. I'll have to work on that. And I will."

"Just give it time. Really. He's not much different than when you knew him in school. Smarter, more notches on his bedpost . . . a lot of notches." I grin and am finally gifted with one of Kendra's big white smiles. "He's protective."

"I'll say." She winces.

"He's that way with all of us. Including Wendy."

"Wendy?"

"Our personal assistant."

She frowns. "I thought your assistant's name was Annie?"

"Uh, she is. Technically. Wendy was before her. She's coming back this week. She'll help keep Bo and Royce in check."

"She out on leave?"

"Yeah."

"Maternity?"

My heart sinks. I hate talking about what happened, but if Kendra's going to be our attorney, she's going to be in the know about everything within this company.

"No. She's been out for the past two months, healing after getting shot on one of our cases."

A dark-brown eyebrow cocks up on Kendra's forehead. "Shot?"

I lick my lips and sit back in my chair. "Yeah. It was touch and go for a little while there. We dealt with a case in Montreal—"

"This happened on an international case? Parker, there are so many legal ramifications that can come back to haunt you if this employee sues International Guy . . . which is within her legal right, by the way."

I wave my hand. "There probably are. Except we have nothing to worry about with Wendy. She's all about IG and has become very much a member of the team and our family. She has as much vested interest in IG as we have. Plus, her fiancé is wealthy. Oprah Winfrey wealthy. She doesn't need to sue us."

Her lips tighten, and she pulls out a legal pad. "I'll trust you on your word for now until I've met and assessed her myself. I think you need to provide me with the files for your last six months' worth of cases. I may need to do some serious follow-up paperwork to ensure the company's holdings are not at risk."

I grin wide. "Well, the good news is, Royce has been keeping on top of those things, so he can provide you with the files and the information about what he's done to date."

She closes her eyes at the mention of Royce's name. I can see her body tensing, but she's trying damn hard not to let it show. She opens her eyes and smiles placatingly. "Great."

"Regardless of whatever happened between you and Roy in the past, Kendra, he's a professional. Plus, what happened between you two was years ago. Water under the bridge, right?"

She licks her lips and nods but doesn't respond verbally. To me, that is telling. Basically telling me that she's not as confident in Roy's response to her working here as I am.

Before I can get into the work side of things, my door opens, and Roy enters smiling, with a pep in his step. "Sorry I'm a bit late. Got caught on the phone with a client and was held up . . ." His words just stop when he sees Kendra, as does his forward movement. His entire face goes blank as she stands up.

"Hello, Royce. It's been a long time." She holds out her hand to shake his.

Roy blinks at her hand, then looks to me and back at her. "What are you doing here?"

She drops her hand and stiffens her spine, looking a solid inch taller than before. "I'm your new lawyer."

Roy's coal-black eyes widen, and his lips purse tight enough to make the skin turn white. "This must be a joke." He turns to me. "Park. Brother. Did you hire my ex to work with us?"

I stand up, button my suit jacket, and swallow in an attempt to relieve the instant dryness coating my throat. "You told me to. You wouldn't listen to me when I tried to explain who she was. And you've been working your ass off . . ."

His hand slices the air. "Did you hire the woman I asked to marry me, the same one who turned me down, packed her ass up from our shared apartment, and left me high and dry so she could move to Washington, DC?"

"Fuck me," I whisper, not realizing the ramifications of the decision I made. Shit. "I think I made a mistake."

"You fuckin' *think*?" Royce growls.

This is when Kendra, the smart-as-hell attorney, pipes up. "Be that as it may, we have an ironclad contract, which you signed, giving me six months' employment as long as I don't do something that does not meet the terms of the contract. If you end the contract, you pay me six months' salary in full, except doubled for my inconvenience. Since six months' salary is a hundred thousand dollars, you will owe me two hundred thousand for receiving absolutely no service."

"Damn, you're good," I whisper, shocked at how lethal this woman is.

"The best. Which, I will remind you, is why you hired me and I came so highly recommended by Andre. You will not find a person more qualified or committed for this position."

"I don't care. Two hundred thousand be damned . . . ," Royce states.

I move over to him and place my hand on his shoulder. "Roy, I'm sorry. I didn't know the severity of the break. I wouldn't have . . ." I lose my ability to continue because my heart is hammering in my chest and my throat feels like it's being squeezed by a vise.

"What, Royce? You're still so hung up on me eight years later you can't stand the possibility of working with me? It's work. Business. There's nothing the two of us are better at than business," she attempts.

He steps up close to her, their faces now not two inches from one another. "I can think of at least one thing we were even better at together," he snarls.

Her chest rises and falls, but they stay at a standoff, a stalemate.

"Maybe we can work something out . . ." I try to smooth over my royal fuckup.

Royce grins, his eyes still on Kendra's. "No need. If she can be professional, so can I. We'll give you your six months, but one screwup, Kendra, and you're out on your ass."

She smiles with a bit of a snide edge. "I look forward to the day you find something I messed up. I do exceptional work. You'll see."

"I'm looking forward to being wrong."

"So am I." Her voice shakes at that parting shot before she turns away from him. What she said almost seems to have a double meaning. Is there something she feels she was wrong about too?

Kendra picks up her legal pad and steps away from all things badass alpha Royce. "Parker, I understand you have an office for me?"

I nod.

"Great. No time like the present to get started. Royce, Parker says you have the files for the last six months' worth of cases. I'd like to review them, get myself up to date over the next few days, and then discuss any issue I might find or actions we need to take."

"Fine. I'll have Annie bring them to you." His voice is a deep, rumbling, low, thunderous storm, brewing without breaking.

She nods curtly. "Also, I want to review the employee files, make sure all required documents are up to snuff."

"Not a problem. I have those here." I dig my keys out of my pocket, unlock my bottom-right drawer, and pull out the employee files on me, Bo, Royce, Wendy, and Annie and hand them over to her. "Those are confidential."

"I'm sure my office has locking cabinets?" she replies to my statement.

"Yeah, keys are in the top desk drawer."

"I'll get started now."

"Later in the week, we need to discuss the Pure Beauty Pharmaceuticals case."

She frowns. "You're working with them?" Her voice takes on a testy note. This could be because of the confrontation with Royce and Bo or from something else. I'll have to spend time getting on her level when things calm down a little.

"Yeah, they're our next client. We're going to DC next week. And when I say *we*, I mean you, me, and Royce. The contract needs to be reviewed, anything not in our favor changed, signed, and sent off. I was waiting for our new lawyer before signing."

She closes her eyes for a moment as if she's centering herself before opening them. "Then I better get to work."

"Annie will show you where your office is."

"Thank you, Parker." She turns to head to the door, but when she reaches it she stops. Her shoulders rise and then fall before she spins around. "Royce, I'm sorry this is a shock. It was not my intention. I'm actually very much looking forward to working with you. We always did work well together. At least in our studies and, um, in other ways." Unconcealed hurt flashes across her face before she covers it up.

Roy licks his lips and crosses his massive arms over one another. "Once upon a time, we did work well together, but a lot has changed."

"I understand. I'll be waiting for those files."

"And you'll have them soon," he promises.

She nods and walks out the door.

4

The second the door closes, Royce is on my ass.

"Seeing Kendra was a low blow, brother. A low, *ruthless* blow. I can't imagine what would make you believe it was okay to hire her as our lawyer." Royce's voice is filled with hurt as well as disbelief.

His words sink a well-placed punch deep into my gut where my self-deprecation lives. "Roy, I tried to tell you, man. Repeatedly, you told me to hire the most qualified person . . ."

He clenches his teeth and twists his lips. "I didn't think the most ideal candidate would be the woman who broke my heart and left the pieces for me to pick up and put back together on an empty bed in our once happy home together. I wanted to *marry* her, Park. Give her my name. Raise children with her. We talked about it all the time . . ."

I run my hand through my hair. "What the fuck happened? You made it sound like it was a mutual break back then. How the hell was I supposed to know any different?"

Roy's dark eyes narrow. "I can't get into it. Not now. *Not ever.* I won't. Just know that I am not happy about this. The last thing I need is the one who got away to be prancing around this office tempting me, breaking my cold heart all over again."

"Roy . . ."

He shakes his head, flaps his coat jacket, and buttons it in place on his massive form. It's as if he's putting his emotional and physical self back together at the same time.

"I can be professional. Get us through the next six months. Then, all bets are off. I want her gone. You hear me? *G-o-n-e*." Royce's statement is a promise, not a threat.

I close my eyes and feel the air in the room fill with disquiet from his demand.

"Whatever you want." There's not much more I can do to salvage the situation.

"That's what I want."

"Then you'll have it."

"Never again, brother," Royce warns.

I frown and shoot my gaze his way. His dark eyes lock with mine.

"Never again are you butting into a situation when it comes to me and a woman. Do you understand me? If you do, we'll have problems. Much larger problems than having my ex working at our fucking company."

Shit. Operation Royce Matchmaking is off the table. Sky will be brokenhearted. She'll rally, though. It's who she is.

"Understood."

Royce's jaw tightens, and he looks out the window right at the moment my suddenly revolving door opens and a chipper, familiar redhead bounces in.

"Hooo-weee, who's the African American ice queen who's all kinds of sexy, badass, but chilly response when prodded?"

Royce closes his eyes and sighs.

"That's Kendra Banks, our new in-house counsel."

Wendy smiles wide. "Sweet. Means you're off the hook on all the legal, eh?" She nudges Royce, who gives her a subtle smile.

Wendy narrows her eyes. "Not happy about a shit-hot, badass lawyer taking over your workload? Oh no, what is it?" A frown mars her pretty red lips. "Lemme guess. Bo chasing her tail? I mean, I get it. She looks like Vanessa Williams and Angelina Jolie had a baby together— not that it could happen, both of them being women and all, but she's that freakin' gorgeous."

Royce walks over to Wendy, cups the back of her head, places a kiss on top, and moves away. "Glad you're home, Wendy. I got shit to do," he says evasively, and leaves us both hanging.

"Wasn't I supposed to come in today to talk to the three of you?" She flicks a hand in the direction of the door that Royce just walked through.

I sigh and rub at my forehead. "I fucked up. *Again.*"

Wendy shuts the door before leading me to the couch by my hand. She sits me on the cushion and then places her ass on the glass table in front of me. "Lay it on me, Bossman. I need the goods, because what happened just then was *not* okay. Royce is close-lipped and didn't even look you in the eye. He avoided all talk about the new lawyer, which means something's up about her, and you look as though someone just crashed your Tesla. Give it up."

So, I do. I tell her everything, letting it all out like a whiny little bitch, laying all of my concerns in her very capable hands.

When I'm done, I feel exhausted, as though I've been mentally run over by a bus and need a week to sleep it off.

Wendy's lips twitch and then turn into a big smile.

"You realize you were right in what you did."

I scowl. "How you figure?"

She beams. "If Royce were over Lady Lawyer, it wouldn't have bothered him to have her working here. Might've annoyed him, but not caused that growly, unhinged reaction. If they truly did leave everything in the past, then it would have been no big thing. Right?"

Her logic has merit. "Continue."

She tips her head to the side, her blue eyes sparkling with intent. Uh-oh, this means she's about to suggest some mischief.

"Wendy . . ." I try to warn her off right away, thinking about the ultimatum Royce threw down for me to back off.

"Nuh-uh, there is no way we're not moving forward with a match-making plan. First, though, they need to work together awhile. Get their juices flowing. You know, being around one another like old times. The case in DC is going to help that for sure. Close quarters when working a case—you're always all in each other's faces."

"Or it could hurt the situation and him more. Rather, I could end up being the one in pain having lost my best friend or when Royce takes a swing at me for putting him in the predicament in the first place."

Wendy frowns. "When was the last time you all came to blows?"

I cringe. "Never. We're best friends. Shit gets physical and that friendship dies. Bro code. We can beat up someone else who's threatening our buddy, but we never lay fists on one another unless we're sparring in a boxing ring for fun."

"Huh. I guess I just thought dudes would duke it out when they couldn't get out what they wanted to say emotionally. Interesting. Girls rip each other to shreds verbally and get over it quick. It's almost cathartic in a way, I think. Not that I'd really know, since my first real friends are Skyler, Rachel, your mom, and Roy's mom and sisters, but I watch a lot of *Gilmore Girls* and *Bitch Housewives*."

I grab Wendy's hand and squeeze it. "Minxy, I'm glad you're back."

"You and me both," Wendy scoffs. "I mean, I like the part about having a lot of sex with the goal of getting me knocked up, but I need a breather." She blows out a tired breath. "Mick is taking on the getting-me-pregnant duty like *it's his job*." She grins wickedly. "Not that I'm complainin', but you know . . . a girl's gotta make a guy work for it a little. Space helps."

I blink at her without saying anything.

She frowns and drops her shoulders. "Too much information again?"

I nod.

"Damn. I'll work on that. I'm never sure when it's girl talk versus guy talk."

"Ask Sky."

She brightens up. "That's a good idea."

"Best I ever had, apparently."

Wendy grins. "Besides the new Lady Lawyer issue with Royce—"

"And Bo."

Her face takes on an expression of shock, eyebrows raised, blue eyes bright. "He's into her too?"

I let out a gruff response. "No. He despises her. Apparently, he knew more about her past with Roy, and he's not happy she's here. Which means we've got a surly Bo and a broody Royce. Not a good combination."

"Ahh, I see the dilemma. I'll work on them."

"Much appreciated."

"Course. Now what did the three of you want to talk to me about anyway?"

"Ugh, well, I guess since I'm not going to be getting them in a room with me anytime soon, I'll do the honors."

"Honors?" she asks.

I stand up and walk over to my desk to grab the document Bo, Royce, and I have already signed. "An offer for you to officially become the new chief information officer for International Guy. It comes with a pay increase, a new title, more responsibility, and unlimited access to pretty much everything here."

She snickers. "Like I didn't already have that." She points to her chest. "Hacker, remember?"

I smile softly at her and hand her the letter and attached contract.

Wendy scans the contract and reads through the letter. "This position comes with a three-year term with automatic renewal unless both or either of us wants to terminate the employment. You're committing to me for three years . . ." Her voice is hoarse and breathy.

"Yeah. And we want you to commit to us too."

"Can I take this home and share it with Mick before I sign?"

"Of course. You're committing three years of your life to IG. I'd be disappointed if you didn't talk to your mate about it."

She sniffs and places the document against her chest as if it's a cherished item, not pieces of paper.

"I want you to know this means a lot, Parker." She sucks a breath in, and her watery blue eyes rise so that her gaze reaches mine. "I'm flattered."

I smile and place my hand on her shoulder. "We're honored to have you as part of the team and want to make an official commitment to back it up. Take the agreement home. The three of us have already signed. Once you've reviewed it, and hopefully signed it, you'll be moving into your new office."

Her eyes widen to the size of saucers. "I'll have my own office?"

"Yep, the one next to reception so you can keep an eye on Annie and the rest of us."

"Awesome . . . ," she breathes.

"I'm glad you think so. For now, though, maybe you can check in with Annie. She's got a lot to take on. She's been doing well, but she's not you. A lot of things we didn't punt her way, knowing you were coming back."

"Damn straight." She winks at me.

"Also, perhaps you can feel out Bo and Royce. Try to see where their heads are at over Kendra?"

"You want me to wade in." She chuckles.

"Uh, yeah. Obviously."

"Nothing's changed. Not even after two months." She shakes her head as though she's enjoying her own joke.

"Except the facts that you're being promoted; we've hired a new personal assistant and a corporate lawyer; you're getting married; Skyler will be working in Boston for the foreseeable future; and she has a superfan/stalker sending us both weird messages. And my brother is bisexual. Nope, nothing much."

***

Three days later. To say the tension in the room is so thick you can cut it with a knife is wildly understating the obvious.

Kendra's eyes and body language are fierce and a force to be reckoned with. She sits stoically, face forward, gaze set directly on me, ignoring the two men sitting to her left.

Bo is in the middle seat, sneering at Kendra every time he looks at her. Royce is ignoring everything, his attention focused entirely on his phone. Hell, he could be checking the scores from last night's games or the stock market, or maybe even playing sudoku for all I know.

God, this sucks. *Where is Wendy anyway?*

Speaking of my savior, she enters the room, a tablet in hand. "Sorry to be late, but I've been digging into this corporation and thought you'd want to be in the know on their current projects and legislative interests."

A weight the size of Massachusetts lifts off my chest at the sight of our own Moneypenny. I offer Wendy a grateful smile as she enters then leans against the ledge along the wall of windows at my back.

"Kendra, let's start with you. Please tell us where we're at with Pure Beauty Pharmaceuticals. We're leaving Monday, and I want to be as up to date as possible." I address our new hire.

Kendra, dressed in an orange silk blouse, a fitted beige tweed skirt, and a cream three-quarter-sleeve jacket, digs into the files in front of her. She stands and hands each of us, including Wendy, a copy of something.

The woman is always prepared.

Bo snarls at her but takes the document, continuing his adolescent behavior toward the seemingly unaffected Kendra. She takes his attitude and tosses it aside as though it's an old, used-up tissue.

"What I've given you is an updated contract signed by the CEO of Pure Beauty Pharmaceuticals."

"Updated?" Royce asks, scanning the document.

"Yes. I found the first one unacceptable." She stares blankly at him.

"I worked that contract myself," he states with a churlish note and a hypersensitivity that can't be missed by anyone within a five-foot radius of the man.

She offers a disingenuous smile in response. "Thank you for getting it moving along in the process. However, the old contract was missing a few necessary items and one very important clause."

He frowns but stares at the new contract. "Which would be what?"

"An out clause."

"Why would we want out?" Bo spouts.

"Well, in my experience, if the consultant gets into a case and encounters a moral concern or a possible risk to the consultant's reputation with continuing said work, the consultant would want the contract to provide a legal out without risk to its holdings or, by terminating, be in a breach of the contract. Basically, it's a protective measure."

I scan the document and note the new legal verbiage she added. "This is a great addition, though from your experience on Capitol Hill, do you have any concerns about us working this case?"

Kendra's mouth tightens. "Not based on professional reasons, no."

"Meaning you have a personal issue with Pure Beauty Pharmaceuticals?" I counter.

"Besides the hinky business surrounding money and medicine when it comes to Big Pharma, yes, I have personal reasons. Many of these entities want to cut corners and take risks with their products. Risks that, as a woman, I wouldn't want for myself if I were to get a beauty treatment. Low-quality product, expiration dates being ignored, and more. However, this contract basically just hires the team to work senators on behalf of the client to aid in the support of legislation.

I don't know what that legislation is, which immediately makes me uncomfortable. I'll want a copy the second we arrive at their offices."

"Good plan. Anyone else?" I ask.

Wendy steps closer to me while pressing buttons on her tablet. "Yeah, I have some concerns. When I did my research on this company, their name popped up a couple of times on animal rights activists' blogs and sites, claiming they use animals to test their products." She makes a stink face, one I see go around the room like a wave at a sporting event. Apparently this group is not big on the idea of innocent animals being used in any form of testing.

"Anything concrete on those claims?" I ask, an uncomfortable tingle tickling the back of my neck.

She shakes her head. "No, just conjecture at this point. Nothing proven. I'm going to keep poking around. As far as I can tell, there's not a lot of press on this company, which is odd for someone trying to get a bill passed. Usually big money comes with big names. It's as though they've flown under the radar of the press and politics up until now. I'm still working to connect the dots on what products they actually make, and I'm not having an easy time of it."

Royce sits up, his expression thoughtful. "You think they're a new company?"

"And able to afford a five-hundred-thousand-dollar contract consulting with us?" I also gear my question to Wendy.

She shakes her head. "No. It says on their website they've been in business thirty years."

"Anyone can lie," Bo adds, and then looks at Kendra. "I've known a lot of liars in my day."

Her jaw goes tight, and she firms her spine like a soldier readying for battle.

I ignore him but plan to have a word about his attitude regarding Kendra when we're alone. "Have we gotten any money yet?" I ask Royce.

"Yeah, twenty percent deposit up front, as with all clients," he confirms.

"Since we've gotten a hundred thousand up front, I say we keep looking into them and make the meet on Monday. It will be Roy, Kendra, and me with Bo on point to take the helm here."

"I don't think my inclusion is necessary now that you have Kendra. Besides, I have another client I'm working where I could use the man-hours. Not to mention we still need to prepare for Madrid," Royce announces.

"What's Madrid?" I pull up my e-calendar on my computer.

"Pop star." He taps the top of his phone with his index finger.

"Pop star. As in, a music artist?" I confirm.

Bo's eyes light up like a bonfire on a sandy beach in summer. I grin, noting his excitement and enjoying the disappearance of the surliness for a moment, however brief it may be. I'll take what I can while it lasts. He's been an absolute pill to be around in the three days since Kendra arrived. Maybe the pop star case will pull him out of it.

"Juliet Jimenez, native to Madrid. Little thing. They call her JJ for short. Voice of an angel, looks of a child even though she's in her twenties. We're going to sex her up and teach her how to be confident, forward, and have stage presence."

I swear, every time we get a new case, I'm surprised by what we're asked to do. It would seem our reputation precedes us as being unorthodox, because none of our cases are the same or have any consistent need. It's always different.

"Interesting," I say around a yawn, proving that I'm not exactly jumping for joy at the idea of jetting off to Madrid.

"Very *interesting*. I'm all over that case." Bo grins.

"Makes sense, especially if I can sit that one out," I toss out in the hopes it will land a three-pointer with the team.

Royce frowns. "Yeah, I'm not thinking so, but we'll discuss it as we get closer. The client specifically asked for you. Apparently, they're familiar with the work you did for the Milan job and want similar results. That means they requested you and Bo. I'm odd man out."

I inhale long and slow, feeling like I'm never going to have a time where I can just be. Stay in Boston for a couple of months straight and have any form of a normal life.

A normal life.

I'm not even sure I'd know what that looks like. Between my celebrity girlfriend, our stalker/superfan issue, my staff up in arms, and traveling around the globe, I can't decide if I'd rather be behind the desk or grilling out on a patch of land with my girl, tossing a ball to an excitable puppy.

The image imprints on my mind: Sky in a pair of booty shorts, a golden retriever puppy nipping at her heels, waiting for her to throw a ball while I grill some steaks off our porch. Nothing but green trees and fields for days, the setting sun on the horizon washing my girl's body in an earthy glow.

"Park . . ." Royce's voice cuts my daydream like a hot knife through butter.

I scowl as the image disappears and Royce's mug is in my face.

"Where'd you go, brother? I said, We done here? I've got business to take care of."

"Oh yeah. Fine. I think we're all headed in the right direction."

Bo looks over at Kendra. "At least some of us are. Catch you on the flip, Tinker Bell, Roy . . ." He moves out the door, then tosses a wave of a hand over his head. "Park. Peace." No goodbye to Kendra, but then that would be giving her attention and acknowledging her presence. He's been doing a damn good job of avoiding her all week.

Kendra stands and presses down the lines in her skirt. "Well, if we're done for the week, I'll take my leave to pack and get ready for the trip too."

I stop her with an arm to her wrist. Wendy sees the move and rushes out. "Bye, guys. I'll be in touch next week," she says, and shuts the office door.

"He'll come around."

She tips her head to the side, and her hazel eyes hit me with hurt in her gaze. "Who? Royce or Bo? Neither of them wants anything to do with me."

"It will take some time, but they're good guys. Known 'em for what seems like forever. They will come around," I promise, although I know it's rather empty since I'm not exactly sure they'll get past their issues with her. I can only hope they will be the guys I know them to be. Fair and free of judgment.

She nods, straightens her shoulders, and pushes a lock of hair behind her ear. "It's fine. I've dealt with worse in my day. This too shall pass."

I narrow my gaze and squeeze her hand. "Something tells me you've dealt with a lot worse. Information that, if shared, could go a long way toward healing some of the hurt left behind by your departure all those years ago?"

"Parker, don't go there." Her lips tighten, and she holds her legal pad against her chest.

We stare at one another for what seems like long minutes, neither of us speaking or willing to back down. I finally take the high road and give her the out. "Okay. Just know that if you ever want to talk, I'm here. We're a team at IG, even if it doesn't feel that way right now. Underneath it all, there's a lot of comradery and respect. The guys will come around, you'll see."

She gifts me a gentle smile. "I hope you're right, Parker. I really do."

"Shall we head out for the weekend? My girlfriend is ordering Chinese in and plans to have a Netflix marathon—whatever that entails. I'm going to suck it up because, when the game is on, she doesn't say a word."

Kendra chuckles.

"You have anyone special to go home to?" I ask, pressing a little.

"Just the family. I've been gone a long time. Much to make up for. Besides, I'm needed here." She moves out the door and off to her office.

"Yes, you are, Kendra." I look at Royce's door and think back to him telling me how he wanted to be settled. "Maybe more than you ever thought possible," I whisper to myself, and head to the elevator. I press the "Penthouse" button and place my thumb over the reader. It pings its acceptance, flashes green, and starts to rise.

The double doors open to the entryway of Skyler's pad. "Honey, I'm home!"

5

Pure Beauty Pharmaceuticals is located west of the White House and downtown Washington, DC, in a little neighborhood called Foggy Bottom. We took the Metro from our hotel downtown because Kendra said it was faster than getting into a car in DC traffic. Since she recently lived here, I deferred to her experience.

A driver waiting outside of the George Washington University Metro station takes us the last half mile to the Pure Beauty Pharmaceuticals plant, which is also where its primary corporate offices are located.

Now we're inside a waiting room surrounded by glass with a great view of the Potomac River. I stand staring out at the river until a raven-haired woman in a very expensive suit approaches. Her skin is flawless and the color of a shiny new pearl. Her eyes are a dark green that matches the silk blouse she has underneath sharp black Armani threads. Her forest-green snakeskin stilettos give the look a stylized pop, but put together, the entire ensemble reminds me of a dark horse. As though she's got her armor on and is ready for a battle. Perhaps she is, since they called in our team.

She shakes my hand with a surprisingly firm grip. "Hello, I'm Vivica Preston, the CEO of Pure Beauty." She then extends her hand to Kendra.

"Parker Ellis, CEO of International Guy, and our in-house counsel, Kendra Banks."

Vivica's dark eyebrow cocks suspiciously, and she smiles. "I believe we know one another through local acquaintances, Kendra. Lovely to see you back in DC, and so soon."

Kendra doesn't return the gesture. "Yes, well, I had hoped I'd have a break from all things Chocolate City, but the government seems to be calling my name."

"Hmm. All right, well, please follow me; everyone's waiting."

"Everyone?" I question.

"Yes." She doesn't offer more by way of an explanation before she's spinning on her stilettos and leading us down a long hallway.

Once we get to what I assume is a conference room, she opens one of the double doors and holds it for us to enter.

Sitting at a table are five men dressed in the standard business suits and ties. Three seem very young, and two in middle age.

"Everyone, this is Parker Ellis, the CEO of the company I hired to assist us with wooing Senator Birchill and Senator Portorino. With him is someone you may or may not recognize, Kendra Banks. Corporate attorney, representing International Guy. She recently left government relations to move into the private sector, and it seems the private sector brought her back home."

A few rumbled chuckles come over the men as each of them stands to shake our hands. Vivica introduces three of them as working for Pure Beauty Pharmaceuticals. However, surprisingly, the older two are names I recognize, seeing as one is Senator Damren, the former Democratic senator from Delaware, and the other is Senator Kemper, the current Republican senator from Louisiana.

"Please take a seat, Mr. Ellis, Ms. Banks." Vivica gestures to two empty leather chairs at the table.

Once we get settled next to one another, I glance over and notice that Kendra is sitting in what I like to think of as her warrior pose. Back ramrod straight, shoulders so stiff you could balance a stack of books on each one of them. Her knees are glued together, shins and feet tucked under her chair. She's placed her folded hands primly on the table, and her hazel gaze is cool and locked on Vivica.

I watch Vivica walk to the front of the table and pick up a remote control. A screen has been pulled down along the wall opposite us. "Now that we're all here, we can get started." She presses a button, and the image of a stodgy woman in a poorly made brown suit comes alive on the screen. "That's Senator Birchill. She's one of the senators we need to sway to vote in our favor on the upcoming bill that's currently in committee review."

"Actually, I've got news on that front. The committee met yesterday. I've got them all confirmed to agree to set the bill for a vote next week," Senator Kemper announces with a smugness I don't care for.

Vivica smiles. "You believe that everyone on the committee will vote in favor of the bill?"

He laughs, his jowls jiggling along with his rotund belly. "Those folks down there don't know what hit 'em. All they see is the number of jobs the new law will bring to their industry and the money to be made."

Senator Damren grins. "When you promise two new plants and fifty thousand more jobs, which will bring in a lot more tax dollars, it's a pretty easy sell. Unfortunately, getting Birchill and Portorino swayed to vote in favor of the bill next week is far more difficult. Our lobbyists have been working the House and Senate for months on this bill and were able to ascertain that those two will be the deciding factor. If they agree, several more who are on the fence will fall into line alongside them."

"Speaking of the bill, I'd like to see a copy of what's being considered," Kendra interjects.

Vivica nods at one of her staff members, who brings out two copies and hands the documents to Kendra and me.

I lean forward. "What I want to know is what is inside the bill that makes them *not* want to vote in favor of Pure Beauty Pharmaceuticals. It would stand to reason that if the bill you're trying to pass helps build two new plants and brings that many new jobs to our country, and thereby our taxpayers, I would imagine this would be a win-win for everyone involved."

Vivica crosses her arms over her chest in a defensive posture. "Nothing that warrants a true revoke, I assure you."

I smile placatingly at her. "Try me."

She firms her jaw. "For one, they are under the impression that the bill will allow us and other companies to test our products on animals."

"Will it?"

One of her staff speaks up, a man very likely just out of college but with an intensity to his expression I can't ignore. Probably comes from generations of politicians. "It won't *not* allow animal testing."

I shrug. "Then why don't you just adjust the bill to change the wording that animal testing is strictly prohibited? End of problem."

Senator Kemper's eyes blaze with white-hot fury. Apparently I've touched on a sore spot with the bulldog. "Would you have us write legislation that lists *all the things* a company *can't* do in order to get work accomplished? The damn things would be a thousand pages long. It's preposterous!"

"It's not something we see as a practical way to achieve our goals, Mr. Ellis, though we appreciate your input," Vivica adds smoothly. "Besides, animal testing is part of our business. We cannot sell our drugs—prescription or over-the-counter medications—nor any of our beauty treatments without testing them on living, breathing entities first. Our priority is the safety of mankind. Even your toothpaste is tested on guinea pigs to ensure human safety before distribution."

A sour taste tinges my tongue, and my breakfast starts to swirl in my stomach.

Needing to change tactics before I hurl, I get to what I most need from them. "Excuse me, I may be out of line here, but what is the goal of the bill?"

"To bring in jobs and tax dollars . . . ," Senator Damren blurts out.

I wave my hands. "Forgive my ignorance once again. Pure Beauty hired my team to schmooze a couple of senators into voting in favor of something you want passed. I need to know why you want this passed in order to proceed with the best possible plan of attack."

Vivica purses her lips and then braces on the table, her green gaze searing mine. "The bill will give Pure Beauty, actually *all* pharmaceutical companies, the ability to distribute our products faster and with fewer hoops to jump through with the FDA. For example, their health risk investigators can hold up a product launch or a factory distribution because of something as simple as a security door being left open because a staff member left to smoke a cigarette and forgot to make sure it shut all the way."

I raise my own eyebrows at that. Seems outrageous to stop something moving forward because of such a simple human error.

She continues. "The agency can also choose not to approve a current drug because the number of tests run on a new product missed the positive mark by a tenth of a point. A teensy, tiny speck in the whole of the pie. We're pushing for more wiggle room in best practices so that we can move more product and hire more staff. This is a billion-dollar problem we need fixed, and these two individuals are standing in the way of allowing us to expand our business, provide what consumers need, and create more jobs in a bleeding economy."

Wow. Two people impact the fate of an entire company, two plants, fifty thousand new jobs, a load of money in new tax dollars to the local, state, and federal governments, and a billion consumer dollars. Incredible. I can see why the majority are in favor.

"And what is it these two senators specifically have a problem with?" I ask, tipping my head thoughtfully.

Vivica smirks and points to the screen. "Senator Birchill, Republican from Colorado. Huge supporter of the Environmental Protection Agency. Seems to believe that the locations we've chosen for the new factories are not 'environmentally friendly,' in her words. She doesn't like the idea that we're going to remove some trees and vegetation and build a three-million-square-foot factory in Jackson, Wyoming, outside of the Bridger-Teton National Forest and Yellowstone."

One of her young staff butts in. "It's the perfect location. Affordable, close to the West Coast and the north end of the country. The second plant will be placed in northern Texas and serve the south and east side of the country."

"So, she's a go-green, granola-crunching kind of gal?" I toss out to see if I've hit the nail on the head.

Vivica smiles. Wow, she's a whole helluva lot more attractive when she smiles genuinely. "You could say that. Yes. Your job will be to get her to see the positives of the new factories and steer her thinking away from the environmental negatives."

I shrug and rub at my chin. Doesn't sound too hard. I'll review the build plans, the location info, and see just how much damage will be done and how much damage could have been done. A lot of times it's a matter of comparing apples to apples to get someone to see that the positives outweigh the negatives.

"And Senator Portorino?" I tap the bright-white sheets of paper in front of me.

"Loves dogs. Has dogs instead of children," another of Vivica's staff notes. "Wants a guarantee that we won't test on animals at our new facilities. We can't make that promise."

Just when I thought my stomach had settled, a squeezing, uncomfortable sensation picks back up in my gut. Thinking of the ginger-haired cat, Spartacus, at Alexis's office in Montreal and how much I enjoyed the sleepy feline, I can't imagine someone wanting to test anything on the little guy unless it was a comfortable office chair specifically made for office cats. Thinking about Spartacus reminds me of my rather recent desire for a pet. Sky would love an animal, and with her movie being stationed in Boston, a pet might very well be a possibility. I wonder if she'd want a cat or a dog. Probably a cat since she's living in the penthouse of a building in downtown Boston. I'll have to discuss it with her later.

Vivica presses the button on the screen and brings up a picture of a woman in a business suit, wearing a pair of tennis shoes, with three leashes dangling from her hands connected to three different breeds of small dogs walking ahead of her along a busy city street.

"Loves dogs," I whisper in Kendra's direction while evaluating the small, olive-skinned, dark-haired woman. Not bad looking. Woman in her late forties. Gold hoops in her ears, hourglass figure, hair pulled back into a thick, tight ponytail at her nape. If I had to guess, I'd say she was Italian and married an Italian since her surname is Portorino.

"We'll get our team started on compiling some deep analytics of both women. Are they currently living in Washington now? I'd like to stop by or visit their offices, see if I can get a meet with them."

Vivica smiles and Senator Kemper laughs.

Senator Kemper speaks first. "You think you're just going to walk into their DC offices and get a meet on the fly? Son, you've got a lot to learn about politics and DC."

Kendra abruptly stands up and places her hand on my shoulder. "No worries. I'll bring him up to speed on all things Washington." She directs the rest of her commentary to Vivica. "We'll review the bill, assess the analytics, and do some recon on our targets. Once we have our plan in place, we'll contact you, Ms. Preston."

The woman nods in response. "Great. My team has compiled additional preliminary information on both Senator Birchill and Senator Portorino. Things we know about them, possible things we can remind them we have against them if they choose not to be swayed by your methods." She grabs the two stacks from her staff and hands one to me and one to Kendra.

I grab the files and tuck them under my arm. "We'll be in touch." I stand and follow Kendra out of the conference room.

She doesn't say a word and neither do I until we've returned to the Metro station and are sitting on the train watching the scenery go by.

"What did I just sit through?" I ask Kendra, feeling as though I've been sucker punched and not knowing why.

"A political hit," she answers flatly, her expression a mask of annoyance.

"A political what?"

"They want us to ruin Birchill's and Portorino's reputations."

I narrow my gaze. "How did you get 'ruin their reputations' from attempting to get them to vote yes on a bill the client wants passed?"

Her lips curl into a disgusted grimace. "Birchill is the top environmental protector in the Senate. She's known for it. She doesn't back down. Ever. It's why she's in the position she's in for the state of Colorado. The entire damn state is green, for crying out loud."

"Okay, so how does that correspond with ruining her reputation?"

"If what I suspect is true, not only are these factories going to be huge and eliminate a good chunk of trees, animal life, and natural resources, but her supporting the bill will give other prospective factories the ability to affect the environment as well. Any company claiming they can create thousands of new jobs and generate millions in tax dollars will be using this bill as carte blanche to destroy the land and pollute the air and flood the market with possibly dangerous products."

An itchy burn starts under my arms, making me feel sweaty and uncomfortable.

"And Portorino?"

"Is a vehement defender of animal rights. She's also the strongest advocate in the Senate for the Humane Society in DC. Their headquarters are located here, and she's a regular at their offices as well as their dinners, charity events, et cetera. She's been staunchly opposed to animal testing of any kind. If she were to change her vote for this bill, it would ruin her reputation as someone who stands up for the little guy, for the innocent. It would be better for her to resign than vote yes on this bill. There's nothing we're going to be able to do to get her to see it another way."

"Hmm. I want to get Wendy on them and find out more from our analysis. Let's spend tomorrow going through the bill and all the documents they've given us. We'll review whatever Wendy finds, and then have a meet with each. Do you have any ideas on that? This was your playground before it became mine." I smile graciously, wanting her to know I trust her judgment and experience completely.

"I'll ask around tomorrow. Check in with a few contacts. I'm sure we can find out where they usually go to lunch or dinner, maybe corner them on the street coming or going from their buildings."

I stare out the window as we pass by Georgetown. Washington really is filled with green trees and beautiful views once you pass through each neighborhood. I even enjoy the female Metro voice. Sounds almost British, reminding me of Geneva James back in London. I wonder if we'll be seeing her soon since her movie is going to be produced in Boston.

"It's as good a plan as any." I smile softly and continue to watch the world go by.

The conversation between us ceases, both of us lost in our own thoughts since the plan is in place for tomorrow. Still, there's an uneasy feeling twisting at my gut. The idea that this company was so nonchalant about animal testing makes me want to learn more about what they're doing, including when, where, and how often. I also don't like the idea of a giant factory being placed at the edge of a national forest. That can't be good for the environment, regardless of the jobs or money it will bring to the economy or the government.

Right now, all I can do is learn more about Pure Beauty Pharmaceuticals, the bill, and the two senators they want us to sway in their favor.

Knowledge is power.

***

The next day, Kendra and I are sitting in the suite we ended up having to share. Something was wrong with our booking. The hotel screwed up, and there weren't additional rooms to move us to. Regardless, it has two separate bedrooms and bathrooms with a living room and kitchenette space between them. When I texted Sky to tell her about the mishap, she laughed her ass off. Thought it was funny that I was worried about telling her I had to share a suite with another woman. Especially since she knows what went down between Roy and Kendra years ago. She thinks the situation will provide a good way for me to get to know the Kendra she is now, versus the young girlfriend of my best bud back in college. I explained repeatedly that I wasn't planning to dig any deeper into Kendra's past for fear of losing my best friend and business partner in the process. Nevertheless, I am very intrigued by why she moved back to Boston after living in DC for the past eight years.

"This bill is bad news, Parker." Kendra breaks through the silence. She's sitting on the couch dressed in a pair of lounge pants and a hoodie. I'm in much the same casual garb, only mine is jeans and a tee.

"Why's that?"

She shakes her head and holds up the bill, scanning a section that has her interest piqued.

"If this bill passes, basically it gives Pure Beauty Pharmaceuticals, not to mention drug companies in general, free rein to test on anything they want. They can also release the products in what they're calling the 'beta phase' as long as the product has passed two tests on living beings. Which means they can skip human trials altogether."

"Seriously?"

She nods. "Yeah. So they can do their tests and, if they get the anticipated results, they can choose whether or not they want to do the beta phase, which is where humans come in. Usually a cosmetics company will get focus groups that are either volunteer or paid, sometimes both, to try new products. Drug companies get their patients for drug trials a little differently, but in either instance, the bottom line is this: if they want, they can skip human trials and release a new product."

"I'm still hung up on the animal testing part."

She frowns. "I've heard about this company, Parker. I didn't want to go into detail because it's only conjecture. A friend of mine here in DC is an animal rights activist, and she says Pure Beauty Pharmaceuticals is connected to PB Resources."

"What's PB Resources?"

"A company that deals in medical testing but also, and here's the kicker, breeds animals just for animal testing. Animals are born in a laboratory just to be test subjects in a variety of ways, much of them cruel. We're not talking a few blood tests or needle pricks. They go beyond mice and guinea pigs, like Vivica mentioned. They use dogs and cats in a *lot* of testing."

I pull out my phone and hit "IG."

Annie answers. "International Guy, Annie speaking. How may I help you?"

"Annie, this is Parker. I need to speak to Wendy. Now."

"Oh yes, okay. Um, is there something I can help you with? I mean, now that I'm your official assistant?"

I clench my teeth and breathe through my nose, trying to dispel the immediate irritation at her not giving me what I want right away, and try to understand that she wants to be seen as helpful and do a good job. "No, thank you. I need Wendy's technical expertise."

"Oh okay." Her voice drops sadly. "Yes, let me get her for you. I hope you're having fun in DC." A beat of silence passes as I realize she's waiting for me to respond to her.

"Business, not pleasure, Annie. Wendy, please?" I push the words out in a barely concealed growl.

"Yes, of course. Right this minute," she says, and finally the phone starts to ring.

"Yo, Bossman. To what do I owe this great pleasure?"

"You in front of your computer?"

"Now that's just about the stupidest question I've heard all day." Her tone is joking, but I'm in no mood.

"Cut the snark. I need you to look up PB Resources and tell me who owns them and what they do."

"PB Resources, got it."

I can hear her typing wildly in the background.

"Looks like a medical research laboratory. Huh, this is weird."

"What is?"

"Some of the same names that you had me look up for Pure Beauty Pharmaceuticals came up. A few of the board members are the same. Oh shit . . . no way."

"What?"

"Well, while I'm doing this, I'm pulling up some deeper info. You know, the kind you're not supposed to be able to get, but I do because I'm the shit—"

"Wendy, please, just tell me what you've found." I let out an exasperated sigh and rub at my forehead, a headache forming.

"Turns out Vivica Preston is the wife of Jeffrey Preston, the CEO of PB Resources. From what I'm seeing in their financials, board of directors, and investors, it looks as though Pure Beauty Pharmaceuticals and PB Resources are fully in bed together. Though, shockingly, it's on the down low. There are no public mentions of the two together, and even the married couple is never seen at the same functions."

"Why would that be?"

"I don't know, but my freak-o-meter is clanging loudly. I need to dig further, go to places you wouldn't even believe existed in my funky poaching."

I grin. "Don't make it sound dirty."

"This shit *is* dirty. All incestuous and . . . Oh shit. No. Eww. Man." Wendy's voice falters.

"What?"

"The USDA has cited PB Resources a bunch of times."

"What's the USDA?" I run through a variety of acronym possibilities in my head to no avail.

"The United States Department of Agriculture."

"Uh, okay. How does that relate to anything?"

"They cited them for Animal Welfare Act violations."

And my stomach twists and turns, the coffee I just drank now feeling like a pool of acid in my gut. "Does it give a list of the citations?"

"Yeah, it's bad. Really bad. Ugly shit. They make dogs swallow lipstick to see what happens both internally and externally so that they can say it's safe for human children if they accidentally eat it. They've literally poured bottles of nail polish all over animals' hair to see what happens when they lick it off and ingest it."

"Fuck!" I growl into the phone, my heart beating furiously in my chest.

"Jesus, tons of dead animals were found tossed into a plastic garbage bin, one on top of the other, dozens deep. The last was because all of their throats closed up because the scientists put the formula they were testing for lip injections in the animals' mouths, but it had a glue-like consistency when it met the saliva, and they all choked and died of asphyxiation. Seems it took 'em a while to get the chemicals in the lip filler right."

"Oh my God, Wendy." I cover my mouth.

"Ugh, Park. They got cited once for leaving the animals locked in their tiny cages over the weekend with no new food or water for two full days." She gasps, and that acid in my stomach starts to rise up into my throat.

"Wendy . . ." I swallow down the desire to vomit but just barely.

"Poor babies. Another citation was for another accident where a staff member locked newborn kittens in a freezer until they froze to death overnight. They were only a week old."

On that last image, I can't take it anymore and rush over to the kitchen and vomit into the wastebasket. Kendra comes up behind me and runs her hand down my back. "I got you, Park." She uses the name she used to call me and moves out of the room. Her strides are quick when she comes back with a wet washcloth that she puts on the back of my neck. I'm clinging to the phone in my hand while the rest of my lunch and afternoon coffee leaves my stomach.

Kendra takes the phone. "Wendy? Yes, this is Kendra. What happened?" I ignore their conversation to focus on breathing and settling my now empty stomach. I wipe my mouth with the wet cloth, wash my hands in the sink, and suck down a bunch of cool water. My throat now feels like I swallowed a handful of razor blades. Once I've soothed my thirst, I grab the garbage bag and tie it off, planning to call housekeeping and have it removed.

Kendra comes back to me, her eyes blazing with hate and anger. "I heard you, girl, and I'm all over it." She speaks into the phone. "Mm-hmm. I'll take care of him. Yes, I'll have him check in with you later. Thank you." Kendra ends the call and sets my phone on the counter. "It seems that Pure Beauty is definitely connected to PB Resources, and based on seeing you tossing your cookies and listening to Wendy lose her mind over the phone, we're going to need to take a new approach on this case."

"There is no way I'm helping them make it easier to hurt animals or humans."

"You willing to lose half a million on that decision?" she asks point-blank.

"No. I'm not. More important than that, I'm not willing to lose my soul over half a million either."

Kendra's lips twitch into a small smile. "Looks like we need to get to work."

"How so?"

"Proving that consulting for Pure Beauty goes against our reputation and the goodness of our brand. As it turns out, it seems like we're going to need that termination clause."

I smile wide. "Hiring you: great decision."

"Now you just gotta convince the boys of that too." She tilts her head and grins.

"This will go a long way toward doing that. A long way. International Guy does not sell their souls to the devil for anything. Not the death of innocent animals, or a bucketload of money."

"I knew I made the right choice taking a chance on you, Parker. Even with the past rearing its ugly head, something deep inside told me that International Guy was where I was supposed to be. You just proved that right now."

"What you're feeling, Kendra . . . it's mutual."

"Well, Parker, that's great and all, but we still have a problem. Taking them down is going to hinge on us making some moral decisions over business ethics. Are you prepared to dive down that rabbit hole and risk IG's future? Everything we do and share is going to walk the razor's edge of ethical business conduct. Two wrongs don't necessarily make a right, even if it seems like it should. Legally we can be sued for sharing with outside parties anything we've found on Pure Beauty."

"Are you saying there's nothing we can do to make this situation right?"

She shakes her head. "No, that's not what I'm saying at all. We'll do everything we can to mitigate any fallout, but we need to be prepared for blowback."

"Let's be smart and cut the risks down as much as possible. However, in life, taking the moral high road can cut deep in order to be able to sleep at night. Plain and simple, I want to rest easy. I can't do that knowing the dark side of mankind is winning. Between blackmail and animal cruelty at its extreme, something has to be done. Someone has to take a stand. International Guy is nothing if we don't lead by example."

6

"Bro, that goes beyond cruelty. I mean, I understand that medicine needs to be tested somehow, but this is beauty shit—a want, not a need—and what they're doing is wrong. Flat out. Fucked up." Royce's deep voice rumbles into the room through the speakerphone.

It's now much later in the day, well after my earlier meltdown, and I'm pacing the room talking to my brothers. I've read through what feels like endless damning information Wendy sent my way after I had my moment with the garbage can.

"I don't want to make money off the backs of animals," Bo interjects. "If I did, I'd be a fuckin' cowboy and, at the very least, have a horde of cowgirls to ride in between working long days on a ranch. I much prefer straddling my motorcycle over a horse, so that's out," he says, his normal brand of humor taking the edge off my anxiety over what we've gotten ourselves into.

This is the first time we've ever been hired to work a case none of us want to continue. We've never not made good on our promise to provide the client what they need. Only this shit they want us to do goes against everything we believe in. It's not something we can back down from or look the other way on. Still, this client could destroy the business we've built, and I'll do anything to make sure that doesn't happen.

I rub at my temples. "Guys, these fatheads in the industry . . . Us bailing on them could hurt IG. Big-time. We have to be smart. Prove that the two senators are not going to be swayed and find a way to get out without getting burned. Kendra's already looking into the best way to spin our termination. Thank Christ she put that clause in there. It's going to save our asses."

"Parker, I'm not real comfortable with just walking away from this thing. They'll find someone else to bully, along with additional ways to burn those two senators. Did they give you what they have on them?" Bo queries.

"Yeah." I sigh long and deep, letting all the air out of my lungs. "Senator Birchill had an abortion at sixteen. It's hidden in her records, but they found it. She's a Republican, and her stance on that particular issue has been pro-life. That makes her a hypocrite and a liar in the party's eyes. It could easily ruin her."

"Jeez-us. These guys will release the information too," Royce adds.

"Yeah."

"And the other, the Democrat from Illinois?" he queries.

"This one's a little loose as far as reputation-ruining info. The senator has a sister in drug rehab. Repeated stints. The senator's platform is to be strict on drug laws. She could spin that this is why she's so firm, but it goes against the fact that she spoke on her sister's behalf at her sister's third-strike hearing in court. The sister had been caught with a bag full of drugs, enough that the DA added intent to sell to the charges. The judge was a friend of Senator Portorino's and somehow managed to find a way around the three-strikes provision. This allowed the sister to be released into rehabilitation one last time instead of bringing down the hammer, which is what should have happened."

"Basically, the judge went easy on Portorino's sister, which is the exact opposite of what she's proposing for other perpetrators in the same situation," Bo surmises.

"Bingo," I agree.

"Politics suck," Bo grumbles. "It's all he-said/she-said bullshit, and everyone's a liar and a hypocrite. You can't trust anyone to protect the public at large anymore."

"I feel ya, brother. In the meantime, Roy, you mentioned not liking letting these guys off. What would you suggest we do that will not hurt us?"

Roy sighs, and it sounds heavy and weighted through the line. "I'm thinking you talk to these senators, explain a bit more about what's going on, and use Kendra's contacts in Washington to spread the word about PB Resources being a kiss away from Pure Beauty Pharmaceuticals and what that means for the bill in general."

A light bulb goes off. "Kendra!" I screech out of my door into the open living space. She opens her door, her body encased in workout clothing. "Can you come here, please?"

As she moseys over, her workout clothes show off her toned body and bangin' booty. Damn, I knew she had some junk in the trunk back when we were in college, but it was never this round and high. Her girlish form turned far womanlier over the years. Even the crop top sports bra thing she's wearing is showing a few inches of hard abs. Looks like she might even have a bit of a four-pack going on. Royce would be drooling right about now if he were here.

I rip my eyes away from her body when she steps through my door, hands on hips and a tight jaw.

"You bellowed?"

I smirk and shake my head, giving her the moment of humor her comment warrants. "Do you know a bunch of senators personally?"

She nods. "Yeah, I have a handful of pretty good friends in Congress, why?"

I grin. "Well, I discussed with the guys the conversation you and I had. They don't like the idea of Pure Beauty getting away with terrorizing animals or these two senators for personal things in their lives either, and they agree with taking some well-calculated risks. We need to open up this can of worms and spread this information all over Washington." She frowns. "As we discussed before, Parker, we have a strict confidentiality agreement with Pure Beauty Pharmaceuticals. We have to be careful about breaking that, or they can sue International Guy for everything we have."

"Fuck." I run my hand through my hair, the curls on top more prevalent than normal.

Kendra taps at her chin. "However, that doesn't mean we can't talk about PB Resources. There is nothing in our contract regarding what we found out about them and who their clients are. We just have to be careful with how we share the information. If the person we're talking to comes to their own conclusions about the connection between PB Resources and Pure Beauty, it's out of our hands."

I grin maniacally at Kendra. "You are brilliant."

"This is true," she states with zero emotion, though I can see her eyes twinkling with mirth.

"Kendra's brilliance aside, how are we going to keep this information from Pure Beauty?" Roy interjects.

"Let me handle that part," Kendra offers. "There's no reason why I wouldn't have lunch or dinner with old friends while I'm working a case in DC. Sometimes the best way to hide information is to put it right out there in the open for everyone to see."

"More brilliance." I grin.

"Thank you. Now if you're done, I'm going to head down for my run. I'll be back in time to meet for dinner. Let's see if we can nail down Senator Birchill tonight."

"I'm in. Guys, we'll be in touch."

"Stay safe, bro," Bo says.

"Peace," Royce clips, and hangs up.

"Have a good run. I'm gonna spend a little time reviewing more of these documents, maybe call Skyler."

She smiles softly. "You do that. Casual clothes tonight. Senator Birchill is a down-to-earth woman."

I make a stink face. "I remember her brown, ill-fitting suit. I figured she was probably more of a jeans-and-boots type of woman."

"You got it. See you soon." Kendra waves over her shoulder as she heads for the door.

When she leaves, I flip open my phone and dial Skyler's number, hoping I'm catching her at a good time.

It rings a few times before a male answers the phone.

"Skyler Bear's phone!" the jovial voice says.

I close my eyes, pinch the bridge of my nose, and let out the breath I was holding while waiting to hear my girl speak. This guy is not the calming, sultry voice I'd hoped to hear. Hell, I never want to hear another man answering my woman's phone unless it's Nate and he has a damn good reason to.

"Rick, it's Parker. Why are you answering my girlfriend's phone?"

"Duuuuude!" He drags out the greeting so it sounds like the word has twelve *u*'s in it. "So good to talk to you. I'm running lines with yo' girl, bro! Isn't this awesome? We get to work together for, like, ever, man! I'm so super stoked about this. We're gonna be best buds!"

Best buds. With Rick the Prick. Not likely.

"Yeah, uh, that's great, Rick. Is she there?"

"Totally," he says with exuberance but no motivation to put her on.

"May I speak with her?" I roll my eyes and try to keep the irritation out of my tone.

"Oh, naw, man, she's in the head. Be out in a second, though. Unless she's dropping a deuce."

Sweet mother. This guy. How he gets roles must be strictly on his ability to look good on camera with his shirt off, because he's dumb as a rock. Then again, I'm certain with my woman's talent and experience, she can make any actor look good.

"That's . . . I'm not even going to address what that is. Just have her call me when she has a moment."

"Naw, dude. Want to talk to you, man. Tell you how grateful I am for the tips you gave me. Those were stellar, and the movie was rock solid because of it. Also, it helps when Sky and I have to do some sexy scenes in the future. This *A-Lister* movie is going to have me all over her body, dude. Gotta know her man is cool with it."

Cool with it? Am I cool with Rick the Prick having his hands and mouth all over my woman's body? Absolutely not. Fuck me.

I grind my teeth and breathe through my nose like a pissed-off bull. "I'm going to aspire to be . . . cool with it."

"Awesome, dude. I'm looking for places here, and Skyler's pad is the shit! She says maybe she can have the lease changed over to me in the next few months when I move here and filming starts. She said something about finding a bigger place. You two shacking up?" That is the million-dollar question. One that we haven't broached together.

Why the hell is she planning a bigger place? She's one person. It makes no sense. Unless, as Rick said, she is planning on the two of us moving in together. I think back to all the new clothes for me hanging in her closet. The desire she has for me to feel at home in her space. Sleeping beside her every night I'm in Boston, whether it's at her pad or mine.

Shit. Are we already living together without actually calling it what it is? Damn.

My mind is swirling with images of us making a place *our* home. Hers and mine. Together. I've never lived with a woman before and never wanted to.

Until this moment, right now.

I need to talk to Sky about it, see where her head is at, as well as her heart. More and more I'm faced with the fact that this woman is the only one for me. Long-term. Picket fences. Animal sharing. The whole nine.

Pushing those thoughts to the side, I focus on the call. "I'm glad I could help, Rick. Please have Sky call me back . . ."

"Ah, here she is. Guess it was just number one. Sa-weetness. Skyler Bear, your dude is on the phone. We were catching up—you know, bro business."

I cringe and shake my head. That guy really needs to install a filter between his brain and his mouth.

A bustle of noises can be heard, and then nothing but my sweet, sexy woman's sultry voice is in my ear, instantly bringing me to my happy place. "Hey, honey . . ."

"Peaches," I rumble into the phone, noticing my own voice is thick with need and desire at just hearing her speak through the line.

"I miss you already, and you've barely been gone. Wondering if this is a new downside to living in Boston?"

"There's a downside?" I chuckle.

She laughs lightly, and it's music to my ears.

"I imagine you might miss the hubbub of New York. Having been settled there for the last few years, your friends . . ."

Skyler's laugh fills my ears. "Honey, the only friend I have in New York is Tracey. Sure, when I tell her I'm planning on relocating here long-term, she's going to have a bit of a shit fit, but that's how best friends are. Ultimately, she'll be happy for me."

Long-term.

There's that phrase again.

"So, you're planning on longer than the *A-Lister* series . . . ," I hedge, anxiety rippling up my spine and wedging somewhere in the spot where my insecurities lie.

"Are you not . . . um . . . planning to have me around for the long run?" Her voice shakes a little, but I can tell that she's trying to be tough and act like it doesn't bother her one way or the other whether I want her in Boston forever or not.

"Hmm, well, I guess that depends on where I'll be. If it's lying in a bed next to you, and that bed happens to be in Boston, or the surrounding area, then I'll likely be the happiest man in the world. What are your thoughts on cats or dogs?"

"As it pertains to what?" Her tone sounds confused.

"Having one. As a pet. There was this cool cat named Spartacus in Montreal that I took a liking to. I'd always considered myself a dog person, until I met that cat. Now I'm open to either . . . or both. Especially if you'll be around for the next few years. It would limit the amount of times we need to have a pet sitter or board our animals if there are two of us managing them."

"Our animals?" Her voice rises with the question.

I grin thinking about my sweet girl with a fat ginger cat on her lap and a dog at her feet when I come home from work.

Fucking bliss.

"Are we getting pets together, pretty boy?" she teases.

"I don't know. What do you think? I've been considering a pet since Montreal, and I can't get the image of you hanging out with a furry friend out of my head."

"Mm-hmm, and would this vision include us living together in the same house, you know, for the sake of the animals?"

I bite down on my lip, wondering if we should be having this conversation face-to-face or not. It's a big step. *Huge.* Still, she's ripe for the discussion, and I can't find a reason not to just put it out there. "Maybe. Is that something you want?"

"Parker, are you suggesting we move in together and get a dog and a cat?" She laughs lightly.

Am I?

Yeah, I am.

Shit.

Hell.

Bomb dropped.

"What would you say if I were?" I hedge, worrying maybe I'm suggesting something way out of left field and she really hasn't been thinking about shacking up. Maybe I've taken her moving here and buying me a wardrobe all wrong. It could be she was just being thoughtful instead of making a statement about my position in her life.

"I'd say: sign me up, honey! I'm dying to start house shopping here in Boston, but I wasn't sure if you wanted to take that next step. Parker, I want to make a life here. Settle down. Buy a home. A *real one* with a front yard and a porch like you talked about having with your grandparents. Is that something you're ready for?"

I lick the front of my teeth and mull it over for a few moments. "It's not something I'd ever wanted before with another woman, but I find that, with you, I want it all." I swallow down the fear and anxiety creeping along my throat. Sweat beads at my forehead as the thought of something so final hits me. Skyler and I sharing a home. Buying one, together. It's a huge commitment, only one step away from marriage. And for the first time, the thought of marriage to a woman after Kayla doesn't make me want to bolt.

"Really?" Her voice is filled with so much excitement and joy, it washes away the fear pressing against my chest.

This is right. Skyler and me.

"Yeah, baby. Really. Sky, I want to be with you as much as possible. When I'm home, it's your body that I want to lie next to. It's your lips I want to kiss good night. It's your face I want to see every morning when I wake up. And of course, if you add in a cat or a dog or both, whatever you want, I'd be down for that too."

"Honey . . ." She sounds choked up.

"Yeah?"

Her tone starts out as a whisper and grows in volume. "I want all of that too. And I want a big, fat cat and a giant dog. If we get them as a puppy and kitten they'll be new together and love one another. It would be perfect!"

And it would. Be perfect.

"Then it's settled," I add with finality.

"What is?"

"We're getting a cat and a dog. And a home. Together."

"Oh my goodness!" She squeals. "Just to be safe, let me get this straight. When you get back from DC, we're going to go house shopping. Together. Me and you. Because we're making it official and shacking up."

"Shit . . ." I rub the back of my neck. "Yeah, Peaches, we're moving in together."

"Oh. My. God. I'm so excited!"

I envision her jumping around the penthouse.

"Parker! I can't wait to start looking for houses! I'm going to call Wendy and Mick. See if anything is available in their area. They're twenty minutes out from the IG offices; it's secure, and it's just perfect! I'll bet we could even find something that had a pool house or something similar that we can have Rachel and Nate move into if they want. Otherwise, they can stay in the apartment above the IG offices. Honey . . ." Her voice seems to shake instead of the warm and sultry tone or previous excitement.

"Sky, what's wrong? I thought you'd be happy." I frown and start to pace again. Dammit, I knew we should have had this conversation when I could hold her, touch her in some way. Give her the reassurance we both need right now.

She clears her throat. "I am happy. *So happy.* I don't even know how to be this happy. I'm going to buy a home with my boyfriend. I'm moving to Boston for good. And . . ." She sniffles. "And we're gonna get pets! I've never had a pet because of my work and the amount I traveled, and I can't wait to pick them out with you. This . . . th-this is the best day *ever.*" Her voice stops on a small whimper.

"God, I wish I were there with you. Peaches, don't overdo it. We have plenty of time. How's about you start looking for places, and get some ideas. Just keep in mind, I'm not riding on your coattails. We need to find something that we both can manage financially."

"Um, well, I kind of already looked at the house prices in Mick and Wendy's area when we went over there the first time, and honey, it's pretty pricey. Definitely not out of my price range by a long shot, and of course, I'll be selling the penthouse in New York too. I have to make sure that whatever we get is in an area that is the most secure. That's not something you should have to worry about, and of course, I need to make sure Rachel and Nate have a place, and . . ."

An uncomfortable tightening of my balls makes me lose my ability to speak. On the one hand, there's a voice in my head speaking loudly, needing to be the provider, pay for our home, and bang on my chest like the caveman I am. Another much smaller voice is reminding me that my girlfriend, the woman who I'm settling down with, has some serious security needs that must be met in order to ensure her safety. These safety measures are something we cannot scrimp on in order to save a buck, as much as I'd like to provide everything for my mate. I have to let her find what she needs and contribute in whatever way is most appropriate.

"Why don't you look at places for now. Get some ideas in mind, and we'll discuss. I'm not going to push you to downgrade your comfort or luxury for me, but I want to make a hefty contribution and feel as though I have done so. Understand?"

"Yeah, honey, I understand perfectly!" The joy is back in her tone. "And I love you. I love that we're moving toward the future and going to start looking at buying a home together. This is more than I could have ever dreamed of. You're giving me everything I could have ever wanted out of life. Love, a home . . . a family again." The sniffles are back, but I can tell she's trying to rein it in.

"Sky, it's the same for me. I want a home we can settle into for a long while, if not forever, with our pets, and one day maybe even our future children."

She gasps. "Children. Oh my . . ."

"You want that with me one day, right?" My heart starts pounding. I can't believe we're talking about a home and children. Skyler has changed me beyond anything I could have ever anticipated. Before her, it was nothing but my playboy ways and an endless sea of women available for the taking. Not that I partook that much, but still. The options were open. That door is now closed, and there is nothing more I want out of life than to set up house with her.

"Totally want that. More than anything." Her words are thick with emotion and a bit of awe.

"All right. One step at a time. Yeah?"

"Yeah. One step, honey. A house and pets."

"That's right, Peaches. A house and pets."

"It's the most perfect start ever, Parker." The awe is still in her voice, and I wish I could taste it on my tongue, kiss the living daylights out of her. Seal this deal the right way.

I smile wide knowing that I've gotten to her. "Since we have that settled, why in the world was Rick answering your phone?"

She groans. "Ugh! The guy has boundary issues. He thinks of me as a sister. Says we're going to be the best of friends, and you and he are going to have a bromance when he moves here. He's even talking about bringing his girlfriend along."

Girlfriend is the magic fucking word of the day, outside of *long-term*.

"Girlfriend?"

Sky chuckles. "I knew you'd pick up on that. Yes, he has a girlfriend. Apparently, a sweet girl he's been dating for the past year, but totally under the public radar. Only his closest friends know about her. They've been close-lipped about it, but I think he's going to marry her."

"Really?" That has me smiling huge. Rick the Prick with a ball and chain . . . now that's an idea I can work my head around.

"Yeah. She's religious, though. They haven't had sex," she whispers, the words sounding muffled as if she covered the bottom of the phone with her hand.

I frown. "Uh, say what?"

"Mm-hmm. He says it's giving him the worst case of blue balls in the world, but he's in love with her and respects her decision to wait until marriage."

"Hence the push for the nuptials, I'd imagine."

"That's my guess. I think it's cute, though, that he's willing to wait. Would you wait for me?"

Not sinking balls deep in Skyler Paige for months on end? "Hell no! I waited long enough."

"You waited like two days. That's nothing."

"More like an eternity. When a man has the likes of you in the wings, every minute of waiting to be with you intimately is like waiting a freakin' year."

"You're a pig," she teases.

"Oink, oink." I laugh out loud, the sound ricocheting off the walls, making me feel less alone. God, I miss her.

She chuckles along with me. "I'm just kidding, honey. You know I wanted to be with you the night we met. I looked at your tall, built form, those clear blue eyes, that thick hair, and I was a goner from the very first night. All I wanted to do was put my mouth on yours and go wild."

"We got there in the end, didn't we?"

"Yeah," she whispers shyly. "And now we're going to shack up and get fur babies. Any special requests on animal breeds?"

"I think I'd like a ginger cat," I suggest, thinking back to Spartacus, the cool lap kitty.

"You got a thing for redheads I should know about?" she taunts.

I grin. "Only furry ones, baby."

"And dogs?"

"What would you like?"

"I'm thinking a golden retriever." She says this with a whimsy I can tell means she's been thinking about this longer than just this conversation.

"You got a thing for blonds?" I toss back at her.

She continues poking me back. "Maybe . . ."

"Well, then it's settled. We'll get a ginger cat and a golden retriever."

"Eeek! I'm going to start looking at animal shelters right away!"

Of course my woman is planning to save an animal. It's who she is.

"Works for me. I'm absolutely down with saving an animal." Which reminds me of the case we're on and the concerns we have regarding Pure Beauty. "You start your search, and no practicing any of the kissing or sex scenes with Rick the Prick while I'm gone."

"Honey, we don't usually practice those. We save that kind of thing for live rehearsals on set. No need to be putting my mouth anywhere near his when I don't have to." She makes a gagging sound that has me smiling like a crazy person.

"That mouth is all mine."

"Yeah."

"Don't forget it," I remind her.

"I won't."

"I gotta go. The sooner I can get done with this case, the better. I'm not happy about it."

"You want to talk about it later?"

"Nah, we'll talk about it when I get home. Nothing you need to worry about."

"Okay, honey. I'll send you pics of anything I find."

"I'd love that. And, Peaches . . ."

"Yeah," she says in a breathy timbre that goes straight to my dick.

"Can't wait to move in with you."

"I can't either. Have a good rest of your night."

"You too."

"Love you!" she says, and then a kissing sound pierces my ear.

I chuckle. "Don't ever stop!"

"Not possible!" she says, and hangs up. I stare at my cell, roll my shoulders and neck, and imagine my girl bouncing around her penthouse at the news that we're shacking up. I'll have to get with the guys soon, toss back a few beers, and give them the good news.

Somehow, though, I don't think they'll be surprised.

7

"Senator Birchill! I thought that was you!" Kendra gushes with a dramatic exuberance I've not heard from her before.

"Ms. Banks? I thought you'd moved on to greener pastures in Boston." The stodgy older woman sets down her BLT.

Kendra smiles genuinely at the woman, which surprises me. I hadn't realized that she actually knew Senator Birchill directly.

"Yes, well, work has brought me back to DC on business, funny enough."

Senator Birchill shocks me when she pats the empty barstool next to her. "Well, why don't you and your friend join an old woman for a meal?"

"That's very kind of you, Senator," I say, and hold out my hand. "Parker Ellis. Nice to meet you."

She smiles wide, the curly ends of her short hairstyle swaying as she rocks my hand up and down. "Well, aren't you a strapping young fella. Kendra, looks like you caught a live one, dear."

Kendra laughs. "This is not my man, Karen; he's my boss."

The woman's shrewd brown gaze looks me up and down. "Shame. You deserve a good, handsome man such as Mr. Ellis."

I grin and pat down my T-shirt, having dressed according to Kendra's suggestion about casual attire. "Why, I thank you very much, and I hope my girlfriend back in Boston feels the same." I cock an eyebrow and then wink at the woman.

She shrugs as Kendra and I take seats to her right, Kendra in the middle, me on the outside.

"Kendra, dear, you've always been too slow on the uptake when it comes to men. You need to get yourself out there more. Get past that sickness you suffered and move on to brighter and much . . . bigger things. Like a six-foot beefcake!" she teases good-naturedly.

Kendra laughs accordingly, only I don't. All humor is lost on me when I pick up on the part where she mentions Kendra being sick. I mean it's been a long time since we've seen one another, but what this woman is inferring is that Kendra had a pretty serious medical condition at one point or another. One that obviously affected her life, if the senator's words can be taken seriously.

"Oh, you know it's all about the fact that I love my job. I can't fit a man into my career. Too much to do, cases to win." Kendra waves her hand in the air. "Enough about me; let's talk about what's happening in the Senate right now."

Wow. She's good. Though she could have mentioned the fact that she knows Senator Birchill far better than she let on. It seems as if the two women are friends.

"Eh, all boring stuff. I want to hear more about you moving to Boston. That fella you were hung up on back in the day still there? Have you run into one another? What was his name? Ray . . . Ron . . ."

Kendra sits up straighter and coughs. "Uh, no, no, not going there. Moving was the right decision for the family, as you know."

I want to dig into the juicy bit the senator just shared.

"I'm thinking the name you're referring to is Royce, Senator."

The woman smacks the bar and points at me. "Roy . . . Royce! Yes. That was it. When we met, and she was a sweet young thing just getting back from her 'all clear' and the last stint in the hospital, I remember her being totally gaga over some big black hunk of a man she'd left in Boston."

Kendra places her hand on the senator's arm. "Karen, Parker and Royce are friends. We work together now. Can we drop this? Please." Her tone is direct yet still holds the twinge of a needy plea.

Karen's eyes practically bug out of her head. "Shoot. I didn't mean to make things awkward for you, dear. I'm sorry." She pats Kendra's hand in a motherly way.

My spidey sense prickles at the gesture. Senator Birchill is a whole helluva lot more than just a friendly acquaintance to Kendra. This woman is someone who matters to her. Which means Kendra hasn't been completely honest. By the sound of it, she hasn't been completely honest about a lot of things. My hackles rise, and I clench my teeth. Kendra's hazel gaze flicks to mine, and she bites down on the side of her lip. It's a move she used to do when we were in school and she was pondering something difficult.

"It's funny that we ran into you, Senator. Your name actually appeared in a case we're working." I bring the conversation back to professional ground so that we can finish this and get back to the hotel, where I can ream Kendra's ass for hiding her relationship with the senator. Not to mention, when she left Royce eight years ago, she was pining away for him. Part of that time she was sick with none of us being the wiser. Not exactly a crime, but a full lie by omission. I wonder if Royce knew she'd been sick. Was that part of why she left? How sick was she?

Too many thoughts of the past are mingling with the present, none of them technically involving me, but anything that involves Royce involves all of us. My loyalty is to him first.

Kendra clears her throat. "Yes, actually a bill has come up we've been consulted to work on. The one being championed by Senator Kemper—"

"That dirty blowhard! I don't know how that man can sleep at night. If you're working with him, you better cut your losses quickly, dear. He'll take you down to the ground and never look back. That man is not a good guy. He's all about how much money can be hidden away in his back pocket. And that Pure Beauty, the things they want to do . . . my goodness. It would turn your stomach. Cutting down all those trees, destroying God's green earth for the benefit of what . . . so a rich woman can get more crap pumped into her face quicker?

"Whatever happened to aging gracefully? Living with what God gave you and being happy to be alive instead of worrying about how many lines you have on your face?" Her expression contorts to one of disgust. "Who decided that smile lines are a bad thing? You know what's a bad thing? Putting fillers into your face. Testing those fillers on animals so that you can look five years younger. Cutting down thousands of trees that give life-sustaining air!" Her face turns beet red.

"I can understand you're upset." I put my hand out to grab her attention. "We agree with you. Completely."

She narrows her brows. "You do? Well, then why are you working with those losers?"

"We didn't know the full details behind what they wanted us to do. Now we're in a difficult position," Kendra adds. "Turns out, PB Resources' primary client is Pure Beauty Pharmaceuticals."

The senator's eyes widen to the size of bowling balls before her lips twist into a snarl. "That is bad news. They do dangerous things to animals. Do you have proof they're working together?"

I lick my lips and lean forward. "The CEO of Pure Beauty Pharmaceuticals and the CEO of PB Resources are married. Many on their boards of directors and investors sit on both boards. That's really all we can say without being sued."

The senator's nostrils flare, and she purses her lips. "Well, isn't that interesting. This changes everything. Once the other senators hear who's backing this bill, they're going to be none too happy."

"Unfortunately, according to Kemper, the committee will approve the bill for vote by the rest of the Senate. There's only your vote and—"

"Portorino's vote," she guesses immediately.

I nod.

"You didn't just stop in to have dinner." Her comment is a statement, not a question.

Kendra swallows slowly and shakes her head. "No, Karen. We didn't."

"I see. What do they have on me?" She taps the bar top as if this is just another day in the world of suits and skirts.

Kendra twists her fingers in her lap. It's the first time I've ever seen her react in any manner other than perfect professionalism. She's rattled by this, and it shows in her body language and the sullen expression marring her pretty face.

Given the pain I can see in her eyes, I jump into the fray first. "You made a difficult decision in your past, when you were sixteen. They know about it." I lay it out directly, sparing Kendra the shitty task of having to admit we know about her friend's abortion.

The senator closes her eyes, and when she opens them, they are glassy and unfocused, but her expression is completely devoid of emotion. She fixes her gaze on a point across the bar, not making eye contact with either of us. Her curly hair covers most of her face, but I can see that she's lost in a memory.

Her voice sounds as though her vocal cords have been dragged over a cheese grater when she finally speaks. "I was raped. Did they bother reading you that police report?"

An ugly clawing sensation rips at my chest. I fist my right hand, wanting to punch those dirty bastards in the face. Repeatedly. Perhaps until they can no longer breathe.

How can these people sleep at night? They had to have known why she had the abortion in the first place. To use something so hideous against a woman who was violated? I can barely contain the rage swirling inside me.

I don't know many women, if any, who would want to raise the baby of a man who'd violated them. To have a constant reminder your whole life of one of the worst moments of your life. No way. On top of that, the woman was a mere girl. Sixteen. A child herself.

"He grabbed me while I was walking home from the library. I used to go to the local library's resource books and type my papers out. He was twenty-five. Strung out on meth. He pulled me into the bushes, held me down at knifepoint, and took my innocence. Strangled me until I lost consciousness and left me for dead. Somehow, I survived. The librarian found me. Called the cops and an ambulance and stayed with me. Except he didn't leave me just with the memory of the wretched experience, he left me pregnant."

I close my eyes and imagine my mother in the role, stumbling upon a raped teen who was close to death. I shiver and suck in a huge breath, trying to stop the anger seething through my veins, boiling my blood, making me hot all over.

"Eventually the authorities caught him. Put him away for life. Still, I couldn't bear to raise his child. So I had an abortion. My records were sealed as a minor. I swore that day I'd never take a life again. Not ever. No matter what happened. Which, in the end, did enough damage because I've never let a man get close to me again. Childless, husbandless, I chose to live a solitary life. Then, I went into politics. Now they want to take that away from me too? The only thing I have in this life." She shakes her head and tosses back the dregs of what looks like a Coke. "Sometimes, I hate politics. Other times, it's all I live for."

I stand up, no longer capable of sitting. "Time to go. Kendra?" I say, gesturing toward the door.

Her brows furrow, and she eases off the stool. "Karen, let's talk a little more tomorrow. We want to put a stop to what these people are planning to do, but we have to be careful. Information cannot come back to us."

Karen smiles maniacally. "Oh, don't you worry about that. I'll have my nephew looking into the company as soon as I finish my dinner. He'll find the connection himself. Looks like the next couple of days are going to be a shit storm of sharing information."

I place my hand on her shoulder. "You may not want to do that. They know about your past and have no problem using it."

Her lips flatten into a thin white line. "My past has stayed hidden long enough." She pats my hand on her shoulder. "Don't you worry about me, son. This old bird can take care of herself."

I squeeze her shoulder and turn to leave, allowing Kendra a private moment to say her goodbyes.

The second we get in our rental car, I'm on her like flies on shit.

"What the hell were you thinking not telling me about your connection to the senator before we approached?"

Kendra's nostrils flare, and she turns her body to the side to face me directly. "It was a long time ago. I interned in her office for six months when I was preparing for the bar exam. She was good to me . . ."

"Obviously the two of you had a connection. Did you think to share that with me? Maybe *before* we agreed to take this case?" My voice is as tight as a drum and just as thunderous.

"I didn't know we'd be working with or against her in any capacity. I was just as surprised as you were when her picture appeared on the screen at the meeting yesterday, okay? I'm sorry, Parker. I didn't know." Her tone loses its edge, which eases my own ire considerably.

I lick my lips and inhale fully. "You're too close to this one, Kendra. You shouldn't be here."

Her gaze on mine is like two red-hot laser beams. "There's no way I'm backing out now. They're going to try and ruin someone I care about. They're working with a company that openly tortures animals and pretty obviously has some seriously deep pockets and contacts high on the Hill or they'd be shut down already. Not a chance I'm bailing on this until we ensure that bill does not pass."

I slam my hand against the steering wheel. "Fuck!"

For a full two minutes I grip the wheel as tight as possible and try to let my anger and frustration seep out of my body so that I can drive safely. Kendra doesn't say a word. Either she's content with the silence, or she needs it to bring her own unraveled emotions back in check.

"What was she talking about when she said you were sick and in the hospital?" I turn my head to focus on her face, waiting to see what her microexpressions tell me.

A flash of intense pain races across her gaze for a single moment and then disappears.

"Parker, my past and personal life are not open for discussion. I don't ask about yours; I expect the same respect to be given to me."

I narrow my gaze. "Your past just walked right up and smacked us in the face with a legal situation that could destroy my company. I need to know if there's anything else that could potentially harm me or my partners."

She shakes her head. "Not true. My time in the hospital and my past with Royce have nothing to do with this case. I'd appreciate it if you let that portion of what she said go. It's not relevant, and frankly, it's not something I want to delve back into." Her words are forthright.

For a couple of seconds, I take in her face. Angular shape, rounded cheekbones, perfectly sculpted eyebrows, plump, full lips, a small chin and nose. The woman's beauty is absolute, which is partly why Royce is so burned over her leaving all those years ago.

She was sick? How sick?

A needlelike sensation buzzes at the base of my skull. It's that feeling I get when I want to know more . . . need to. Grinding my teeth, I decide I'm going to have Wendy look into her past. Hell, knowing our crazy minx she's probably already done the deed but is keeping the goods to herself out of respect for her new colleague.

"Fine," I lie, knowing there isn't anything I won't do to ensure that Royce and this company are protected. If she has skeletons in her closet,

I want to know what they are and how they could possibly impact my brother or the business. Once I know what she's hiding, I'll make the decision then if I want to expose her secrets or not. For now, I'll cool my jets and focus on the case.

Hell, all I want now is to get out of Washington, DC, and get back to Boston where a wicked-hot blonde is searching for fur babies and a house with a porch.

"Thank you, Parker." She eases back against the seat and buckles her seat belt.

I do the same and start the car.

"Let's just hope we can get through this case unscathed and with our company intact."

"We will. On that I'll stake my career. We are not going down with their ship." Her words are a promise I hold on to, because I'm going to need to trust her if I have any hope of making it out of this political nightmare.

***

A banging on my door has me jumping out of bed a little wobbly legged and panting like I've just run a marathon. The door flies open, and Kendra is standing behind it. Her hair is wet, and she's wearing a giant Harvard T-shirt that hangs down to her knees, showing off a pair of spectacular bare legs. She looks at me from top to toe.

"Damn, Park, you grew up." She grins, looking her fill. "I mean I always knew you were cut, but good Lord." She fans herself with what looks like a half-folded newspaper. "Now I know how you scored yourself a Hollywood star. If I had all of that in my bed, I'd hold on tight too." She stares, tipping her head to the side but not coming in past the doorway.

I place my hands on my hips, thanking God himself that I wasn't dreaming of Skyler and don't have morning wood. I spy my jeans on the floor, scoop them up, and tug them on. "Is there a reason for your impromptu wake-up call?"

She runs her gaze up and down my body once more and shakes her head, then focuses on the paper. "You're never going to believe this." She opens the paper and holds it out to me.

I reach for it and scan the headline.

Senator Birchill's Childhood Tragedy Revealed

"Holy fuck!" I read through the article. It's all there. Her rape at sixteen, how she went through a horrible bout of depression afterward. She speaks on the fact that she'd gotten pregnant by her rapist and made the hard choice to have an abortion. Her story is so well written I have tears pricking at my eyes. "I cannot believe she revealed it all."

"Smartest decision she could make." Kendra crosses her arms over her chest. "Take the offensive. Be the first to release your secrets in your way, with your voice, and they can't use it against you." She moves over to the TV and turns it on to one of the morning news programs.

As expected, the senator's story is the lead.

The two of us listen as the newscaster expresses his deep sadness for what the senator went through. I flick the channel and stop on the senator herself.

Her voice sounds confident and assured as she speaks. "Which is why I'm pro-life now, but I don't begrudge anyone who's pro-choice. I've gone through the hell of giving up a child due to depression and having been victimized. As a child, I did what my parents encouraged me to do. If I could do it again, I'm not sure I'd make the same choice. Still, it's the reason I am who I am today, in the position I'm in, protecting other women who might have to make a similar choice. I want to encourage them to choose life if at all possible. And that's my stance," the senator states emphatically while standing in front of what looks to be a podium.

"Damn, she works fast," I whisper.

"You have to in this business. If you're lucky, today's news is tomorrow's trash. It's best to get it out in the open and move on as quickly as possible. And look at her numbers. The public is eating it up. They're calling her strong willed and heroic for coming clean with her past. Amazing . . ." She shakes her head.

"So it seems. My guess, this means she can say whatever the heck she wants about Pure Beauty since the big bomb has dropped."

Kendra smiles as my cell phone rings.

I grab it off the nightstand and notice the Washington, DC, prefix. "Parker Ellis . . ."

"Mr. Ellis. This is Vivica Preston. I'm sure you've gotten a gander at the news this morning?"

"Yes, I have. I was just discussing it with my counselor."

"It puts a bit of a hole in our plan to force the senator to vote our way. Until we can find something else on Senator Birchill, work Portorino."

A tremor ripples through my body. I clench my teeth and try to hold back the snarl. "It definitely makes our job nearly impossible." I set up the "failure" part of our plan to help back the need to terminate the contract.

"Yes, we understand. Work Portorino. We need her agreement. We'll review the other senators and see who else might have something we can use. I'll be in touch," she says briskly, then hangs up without another word.

I hit the "Off" button for the TV and groan out loud, fisting my hands at my sides. "I do not want to work with these people. They disgust me."

Kendra nods. "I'm setting our distribution of information plan into motion. Today, we meet with four more of my friends on the Hill. We'll tell them about PB Resources and the connection to the cosmetics industry. What we need to do, though, is get more information on PB Resources. Where are they located? What else can we find?"

"You mean, you want to go visit the lab itself?"

She grins. "No. I want Bo to go visit. Back in the day, he was pretty handy at a little *b* and *e*." Kendra waggles her eyebrows like she knows something I don't.

I raise my eyebrows up into my hairline. "Is my lawyer suggesting we break the law?"

She smirks. "Only a little bit, and only if he truly believes he can get some damning pictures as evidence of what they're doing to animals firsthand."

The breaking and entering is absolutely *not* happening. However, another idea enters my mind like a shot in the dark. "Oh, I've got an even better idea." I pick up the phone and dial a number.

"Yo, Bossman. What wishes can my magical technical prowess grant you today?" She laughs at her own joke.

I smile. "Need you to do some hacking. Supersleuthing-type stuff."

"Ohhh you're talking dirty to me. I won't tell Mick." Her voice dips conspiratorially. "What you got?"

I roll my eyes and stop at the window, peering over DC proper. "Need you to hack PB Resources and find out if they have any job openings. Then I need you to get Bo on a plane and into that company as a new hire ASAP." I can hear her fingers clacking against the keyboard in the background.

After a few moments of silence, I break the quiet. "Can you handle it?"

"Pshhht, child's play. Next time ask me to break into the Department of Defense and get him a job, and we'll chat about difficulty." She guffaws, then hums. "Oooh, they have a job as a janitor and one as a lab assistant. Oh, please let me force him to clean toilets." Her voice rises with unbridled glee. "It would make my whole year, Parker. Pretty please!" she begs. "I promise to not ask for anything else all year! Swear! Cross my heart and hope to die!"

The *die* part makes my smile slide right off my face, reminding me of her recent stint in the hospital from a very real gunshot wound. "Too soon, minxy. Too soon."

She groans into the phone. "Sorry. Seriously, though, can I make him the janitor?"

"We need him to get into the lab . . ."

"What is it?" Kendra asks from over my shoulder.

"Wendy found jobs at PB Resources for a janitor and a lab assistant."

"Janitor," she says flatly.

I frown even though a squeal can be heard from my phone. I hold it away from my ear. "Why janitor? Wouldn't we want Bo to get into the lab, get close to what they're doing?"

She leans against the bed. "No. For one, I don't want to put him into a position where he wouldn't know what to do. Lab assistants need to know the business. He doesn't. Second, I would never ask him to do something I wouldn't do myself. What if they ask him to inject an animal or worse, hurt one?" She shivers. "No. Janitors usually have access to most of the building. He could probably get a lot more information in that role. Plus, it's not hard to clean bathrooms, mop floors, and the like. He'd be a shoo-in."

"Yes!" Wendy cheers into the line. "Please let me tell him he's going undercover as a janitor!"

I chuckle at her excitement. "No, crazy girl. I need to speak to Bo directly about it. Just set it up and make sure that, if at all possible, he can start the job first thing tomorrow or the next day. We need some damning evidence on the way this company is treating their animals immediately or this case is going to bury us."

"Got it. I'm on top of it, Bossman. I won't let you down."

"You never have, Wendy. Text me when you've got it set up. Can you transfer me to Bo?"

"With pleasure."

8

Two more days down the drain, and I'm irritated with a serious case of blue balls. Skyler didn't have time for a little phone sex last night, but she did have time to send me a fuckhot picture of her in nothing but her underwear before she jumped on a plane to visit Tracey and sign some contracts on the *A-Lister* movie.

I rub my thumb over her scandalous picture. She's wearing nothing but red lace. Her face is hidden by her hair, but I know that body like I know my own dick. Every curve, subtle dip, the muscular roundness of her calves . . .

My mouth waters as my phone buzzes in my hand. "Lovemaker" comes up on the display.

I hit "Accept" and put the phone to my ear; all thoughts of my golden goddess disappear in the hope that Bo has the goods. "Tell me you've got something!" I half beg. I'm tired of being in DC, visiting stuffy senators and pretending to work with a company that goes against everything I believe in as a human being.

"Boy howdy! I'm coming at you from the astute janitor's closet at PB Resources, where the shit they are hiding is unconscionable. I actually couldn't eat dinner last night or breakfast today, and that's after only one full day of work."

A grimace steals across my face. I don't want my brother to have to deal in grotesque shit any more than I want to myself. "I'm sorry, brother."

"Naw, it's fine. Had to be done. I'm going to send you some quick pics I took. One a bit damaging but not enough to wound them. The worst so far is of a couple of dogs that are skin and bones, definitely malnourished. I went back in after I hit the vending machine and snuck the two dogs a couple of beef jerky sticks each. Today my overalls are loaded with treats just in case."

I smile at the image of Bo sneaking dogs beef jerky. No matter how many women he loves and leaves, he's a good guy with a huge heart.

"There's a room I haven't been into yet. It's not on rotation until tonight. I have a feeling that's where most of the hinky shit goes down. I'll let you know what else I find."

"Okay. And Bo . . . thanks again for doing this. You didn't have to, but the fact that you want to make things right and are taking a hit for the team means a lot."

Bo growls in clear frustration. "Shut up. I own a fat chunk of IG. It's my ass on the line just as much as it is yours and Royce's. We're a team. More than that, we're family. We don't let scumbags fly on our radar. Keep your phone on, and I'll send you whatever I can. I want out of this place soon. I've cleaned enough filthy rooms to last me a lifetime. As a matter of fact, I'm giving my housekeeper a raise for cleaning my bathroom alone. That woman's a saint!"

Laughter fills my lungs and has me barking into the phone so hard my gut aches with the motion. "Wendy wanted to be the one to tell you about the janitor role. She was itching with glee."

He lets out a groan. "She would! I'm going to have to find interesting ways to get her back. Maybe I'll send her pictures of the presents these losers leave me to clean. Yeah . . . that ought to do it."

A snicker leaves my lips as I try to cover my mouth and hide the noise. The last thing I want to get is a copy of whatever those particular pictures would contain.

"Anyway, I'm out, Park. I'll keep you posted. I've got some floors to mop and some spying to do. Later."

After we end the call, my phone pings, and I open the texts from Bo. One shows an image of at least six rats in a cage littered with shit and piss. Gross, but not enough to get them on the chopping block. The second picture is of two floppy-eared dogs. Their ribs are completely visible, and they're huddled together, obviously scared out of their minds. I clench my teeth and breathe slowly through my nose. Anger will only cause me to screw up this case. The important thing to do right now is keep a level head with the promise of retribution in the very near future.

I save the images and forward them to Kendra, Royce, and Wendy. The five of us are operating at full disclosure, each one of us working our own angles. Royce and Wendy are digging into the financials and clients to see if we can find any additional avenues and doors to blow open. Bo is working the lab. And today, Kendra and I are meeting with Senator Portorino.

Yesterday we spent the day meeting with lobbyists, a congressman, and two senators. We slipped each one the damning information about the connection between PB Resources and Pure Beauty Pharmaceuticals and what the bill would mean to public safety at large, not to mention the rumor of their treatment of animals in their testing practices. Senator Birchill is on her own mission to take them out regarding the environmental concerns of removing thousands of trees and destroying the natural landscape bordering a very popular national park, along with the amount of pollution those factories would be pumping into the air and water.

Unfortunately, as I see it, in the eyes of local politicians, her argument is weak. The benefit of the factories bringing in tens of thousands of new jobs and tax dollars to a downtrodden economy would far outweigh a little smoke in the air or the cutting down of a portion of a huge forest. The general public doesn't usually see the long-term ramifications of such a decision, only the short-term benefits. And jobs and money are big benefits. It's what the bill includes that needs to be brought into the spotlight. The ability to skip crucial steps in medical testing that ensure consumer safety. The fact that they're abusing innocent animals in order to produce their products. Medical and cosmetic safety and possibly being able to tweak the moral compass of mankind are the best arguments we have to defeat this bill.

Grabbing my sport coat, I head to meet Kendra in our shared living room.

"I'm so done with being in DC. How the hell did you live here for eight years? The negativity in politics is insufferable."

She grins. "Depends on which side of politics you're on. When you're fighting injustices, it can be a lot of fun. Kind of like a superhero or vigilante, working to achieve justice for the good of all people. I did it by taking cases that protected the public and the interests of good, honest-working corporations, not by wearing spandex and fighting crime."

I slip on my khaki sport coat with the tan suede patches at the elbows. It pairs nicely with my navy slacks and the yellow lined tie Skyler added to my new wardrobe at her house.

The idea that soon I'll be thinking *our* house makes me smile wide. That little bit of positivity about our future helps me feel pounds lighter. I can handle this case, get through it. Hell, I can survive anything if my reward is coming home to Skyler.

"What's got you smiling so much? You've been nothing but a grump since we had our 'come to Jesus' moment with Senator Birchill."

I tip my head to the side and decide if I'm going to share something so personal. She petitioned me to keep her personal life to herself, but behind the scenes, that's not at all what I'm doing. I'm still waiting to find out more about the eight-year block of time in her life I don't know about. If Kendra wants to have the same connection the rest of the IG team has with one another, she's going to have to open up. At the same time, we'll need to be open with her, build that bridge to comradery.

"Skyler and I have decided to start house shopping together as well as look into adopting a dog and a cat."

She cocks a sculpted brow. "Wow. Big step. Have you been together long?"

"On and off for close to a year."

"On and off?" She picks up on that fact like a hawk on a skittering rodent in an open desert.

"Well, one time off, for a couple of weeks. We had a bit of a bungle in some information. We worked it out and are stronger for it. We've just decided to shack up, forgo the two houses since, when we're in the same city, we're together every night anyway. Plus, Skyler made the huge leap to move to Boston to be where I am, and it's now up to me to make a similar overture."

"You planning nuptials anytime soon?"

The question practically lays me flat, like a tidal wave just hit me and slammed me back a foot. I lean against the edge of the couch and sit my ass on the arm. "Not at this time."

"Hmm. Interesting. Buying a home and getting pets together is usually something a married couple does after they . . . you know . . . say 'I do.'" She leans her elbows on her knees and stares up at me blankly, allowing her comment to wiggle its way into my subconscious.

I nod. "This is true. Skyler and I already have an unconventional relationship, with her being a celebrity and my being . . . well, not a celebrity. We have our own way of doing things."

She stands, grabs her pristine white jacket, and puts it on over a mustard-yellow blouse that ties in a silky bow at the neck. Her skirt is black, as are her stilettos, though they have a slim gold strap that wraps delicately around the ankle. One thing about Kendra: the woman knows how to dress. She does not need any tips. Everything she wears is a perfect combination of slinky, elegant, and professional. Basically, sex on a stick for the average suit-wearing businessman.

Kendra is the type of woman who any man would be lucky to have on his arm. Beautiful, classy, and intelligent. Which is why it's so easy for me to see her long feminine fingers looped around my brother Royce's bicep. Not only would the two of them together be a jaw-dropper to look at, they'd make beautiful progeny. Something I know my brother wants with all his heart. A family of his own to raise and protect.

The only question is, Does Kendra want the same things? With her being so tight-lipped about her past and her personal life, I'm not so sure they're even in the same galaxy, let alone on the same page.

***

"Senator Portorino?" I approach the petite olive-skinned woman. Her eyes are a dark brown that matches her espresso-colored hair, and she has a curvy, hourglass shape. A true Italian from top to toe.

She narrows her gaze. "Yes?"

I hold out my hand. "I'm Parker Ellis, and this is my attorney, Kendra Banks. We're in from International Guy, located in Boston."

She frowns. "I'm afraid I'm not sure why you're here." She glances around as if there might be someone else I'm meant to speak to.

"If we may sit, I can explain. We won't take up too much of your time."

The senator's gaze turns icy. "I'm not sure who you are, and I don't have a lot of time for lunch before I have to be back."

Kendra steps up from behind me. "It's about your sister. The one doing a six-month stay at the Betty Ford Center in Rancho Mirage, California, paid for by your husband's brother. Interesting why your husband's brother would get involved in your sister's sobriety, unless . . ."

"Sit down," she states, a pinched expression marring her pretty face.

We both take a seat and wave off the waiter when we do.

"Look, Senator Portorino, we mean no disrespect," I start, attempting to curb the harsh approach we had to take in order to get her to speak with us.

"Could have fooled me." Her voice is dripping with disdain.

I take a deep breath and try to smooth over the edges of her irritation. "We didn't want to bring up your sister; however, the people who hired us to help them do. We're trying to avoid the smear campaign they're planning to run on you if you don't vote yes on the pharmaceutical- and cosmetics-testing regulations bill coming up for vote in a few days."

The senator tips her head back and laughs, her long straight hair shifting back behind her shoulders with the movement.

"This is no joking matter."

"You're what? Blackmailing me? Do you think I'm stupid enough to agree to the terms of a blackmailer? I wouldn't have been in politics so long if I had. I have nothing to hide."

I shake my head. "First of all, we're not blackmailing you. Second, Pure Beauty Pharmaceuticals is prepared to release the information on the last 'get out of jail free card' your sister was given by Judge Mastery. Not only would that hurt your reputation, it could absolutely hurt the judge for not having recused herself when seeing your sister was the one on trial. She knew you personally and that the defendant was your sister."

Senator Portorino crosses her arms over her chest defensively. "For one, it was a small drug charge. She would have gotten a few years at most, with release in one year with good behavior. Instead, we agreed to a one-year term in a rehabilitation center. The same one she's still in and where she's doing beautifully. I'm not afraid of what the press will bring. Pure Beauty needs to work harder if they want to hurt me."

"What about the judge?"

She shrugs. "Mandy retired a month after that case. She's moved down to Florida, so she can play bridge and visit the beach."

I smile wide at Kendra. "This is great news. I can't wait to tell our contact."

The senator frowns. "You're not a very good blackmailer if you're happy I'm unconcerned with the information you have on me. Besides, even if I were asked to resign, which I highly doubt would occur, this is my last term."

This time, Kendra grins. "Senator, here's some additional information on Pure Beauty Pharmaceuticals that you don't know. Some of your colleagues might not take kindly to the fact that the lab this company is in cahoots with is PB Resources."

That name must tweak her, because a disgusted grimace slips across her lips. "That company is disgusting. They have one of the largest puppy mills, but no one can prove it. They've been raided and have received numerous citations for mistreating their animals, but they pay the fines and then carry on, business as usual. No one can find the mills. I can't even imagine the poor innocent babies bred for the sole purpose of being tortured for the sake of the perfect long-lasting lip stain or wrinkle filler." She shivers and winces.

"We can't either. That's why we're going to do everything we can to make sure this bill is defeated. Not only is it unacceptable what they're doing to animals, but the half-assed measures they want to take to release their products to the public at large are frightening," I add.

She nods. "Well, I don't care what they try to do to me. I'm not voting yes on that bill, and with this nugget of information, I know three other senators who will be voting no too."

I grin. "Excellent."

Kendra interjects, "Please, if you would, keep this meeting and our involvement to yourself. We're doing our best to avoid a legal suit ourselves."

She crosses her heart with her index finger. "My word is my bond."

And with her, I believe it. "Thank you. We'll let you get back to your lunch."

"Good luck, Mr. Ellis, Ms. Banks. I'm rooting for you."

"Appreciate the gesture. I fear we're going to need it," I finish, then pull out Kendra's chair and walk with her out of the restaurant.

The second we're on the sidewalk, Kendra turns to me. "That was risky, giving her the information like that in the open."

I sigh. "Sometimes you've got to look like you're doing what the bad guys ask in order to secure their belief that you're on their side. If we'd had a clandestine meeting somewhere and were caught, there's far more plausibility that we're setting them up. At this point, we're working out in the open, visible to everyone. Speaking of . . ." I pull out my phone and visit the recent calls, choosing the one I know as Vivica's number.

"Preston," she answers.

"Yes, Ms. Preston, it's Parker Ellis. We've got an update. One I'm afraid, once again, you're not going to be happy with."

***

The next morning I'm sitting on the couch in the living room across from Kendra, who's in the single lounge chair. My cell phone is on speaker on the coffee table in front of us.

"We're just waiting on Bo to call in," Wendy says.

I swear the silence is deafening. We haven't gotten any additional good news, and it looks like we're going to be eating crow unless Bo has something of substance for us.

"Guys?" Bo's voice booms through the line as if my phone is on volume one hundred.

"Damn, dude. Turn it down a notch," I suggest.

"Okay, we're all here," Wendy states.

I clear my throat. "First, I'll go over what we've found here. Senator Portorino is not threatened by the information Pure Beauty has on her.

Senator Birchill went public with their damning evidence on her. This means that both of them are going to vote no on the bill regardless of what the company tries to do to them. In theory, this all sounds great, except during my update call with Vivica Preston, she notified us that Senator Kemper and Senator Damren have been schmoozing additional yes votes, and according to them, they have them. The yes votes now outnumber the no votes by five."

"That sucks!" Wendy states. "How can these people not realize how dangerous this company's plans are to the public? Skipping steps in testing, not to mention working with a horrible lab that mistreats animals . . ."

"Yeah, guys, and it's worse than we thought. Remember that rumor about puppy mills?" Bo questions.

Kendra leans over to get closer to the phone on the table. "Senator Portorino says that there's no proof the mill exists."

"Oh, it exists, and it's bad. They have hundreds of animals being bred right on site at the lab."

"No!" Kendra gasps. "How did the USDA miss that in their repeated citations?"

"Probably because the entire mill is underground," Bo says.

"Where did you get your information, brother?" I ask.

"From my own freakin' eyes, and I'm adopting a fucking dog, cat, or gerbil as soon as I get home. We all need to. This shit is bad. When it splits open there are going to be hundreds, maybe even a thousand animals that need homes. All breeds. All varieties. It's awful . . ." His voice lowers, and it sounds like he's taking a breather.

"Did you get proof?"

"Who the fuck do you think I am? Please. Don't insult me, Park."

I lift my hands even though he can't see it. "Brother, no insult intended. I apologize. Tell us what you saw; walk us through what went down."

Bo chuckles. "I'm pretty sure you don't want to know exactly what went down, because it was a tall blonde named Stephanie who works as a lab tech in the supersecret program. She apparently digs a man in uniform . . ."

"A janitor's uniform!" Wendy blurts out, and the rest of us laugh, a much-needed reprieve from the seriousness of the situation we've been facing all week.

"Hey, where there's a will, there's a way. And believe me, Tink, I always find a way."

"You're ridiculous," Wendy fires back.

"Says the woman who wears a collar like a pet!"

"All day, every day. At least I don't get my jollies off on anything with two legs!"

Royce interrupts their fiery banter. "Hey, hey, hey, calm down. That's enough."

"Sorry, Royce. It's been three days since I've thrown barbs with the jackal. We're overdue," Wendy admits good-naturedly.

"True dat. Miss you, Tink," Bo mumbles through the line.

What would these two do if they couldn't tease one another? A tremor rips through me. They'd probably find one of us to lay their brand of communication on.

"Anyway, back to my story before I was so rudely interrupted by a big mouth in Boston . . ."

Wendy growls through the line but doesn't follow up with a quip of her own. My mind supplies the image of Royce putting a big paw over her mouth to keep her quiet.

"When I got the lab tech all sated and happy, I promised to rock her world if she showed me where they kept all the puppies. Said I was enchanted by the work they did there, blah blah. She brought me to a specially marked elevator on the third floor. It's backed into a corner and is rarely used because it's supposed to only go between floors three and five. However, there's a random small door under the buttons with a key card swipe inside. She swiped her card, and the elevator went down way more than three floors. More like seven or eight."

"Nuts . . . ," I whisper as Kendra puts her hand over her mouth.

"When the elevator opened, it was to a floor that smelled of antiseptic and wet animal mixed together. She took me down a hall that had at least twenty doors. Behind each door was a different breeding room. When she wasn't looking, I snapped pics of at least four of them. Should be enough to damage them. Except it gets worse . . ."

"Jesus, brother, not sure if I can take more, and you just got started." Royce's deep, growling tone coupled with the volume of his timbre echoes through the room. Kendra closes her eyes at the sound. It's not the first time I've seen her react to my brother, and I doubt it will be the last.

Bo clears his throat and sighs. "She took me by this room they call the 'dead zone.' We didn't go in that room, but I could see through a window there was a guy tossing animals into some type of acid."

"Dead animals," I clarify.

"No, brother. These animals were not dead. They looked sick. Malnourished, but most of them were alive and breathing until he dropped them into the giant vat. Hold up . . . shit, I'm gonna be sick," Bo says in a muffled voice, and then his part of the line goes quiet.

Not one person says a thing for a long time. My entire insides feel like they're revolting. My stomach is in knots, my skin is hot as fire, and a pounding like someone hitting a bass drum picks up against my temples. The pendulum has swung to one of the worst possible scenarios. They're essentially frying animals alive to get rid of them after they've tortured them with whatever crap they put them through.

Eventually Bo comes back on the line. "Back. Sorry. I just . . . Talking about it brought it all back up. Literally."

I take a few calming, deep breaths and focus my gaze on the phone.

"Everyone . . . I want them to burn in hell. Kendra and I have skirted the boundaries of business ethics more than I care to repeat.

What they are doing is wrong. If we have to break every rule in that contract, I say we do it. Consequences be damned. Whatever it takes, this has to stop now. Are you in?"

"Agreed," Royce says.

"Fuck yeah!" Bo states.

"Absolutely," Kendra adds.

"Damn straight," Wendy chirps.

"It's time to put our heads together and be smart. This is what we need to do . . ."

9

"Mr. Ellis, Ms. Banks, come in. Please have a seat." Vivica gestures to two open seats at the same conference table we sat at the first time we were here.

"Thank you." I hold out a chair for Kendra. She sits, and I take my own seat.

Vivica sits across from us and laces her fingers, placing her hands on the top of the table. "I was surprised to get your request for a meeting so soon. I hope that means you have good news and were able to sway the senators?"

Beside me, Kendra leans over her chair to her briefcase, where she pulls out a stapled set of documents and hands them to our client.

"Unfortunately, we do not have good news. We are terminating our contract."

Vivica frowns as she reaches for the documents. She scans the termination notification Kendra drew up that I've already signed. "Termination?"

"Yes. Some disturbing information has come to our attention that goes against our moral code and business practices, which has forced us to make the difficult decision of ending our contract with Pure Beauty Pharmaceuticals."

"Is this about Senator Birchill's announcement the other day?"

I rest my forearms on the dark mahogany tabletop and tip my head. "No. Though, while it does not quite meet the criteria for termination of the contract, attempting to ruin a woman's reputation by making her violent rape and subsequent abortion public knowledge does go against our personal morals."

Kendra leans back in her chair and smiles. "It has come to our attention that Pure Beauty Pharmaceuticals is working with PB Resources."

Vivica narrows her gaze and twists her fingers together so tight the knuckles turn white. "What do our client relations have to do with our contract with International Guy?"

"We've been informed that PB Resources has questionable product-testing practices as it pertains to using animals as testing subjects. International Guy supports the Humane Society with a substantial yearly charitable donation, and working with a company directly connected to PB Resources will negatively impact our reputation generally plus specifically with the clients we work with who are animal rights activists."

Vivica's face reddens, and her jaw goes tight. "I can assure you that our relationship with PB Resources is limited—" She is lying through her teeth, and I cut her off.

"We are aware that the CEO of PB Resources is your husband. We know for a fact that your company uses PB Resources solely for your product testing. While there is no crime in that, there is substantial circumstantial evidence that you and he have collaborated to hide numerous violations of animal abuse statutes. Additional proof can be found in the citations PB Resources received last year when they were injecting dogs' faces with lip fillers that your company manufactures."

Vivica picks up the contract. "We've paid you a hefty deposit . . ."

Kendra steeples her fingers. "Which is nonrefundable. We are releasing you from any additional costs that we've incurred since our arrival a few days ago in DC. We will cover the expenses for flights, hotel, and ancillaries from the deposit given, though it is our right to continue to bill you for them." Kendra perks up and smirks.

"I'm going to have our lawyers review this. We do not take professional *thievery* lightly and will act accordingly." Vivica's gaze narrows as she presses her hands to the top of the table and stands, her shoulders hunched over in a menacing pose I think is meant as a warning.

Kendra pushes her chair back and clasps her hands in her lap. "Are you threatening us and our business for wanting to cancel our contract?"

"We've never had a company go against our wishes. You would be wise to think about this decision before leaving DC without meeting your end of the agreement. Our reach is long and our finances endless."

"That's enough." I stand, pushing the chair back, and button my suit jacket. "We've notified you of our intention to terminate the contract. You do not have a legal leg to stand on. What I would suggest is that you get your affairs in order. Something's brewing, and I wouldn't want to be smack-dab in the middle of it when the storm hits."

"Is there something you want to tell me, Mr. Ellis?" Vivica cocks a dark brow and glares.

"By attempting to get this bill passed, knowing what you're doing behind the scenes to make that happen, it's your ass that's in a sling. You've opened up Pandora's box, and she has a wicked temper. I'd prepare for the fight of your lives," I say.

"You think you're the only company that does its homework, Mr. Ellis? I know all about you, Royce Sterling, Bogart Montgomery, and Wendy Bannerman. You've got three Harvard grads and a high school dropout runaway on your team. Not to mention the fact that you're dating Skyler Paige, the most recognized celebrity in the nation, if not the world. What do you think the press would do if some of your skeletons got out of the closet?"

I shake my head and cross my arms over my chest. "I've got nothing to hide. My past is what it is, the past."

"Really? You think your old girlfriend, Kayla McCormick, would say the same, or the ex-friend, Greg, you and your partners pushed out of his rightful twenty-five percent of International Guy? He was in on the initial brainchild for the company, from what I understand, and then the three of you kicked him to the curb. And what of Ms. Bannerman? Getting shot on a case. I wonder how your future clients would feel about that tidbit of information that was kept out of the national press because it occurred in Canada. I'll bet the media would love to know some of these details. Right or wrong, the tabloid press can spin a tale that would look bad not only for your girlfriend and her celebrity status, but for your business."

My heart pounds so hard I feel as though it's going to beat right out of my chest. I clench my teeth and tighten both hands into fists, wanting nothing more than to strangle this disgusting human where she stands.

Instead, I reel in my anger and put it on the back burner. "Good luck with your smear campaign," I say evenly. "Pure Beauty hired us knowing this information. How will it look for you if you release anything that could defame us? I'm not afraid of you or your billions," I sneer.

She smirks as if she doesn't believe me.

I continue undeterred. "What I am afraid of is women using your products and ending up disfigured due to rushed tests or miscalculations in the chemical makeup of the products because you didn't go through a thorough testing process. Or worse, dying because you decided to skip a few steps in order to make more money by cutting a few additional corners."

Her gaze turns to white-hot points of anger, but I move ahead, undaunted.

"I'm afraid of animals being mistreated and killed in order to make the perfect shade of lipstick. I'm afraid of a forest being destroyed and changing the face of America's landscape in order to do more of your dirty work. Everyone has a past, Ms. Preston. I'm not ashamed of mine. It's part of what made me who I am today. My partners, the same. And as it pertains to Wendy Bannerman, her future husband is Michael Pritchard; I'd think twice about going against his woman. He's extremely territorial and has zero problem using all of his many, many billions and contacts to protect her honor. I'd love to see you in a battle against MP Advertising. In fact, I'd pay to watch it happen."

On that note, I open the conference door and gesture for Kendra to walk through first as I look back at Vivica. "Feel free to have your counsel contact Kendra, not that there's anything you can do. We do our homework too and are very . . . *thorough.*"

Vivica's mouth twists into a snarl before she laughs dryly. "You're going to regret this. International Guy is all of five employees strong, and maybe brings in eight to ten million a year?" One side of her face lifts into a haughty expression. "We're a billion-dollar organization with hands in every political pot from the East Coast to the West. Enjoy your last days in DC, because when you get home, you will feel the strain of the decision you made today. And that is a *promise*, not a threat, Mr. Ellis." She smiles, and I swear she learned that charm from the devil himself.

"Be careful of your karma, Ms. Preston. You never know when it's going to turn around and kiss you, bite you in the ass, or cut you off at the knees."

***

"Step one is done," I say into the phone's speaker. Kendra is pacing the room like a rat in a cage while I sit back sipping the whiskey I ordered from room service even though it's only just after one in the afternoon.

"Turn on the TV," Wendy announces through the line with utter glee in her tone.

Kendra finds the remote and flicks it on to one of the cable news shows. A newscaster is watching the screen behind her, one hand held up to her open mouth, covering what looks to be an expression of pure disgust. The screen shows hundreds of puppies, cats, pigs, goats, and a variety of other animals locked in minuscule cages. Another shot shows dead animals stacked in a freezer where it's obvious they're being stored before being disposed of.

"Oh my God . . . ," the newscaster says, and I wince as a team of cops moves through the rooms. One room looks like the location that Bo said they called the "dead zone." A man is being cuffed, screaming at the top of his lungs how he's just doing his job. Dogs strapped to the table behind him are whimpering and shaking. Two officers pick up a few animals, cuddling them in their arms before moving out of the room.

The camera moves into another room. Inside, there are animals in plastic cubes, a variety of medical testing being done. The scene is utterly gruesome when it pans past an animal foaming at the mouth, eyes rolling back in its head.

The newscaster looks away, tears pouring down her cheeks. "And . . . a-and . . ." She clears her throat, stares at the camera straight in front with a determined look, and wipes at her tears. "Authorities have raided PB Resources after having received snapshots of a hidden animal mill and mistreatment of multiple animals in their testing facility. The laboratory is the sole testing facility for one of the nation's largest cosmetics companies, Pure Beauty Pharmaceuticals. According to reliable sources, Pure Beauty has managed to sponsor a bill that is due for a vote in the Senate tomorrow that would allow the company and others to cut corners on product testing, skipping the human trials phase completely in order to speed release of products to the public."

The newscaster grimaces. "Social media activists have organized a boycott of Pure Beauty products and released a comprehensive list for consumers." A huge running list of some of the most well-known brands for makeup, lotions, and nail polishes appears across the screen. "And if you're visiting your plastic surgeon, be sure to double-check that the fillers you're receiving are not the ones that have done this." The screen behind her shows one of the pictures we've already seen of the dogs that have been injected with jacked-up fillers to their faces.

I open my mouth in awe as I watch the authorities tear through the facility where we had Bo digging for information.

"Bo, you on?" I call out.

"Hell yeah, bro. Watching and tipping back my beer from the comfort of my bed in my hotel room as we speak. On the first flight out tomorrow morning. Going to see if I can find me a chicklet to warm my bed this evening before I head out."

I chuckle, my eyes still glued to the images of the Humane Society sweeping in and helping the animals in the worst condition first.

"Good work on this. You saved our asses. The threats she made . . ."

"Park, brother, we all have things we'd like to keep in our past . . ." Roy's deep voice penetrates the crackling speaker.

Kendra stops midpace and stands still, Roy's words hitting her like an arrow to a bull's-eye.

"But you gotta remember," he continues, "we work as a team. One of us gets hit, the other comes out swinging. This business is our baby, and we're proud of it. That does not, however, take away from the fact that we are going to back one another up before anyone can hurt a single hair on our heads."

"Says the bald guy!" Wendy snorts, which has me smiling.

"True, brother," I admit. "I'm just glad this all worked out. I'm still wondering if we're going to get any backlash from Pure Beauty. They had to guess this was our doing. The timing is suspect to say the least. If they—"

"Suspicion is one thing; proof is another. If they try, we'll be ready," Royce says with a conviction I'm not yet capable of feeling since I'm still reeling in the middle of this. "We've got our ducks in a row, and Wendy's on watch. If they try something, we'll know it's coming."

"Honestly, I think they're going to have a lot to get through legally. The fines, the citations, the laws that they've broken are a legal nightmare. Revenge on us would take a lot of energy and effort they can't spare right now," Kendra adds smartly.

I tip my head from side to side, evaluating that information and letting it soothe my nerves.

"Plus, have you seen the stock market?" Royce says, a smile in his tone.

"Yeah, I couldn't wait to open the paper and check the Nasdaq," I say dryly.

"Well, if you had, you'd have seen their stock is in the shitter. They're going to be bankrupt. Everyone has sold their stock. My guess, they don't want to be in bed with a company like that. So even if they wanted to come after us . . . what money would they do it with?"

A subtle warmth flares in the center of my chest and spreads out like the sun's rays lighting me up from the inside out.

"Excellent." I sip my drink and watch the TV.

Kendra hits the remote and changes the channel. Every station is airing the takedown and talking about Pure Beauty and PB Resources.

The last one Kendra stops on has an image of Vivica and her husband being removed from their home in handcuffs. Side by side.

Maybe they'll have a cell for two. A tiny, dark, dank hole in the ground for two would work smashingly. I smile wide at the image and lift my glass in salute to justice being done.

A-fucking-men.

***

In the two days after the takedown, we got everything situated with the senators, made sure the bill did in fact fail, and gave our statements to the authorities, even bringing up the threat that they would blackmail us for ending our contract. Finally we were able to hop on a plane and head home. I hadn't talked to my girl in two days, just had a series of missed calls and follow-up voice mails and texts.

Now that I'm home, I face plant right onto my bed. Skyler sent me a text while I was in the air saying she was out of town still, in New York. For a moment when I saw that message after getting back from a shit case, I was man enough to admit it pissed me off. All I wanted when I came home from DC, after working the case from hell, was to walk right into the arms of my woman. I'd soak my senses in her peaches-and-cream scent, dip my wick into her heat, and let the entire week go. Instead, I got a fucking text.

No woman. No comforting arms. No tight heat to lose myself in.

The rational side of me understands that she has to work, and our jobs often call us both away at inopportune times. Still, I'm in full sulk mode with no hope of getting out of it anytime soon.

The smooth cotton of her pillowcase against the skin of my face eases my irritation when I catch a whiff of her scent from the last time she stayed here. Mostly we've been at her place since it's so conveniently located to IG. Though I'm glad I came here. I don't want to taint her pad with my doom-and-gloom mood.

That case rattled me. Like a damn snake, it sank its fangs into my jugular, and its body squeezed until I lost my breath. That's how I felt.

I roll over onto my back and stare up at the ceiling. The things that company was willing to do to get what they wanted were beyond the pale. It disgusts me on so many levels it has me worrying about humanity. Is everything really that fucked up in the world outside of the sphere of IG and the clients I usually work for? Am I that ignorant of the destruction going on in the world outside of my own existence?

A sour taste in my mouth has me hauling my ass out of bed and shuffling into my bathroom. I take my time brushing my teeth, pulling off my dirty clothes, and stepping under a hot spray of water in the shower. For a few minutes I just let the heat ease the tension in the muscles of my back and neck. I look down at my flaccid cock, too tired to even give it a yank and tug. The release would help me sleep, but without the emotion and connection from Skyler's touch, I'm not interested tonight.

Going through the motions, I wash my body as if on autopilot. The same goes for shutting off the water, drying off, and pulling on my robe.

When I exit the shower the sight that greets me is beyond gorgeous.

My woman is sitting cross-legged in the center of my bed in a pair of jeans, a tank, and a smile. Her hair is tumbling into golden waves down her back and over her shoulders. Her presence is not the biggest surprise. It's the two fluffy balls bouncing in and out of her lap that have my attention. One yellow, one black.

"What are you doing here? I thought . . . I . . ." I watch in shock as she lifts up the two furry friends.

I hustle over to the bed and take the black puppy into my arms, lift him up, and he licks my face with his long pink tongue. "Who are you, buddy?"

Sky gets up onto her knees, holding the yellow puppy against her chest. "Well, officially, that animal is 707 and this is 1116. They don't have real names," she says sadly. "Which means we get the honor of giving our babies names." Her smile is bright and reminds me of the sun peeking out over the horizon on an otherwise dark day.

"Peaches." I rub her bicep and look at her face. Even with the smile, I can see the underlying sadness.

"Bo sent me photos of the hundreds of animals needing a home two nights ago. I got Tracey and my PR team on it and flew down there yesterday morning to visit the mass shelters that had been set up. I recorded a piece for the news that they could use, then signed tons of headshots that Tracey had printed at the local print place, and we helped coordinate a mass adoption event. I encouraged anyone and everyone to come out and pick up an animal to adopt. If they did, they'd get a signed headshot of me and a raffle ticket entry to have a private lunch with me and my boyfriend next month. Hope you're cool with that."

"Yeah, yeah, baby, I'm cool with that." I cup her head and bring her forehead to my lips, where I plant a long kiss, letting her soft skin and scent mix with the puppy breath surrounding us. "What about these guys? Two dogs?"

She nods. "I love them. This one is a golden retriever mix of some kind. That one is a German shepherd. They were caged together, and anytime the animal workers tried to separate them they freaked out. Barking, whimpering, whining. It was awful. When I petted their heads they both licked my hands, and I just knew they were meant to be ours. Is it okay?"

I kiss her lips right as the yellow one licks both our faces. We both start laughing, and Sky kisses the dog all over its furry head.

"What are we going to do with two of these guys?" I laugh and stare at the happy face of the dog I'm holding. "And what are we going to name you?"

"I may have an idea . . ." She grins, her shoulders going up toward her ears with her shyness.

I inhale long and deep, letting the sight of her holding a sweet puppy sear into my memory. "Lay it on me."

"Well, this one is a she and is so happy and joyous, and she's golden like the sun. I was thinking Sunny."

"Sunny." I try out the name for myself.

The dog in her arms whips its head around to look at my face. "Guess she likes it and already knows it."

"I may have been calling her that for a full day," she admits, her cheeks pinkening with embarrassment.

"I love it. And this bruiser?" I cuddle the dog in my arms.

"Midnight," she suggests.

"Midnight." I stare at the dog's pitch-black fur with small tufts of tan peeking through around his face and belly like stars coming through a night sky.

"Sky, Sunny, and Midnight. I love it."

"Yay! Did you hear that, Sunny? Daddy loves it! You're going to be so happy with us as your parents." She snuggles the dog, leans over, snuggles Midnight, and then kisses me hard, one of her hands wrapping around my neck and holding me close. "I love you."

"I love you, and I love that you saved these dogs. It makes the hell we went through all the more worth it."

"I figured you might think so. When Wendy told me what happened and Bo asked for my help, I was all over it. Last I heard, they only had two hundred more dogs to find homes for. They're going to distribute them to shelters and rescues farther away to get a larger reach. It was pretty easy to get the farm animals distributed—all of the local farms were willing to take on the pigs, goats, and chickens. The schools, universities, and pet shops took in the rodents. All that was left were a ton of cats and dogs. Mostly dogs. And the whole team adopted animals. Wendy and Mick took home a two-year-old Jack Russell–beagle mix they named Lauren. Royce took home a female pit bull he named Halle. And Bo—"

"Bo adopted an animal?" I'm pretty sure my eyes are wide with surprise. "I thought he was joking the other day when he said it."

"He probably was serious, because there was this white fluffy cat that would not leave him alone. He said any female that rubs all over his legs and marks her territory deserves to be with him. Said he could understand her logic because he's hard to resist."

Fuckin' Bo! I laugh so hard at that, my gut aches.

"Get this!" Skyler smiles prettily, and I'm reminded once again how much I love her plump, glossy lips. "Do you know what he named the cat?"

I shake my head and laugh. "No, what?"

"Snowflake."

"You're kidding."

She giggles like a schoolgirl sharing some gossip. "Nope. He said that any female that can nail him down and make him commit must be one of a kind, just like a snowflake."

"Well, there you go," I get out through more laughter. "Also, it's good he went with a cat. They need a lot less supervision. What about Kendra?"

She frowns. "Actually, she didn't adopt. Said she couldn't right now, but when she got her own place, she'd consider it."

"Her own place?" I pick up on the part I hadn't heard before.

Skyler shrugs. "Didn't she just move here?"

"Yeah, I guess. And I know her family is here, so she must be staying with them for the time being." Seems odd, though, because she's a very independent woman. Her living with her parents for any length of time does not strike me as her normal MO. This bit of info reminds me that I need to get the lowdown from Wendy about what she found on Kendra while I was away.

"Probably." Sky sighs.

"You know, it's all really sad, but I feel good about taking PB Resources and Pure Beauty Pharmaceuticals down. I've talked to the guys, and the hundred thousand dollars they gave us as a deposit to work the case? We're donating it to the Humane Society to help get these animals help, especially all the sick ones they mistreated."

Sky grimaces and cuddles Sunny closer. "Honey, it was awful, the amount of sick and broken animals. Some had to be put down; they were too far gone to help. They were suffering terribly. If you guys and Bo hadn't found that secret mill and lab, I shudder to think what would have become of all of these animals, even our babies, Sunny and Midnight." Her voice is but a whisper as she places her chin on top of the head of her new fur baby as if the dog has always been hers.

God, she's going to be an incredible mother one day. Not soon. Not even within the next year, but down the road when we're ready. These pups will go a long way toward us determining the path toward a family. For now, I'm pretty happy having my girl and two new fur babies to call my own.

"Let's get these two settled and order some takeout. What do you say?"

"I say, whatever my man wants, my man gets. I've missed you." She sets Sunny down to explore, and I do the same with Midnight. Her arms come around me, and she rests her face in the crook of my neck.

With Skyler in my arms, two fur babies poking their noses around my bedroom, my world is back to peaceful. Not the first time the thought has simmered within me, but it's a wonderful feeling every time. Being in Skyler's arms is where I feel at home.

10

"Puppies. You had to have puppies. Not fully grown animals that know when and where to use the bathroom and bark only if there's a reason, but puppies that yap at anything and then piss all over my floor mats." Nate tosses back a handful of napkins to us in the rear passenger seats.

I grab the stack and hand them to Skyler. She's much smaller and capable of patting the newest accident Sunny made on the floor mats of the SUV.

"Technically they're *my* floor mats," Sky says. "You're just mad that I didn't run the dog situation past you first."

"Yes, yes, I am. I wouldn't have bought carpeted mats. Now I have to take the car through the cleaner."

Skyler purses her lips and shrugs. "Sunny didn't mean it, did you, baby girl?" She nuzzles the crown of Sunny's furry head.

Midnight, however, is a stud. He's standing tall, his nose stuck out the window, his ears alert to what's happening. Sunny is a mess. A beautiful mess my woman is in love with.

"It's not her fault. The car is a very exciting place, isn't it, baby girl? I know. Don't worry, we'll get to Daddy's building and your second home soon." She coos to the dog as if Sunny understands everything she says. Then again, maybe she does. The dog is focused on every word coming out of Skyler's mouth as if it's God himself speaking.

As Nate turns the corner of our building, Skyler pats his shoulder. "Stop in front. Sunny and Midnight need to learn to piddle in the grass."

Nate shakes his head curtly. "There're paparazzi out front."

"I don't care. My dogs need to pee."

"They can wait until we've got you secured in the building, and I'll take the dogs."

"Stop the damn car, Nate. My babies need to go. Now."

"Didn't she just go a few minutes ago?" he snidely remarks.

Skyler narrows her gaze and sends invisible daggers his way. "Midnight did not. He's been very good, and I want to encourage it. Just stop the damn car."

Nate's mouth tightens, and Rachel snickers behind her hand, not saying a word. My guess, she knows her husband's mood is questionable and doesn't want to poke the bear any more than Skyler already has.

"Wait until I can get around the car . . . please," he growls to Skyler.

When he exits the car, Rachel follows.

"Ohhh, you're in trouble with your bodyguard," I tease Skyler.

She pouts and narrows her gaze at me. "He works for me."

I smile. "Maybe you need to remind him of that fact, but honestly, Peaches, he's just doing his job. Your safety is his first priority, not whether or not your dog needs to piss."

"Our dogs," she reminds me, not that I need it. I've got Midnight on my lap. The boy has taken a liking to me. He's decided I'm his person, which works for me because he's cool as hell. Sunny is a sweet girl who loves her momma, but they both seek attention from the two of us. Still, they sleep right next to one another and seem to stay close to us, no matter what room we're in. So much so that, when we took a much-needed shower together, we came out to find them cuddled together outside of the shower, awaiting our exit.

It hurts my heart to know that they are afraid of being without us. I don't know what they went through at the lab, and I don't want to know. I'm just determined to make sure that they have a good life.

Nate opens our door as Skyler hooks each dog's collar with a leash. She hands me Midnight's and lifts Sunny out of the car.

The paparazzi go wild as she exits, the dog in her arms.

"Skyler, Skyler, is that your new dog?"

She waves good-naturedly as she walks Sunny over to the patch of grass near our building.

"What's its name?" another pap hollers.

I follow Sky's lead with Midnight.

"Parker, Parker, did you both get a dog, or are they Skyler's?"

"What are their names?"

They continue to take pictures as Nate and Rachel keep them a safe distance from us.

"Okay, baby girl, now I know you have an audience, but just try for Momma, okay?" She pats Sunny's head. The dog does not like the attention, tucking her tail between her legs and leaning against Skyler.

I set Midnight down next to Sunny, and he immediately walks over to the tree, hikes his leg, and does his business. "Good boy! That's a good boy." I ruffle his scruff at the back of his neck, and he looks up at me, tongue lolling out, happy as a clam.

Sunny seems to figure out what we want her to do and crouches and pees a little. Skyler jumps up and down, clapping wildly as if her dog has just performed the most amazing trick in the universe. "Good girl!"

Sky pulls out treats from her bag and continues to praise Sunny and then Midnight. She looks up at me from where she's crouching. Her eyes are a golden honey color today and filled to the brim with happiness. Immediately my heart swells, and I cup the side of her face, caressing the apple of her pinkened cheek, wanting to touch and feel her joy myself.

"They are so smart," she says to me, pride overflowing in her tone. I smile down at my girl. "Yes, they are."

"Should we introduce them to the paps so they'll back off?" she asks me.

"No," Nate growls.

"Yes," I say at the same time.

Nate's shoulders stiffen, and he shakes his head.

When the dogs have sniffed the entire patch of grass and tree, we pick up our respective animals and Nate leads us over to the paps. The cameras go crazy, snapping pics.

"Are those your dogs, Skyler?" a respectful one I've seen before asks, but doesn't try to approach.

She nods happily. "Yes, Parker and I have adopted these two dogs from the horrible mill that was just taken down by the Humane Society recently. This is Sunny and her best friend and now brother, Midnight."

I dutifully hold up the dog, and surprisingly he's not at all afraid of the cameras; instead, he seems to grow taller, stretch his neck out, and preen. I should have named him Stud.

"You say that you adopted these dogs. Can we assume that you've adopted them together?"

Skyler beams and nods. "Yep." She snuggles into my side. "We're going to raise fur babies together." She looks up at me, and I kiss her right then and there. Every time I look at her, I'm lost to her beauty all over again.

"We wish you luck!" one of the paps says.

"Yeah, cute dogs!" another calls out.

"Thank you. And remember, save a dog, save a life! Beauty lies within, and we don't need to torture innocent animals to create products that make us more beautiful. Beauty starts from the inside," she says poetically before setting her dog down and curling the leash around her wrist. "Come on, Sunny, let's go meet the IG team. Bye!" Sky waves over her shoulder and moves toward the building, flanked by Nate and Rachel. I follow right next to her with Midnight leading the charge.

Once we get inside, Nate leaves us to go take the car to the garage, but Rachel stays with us.

The small blonde keeps her eyes peeled as we go through security and to the elevators. Once we step on and the doors start to close, a hand stops them. "Wait!" a rather squeaky voice says.

I press the open-door button as Benny Singleton enters the elevator. Internally I growl but find I must be doing it out loud, because the sound is rippling off the walls of the small space—until I realize it's not me who's growling. It's Midnight.

Benny flattens his body up against the wall of the elevator like the pussy he is. "Whoa, boy. Uh, Sky, can you help me?"

She dips down and scoops up Midnight. I do the same with Sunny.

"He's protective of his family. Aren't you, boy." She wiggles her fingers under his chin and holds him close.

"I love dogs too!" Benny starts reaching out to pet Midnight, but he starts growling again.

Rachel puts her hand up and catches Benny's wrist midair. "Dude. Don't touch the dog. He bites," she warns.

Technically we don't know if he bites, but with the way he's got his little puppy lips pulled back and his eyes focused on Benny, I'd say she was wise to warn him.

Benny snatches his hand back. "Yikes. Well, okay. Sorry, Midnight. What about you?"

The stupid guy moves to pet Sunny in my arms. Midnight growls and Sunny cowers, burying her face into my armpit.

"Look, the dogs are new and have been through a lot. They don't want to be touched by strangers. Step back," I demand, my tone brooking no argument.

Benny's eyes widen, and he puts his back against the far end of the elevator. "Sorry. I just, you know, love dogs. Sky, I didn't know you were a dog fan. We should totally take your dogs for walks together," he suggests, his eyes scanning Skyler's jeans-and-tank-clad body. She has an array of dangling necklaces and a plethora of bracelets and rings tinkling with every movement.

"Um . . . I . . ." She starts to let the guy down easy, but I have zero tolerance for this prick.

"We've got it covered. Besides, soon she won't be living here."

He frowns. "Really? Where are you going? Back to New York?"

I put my free arm around Sky. "We're buying a house together."

"You're . . . oh, you're moving in together. I see."

"Yeah, so I'll be taking the dogs for walks. Thank you, though, for the gesture," I say dryly, leaving no room for him to think I'm not being sarcastic.

He rubs the back of his neck, and his head twitches not once but twice. "That's, uh, yeah, I'm sure that's good for you," he says to me, but avoids looking at Skyler.

Weirdo.

The elevator dings, and I realize it's IG's floor. He must be higher up in the building. I need to have Wendy or Nate find out. Our first check on him was pretty clean. Nothing strange in his record besides changing jobs regularly.

Rachel leads Skyler out of the elevator and holds it open for me.

"Bye, Skyler. I hope to see you again soon! We should have coffee together again," Benny calls out.

I place my hand on her lower back. "I don't think so . . . *friend*," I snarl, and narrow my gaze, making it very clear what I think about his idea.

"Uh, yeah, okay. Have a good day, Skyler." Benny waves like a loon, but I'm pushing Skyler forward, so she doesn't return the gesture.

"What is with that guy? He acts like we're friends, and we spent literally a day together shooting a commercial when we were children.

Then I run into him that one time, and what . . . we're BFFs?" Skyler grimaces.

I loop my arm around her shoulder. "I'll handle it."

She laughs but doesn't say anything as we make it to IG's office, dogs in our arms. The second we open the door, Annie stands up at her desk.

"Welcome home, Mr. Ellis, Ms. Paige."

"Annie, you may call me Parker."

Skyler shrugs. "And I'm just Sky. We're all family here, Annie."

Annie's smile becomes big, and a flush of red rushes up from her chest to pinken her cheeks. She covers them and stares at the bundles of doggy love we have in our arms. "My goodness, who are these little friends?"

Skyler brings Midnight over to Annie and introduces him. The dog is perfectly fine with Annie. I set Sunny down, and she moseys around the office to snoop.

"Is that your dog, Parker? I just got a golden retriever too! I rescued him like Skyler said to do in her news announcement." Her statement is proud and more confident than I've heard her speak before.

"Yes, they are *our* dogs." I look at my woman as I put more inflection on the *our* part.

Sky smiles huge. "Parker and I have some news!"

"Oh . . . I thought I heard your voices." Wendy enters, her red cap of hair slicked back with the top poufed up into an interesting bouffant style. She's wearing fingerless neon-green fishnet gloves that match her green suede stilettos. Her black pants are a skinny-fit style that hits right at the ankle. On top, she's wearing a white torn T-shirt with a white three-quarter-sleeve blazer. The shreds on her shirt run down the center and offer peeks of her yellow lace bralette underneath. In her ears are a pair of long, dangling, chandelier-type earrings. Her new collar and padlock ever present.

"You look like a rock star." I set my hand on my hip, the other bracing my chin as I assess her.

"Because I am a rock star? Hello? Have we met?" She grins and opens her arms, pulling me into a deep hug.

I wrap my arms around her and breathe in her coconut-and-sunshine scent. "Some things about you never change," I whisper into her ear, but hold her close.

"Which would be my sparkling personality?"

"You always smell the same."

"I don't wear perfume."

"I know. It's all you. Ask Mick about it sometime. See what he says. If he's into smells like me, he'll know what I'm talking about."

She pulls back and smiles, her bright daylight-blue eyes shining happily. "How you doin', Bossman?"

I release her and gesture to our new furry babies. "Pretty good, considering."

"Oh my God! These are the perfect doggies! Well, except for my Lauren." She beams up with pride.

"Lauren?" I snicker, vaguely remembering Sky mentioning something about Wendy's dog's name. "You named your dog Lauren?"

She puffs out her bottom lip. "Yeah. Like Sophia Loren but spelled *L-a-u-r-e-n* because it's cuter. Mick was obsessed with Sophia Loren . . . before he met me, that is. Now his obsession is focused on me." She winks and pulls her phone out of her back pocket and opens the screen to her background, which shows a picture of Mick holding a blondish-red dog. Mick is not smiling, but he is holding the dog protectively. "My Lauren is a total Mick magnet. Understandably. We're both Daddy's girls." She smiles saucily.

"Whatever, minxy." I sigh and focus my attention on Skyler until Bo enters the room.

"Bro!" He walks over to me and pulls me into a man hug, slapping my back hard. "Glad you're home."

I step back and notice a few long white hairs on his black T-shirt. I pluck one off and hold it up. "Snowflake?"

He shrugs. "What can I say? The pussy loves me."

"Gross!" Wendy punches him on the arm as she passes behind him to hug Sky and meet the dogs.

"I've got something for you, but I left it in your office," he says mysteriously.

"Oh yeah? Should I be scared?"

Bo grins and hooks me around the neck. "Any other day, maybe. Today . . . no. I think you're going to like this surprise."

"Honey, I'm going to take the pups up to the penthouse, get them connected to their second home."

"Okay. See you for lunch?"

"I'll make my specialty!" She shimmies toward the glass door where Rachel is standing, our dogs in tow. "Say goodbye to Daddy."

"Daddy?" Bo teases.

"Shut up, Snowflake."

He grins and pushes me toward my office. "What's her specialty? Is that code for a lunch quickie?"

I laugh. "No. Her specialty is peanut butter and jelly sandwiches."

"No shit?"

I shake my head and chuckle. "No shit. Though the quickie is a given."

"Word," Bo states approvingly.

When we get to my office, he opens the door and I walk in. At first I don't see anything out of place, until I walk around to my desk. Sitting in the center of my chair is a full-size sleeping ginger cat.

I look up at Bo and grin wide. "You got me a cat?"

"Everyone needs his own pussy."

This time I punch him on the other arm.

"Dammit, you and Wendy. Stop hitting me. I'm going to have bruises, which means I'll have to go out and find a chicklet to kiss them better." He pauses dramatically. "Actually . . . maybe you ought to hit me again." He waggles his brows.

"Don't tempt me," I snarl playfully, then turn my chair. The ginger cat's head lifts up, and I'm staring at his startling green gaze. "What's its name?"

"*He* doesn't have a name. I thought we should leave that up to you. He was used to breed the females. Vet who checked him over said he's about a year or two. He's apparently mild mannered and chill as fuck. I've had him here since shortly after I got off the plane, and he's been cool. Sits in the sun. And get this . . . he chose your office, and he's had the run of the place."

That comment has me smiling. Memories of Spartacus back in Montreal send a few pleasant images dancing through my mind until I remember I already have two new puppies. Adding a cat to the mix right now is not a good idea. "Bro, I can't take him home . . . the pups—" I start, but Bo cuts me off with a wave of his hand.

"Talked it over with Roy, Wendy, and Annie. We're all good to have him as our office cat. Every office needs a little pu—"

I clamp my hand over his mouth. "No. Just . . . no."

Bo licks my palm, and I fling my hand off his face and rub it down my pant leg. "You licked me!"

"You put your hand on my mouth, bro. I can't be held responsible for what happens when a piece of flesh is near that orifice."

"You're disgusting."

"I resemble that comment." He bites his bottom lip through a grin.

"This is amazing, but how are we going to take care of him with the travel . . ."

"Annie offered to clean the kitty box every day and feed and water him when she gets in and again before she leaves. He's a cat, bro. They don't need much. We all agreed to leave our doors open at night so he could have full run of the place. That's several thousand square feet for one animal. He'll be the goddamned king of the castle. He's been here two days, and he loves it. Look at him."

I look down at the red-haired cat in my black leather chair. He lifts up a paw and takes a leisurely lick before yawning and putting his head back down and closing his eyes.

"What are you going to name him?" Bo asks.

I look down at my new friend. "Well, if he's the king of this office and a ladies' man, I think I'm going to name him Zeus."

"Righteous name, bro. Perfect."

"Now I just need to get him out of my chair so I can work."

Bo laughs heartily while backing away and moving to the door. "Good luck with that. The dude has claimed your seat. You're going to have to fight him for it."

Not scared in the slightest, I lift up the cat and set him on the floor. Zeus sits primly, licks his arm and then his paw. He looks up at me with his emerald-green gaze and meows.

"This is my seat, Zeus. Deal with it," I say in response.

Zeus tips his head and then jumps into my lap. He spins around in a circle, lays his body down, and looks up at me. Then he meows before putting his head down and closing his eyes.

I run my fingers through his silky-soft fur. "Fine. I guess we can share it."

SKYLER

"Birdie, I know we sent that press release out regarding your moving to Boston, but are you really sure this is the right decision? I mean, you're an action girl, a city girl," Tracey says.

I frown. Actually I'm not really, at the heart of me. It's just that the job has always taken me to big cities, from Los Angeles to New York. Once Tracey settled her business in New York, it made sense for me to live there too. Plus, it's a five-hour plane ride to LA or seven to eight from New York to Paris and the other locations in Europe I may be filming.

"It's doesn't really change much, my living in Boston, not that it's a small city," I tease.

"It changes everything."

"How so? I'm still on the East Coast. The same flight time away, plus it's way easier for the *A-Lister* series—and big hello? My boyfriend lives here, and we're moving on to the next step. I'm so excited! I can't believe he was pretty much the one to suggest it."

She makes a gagging sound. "That surprises you? He's dating Skyler Paige, the world's most sought-after actress. Everyone wants a piece of you."

Her words settle uncomfortably in my gut and leave a sour taste in my mouth. "He doesn't want a piece of me, Flower. He wants *all* of me. Body and soul. This is serious."

"Hmm, I guess I'll believe it when I've spent more time with him and the two of you together."

"Totally!" I grin, liking her tone changing from a Debbie Downer to a more pleasant sound. "You'll have to come out for the movie anyway, so we'll spend a lot of time together."

My dogs rush into my bedroom and follow me into the bathroom, squirming around and making whimpering noises.

"Hey, Trace, I gotta go. The babies need to go outside."

"Ugh, I still can't believe you rescued two dogs. Crazy woman. Like you have the time for dogs."

"Well, hopefully in the very near future, I'll have a lot more time." I pet my pooches and ponder the idea of a new acting academy I had. Still want to talk to Parker about it, though.

"What does that mean?" Tracey says with a note of strain in her voice.

The dogs bang into my legs again. "Trace, I can't talk about it right now. I've gotta take the babies out soon. We'll talk later. Love you, bye!" I cut the connection and call out to Rachel, who's somewhere in the house. "Rach, I gotta go take the pups to piddle again!"

I stare up at the empty mirror in front of me and fluff my hair while thinking about the case Parker was on and how he took down Pure Beauty Pharmaceuticals and PB Resources. What they did was risky, and after hearing the full details, I was scared he or his company would be caught in the backlash, but the severity of what was found in that facility and the ties to Pure Beauty were astronomical.

It reminds me to check all the brands of my makeup to ensure I'm not using one of their products. Opening my cosmetics drawer, I scan a few of the tubes and packs of eyeshadows and lotions. I immediately recognize some of the names that were on the extensive list I'd seen on the TV the other night. I toss the few pieces straight into the trash. I'll buy new, organic makeup. Spying a tube of lipstick, I grab it and note it's a cherry red, but it comes from one of the brands that were cited.

I grimace and plan to toss it when an idea comes to me. I look up at myself in the mirror.

Brown eyes not too far apart or close together. Long, crazy blonde hair that could use some taming. Full bow-shaped lips. Arched eyebrows and high rounded cheekbones. What price would I pay to stay young and feel beautiful?

I wince at my image, uncap the lipstick, and touch the mirror with the red tip.

BEAUTY LIES WITHIN

I write the three words on my personal mirror in order to remind myself never to take for granted what I have right in front of me. Any price is too high to contort what genetics and the Lord above have given me. I mean, I understand the pressure to stay young and look young, but more than that, I appreciate that aging shows I've experienced life. Laugh lines mean I smile all the time. Wrinkles between my brows and at the creases of my eyes mean I've grown older, learned more, changed, and lived every day to the fullest. Right then and there, I make a promise to myself not to get swept up in the trap of not being good enough, young enough, or pretty enough for the people around me, my fans, or my man. I live for me. My beauty lies within as much as I hope it shows on the outside.

Decision made, I pat my legs and holler for my pups. "Come on, guys, let's go piddle and then pick up Daddy for lunch. How about it?" I say as my babies bounce around my legs.

Aside from Parker, there's nothing I love more on this earth than these two dogs. They've already completely owned my soul in three days.

Midnight sits properly like a good boy as I latch his collar. Sunny spins a circle around my legs a few times before copying her brother.

"Good girl, good boy." I pet both of their heads as Rachel approaches.

"I've been thinking. What if we put some grass out on one of the patios?" she suggests.

I frown. "Like Astroturf?"

She shakes her head. "No, like a patch of grass. Nate could build you a platform almost like a gardening planter box, but instead we could put sod down, and the pups will have a place to go potty that's not in front of the building, all the way down the elevator, and where the paps can get shots of you every thirty minutes."

My heart beats hard, and I glance over at the second patio. There's not much on it but a small dinette and a few plants with my yoga mats. "That could totally work. How fast do you think he could do it?"

Rachel smiles, her blonde ponytail curled over one shoulder. "Pretty fast since I already sent him to the hardware store to pick up the stuff and get the help."

"Awesome," I say. "You are the shit, Rach."

"Don't I know it!" She winks. "Come on, for now we're still on dog training."

"Cool. And when we're done I need to stop and get Parker for lunch."

"How about I drop you off at his office and take the dogs down. Then ring me when you're headed down, and I'll meet you at the front of the building. As long as you're with Park, you're fine."

I grin. Yes, I am. Having that man on my arm is like walking eye candy. I'm one lucky duck, for sure. "Good plan."

We get in the elevator, and she lets me off at the IG offices. I enter and find Annie on the phone. I point to Parker's office, and she nods and waves me in.

When I get to his office, I'm surprised to find the door open. He usually wants quiet and privacy when he works.

As I approach, I hear his voice, softened and sweet as if he's cooing at someone. I stop at the edge of the door and peek in. He's at his desk, and on top of his blotter right in front of him is an orange cat. He's so focused on the cat he doesn't realize that I'm there.

"Zeus, now I understand that you want to sleep all day in my lap or on my desk. You need to pick a new spot, brother, or this thing between us isn't going to work out."

I chuckle, and my man's blue-eyed gaze lifts to meet mine. "Hey, baby . . ."

"Who do you have there?" I enter, gesturing to the new cat.

"A present from Bo. He rescued this guy for me when he took home Snowflake. I've named him Zeus."

I run my hand over his head and down his fur. "He's even softer than our pups."

He grins. "I know. And he's a total lap kitty. Wants to just hang out with me."

"Well, you wanted a ginger cat, and looks like you've got one, but what about our babies? I'm not sure how that's going to work out with us training the new dogs."

He grabs the cat and puts him on the floor. Zeus promptly walks over to a two-foot slice of sunlight on the carpet near Parker's desk and drapes his body along it. His fur gleams a burnished red gold.

"The team decided he could be an office kitty."

"Yay!" I clap my hands, but not too loud so as not to disturb Zeus and his sunbathing, while I lean my booty against Parker's desk. "I love everyone here. We all have fur babies and now an office cat."

Parker stands up, wedges himself between my knees, and cups the sides of my neck, lifting up my chin with his thumbs. "Me too. But you know what I love more than all of that combined?" He cocks a sexy sculpted brow and grins.

I bite down on my lip and then lick it slowly. His gaze clocks the move, and his nostrils flare a tiny bit before he leans closer.

"What?" The word comes out breathless at his nearness. His citrus-and-woodsy scent invades my senses. I loop my arms around his back and my legs around his hips, locking my ankles at his thighs.

"You know . . . ," he taunts.

I smile and press closer to his mouth. "Tell me anyway."

"I love you more than anything."

"Mmm." I sigh into his mouth as he kisses me, taking away any thoughts of fur babies, kitties, potty training, patio boxes, and anything in between.

His tongue dips in, and I can taste the richness of his coffee along with his own unique flavor. I sit up and plunge my own tongue in, wanting a deeper taste. Parker runs his hands down my back until his fingers reach the hem of my shirt. He lifts it up a few inches so he can tease the bare flesh he's found. He loves to touch me skin to skin.

When he's thoroughly explored my mouth, nibbled on my lips to distraction, and run his lips down the column of my neck where he repeatedly inhales my scent, I finally sigh and push at his chest. "Rachel is waiting for us with Sunny and Midnight. I thought we could pick up some sandwiches at the café and take them to a park. The paparazzi have gotten a lot of pics of me and the dogs, so they're kind of bored and not as many are there. We should be able to trick them by getting the sammies, getting into the car, and having Rachel take us to the park. What do you say?"

"Sounds perfect, Peaches. Let me make sure Zeus is settled."

As I stand in front of his body, I feel a buzzing sensation against my belly. I chuckle as he backs up and pulls out his phone. He reads the display, and his jaw goes tight, his gaze narrowing in on the phone.

"What is it?"

I can hear him grind his teeth. "Nothing."

I place my hand on his chest. "Don't hide things from me. You're upset. I want to know why."

He inhales long and slow before he shows me the text.

From: Unknown
To: Parker Ellis

YOU TOOK HER AWAY FROM ME. YOU CAN'T BE TRUSTED.

A foreboding tickle picks up at the base of my neck. "I thought the freak had given up. We had a good break, and the last text seemed nicer. What do you think it means?" I swallow around the sudden dryness in my throat and wring my hands together, an electric energy nipping at my nerve endings, making me feel unsteady.

Parker's voice is tight and his words measured when he replies, "Obviously, whoever it is has gotten word that you're staying in Boston. Did you tell anyone in particular?"

"Yeah, the entire world!" I say with a hint of panic. "I met with Tracey a few days ago in New York while you were in DC. We had dinner, and I told her I was moving here and we were going to start house hunting and animal rescuing. Tracey sent out a press release regarding my official involvement in the *A-Lister* movies along with my quote regarding how I was excited to be moving to Boston and would be closer to my friends and boyfriend."

"Apparently, our little friend"—he shakes the phone mockingly— "doesn't like the idea of your moving. That could mean the person lives in New York or somewhere close enough to follow you there."

I shake my head and run my hand through my hair. "Or it could be someone who's mad that we adopted pets together. We just talked to the press this morning. Maybe the guy saw that we were a serious couple. Add in the fact the press release went out to the masses, and we're back to square one."

He lets out a tortured breath as his phone buzzes again. This time we both look at the screen when he opens it.

From: Unknown
To: Parker Ellis

LESSON LEARNED. NOW IT'S YOUR TURN TO
LEARN A LESSON.

"Oh my God." I cover my mouth with my hand. "He's going to
hurt you. I just know it. He's mad, and he's going to hurt you!" Tears
prick my eyes, but they don't have a chance to fall before Parker has
me in his arms.

"Shhh . . . nothing is going to happen to me. We're fine. We'll
handle this. Sure, the tension may have ramped up, but that doesn't
mean the person is going to strike. We haven't had anything in the way
of physical ramifications."

I swallow, and my voice cracks with emotion. "Yet! He hasn't done
anything to us yet! It's only a matter of time. I can't bear to lose you,
Parker."

He dips his face into my neck, pressing my body tightly to his. Each
of his arms is like a secure barrier from anything and everything that
might be out to get me.

Safe.

I feel safe in his arms.

"Just breathe, baby. Nothing's going to happen. We'll get Nate and
Wendy on this right away." His hands smooth up and down my spine.

"Honey . . ." The word scrapes out between my lips. "I can't lose
you."

He holds me at arm's length until our gazes meet. "You are not
going to lose me. This is a prankster. A loser who's attached to you in
an unhealthy way. They have done nothing but taunt us. Right?"

I lick my salty lips and nod.

"Right. Which means the person is a coward. We just have to be
smart, and we are. Now come on. Our dogs want to go to the park,

and I need to feed my woman a sandwich since she's not making me her specialty."

"We can have them for dinner?" I suggest.

"Anything you want." He pulls me against his chest.

"I only want you, our pups, and our friends . . . and Zeus."

He chuckles, and it takes away some of the fear and anxiety. "Absolutely Zeus."

He dips his head, kisses my lips, and wipes away the few tears I shed. "No more worrying your pretty head about this. I'm on it. Okay?"

"Okay. Just don't keep things from me. I need to know what's going on or I'll be more afraid."

Parker hooks me around the waist and urges me toward the door. "Let's go chat with Wendy really quick, and then we're off to the park. It's nothing but blue skies, green grass, and our new babies." He squeezes my shoulder lovingly.

"It's just us. Against the world."

"That's right. You, me, and our pups." He winks, and I smile knowing that he'll stop at nothing to find this person. I just have to hold tight and trust him to take care of me and our new little family.

The end . . . for now.

If you want to read more about the guys—Parker, Bo, and Royce—from International Guy, get your copy of *Madrid: International Guy Book 10*.

In the tenth installment, a music label hires International Guy to transform Juliet Jimenez, an angel with a beautiful voice, into a chart-topping, pop-star sex vixen. The client wants the same results they had from their fashion show in Milan, so Parker brings along the sex maestro himself . . . Bogart Montgomery.

With Skyler's movie plans for the *A-Lister* series ramping up, Parker suggests she come on the trip. Her inclusion on the job proves instrumental to a successful outcome.

ABOUT THE AUTHOR

Photo © Melissa McKinley Photography

Audrey Carlan is a #1 *New York Times* bestselling author, and her titles have appeared on the bestseller lists of *USA Today* and the *Wall Street Journal.* Audrey writes wicked-hot love stories that have been translated into more than thirty different languages across the globe. She is best known for the worldwide-bestselling series Calendar Girl and Trinity.

She lives in the California Valley, where she enjoys her two children and the love of her life. When she's not writing, you can find her teaching yoga, sipping wine with her "soul sisters," or with her nose stuck in a steamy romance novel.

Any and all feedback is greatly appreciated and feeds the soul. You can contact Audrey through her website, www.audreycarlan.com.